ALEXANDER: THE ENDS OF THE EARTH

VALERIO MASSIMO MANFREDI is the professor of classical archaeology at Luigi Bocconi University in Milan. He has carried out a number of expeditions and excavations in many sites throughout the Mediterranean, and has taught in Italian and international universities. He has published numerous articles and academic books, mainly on military and trade routes and exploration in the ancient world. He has published nine works of fiction, including the 'Alexander' trilogy, translated into twenty-four languages in thirty-eight countries, whose film rights have been acquired by Universal Pictures in light of a large international production. He has written and hosted documentaries on the ancient world transmitted by the main television networks, and has written fiction for cinema and television as well.

He lives with his family in the countryside near Bologna, Italy.

IAIN HALLIDAY was born in Scotland in 1960. He studied American Studies at the University of Manchester and worked in Italy and London before moving to Sicily, where he now lives. As well as working as a translator, he currently teaches English at the University of Catania.

Also by Valerio Massimo Manfredi

ALEXANDER: CHILD OF A DREAM

ALEXANDER: THE SANDS OF AMMON

SPARTAN

THE LAST LEGION

THE TALISMAN OF TROY

To Christine

First published 2001 by Macmillan

This edition published 2002 by Pan Books
an imprint of Pan Macmillan Ltd
Pan Macmillan, 20 New Wharf Road, London N1 9RR
Basingstoke and Oxford
Associated companies throughout the world
www.panmacmillan.com

ISBN 978 0 330 51860 4

Originally published 1998 in Italy as *Alexandros: Il Confine Del Mundo* by
Arnoldo Mondadori Editore S.p.A., Milano

Typeset by SetSystems Ltd, Saffron Walden, Essex
Printed and bound in the UK by
CPI Mackays, Chatham ME5 8TD

Visit **www.panmacmillan.com** to read more about all our books and to buy
them. You will also find features, author interviews and news of any author
events, and you can sign up for e-newsletters so that you're always first to hear
about our new releases.

VALERIO MASSIMO MANFRED

ALEXANDER

THE ENDS OF THE EARTH

Translated from the Italian by Iain Halliday

PAN BOOKS

ALEXANDER

THE ENDS OF THE EARTH

Lake Balkhash

Aral Sea

Issyk-Kul Lake

Jaxartes

Oxus

(Bukhara) • Alexandria-the-Furthest

Choriene Rock

Sogdian Rock

Bactra-Zariaspa Drapasca

Ortospana

Zadracarta

Alexandria of Aria

Taxila

Sangala

Persepolis

Alexandria

Gulf

(Gwadar) (Pasni) Cocala

Patala

India

Arabian Sea

0 100 200 300 400 500 600 kilometres

0 100 200 300 400 500 600 miles

ALEXANDER'S CONQUESTS (1)

ALEXANDER'S CONQUESTS (2)

SCYTHIANS

(Bukhara)
Oxus

Alexandria-the-Furthest
Cyropolis
Samarkand
Nautaca
Sogdia
Pamir
Sogdian Rock
Choriene Rock
Margiana
Alexandria on the Oxus
Bactra-Zariaspa
Aornos
Drapasca
Karakoram
Susia
Bactria
Ortospana
Alexandria-in-Caucasus
Aria
Antacoana
Alexandria of Aria
Nicaea
Arigaion Ora
Massaga
Aornos
Embolima
Peucelaotis
Bazira
Dyrta
① ③
Taxila
② Nicaea
Bucephala
④ ⑤
Arachosia
(12 Altars)
Alexandria of
Arachosia
Indus
MALLANS
Sangala
City of the
Mallians
SAGALASSIANS
SIBI
rada/Proftasia
Drangiana
City of the Brahmans
Capital of the Mallians
ARIMASPIANS
Alexandria
Alexandria
Pura
Gedroasia
ORITES
Thar Desert
Rhambacia/
Alexandria
Cocola
Patala
(Gwadar)
Indus
(Pasni)
Alexandrou
Limen
India
Indus

Arabian Sea

0 100 200 300 400 kilometres
0 100 200 300 400 miles

ALEXANDER'S CONQUESTS (3)

ANCIENT GREECE

1

THE KING SET OFF again across the desert, taking another route that led from the Oasis of Ammon directly to the banks of the Nile near Memphis. He rode alone for hours and hours astride his Sarmatian bay, while Bucephalas galloped alongside wearing no halter or tack at all. Alexander had understood just how long their journey was going to take, and he sought to spare his horse whenever possible, keen to preserve its strength and vigour.

The march took three weeks under the baking hot sun and they suffered much before the thin green line marking the fertile banks of the Nile came into view. However, Alexander seemed to be immune to exhaustion, hunger and thirst, so immersed was he in his thoughts and in his memories.

His Companions tried not to disturb these reveries because they realized he wanted to be alone in the midst of those endless, desert spaces, alone with his feeling of infinity, with his anxious dreams of immortality, with the passions of his soul. Only when evening fell was it possible to approach the King, and occasionally some of his friends would enter the tent to speak to him and keep him company while Leptine bathed him.

One day Ptolemy took him by surprise with a question

he had been wanting to ask his King and friend for too long: 'What did the god Ammon tell you?'

'He called me "son",' replied Alexander.

Ptolemy picked up the sponge that had fallen from Leptine's hand and returned it to her, 'And what did you ask him?'

'I asked him if all of my father's murderers are dead or whether any of them have survived.'

Ptolemy said nothing. He waited for the King to come out of the tub and then placed a towel of clean linen over his shoulders and began rubbing him dry. When Alexander turned, his friend looked firmly and deeply into his eyes and asked him, 'So do you still love Philip, your father, now that you have become a god?'

Alexander sighed, 'If you weren't here before me now, I would say that this question had come from Callisthenes or Cleitus the Black . . . give me your sword.' Ptolemy looked at him in surprise, but he did not dare reply. He simply unsheathed his sword and held it out. Alexander took the weapon and cut the skin on his arm with the sharp metal point so that a bright red rivulet started running down it.

'What is this, Ptolemy, if it is not blood?'

'It is indeed blood.'

'Quite. It is not the *icor* which is said to run through the veins of the celestial gods,' he continued, reciting from Homer. 'Therefore, my friend, try to understand me, and if you love me then put an end to these pointless gibes.'

Ptolemy understood and apologized for having spoken

in that way, while Leptine washed the King's arm with wine and put a bandage on the wound.

Alexander saw that his friend was truly sorry and invited him to stay for supper, even though there was not much to eat – dry bread, dates and some rather sharp palm wine.

'What are we going to do now?' asked Ptolemy.

'We will travel back to Tyre.'

'And then?'

'I do not know. I think Antipater will send me news on what is happening in Greece and our informers will let us know what Darius is planning. At that stage we will take our decision.'

'I know that Eumenes has given you the bad news regarding your brother-in-law, Alexander of Epirus.'

'Yes, he has. My sister Cleopatra will be beside herself with grief, and my mother too, for she loved her brother very much.'

'But I am sure the greatest grief will be your own. Am I not right?'

'Yes, I believe you are.'

'What was it that brought the two of you so close together, apart from your family ties?'

'A great dream we shared. Now the entire weight of that dream lies on my shoulders. One day we will invade Italy, Ptolemy, and we will annihilate the barbarians who killed him.'

He poured some wine for his friend and then said, 'Would you like to hear some poetry? I have invited Thessalus to keep me company.'

'Indeed I would. Which poems have you chosen?'

'Works by a variety of poets, all of which are about the sea. These endless sands around us remind me of the great expanse of the sea, and then all this dryness makes me long for it.'

As soon as Leptine had cleared away the two small tables, the actor entered. He wore a stage costume and had make-up on his face – bistre around his eyes, his mouth lined with minium, a red dye to create a bitter expression, like those of the masks from the tragedies. He strummed some subdued chords on his lyre and began:

> O breeze, breeze of the sea,
> That wafts swift galleys, ocean's coursers,
> Across the surging main!
> Where will you bear me, the sorrowful one?*

Alexander listened in the deep silence of the night, enchanted by the voice that was capable of any intonation, capable of resonating through all human feeling and passion, capable of imitating the very wind and the crash of thunder.

They sat up until late in the night listening to the voice of the great actor as it mutated through every shade of feeling, wailing through the tears of women, or rising proud as he gave voice to the heroes. When Thessalus finished, Alexander embraced him, 'Thank you,' he said, his eyes moist with emotion. 'You have evoked the dreams that will come to me this night. Now

* Euripides, *Hecuba* (lines 444–445), translated by E. P. Coleridge (1938).

go and rest – we have a long march ahead of us tomorrow.'

Ptolemy waited up a little longer to drink some wine with Alexander.

'Do you ever think about Pella?' he suddenly asked. 'Do you ever think of your mother and your father, of the days when we were boys and we rode all over the hills of Macedon? Of the shining waters of our rivers and our lakes?'

Alexander considered the question for a moment and then replied, 'Yes, often, but it's as though they are distant images, like things that happened many many years ago. Our life is so intense that each hour is like a year.'

'This means, then, that we will grow old before our time, does it not?'

'Perhaps, or perhaps not. The lamp which burns brightest in the room is the one that is destined to burn out first, but all those present will remember just how beautiful its light was during its heyday.'

He pulled the door of the tent to one side and accompanied Ptolemy outside. The sky over the desert was filled with a myriad of stars and the two young men lifted their eyes to look.

'Perhaps this too is the destiny of the stars that shine brightest in the celestial vault. May your night be a peaceful one, my friend.'

'And yours too, *Aléxandre*,' replied Ptolemy, as he moved off towards his tent on the edge of the camp.

*

Five days later they reached the banks of the Nile at Memphis, where Parmenion and Nearchus were waiting for them. That same night Alexander saw Barsine again. She was staying in a sumptuous building that had belonged to a pharaoh and her apartments had been arranged on the upper floors. In the evening the northerly winds brought to these rooms a pleasant coolness as they stirred the blue byssus curtains, as light and delicate as butterfly wings.

She waited for him, sitting on an armchair decorated with gold and enamel friezes, dressed in a light gown in the Ionian style. Her black hair with its violet highlights lay loose over her shoulders and she wore light make-up after the Egyptian manner.

The moonlight and the light of the lamps hidden behind alabaster screens mingled in an atmosphere perfumed with nard and aloe, glowing with amber reflections from the onyx tanks full of water, on the surface of which lotus flowers and rose petals floated. From an openwork screen of stylized ivy branches and gliding birds, came the quiet, gentle music of flutes and harps. The walls were completely frescoed with ancient Egyptian pictures representing scenes in which naked maidens danced to the sound of lutes and tambours before the royal couple on their thrones, and in a corner there was a large bed with a blue canopy supported by four columns of gilded wood with capitals in the shape of lotus flowers.

Alexander entered and looked long and ardently at Barsine. His eyes were still full of the dazzling light of

the desert, his ears rang with the sacred words of the Oracle of Ammon, his whole body emanated an aura of magical enchantment: the golden locks falling on his shoulders, his muscled chest with the scars it carried, the changing colour of his eyes, his slender, nervous hands with their blue veins. Over his naked body he wore only a light *chlamys*, held loosely on his left shoulder with an ancient silver buckle, an age-old inheritance of the Argead dynasty, and he wore a golden ribbon around his forehead.

Barsine stood up and immediately felt lost in the light of his gaze, '*Aléxandre . . .*' she said as he pulled her into his arms and kissed her lips, as full and moist as ripe dates. He pulled her down to the bed and caressed her hips and her warm, perfumed breasts.

But suddenly the King felt her skin go cold and her limbs stiffen under his hands; a menacing air permeated the room, sending all his warrior's senses into alarm. He turned quickly to face the imminent danger and found himself being attacked head on by a body running towards him. He saw a hand raised as it brandished a dagger, he heard a wild, strident cry reverberate around the walls of the bed chamber, and he heard Barsine cry out in grief and in pain.

Alexander quickly pinned the aggressor to the floor, twisting his wrist and forcing him to release the weapon. He could have massacred him there and then with the heavy lamp holder he had instinctively grabbed, but he had recognized the young fifteen-year-old – Eteocles, Memnon's and Barsine's eldest son! The boy struggled

and turned like a young lion caught in a trap, shouting all sorts of insults, biting and scratching now that he was unarmed.

The guards burst in, having heard the scuffle, and they took hold of the aggressor. The officer in command understood immediately what had happened and called out, 'An attempt on the King's life! Take him below and have him tortured before he's executed.'

But Barsine threw herself crying at Alexander's feet, 'Save him, my Lord, save my son's life, I beg you!'

Eteocles looked at her with contempt written all over his face and then, turning to Alexander, said, 'The best thing for you to do is to have me killed, because I will try again and again . . . a thousand times until I succeed in vindicating the life and honour of my father.' He was still shaking, partly because of the excitement and agitation of the scuffle, and partly because of the hatred burning in his heart. The King gestured to the guards to leave.

'But, Sire—' protested the officer.

'Out!' said Alexander. 'Can't you see he's just a boy?' and the man obeyed. Then the King turned once again to Eteocles, 'Your father's honour is fully intact. He died because of a fatal disease.'

'It's not true!' shouted the boy. 'You had him poisoned and now . . . now you're trying to take his woman. You are a man with no sense of honour!'

Alexander moved closer and repeated, his voice firm, 'I admired your father; I considered him my only worthy adversary and I dreamed of one day fighting him in a duel. I would never have had him poisoned; when I have

to deal with my enemies I do so face to face, with sword and spear. As for your mother, she has made of me a victim because I think of her every waking moment; I am tormented by the thought of her. Love has all the strength of a god, love is irresistible and invincible. Man knows neither how to avoid it, nor how to escape it, in the same way that ultimately man cannot avoid the sun and the rain, birth and death.'

Barsine sobbed in a corner, her face hidden in her hands.

'Have you nothing to say to your mother?' the King asked.

'From the very instant you first laid hands on her, she has no longer been my mother, she is nothing to me now. Kill me, I tell you, it is in the best interests of both of you. Otherwise I shall kill you and I will offer the blood of both your bodies to my father's soul, so that he may find peace in Hades.'

Alexander turned to Barsine, 'What shall I do?'

Barsine dried her eyes and composed herself, 'Let him go free, I beg you. Give him a horse and provisions and let him go. Will you do this for me?'

'I warn you,' said the boy once more, 'that if you let me go I will speak to the Great King and I will ask him for armour and a sword so that I may fight in his army against you.'

'If this is the way it must be, then so be it,' replied Alexander. Then he called the guards and issued orders for the boy to be given a horse and provisions before being set free.

Eteocles walked away towards the door, seeking to

hide the violent emotions gripping his soul as his mother called out to him. He did stop for an instant, but then turned his back once again, crossed the threshold, and went out into the corridor.

Barsine called out again, 'Please wait!' Then she went to a chest and out of it pulled a shining weapon together with its scabbard. She rushed into the corridor and held it out to her son, 'It is your father's sword.'

The boy took it and held it close to his chest, and as he did so burning tears flowed from his eyes and made tracks down his cheeks.

'Farewell, my son,' said Barsine, her voice quavering. 'May Ahura Mazda protect you and may your father's gods protect you too.'

Eteocles ran off along the corridor and down the stairs until he came to the courtyard of the palace, where the guards placed a horse's reins in his hands. But just as he was about to leap astride the animal, he saw a shadow emerge from a small side door – his brother, Phraates.

'Take me with you, I beg you. I won't stay here, a prisoner to these *yauna*,' and Eteocles hesitated as his brother continued to plead with him. 'Take me with you, I beg of you, I beg you! I don't weigh much, the horse will manage both of us until we find another one.'

'I cannot,' replied Eteocles. 'You are too young and then . . . someone must stay with our mother. Farewell, Phraates. We will see each other again as soon as this war is over, and I will free you then.' He held his tearful younger brother in a long embrace, then he leaped on to the horse and disappeared.

Barsine had witnessed the scene from the window of

her bed chamber and she felt herself wither at the sight of her fifteen-year-old boy galloping off into the night to face the unknown. She cried disconsolately, thinking of just how bitter the fate of human beings can be. Just a short time before she had felt like one of those Olympian goddesses painted and sculpted by the great *yauna* artists, and now she would gladly have changed places with the most humble of slaves.

2

ALEXANDER HAD TWO floating bridges built so his army could cross over to the eastern bank of the Nile. There he met up with the soldiers and officers he had left behind to guard the country; having made sure that they had behaved properly, he reconfirmed them in their positions, dividing them up so that power over this most rich of countries was not concentrated in the hands of just one person.

Egypt welcomed him on his return from the Sanctuary of Ammon, heaping honours on him as if he were a god and crowning him Pharaoh, but destiny had it that these days of glory were darkened by sad events. Barsine's despair lay before his eyes every day, but an even greater tragedy was looming. Parmenion had two other sons besides Philotas – Nicanor, an officer in a *hetairoi* squadron, and Hector, nineteen years old and deeply loved by his father. The younger man was much taken with the sight of the army crossing the Nile and had climbed aboard an Egyptian papyrus boat to enjoy the spectacle from the middle of the river. Hector's youthful vanity had led him to wear a heavy suit of armour and a very showy dress cape; he stood up at the stern of the boat, straight and proud so that everyone could admire him.

Suddenly, however, the boat struck something, perhaps a hippopotamus which was surfacing at that moment, and it very nearly capsized. Hector lost his balance, fell into the water and disappeared immediately, dragged down by the weight of his armour, his clothes and his sodden cape.

The Egyptian rowers of the boat wasted no time diving in, as did many of the young Macedonians and Hector's own brother, Nicanor, ready to brave the currents and the jaws of the crocodiles, of which there were many in that area, but it was all in vain. Parmenion, on the eastern bank from where he had been watching the orderly arrival of the army, looked on, helpless, as the tragedy unfolded.

The news reached Alexander shortly afterwards and he immediately gave orders to the Phoenician and Cypriot mariners to try at least to recover the young man's body, but nothing came of all their efforts. That same evening, after hours and hours of desperate searching, in which he participated personally, the King went to visit the grief-stricken old general.

'How is he?' he asked Philotas who was standing outside the tent, as though guarding over his father's privacy. His friend shook his head disconsolately.

Parmenion was sitting on the ground in the dark, in silence, and only his white hair stood out in the gloom. Alexander felt his knees go weak – he was deeply sorry for this valiant and loyal man who so many times had irritated him with all his advice to be prudent, with the incessant reminders of just how great his father Philip had been. Now Parmenion looked like an age-old

oak tree that for years had withstood storms and hurricanes and had now suddenly been rent by a bolt of lightning.

'This is truly a most sad visit I pay you, General,' he began, his voice shaking slightly. As he looked at Parmenion he could not help but think of the rhyme he used to sing as a boy whenever he saw him arriving at his father's war councils with his hair which even back then was already white:

> The silly old soldier's off to the war
> And falls to the floor, falls to the floor!

Almost automatically Parmenion got to his feet at the sound of his King's voice and managed to say, his voice broken, 'Thank you for coming, Sire.'

'We have tried everything, General, to recover your boy's body. I would have granted him the highest of honours, I would ... I would have done everything if only ...'

'I know,' replied Parmenion. 'The proverb has it that in peacetime sons bury their fathers, while in wartime fathers bury their sons, but I had always hoped that I might be spared this grief. I had always hoped that the first arrow or the first sword blow would be for me. But instead ...'

'It is a most terrible loss, General,' said Alexander. In the meantime his eyes had become used to the gloom in the tent and he could make out Parmenion's features, distorted in his pain. He seemed to have aged by ten years in a matter of moments – his eyes were red, his skin dry and wrinkled, his hair untidy. He had never seen

Parmenion in such a state, not even during the toughest of battles.

'If he had fallen—' Parmenion said, 'if he had fallen in battle, fighting as he brandished his sword then it would have made some sense to me – we are soldiers after all. But to die like that . . . in those muddy waters, ripped to pieces and devoured by those monsters! O by the gods! Gods above! Why? Why?' He covered his face with his hands and burst into a long, doleful crying that was truly heartbreaking.

Alexander could find no more words in the face of that suffering. All he could manage was to murmur, 'I am sorry . . . I am sorry.' And he left, saying goodbye to Philotas with just one pained look. The other brother, Nicanor, arrived just at that moment, he too stricken by grief and exhaustion, still soaked to the skin and covered in mud.

The following day, the King had a cenotaph erected in memory of the young man and he personally celebrated the funeral rites. The soldiers, all lined up, shouted Hector's name ten times so that his memory would not be lost, but it was not like the occasion when they had shouted the names of their fallen companions on the mountains of Thrace and Illyria in the midst of the snow-capped peaks, under the sapphire sky. In that grave, dark atmosphere, on that muddy water, Hector's name was immediately swallowed up by the silence.

*

That same evening the King returned to Barsine. He found her stretched out on her bed crying. Her maid told him that she had eaten hardly anything all day.

'You must not despair so,' Alexander said to her. 'Nothing will happen to your boy – I had two of my men follow him to make sure he will be alright.'

Barsine got up and sat on the edge of the bed: 'Thank you. You have taken a weight off my heart ... even though the shame remains. My children have judged and sentenced me.'

'You are wrong,' replied Alexander. 'Do you know what your boy said to his younger brother as he left? The guards told me about it. He said to him, "You must stay with our mother." This means that he loves you and he has done what he has done because he feels that this is precisely what he must do. You should be proud of him.'

Barsine dried her eyes, 'I am sorry that all this has happened. I wanted to be a source of joy to you, I wanted to be close to you in your moment of triumph, but instead all I am capable of doing is crying.'

'Tears flowing after tears,' replied Alexander. 'Parmenion has lost his youngest son. The entire army is in mourning and I could do nothing to prevent it. Becoming a god has not done me much good at all. But please sit now and eat with me, together we must seek to regain that happiness which destiny is so envious of and which destiny tries to snatch from us.'

*

Admiral Nearchus received orders to sail for Phoenicia while the army returned by land, along the road that ran between the sea and the desert. As they approached Gaza, an orderly from Sidon arrived with some bad news: 'Sire,' he said, leaping from his horse and not even

waiting to get his breath back, 'the Samaritans have tortured and burned alive Commander Andromachus, your governor of Syria.'

Alexander, already saddened by recent events, grew angry, 'Who are these Samaritans?' he asked.

'They are barbarians who live on the mountains between Judaea and Mount Carmel, their city bears the name Samaria,' replied the orderly.

'And do they know nothing of Alexander?'

'Perhaps they do know something,' said Lysimachus, 'but they don't care. They think they can risk incurring your wrath.'

'In that case they must be taught something more of Alexander,' replied the King, and he gave orders to start off again on the march. They proceeded to Akrai without stopping and from there marched eastwards towards the interior, with the light cavalry of the Triballians and the Agrianians and with the Vanguard fully prepared for battle. The King led them in person, accompanied by his friends, while the heavy infantry, the auxiliaries and the *hetairoi* cavalry remained on the coast under Parmenion's command.

They arrived just as evening was falling and were completely unexpected. Indeed, the Samaritans were a shepherding people and they were all out on the hills with their flocks at pasture. Over a period of three days every village was set alight and the capital, which was nothing more than a slightly larger and walled village, was razed to the ground. Their temple, a modest sanctuary which did not even have a statue or an image of any kind, was reduced to ashes.

The action continued until nightfall on the third day, and the King decided to set up camp with his men out on the mountains and to wait for the following day before setting off on the journey back to the sea. Double sentries were posted on all the surrounding paths so as to avoid any surprise attacks, and fires were lit to illuminate the guard posts and the night passed peacefully. Shortly before dawn the King was awakened by the officer in charge of the last watch, a Thessalian from Larissa by the name of Euryalus, 'Sire, come; there is something you must see.'

'What is it?' asked Alexander as he got to his feet.

'There is a group of people coming from the south. It looks like some sort of delegation.'

'A delegation? And where can they be from?'

'I do not know.'

'There is only one city in that direction,' said Eumenes who had been awake for some time and had already made one inspection round. 'Jerusalem.'

'And what city is Jerusalem?'

'It is the capital of a small kingdom that has no king – the realm of the Judaeans. It perches high up on a mountain and is surrounded by cliffs.'

As Eumenes spoke, the small group had reached the first guard post and was asking permission to pass through.

'Let them come,' Alexander ordered. 'I will receive them in front of my tent.' He covered his shoulders with his cape and sat on his field stool.

In the meantime one of the men from the delegation who certainly spoke Greek was exchanging a few words

with Euryalus and asked if the young man sitting in front of the tent with the red cape on his shoulders was King Alexander. On being told that he was, the man moved forward, the rest of the delegation following behind. It was immediately apparent who was the most important personage in the group – an old man of average height with a long, well-kept beard, on his head a mitre and on his chest a pectoral embellished with twelve stones in various colours. He was the first to speak and to Alexander his tongue – guttural and yet harmonious, syncopated and strongly aspirated – seemed very similar to the Phoenicians'.

'May the Lord protect you, Great King,' came the interpreter's translation.

'Of which lord do you speak?' asked Alexander, intrigued by the use of the word.

'Of the Lord our God, God of Israel.'

'And why should your god protect me?'

'He already has,' replied the old man, 'allowing you to survive many battles and to travel here to put an end to the blasphemy of the Samaritans.'

Alexander shook his head as though the interpreter's words held no meaning for him, 'What is a blasphemy?' he asked, but just at that moment he felt a hand placed on his shoulder. He turned and saw Aristander, wrapped in his white cloak and with a strange expression in his eyes.

'Respect this man,' he whispered in his ear. 'His god is surely a most powerful god.'

'Blasphemy,' the interpreter began, 'is an insult to God. The Samaritans had built a temple on Mount

Gerizim. The one that you have just destroyed, with the Lord's help.'

'And that was . . . blasphemy?'

'Yes.'

'Why?'

'Because there can be only one temple.'

'Only one temple?' asked the King in amazement. 'In my land we have hundreds of temples.'

Aristander asked permission to speak to the old man with the white beard: 'What is this temple like?' he asked.

The old man's voice was suddenly filled with passion and the interpreter translated, 'The temple is the house of our God, the only God who exists, creator of the earth and the sky, of the visible and the invisible. He freed our fathers who were slaves in Egypt and gave them the Promised Land. For many years He lived in a tent in the city of Shiloh until King Solomon built him a splendid temple of gold and bronze on the rock of Zion, our city.'

'And what does he look like?' asked Aristander. 'Do you have an image of him to show me?'

As soon as the old man heard the request he pulled a face of sheer disgust and replied dryly, 'Our Lord has no image and we are not allowed to make use of any images to represent Him. The image of our Lord is everywhere – in the clouds in the sky and in the flowers in the field, in the songs of the birds and in the whispering of the wind through the leaves of the trees.'

'What do you have, then, in your temple?'

'Nothing that can be seen by human eyes.'

'So who are you, then?'

'I am the high priest. I present the people's prayer to

their God and I alone may pronounce His name, once a year, in the innermost sanctum of the temple. And who are you, if I may ask?'

The King looked at the two men, first one then the other, and said, 'I want to see the temple of your god.'

The old priest, as soon as he understood the King's words, knelt down and bent over so that his forehead touched the ground, begging Alexander not to do it, 'Please do not profane our sanctuary. No one who is not circumcised, no one who is not one of God's Chosen People may enter the temple, and my duty is to prevent such people from entering, even if it means spilling my own blood.'

The King was about to lose his temper, as he always did when someone denied him anything, but Aristander gestured to him to control himself and whispered in his ear, 'Respect this man who is prepared to give his life for a faceless god, this man who is not prepared to lie and to adulate you.'

Alexander thought in silence for a short time, then he turned once more to the old man with the white beard, 'I will respect your wishes, but in return I want an answer from you.'

'What answer?' asked the old man.

'You said that the image of the only god is in the clouds in the sky, in the flowers in the fields, in the singing of the birds and in the whispering of the wind, but what is there of your god in human beings?'

The old man replied, 'God made man in His image and likeness, but in some men the image of God has become clouded and obscured by their behaviour. In

others it shines as bright as the midday sun. You are one of these men, Great King.'

Having said this, the old man turned and went back to where he had come from.

3

THE ARMY PROCEEDED on its march through the last part of Palestine and entered Phoenicia. A heavy sense of anguish had spread throughout the army following the death of young Hector, with all of the men taking it as a bad omen. So at Tyre the King offered a sacrifice to Hercules Melkarth in an attempt to clear the sense of oppression with a solemn religious rite.

The city still displayed signs of the devastation it had suffered the previous year, and yet life was tenaciously beginning to bloom once again. The survivors worked hard at reconstructing the houses, transporting materials on their boats from dry land. Some concentrated on fishing while yet others busied themselves in the workshops that produced the world's most celebrated purple dye from the mussels that lived on the rocks. New colonists had arrived from Cyprus and Sidon to repopulate the ancient metropolis and slowly the sense of desolation which had accompanied the ruins was gradually dissolving as works proceeded, as families were reunited, as the ordinary activities of daily life picked up again.

At Tyre Alexander received visits from many delegations representing various cities in Greece and the islands, together with several messages from General Antipater keeping him informed on military recruitment activities

being carried out in the northern regions. He also received a letter from his mother that made a deep impression on him:

Olympias to Alexander, her beloved son, Hail!

I have had news of your visit to the Temple of Zeus which stands in the midst of the desert sands and of the response the god gave you, and I find my heart flooded with the deepest of emotions. I remembered when I first felt you move in my belly – the day when I consulted the oracle of Zeus at Dodona, in Epirus, the land of my birth.

That day a sudden wind brought the desert sands to us and the priests told me that your great destiny would be fulfilled when you reached the other great sanctuary of the god, which stands in the desert sands of Libya. I remembered a dream in which I felt I had been possessed by a god, which had taken the form of a snake. I do not believe, my son, that Philip begot you, but you descend truly from the gods. Is there any other way of explaining your astounding victories, the retreat of the sea before you, the miraculous rains in the burning sands of the desert?

Turn your thoughts to your celestial father, my son, and forget Philip. The blood flowing in your veins is not his.

Alexander realized that his mother was fully informed of every aspect of his expedition and that she was pursuing her own detailed design. Olympias was scheming to wipe out the past completely, making room for a future for Alexander that was totally different from the

one envisaged by Philip and his teacher Aristotle. There was to be no room in this rewriting of the future for even any memory of Philip. He placed the letter on the table just as Eumenes entered with other papers to be read and signed.

'Bad news?' asked the Secretary General as he took in the expression of shock on the King's face.

'No, in fact I should be happy since even my mother is now telling me that I am the son of a god.'

'But you don't look like a happy man to me.'

'Would you be happy?'

'You well know that there was no other way of governing Egypt and being accepted by the priests of Memphis – becoming son of Ammon and therefore Pharaoh. What's more, Ammon is worshipped as Zeus by all the Greeks who live in Libya, all those from Naucratis and Cyrene and soon those from Alexandria as well, as soon as your city is inhabited. It was inevitable, because in becoming son of Ammon you have also acknowledged that you are the son of Zeus.'

While he was still talking, Alexander handed him Olympias's letter, 'The Queen Mother is simply helping you come to terms with your new role,' Eumenes said as soon as he had finished reading it.

'You are wrong: my mother's mind is always some-where between dream and reality, exchanging the one for the other and vice versa. And what is more—' and he stopped here as though undecided whether to divulge such a secret, '. . . what is more, my mother has the power to give substance to her dreams and to pull other people into them.'

'I do not understand,' said Eumenes.

'Do you remember the day when I fled from Pella, the day when my father wanted to kill me?'

'Of course I do, I was there.'

'I fled together with my mother with the intention of reaching Epirus and we stopped to sleep in an oak wood some thirty stadia west of Beroea. Suddenly, in the middle of the night, I saw her get up and go off into the darkness – she walked as though she were floating above the ground and came to a place where there was an ancient image of Dionysus covered with ivy. I saw her there, just as I can see you now, and she called up an enormous snake from underground, I saw her conjure up an orgy of satyrs and maenads, playing her flute, completely possessed . . .'

Eumenes looked at him with worry written all over his face, unable to believe his ears, 'You probably dreamed it all.'

'Not in the slightest. Suddenly I felt a hand on my shoulder and it was her, do you understand? But just an instant before I had seen her playing her flute caught up in the coils of a gigantic snake. And I was there, I was not lying in my makeshift bed. We returned to our camp together, walking along the path for some distance. How do you explain all that?'

'I do not know. There are people who walk in their sleep and they say too that there are people who while they sleep somehow leave their bodies and travel distances, appearing before other people. This is what they call *ekstasis*. Olympias is certainly no ordinary woman.'

'There is no doubt about that. Antipater is finding it

increasingly difficult to keep her under control. My mother wants to rule, she wants to exercise power and preventing her from doing so will not be easy. I wonder what Aristotle would make of all this.'

'That's easily discovered – just ask Callisthenes.'

'Callisthenes irritates me sometimes.'

'That is apparent, and the fact obviously pains him.'

'But he does nothing to prevent it.'

'That's not quite the way it is. Callisthenes has his principles and has been educated by his uncle not to make any compromises in this direction: you should try to understand him . . .' and Eumenes then changed the subject. 'What plans do you have for the near future?'

'I want to organize drama and athletic competitions.'

'Competitions . . . drama?'

'That's right.'

'But why?'

'Because the men need some sort of distraction.'

'The men need to wield their swords again. They haven't been involved in any fighting for more than a year, and if the Persians caught up with us right now, I'm not so sure that we'd—'

'The Persians will certainly not appear now. Darius is busy gathering the largest army ever seen to wipe us out.'

'And you simply let him get on with it? You would rather organize drama and athletics?' the Secretary shook his head as though speaking of pure madness, but Alexander stood up and placed a hand on his shoulder.

'Listen: we cannot now face a tiring campaign to wipe out the cities and the fortresses of the Persian empire one

after another. You yourself saw just how much it cost us to take Miletus, Halicarnassus, Tyre . . .'

'Yes, but—'

'So I want to leave Darius all the time he needs to recruit as many soldiers as he can and then I will take him on. And I will resolve everything in one final clash.'

'But . . . but we might lose.'

Alexander looked him in the eyes as though his friend had just uttered some absurdity, 'Lose? That is not possible.'

Eumenes lowered his gaze. He now realized that Olympias's letter had simply convinced Alexander of something he already believed subconsciously – that he was invincible and immortal. That this actually implied some form of divinity was immaterial given the situation, but would the army and his companions share his conviction and determination? What would happen when on some limitless Asian plain they found themselves facing the largest army of all time?

'What are you thinking about?' Alexander asked him.

'Nothing, it's just that a passage from the *March of the Ten Thousand* springs to mind, the passage that goes—'

'I know,' said the King, interrupting him, 'I know what you're thinking of,' and he began reciting from memory: ' "It was already midday and still the enemy was nowhere in sight, but in the afternoon a large dust storm appeared, like a white cloud of the plain spread over a long distance. A little later they could just make out the flashing of the metal and the spears and the ranks became visible . . ."

'The battle of Kunaxa, the Great King's limitless army appearing like a ghost out of the desert dust . . . and yet

even back then the Greeks won the battle, and if they had charged the centre immediately rather than tackling the enemy's left wing head-on, they would have killed the Persian king and conquered his entire empire. You just organize the athletics and the theatrics, my friend.'

Eumenes shook his head again and made for the door.

'One last thing,' said Alexander, stopping him on the threshold. 'Make sure you choose those works which suit Thessalus's voice and bearing. *Oedipus Rex*, for example, and then—'

'Don't worry,' the Secretary sought to put his mind at rest, 'you know I'm good at these things.'

'Eumenes?'

'Yes.'

'How is the General?'

'Parmenion? He must be completely beside himself with grief, but he doesn't let it show.'

'Do you think he'll be up to it when the moment comes?'

'I think so,' replied Eumenes. 'There are not many men like him,' and he left.

<center>*</center>

Alexander celebrated the opening of the athletic and theatrical games in grand style, inviting all his friends and the most important officers to a banquet. Everyone came, apart from Parmenion who sent an orderly with a note excusing himself: 'Parmenion to King Alexander, Hail! Please excuse me for not participating in the banquet. I do not feel well and I would do your table no honour with my presence.'

It was immediately apparent that this was to be a conversational meal, because there were no dancers nor 'companions' expert in love play, and Alexander himself, as 'head of the symposium', cut the wine in the crater with four parts of water. It was also clear that he wanted to discuss philosophical and literary topics rather than wartime subjects because he had assigned the places near him to Barsine and Thessalus. Then came Callisthenes and a couple of sophist philosophers who were visiting with the Athenian delegation. Hephaestion, Eumenes, Seleucus and Ptolemy were also close by with their female companions – some more occasional than others – while the other friends were arranged in the other part of the room.

Although it was now midsummer, the weather outside was taking a turn for the worse and black rain clouds were gathering over the old city. Suddenly, while the cooks were just beginning to serve the first portions of roast lamb with fresh broad beans, a great thunderclap resounded, making the walls of the house shake and sending ripples through the wine in the cups.

All those present looked at one another in silence for a moment, while the thunder rolled away towards the foothills of Mount Lebanon. The cooks started serving the meat again, but Callisthenes, turning to Alexander with a smile part way between ironic and jocular, asked, 'Since you are the son of Zeus, couldn't you manage something along those lines?'

The King lowered his head for a moment and many of the guests in the room thought he was about to produce one of his explosions of wrath. Even Callisthenes

himself suddenly seemed to regret having made the joke. Seleucus noticed that the historian had turned decidedly pale and whispered in Ptolemy's ear, 'This time he's wetting himself with fear.'

However, Alexander lifted his head and let everyone see his smiling face, not upset in the slightest: 'No, I would never do such a thing; I have no wish to frighten my guests.'

Everyone started laughing. The storm had passed by, for the moment at least.

4

ETEOCLES RODE FOR several days, sleeping only for a few hours each night near his horse. He often woke up, frightened by the calls of the animals of the night and the howling of the jackals; he worried about losing his way or being attacked and robbed of his horse and his provisions. The worst fear of all was that he might be captured by brigands and sold as a slave in some far off place where no one would ever find him to set him free again. In all his brief life he had never had to suffer such anxiety and face such danger on his own, but having his father's sword with him did give him some heart, holding the weapon which had belonged to the great Memnon of Rhodes. The fact that he was physically very well developed for his age also helped, making him seem and feel more adult than he in fact was.

He had no way of knowing that his safety depended instead on the men put on his tail by his hated enemy, the man who had brought dishonour on his father and had conquered his mother in body and soul. Perhaps he really was the incarnation of Ahriman, the genius of the darkness and evil, as his grandfather Artabazos had once said.

Everything proceeded smoothly while Eteocles crossed the inhabited areas of Palestine and Syria, where it was

relatively easy for his escort to camouflage themselves or to mix in with caravans that moved from one village to another bearing wares; but out on the limitless expanses of the desert the two *hetairoi* who were following him had to discuss matters and make a decision. They were two young Macedonians from the royal guard, among the most valiant and intelligent of Alexander's soldiers, and they knew their leader very well. If they failed in their mission and anything happened to the boy, the King would certainly never forgive them.

'If we keep him under observation,' said one of them, 'he will see us, because there is nowhere for us to hide. If we keep out of his sight then there's the risk we might lose him.'

'We have no choice,' replied his companion. 'One of us has to approach him and win his trust. There is simply no other way of protecting him.'

They laid out a plan of action and the following day at dawn, when the boy set off again on his journey, exhausted after a night spent half awake, off in the distance he saw a man alone on a horse, riding in his same direction. He stopped and wondered whether it might be better to let him go on ahead and set off later, or to ride closer to the solitary traveller and thus have some company for at least part of the journey.

He decided that waiting was not a good idea because it would consequently mean having to travel in the warmest hours of the day. He felt sure that one man, alone and unarmed, was certainly no danger and that in any case he would have to face much more difficult situations in the near future. He plucked his courage up,

kicked the sides of his mount with his heels and set off along the deserted track, soon drawing level with the rider, who turned on hearing the noise of the horse. Eteocles, overcoming his own shyness, spoke to him in Persian, 'May Ahura Mazda protect you, stranger. Which way are you going?'

The man, knowing that he would be understood, replied in Greek, 'I do not speak your language, my boy. I am a goldsmith from Crete and I am on my way to Babylon to work in the palace of the Great King.'

Eteocles breathed a sigh of relief and said, 'I too am on my way to Babylon. I hope you won't mind if we travel together.'

'Not at all. Indeed, it would be a pleasure – travelling alone on these deserted roads frightens me.'

'Why are you travelling alone? Wouldn't it have been better for you to join up with a caravan?'

'You are right. The fact is that I have heard so many stories about the merchants on the caravans . . . that they supplement their income by selling off as slaves the lone travellers they meet along their way, whenever they think they can get away with it, so I said to myself, "Better alone than in bad company." At least I can see right across to the horizon, the track is clearly marked and it's not difficult to maintain one's sense of direction – all you have to do is keep going towards the rising sun and sooner or later you'll come to the banks of the Euphrates. The worst is over at that stage because all that's needed then is a good boat and that's it. You can put your feet up and rest until you reach Babylon. But

you look a bit too young to me to be travelling on your own. Don't you have parents or brothers?'

Eteocles did not reply and for a moment all they could hear was the noise of their horses' hooves on the desert track, under the empty sky. The man spoke again, 'Sorry. I shouldn't have poked my nose into your personal affairs.'

Eteocles now stared off towards the horizon, flat and monotonous like the becalmed sea, 'Do you think it'll take us long to reach the banks of the Euphrates?'

'No,' replied the man. 'If we keep this pace up we should be there tomorrow night.'

They kept going until evening and then set up camp in a slight hollow. Eteocles stayed awake for as long as he could manage, so as to keep an eye on his new companion, but in the end exhaustion won and he fell into a deep sleep. The man then stood up and walked back in the direction they had come from until there in the darkness he was able to make out the silhouettes of a horse and a man lying down next to it. Everything was proceeding according to plan and so he returned to their camp and lay down himself, snatching brief moments of sleep while remaining alert to the sounds of the night.

When the boy woke at dawn he found that the man had placed a handful of dates with dry bread and a boxwood cup full of water from his water bag on his cape. The water had chilled during the night and was refreshing to drink. They ate in silence and then set off again under the burning sun, in the stagnant, motionless air.

By about midday it was clear that the horses were struggling and so they dismounted and continued on foot, leading the animals by their bridles.

They reached the Euphrates late in the night, becoming aware of the great river thanks to the gurgling of its waters before they actually saw the sparkling of its flow in the moonlight. There was one point where the water rushed against the shallow gravel bed creating a ribbon of foam from one bank to the other – a ford. The soldier moved closer, rode slowly towards the centre of the river, testing the solidity of the crossing, and then turned back.

'It's safe here,' he said, turning to Eteocles. 'If you want, you can cross.'

'What do you mean?' the boy asked him. 'Aren't you coming?'

The soldier shook his head. 'No. My mission is accomplished and I must turn back now.'

'Mission?' asked the boy, increasingly bewildered.

'That's right. Alexander gave us orders to escort you to the border and to make sure nothing happened to you. Another companion has been following us at a distance.'

Eteocles lowered his head, humiliated by such odious consideration on Alexander's part: 'Return to your master and tell him that this will not stop me killing him if I ever meet him on a battlefield.' He guided his charger into the ford.

The soldier, sitting upright on his mount, stood there watching until he saw the boy riding up the opposite bank and setting off along the plain into Persian territory.

Then he turned and headed back to meet his companion who was probably waiting not far away. The moonlight was increasingly strong and things were well illuminated, helped by the chalky colour of the desert, but there was no sign of the other *hetairos*. And the next day, by sunlight, there was no trace of him either, nor was there any the day after that; the desert had swallowed him up.

5

'YOUR SON ETEOCLES has crossed the border into Persia safe and sound,' said Alexander as he entered Barsine's room, 'but one of the men I sent to follow him and protect him has not returned.'

'I am sorry,' replied Barsine. 'I know how close you are to your men.'

'They are like my children. But this is the price I pay for your peace of mind. And how is your youngest son?'

'He remains close to me, he loves me, and perhaps he understands me. And then nature helps protect the young – they soon forget and forgetting comes more easily to them.'

'And you? How do you feel?'

'I am most grateful to you for all you have done, but my life is no longer the same. A woman who is also a mother can perhaps never be a real lover – her heart is always pulled in another direction by other feelings.'

'Are you trying to tell me that you no longer wish to see me?'

Barsine lowered her head, somewhat upset now, 'Please don't make things any harder for me; you well know that I wish to see you every day, every instant, that your remoteness and your coldness hurt me so much. I beg you, please give me some time to recover,

to build a small refuge in my heart for my memories and then . . . then I will know how to love you as you wish me to.'

She stood up and approached him, enveloping him in her beauty and her fragrance – Alexander took her face in his hands and kissed her.

'Do not despair. You will see your son again and perhaps in some not so distant future we will all be able to live in peace together.' He embraced her and left.

On the stairs he met Seleucus, who had been looking for him, 'A ship has arrived from General Antipater with an urgent message. Here it is.'

Alexander opened it and read:

Antipater, Regent of the Kingdom, to Alexander, Hail!

The Spartans have assembled an army and are on the march against our garrisons and our allies in the Peloponnese, but for the moment they are alone. It is vital that they remain without allies. Do as you think you must to ensure that the situation does not change, and thus I will have no need of assistance. Your mother and your sister are both well – perhaps you should consider a new match for Cleopatra. The Egyptian Sisines, the man you asked me to investigate, became a trusted servant of your mother the Queen on your father's death.

Take good care.

'I hope the old man has sent you good news,' said Seleucus.

'Not quite. The Spartans are making a move and are preparing to attack us – we must remind the Athenians

of their commitment. When is the audience with the delegation from their government?'

'This evening. They have already handed Eumenes a note in which they request the return of the Athenian prisoners captured at the Granicus.'

'They haven't wasted any time. But I am afraid they will be disappointed. Is there anything else?'

'Your physician Philip is attending to Darius's wife during her pregnancy, but he is very worried and asked that you should be informed.'

'I see. Tell the Athenians I will receive them after the theatre and ask Barsine to go to the Queen in her rooms. Perhaps she will be of some help.'

He set off down the stairs and met Philip just as he was leaving his quarters, followed by a couple of assistants, loaded down with medicines of all types.

'How is the Queen?' Alexander asked.

'The situation is stable, but very serious.'

'What is the problem?'

'As far as I can make out, the child has turned and she cannot give birth to it.'

In the meantime Alexander had started walking and was heading now for the building in which Darius's wives were lodged together with their court.

'Can you do nothing to help?'

'Perhaps I could do something, but I am afraid she would never let herself be examined by a man. I am trying to train her midwife, but I am not sure it's of any use. She comes from the Queen's ancestral tribe and it seems to me she is more expert in magic than in medicine.'

'Wait, Barsine will come now and perhaps she will succeed in convincing her.'

'I hope so,' replied Philip, but the expression on his face made it clear he doubted it very much.

On reaching the building which had been set up as the royal harem, they saw that Barsine had already arrived and was anxiously waiting for them in front of the door. They were met by a eunuch and shown into the atrium. From the floor above came the sound of suffocated moaning.

'She doesn't even cry out when the labour pains come,' said Philip, 'decorum prevents her.'

The eunuch very respectfully gestured for them to follow and led them upstairs, where they met the midwife who was leaving the room just at that moment.

'Please interpret for me,' said the physician to Barsine. 'I must convince her, do you understand?' Barsine nodded and entered the Queen's apartments. The eunuch in the meantime led Alexander to the threshold of another door and knocked.

A finely dressed Persian woman opened it and accompanied them first to an antechamber and then to a room in which Sisygambis, the Queen Mother, was sitting. She was near a window, on her knees was a roll of papyrus densely covered in script, and she was quietly whispering formulae to herself. The eunuch gestured to Alexander to explain that she was praying and the King stood respectfully in silence near the door, but Sisygambis immediately realized he was there, stood up and came to him, warmly greeting him in Persian. Her face clearly

displayed her worry and concern, and pain too, but there was no sign of unease.

'The Queen Mother greets you,' came the interpreter's translation, 'and she begs you to accept her hospitality.'

'Thank her for me, but tell her that I do not wish to disturb her – I have come only to try to provide assistance for Darius's wife who is in some difficulty now. My physician,' he continued, looking straight into her eyes, 'says that he could perhaps help if she . . . if she were able to overcome her modesty and agree to have him examine her.'

Sisygambis thought deeply, looking back into Alexander's eyes with her face displaying just how much she was moved, and they both felt how strong their feelings were and how distant they were from the formal language of the interpreter. At that moment the silence was invaded by the muffled sound of the mother-to-be moaning, trying to face her ordeal in solitude and pride. The Queen Mother flinched at the sound and her eyes filled with tears.

'I doubt your physician would be able to help even if she did give permission.'

'But why, Great Mother? My physician is most expert and—' he cut himself short because he realized from the expression on her face that her thoughts were travelling in a different direction.

'I believe,' said Sisygambis, 'that in truth my daughter-in-law does not want to give birth.'

'I do not understand, Great Mother: Philip, my doctor, feels that the baby is perhaps not in the correct position for the birth and . . .'

Slowly, two tears ran down the Queen Mother's cheeks; her face bore all the marks of her age and her pain and the words came from her mouth deliberately, like the words of a verdict: 'My daughter-in-law does not want to give birth to a prisoner and no physician has the power to change her decision. She is holding the baby within her, so that she will die together with him.'

Alexander was truly bewildered and speechless and he lowered his head.

'It is not your fault, my boy,' continued Sisygambis, her voice cracking with emotion. 'Destiny created you to destroy the empire founded by Cyrus. You are like the wind that blows impetuously across the earth, and after the wind passes, nothing is as it was before. But men remain attached to their memories, just as ants hold on to leaves of grass while the storm rages around them.'

At that moment there came a much louder cry and then a doleful chorus of moaning from the rooms within the building.

'It is done,' Sisygambis said. 'The last King of Kings is dead, before being born.' Two handmaids entered and covered her face and shoulders with a black veil so that she could give vent to her grief without being seen.

Alexander would have liked to say something, but as he watched her she appeared to him to be like a statue, a simulacrum of the goddess of the night, and he dared not speak. He lowered his head for an instant and then left the room, setting off along the corridor in the midst of the crying and the wailing of Darius's women. Philip

came out of the dead queen's antechamber, pale and dumbstruck.

*

The following day Alexander gave orders for the funeral to be celebrated, for the Queen to be buried in grand style, with all the honours befitting her rank, and for a great mound to be constructed, as was the custom in her native tribe. He could not help but cry as they placed her underground, thinking of just how beautiful and delicate she had been and thinking too of the baby who had never even seen the light of day.

The eunuch escaped that very evening and rode for days and nights until he reached the first Persian outposts near the River Tigris. There he asked to be taken to King Darius's camp, which was on the other side of the river. A group of Median horsemen escorted him for ten parasangs across the desert and at sunset on the following day they brought him before the Great King.

Darius was at council with his generals, dressed like an ordinary soldier with rough linen trousers and an antelope-skin jacket. The only sign of his regal status was the rigid tiara and the solid gold dagger, the shining *akinake* that hung from his side.

The eunuch threw himself to the ground with his forehead in the dust and through his sobbing recounted what had happened at Tyre – the Queen's long, painful labour, her death, the funeral. He even put in Alexander's tears.

Darius was shocked by the news and ordered the

eunuch to follow him into the interior section of the royal tent.

'Forgive me, Great King, for having brought you such sad news, forgive me . . .' the eunuch continued to say through his own tears.

'Do not cry,' said Darius, seeking to console him. 'You have done your duty and I am grateful to you for this. Did my wife suffer much?'

'She suffered a great deal, Your Majesty, but with a dignity and strength befitting a Persian queen.'

Darius looked at him without saying anything. It was clear from the deep furrows on his forehead and from the failing light in his bewildered gaze that his heart and mind were full of contrasting sentiments.

'Are you sure,' he asked after a moment's silence, 'that Alexander actually cried?'

'Yes, my King. I was close enough to see the tears run down his cheeks.'

Darius sighed and sat down heavily on a chest, 'But then this means . . . this means there was something going on between them; tears come when a person dear to us dies.'

'Your Majesty, I do not believe that—'

'Perhaps the child was his—'

'No, no!' protested the eunuch.

'Silence!' shouted Darius. 'Or perhaps you dare contradict me?'

The eunuch fell to his knees, trembling and crying once more. 'Your Majesty, I beg you, let me speak!' he said.

'You have already said too much. What else is there to add now?'

'That Alexander never touched your wife. Indeed, he paid her every respect and concern; he never visited her without asking permission and always in the presence of her maids. He displayed the same regard, if not even more so, for your mother.'

'And you are not lying to me?'

'I would never lie to you, Great King. Everything I have told you is the truth. I swear it in the name of Ahura Mazda.'

'Ahura Mazda . . .' murmured Darius. He stood up, moved the curtain door of his tent to one side and lifted his gaze towards the sky. The celestial vault over the desert was teeming with stars and the Milky Way stretched out from one horizon to the other with its diaphanous light. The camp was dotted with thousands and thousands of campfires. 'Ahura Mazda, Lord of the Celestial Flame, our god,' he prayed, 'make me victorious, let me save my ancestors' empire. I promise that should I win, I will treat my opponent with clemency and with respect because if war had not placed us in this position I would have liked in all sincerity to have asked for his friendship and his affection.'

The eunuch made to go, leaving the King alone with his thoughts, but as he did so he heard a certain fuss coming from one of the entrances to the camp and he stopped. A group of Assyrian horsemen were approaching, escorting a most handsome young man who as he passed looked at him as if he recognized him. The eunuch followed behind the group for a few steps, almost not

believing what he was seeing. The small procession in the meantime had reached the royal tent and when the light of the torches burning there before the entrance illuminated the boy's face, he was certain. It was Eteocles, son of Memnon of Rhodes and Barsine!

6

THESSALUS'S PERFORMANCE IN *Oedipus Rex* was impeccable and when he came to the scene in which the hero puts out his own eyes with the pin of his buckle, the spectators saw two streams of blood run down the actor's mask; a long 'oooooh' of wonder came from the audience arranged on the terraces while the rhythmic lament of Oedipus himself came from the stage: *'Oitoitoitoitoitói papái féu féu!'*

Alexander, sitting in a position of honour, gave long and enthusiastic applause. Immediately afterwards came the performance of *Alcestis* and the audience were even more taken aback when at the climax Death, decked out in Thanatos's costume, sprang up from below ground and proceeded to fly about the stage, flapping his bat's wings, while Hercules sought to bring him down with great sweeping blows of his club. Eumenes had arranged for the stage machinery to be designed by the architect Diades, the same one who had built the assault towers that had brought the walls of Tyre tumbling down.

'I told you he would do a good job,' the Secretary whispered in Alexander's ear. 'Just look at the audience – they're lapping it up.'

At that precise moment Hercules' club caught Thanatos with a direct hit, the hook holding the actor was

released from the swivelling arm and he fell to the stage with a loud thump and Hercules immediately set about massacring him with a series of blows while the public went wild.

'You've done a marvellous job. Make sure that everyone receives a prize, especially the architect who designed the machinery. I've never seen anything like it.'

'Thanks also to our *choregi*, our sponsors: the King of Cyprus spared no expense in financing the sets and . . . just one last thing,' he added. 'There is news from the Persian front. I will inform you of everything this evening after the audience.' Then he left to organize the prize-giving ceremony.

The judges, among whom were some Athenian guests who had been nominated out of courtesy, retired to the council chamber before reaching their decisions: the prize for best stage set went to *Alcestis*, while best leading actor went to Athenodorus for his interpretation of the Queen of Argos with a female mask and a falsetto voice.

The King was disappointed, but he sought to hide the fact and then courteously applauded the winner.

'Don't fret about it,' said Eumenes, 'they've given him the prize for his fairy voice.'

'If I know Alexander then this will not help the Athenian government's petitions at the audience this evening,' Ptolemy whispered to Seleucus.

'No, but even without this decision of theirs they wouldn't really have much hope: King Agis of Sparta is attacking our garrisons and it's best to nip in the bud any temptation the Athenians might feel.'

Seleucus had read the situation well – when the

moment came the King received the Athenian ambassadors and listened carefully to their requests.

'Our city has been loyal,' began the leader of the delegation, a senior member of the assembly with many years of experience, 'we have supported you throughout your conquest of Ionia and we have kept the sea free of pirates, guaranteeing your communications with Macedonia. We therefore ask you to release the Athenian prisoners who fell into your hands at the Granicus. Their families are anxious to embrace them once more, the city is ready to welcome them. It is true that they acted unwisely, but they did so in good faith and they have paid for their mistake.'

The King exchanged rapid glances with Seleucus and Ptolemy, then he replied, 'In my heart I want to satisfy your request, but the time is still not ripe for us to put the past to one side. I will release five hundred men drawn by lots or chosen by you. The others will remain with me as prisoners for some time to come.'

The leader of the Athenian delegation did not make any attempt to discuss the matter; he was well aware of the nature of Alexander and swallowed the bitter taste in his mouth as he withdrew. He knew that the King never went back on any of his decisions, especially where anything connected with politics and strategy was concerned.

As soon as the delegates had left, all the members of the council got to their feet and left in their turn. Only Eumenes remained.

'Well then?' Alexander asked him. 'What is the news you mentioned?'

'You will know soon enough. There is a visitor for you.'

Eumenes opened a side door and showed a rather bizarre character into the room: a nicely curled and evidently dyed black beard, hair combed in the same manner with a calamistrum and showy Syrian clothes. Alexander had some trouble recognizing him.

'Eumolpus of Soloi! But what has happened to you?'

'I have changed my identity: my name is now Baaladgar and I move in Syrian circles where I enjoy a considerable reputation as a seer and magician,' he said. 'But how must I address the young god who is Lord of the Nile and the Euphrates, whose name makes all Asia tremble in fear?' and then a further question, 'Is the dog here?'

'No, he's not here,' Eumenes replied. 'Are you a blind seer?'

'Well then, what news do you bring me?' Alexander asked.

Eumolpus dusted down a chair with a corner of his cloak and sat down after having been invited to do so. 'This time I believe I bring you information the likes of which you have never received before,' he began. 'This is the situation: the Great King is assembling a big army, certainly bigger even than the one you faced at Issus. What is more he is planning on making use of newly designed scythed chariots, terrible devices bristling all over with razor-sharp blades. His base camp will be just north of Babylon where he will wait to see which direction you take. At that stage he will choose the site for the battle. Most certainly it will be a flat plain where he can gain maximum advantage from his numerical

superiority and where he can let the chariots have free rein. Darius no longer wishes to negotiate with you – he is now putting everything into the final clash. And he is sure he will win.'

'What has made him change his mind so quickly?'

'Your inaction. The fact that you have not moved from the coast has convinced him he has the time to assemble all the troops he needs to defeat you.'

Alexander turned to Eumenes, 'See? I was right. This is the only way for us to reach a definitive solution. I shall win and then all Asia will be mine.'

Eumenes turned again to Eumolpus, 'Do you have any idea as to where Darius might choose to fight us? To the north? To the south?'

'I cannot say, but there is one thing I know – wherever you find an open road before you, that is where the Great King will be waiting for you.'

Alexander thought in silence for a moment while Eumolpus watched furtively and then he said, 'We will make our move at the beginning of autumn and we will cross the Euphrates at Thapsacus. Wait for us there, if you have more news then.'

The informer left in a flurry of ceremonious leave-taking and Eumenes remained behind to speak with the King.

'If you cross at Thapsacus then that means you want to move down the Euphrates, just like Xenophon's "ten thousand" . . . am I right?'

'Perhaps, but nothing's certain. I will make my decision when I am on the left bank. For now let the

athletics continue. I want the men to enjoy themselves and have some sort of distraction: afterwards there won't be any time left. We will be under pressure for months, perhaps for years. Who is representing us in the boxing?'

'Leonnatus.'

'Of course. And the wrestling?'

'Leonnatus.'

'I see. Please find Hephaestion for me and send him to me here.'

Eumenes took his leave and set off in search of the King's friend. He found him training for the wrestling together with Leonnatus and saw him take a couple of falls before managing to get his attention. He waited until Hephaestion hit the deck a third time and then said, 'Alexander wants to see you. Hurry up.'

'Does he want to see me as well?' asked Leonnatus.

'No, no he doesn't. Stay here and carry on with your training – I wouldn't like to be in your shoes if you don't beat the Athenian challenger.'

Leonnatus grumbled something as he gestured to another soldier to step forward. Hephaestion washed hurriedly and then went before Alexander with his hair still full of sand.

'You sent for me?'

'Yes. I have a special job for you. Choose two cavalry units, from the Vanguard if you wish, and two teams of the Phoenician naval carpenters. Take Nearchus with you, go to Thapsacus on the Euphrates and provide him with cover while he builds two floating bridges. We will cross there.'

'How much time do I have?'

'A month at the most, after which we will join you with the rest of the army.'

'So we are finally moving.'

'Yes, we are making our move. Say your farewells to the sea, Hephaestion, you won't be seeing any more salt water until we reach the shores of the Ocean that has no end.'

7

IT TOOK FOUR DAYS to assemble the cavalry, the carpenters and the construction materials. Under Nearchus's supervision, the barges were taken apart, the pieces numbered and loaded on carts drawn by mules, and the long convoy made ready to leave the coast. The night before their departure, Hephaestion went to say goodbye to Alexander; when he came back he saw two shadows creep out from behind a tent and approach him furtively. He was just beginning to reach for his sword when a familiar voice whispered, 'It's us.'

'Are you tired of living?' Hephaestion asked Eumenes.

'Put that weapon away – we have to talk.'

Hephaestion took a furtive look at the other character and recognized Eumolpus of Soloi. 'Well I never!' he laughed. 'The man who saved his arse from a Persian stake, leaving a whole army up shit creek in the process.'

'Just watch your mouth, lad,' the informer retorted, 'and listen to me if you want to save your own arse and all the lice that live thereabouts.'

Hephaestion had them enter his tent, astonished at all that secrecy, and poured some wine into two cups. Eumenes took a sip and began, 'Eumolpus has not told Alexander everything.'

'I don't know why, but somehow I had imagined as much.'

'And he did the right thing, by Zeus! Alexander wants to lower his horns and charge like a bull without even considering his own forces, nor those of the enemy.'

'That's the right approach; that's how we won at the Granicus and at Issus.'

'At the Granicus we were more or less equally matched and at Issus we scraped through with a considerable dose of luck. Here we're talking about a million men. Do you understand that? A million men. One hundred myriads. Can you count? I don't imagine you can. Anyway, I've worked it all out – lined up in six rows, they'll encircle us on the right and on the left by over three stadia. And the scythed chariots? How will our men react when they find themselves faced with those frightful machines?'

'Where do I fit in all this?'

'I'll tell you immediately,' said Eumolpus. 'The Great King will send a garrison led by Mazaeus, Satrap of Babylonia, to the ford at Thapsacus. Mazaeus is his right hand man, an old fox who knows every corner of every land between here and the mouth of the Indus, has several thousand Greek mercenaries with him, all of them well seasoned, the type of soldiers who can spit blood when necessary. And do you know what else? Mazaeus has no problem communicating with those lads because he speaks Greek better than you do.'

'I still don't understand what you're getting at.'

'For some time now Mazaeus has been thoroughly

disheartened by a conviction that the empire of Cyrus the Great and Darius has reached its demise.'

'So much the better for us; and so?'

'And so, since the man who passed me this information is very close to Mazaeus, there is a chance that we might reason with the old man. Do you see what I mean?'

'Yes and no.'

'If you get the chance to meet him, speak with him,' said Eumenes. 'Nearchus will recognize him because he once saw him on Cyprus.'

'I will try. And then?'

'There is a chance that we might just lose in battle against a million men. Some help would be most useful.'

'You want me to persuade him to betray Darius.'

'Something like that,' said Eumolpus.

'I'll talk to Alexander about it.'

'Are you off your head?' said Eumenes.

'Otherwise there's nothing to be done.'

Eumolpus shook his head, 'Stupid boys who just don't want to listen to those who know so much more than they do ... do as you wish then, you go on and have your head split open.' He left, followed by Eumenes, and he just missed Alexander who was taking Peritas for a walk along the seashore. The dog immediately started barking in their direction and Eumenes looked first at Peritas and then at the informer and asked him, 'What's your wig made of?'

<div align="center">★</div>

Hephaestion's army took seven days to reach the banks of the Euphrates at Thapsacus, a city full of merchants, of travellers, of livestock and wares of all kinds. Thapsacus teemed with life because it was the only fording point on the river.

Although located in the interior, the city was Phoenician in origin and its name indeed meant 'ford' or 'passage'. There was nothing particularly attractive about it from an aesthetic point of view – no monuments or temples, and not even any squares with porticoes and statues. Nevertheless, it was pleasant, thanks to the hustle and bustle of the people there, the merchants' shouting and the incredible number of prostitutes who plied their wares with the mule and camel drivers who worked along the banks of the great river. The language spoken at Thapsacus was a curious mixture of Syrian, Cilician, Phoenician and Aramaic with the occasional word of Greek.

Hephaestion completed his first reconnaissance tour and immediately realized that for the moment there was no possibility of fording the river; it had already begun to rain up in the mountains and the river was too swollen. The only way to cross was to build a bridge and so the Phoenician carpenters set to work under Nearchus's command. The planks were all marked with red-hot brands bearing letters from the Phoenician alphabet for matching up the tenon joints.

When all the barges were ready, they started assembling the bridge – the mariners brought each pontoon into position, anchored it to the riverbed, attached it firmly to the previous pontoon and then laid out the wooden

planks and raised the parapet. The work had only just begun when Mazaeus's troops appeared – Syrian and Arab cavalry together with Greek heavy infantry. They immediately began disruptive action – incursions to the middle of the river with fire arrows, and naphtha-laden fireboats sent from upstream at night; fast and burning bright they came, globes of flame that crashed against Nearchus's constructions, setting them alight.

Thus the days went by without any progress being made and the moment when Alexander's army would appear, with ten thousand horses and two thousand carts full of provisions and equipment, ready to cross the Euphrates, was drawing near. Hephaestion hated the idea of being behind schedule and he often spoke to Nearchus in an attempt to find some solution. One night, while they were sitting on the riverbank discussing what should be done, Nearchus clapped him on the back, 'Look.'

'At what?'

'At that man.'

Hephaestion looked across to the other bank where Nearchus pointed and saw a man alone, astride a horse, holding up a lighted torch.

'Who can it be?'

'It looks as though whoever it is wants to speak to us.'

'What shall we do?'

'I think you should go over there. Take a boat, get yourself ferried across and listen to what he has to say. We'll try to provide you with cover, if it proves necessary.'

Hephaestion agreed, had himself ferried across to the other bank and stood there before the mysterious horseman.

'Hail!' he said, in excellent Greek.

'Hail to you,' replied Hephaestion. 'Who are you?'

'My name is Nabunaid.'

'What do you want of me?'

'Nothing. Tomorrow we will destroy your bridge, but before the final battle I would like to give you this object and I would like you to give it to Baaladgar, if you see him.'

Eumolpus of Soloi, Hephaestion thought to himself as he looked at the terracotta statuette the man held in his hand, decorated around its base with wedge-shaped characters.

'Why?'

'He once cured me of a deadly illness and I promised I would repay him with an object I was most fond of. This is it.'

Who would have credited it, thought Hephaestion, and I thought he was the last of the charlatans.

'Fine,' he replied. 'I will give it to him. Is there anything else you want to tell me?'

'No,' said the strange character, and he rode off, still holding up his torch. Hephaestion returned to Nearchus who was waiting on the furthermost pontoon that was still intact.

'Do you know who that man was?' the admiral asked as soon as he saw Hephaestion approaching the mooring.

'No . . . why?'

'If I'm not mistaken, it was Mazaeus, Satrap of Babylonia.'

'By Hercules! But what—'

'What did he tell you?'

'That he is going to tear us apart, but also that he is indebted to Baaladgar, or Eumolpus of Soloi; he asked me to give him this . . .' and he showed Nearchus the statuette.

'This means that he is a man who respects his commitments. As for tearing us apart, I have had an idea and within a couple of days we will give him a nice surprise.'

'What idea would that be?'

'I have had all the pontoons that have not yet been assembled transported upstream.'

'You mean all the pontoons we have.'

'Exactly. I'll have them put together in a wood where no one will see us and then we'll load them up with three hundred horsemen, ferry them across the river and attack Mazaeus's camp in the middle of the night, unleashing merry hell. As soon as they have unloaded the cavalry on the other bank, the pontoons will float downstream, and our carpenters will join them all up together. At this stage you will cross the river and provide support with the Vanguard. We will win. They will lose. The Thapsacus ford is ours. Game over.'

Hephaestion looked at him closely; this Cretan with his curly hair and his dark skin certainly knew how to handle his boats. 'When do we start?' he asked.

'We already have,' replied Nearchus. 'Once the idea came it seemed pointless to waste time. Some of my men have already gone on ahead as an advance party.'

8

Nearchus's manoeuvre was carried out two days later, just after midnight. The horsemen were ferried across to the left bank of the river and they immediately started advancing southwards. The pontoons were now empty and a few crewmen waited for a short while so as to give the cavalry time to attack before setting off with the flow of the water down the Euphrates.

When they came near Hephaestion's camp they could hear shouting from the Persians who were being attacked by the Macedonian aggressors. Nearchus immediately gave orders for the assembly to begin and the pontoons were lined up one after the other and moored firmly; while the battle raged in the enemy camp, he managed to reach the left bank and safely anchor the last one.

The attacking horsemen were finding themselves in difficulty, but Hephaestion, at the head of the Vanguard, set off at a gallop across the bridge to offer help to his exhausted men. The battle picked up again even more fiercely than before and the Greek mercenaries, positioned at the centre of the Persian lines, put up ferocious resistance to each charge as it came; indeed, they locked into a square formation, protecting one another with their heavy shields.

Suddenly, however, and unexpectedly, the Persians

seemed to respond to some signal and began retreating southwards. The Greeks, surrounded on all sides and left with no support whatsoever, had to surrender. Hephaestion planted the red standard with the Argead star at the centre of the enemy camp on the left bank of the Euphrates. Nearchus came to him shortly afterwards.

'Is everything alright?' he asked.

'Yes, Admiral. But I wonder how it feels for you to be playing with these nutshell boats when you are used to leading fleets of quinqueremes.'

'One gets by with whatever one has to hand, Hephaestion,' replied Nearchus. 'The important thing is to win.'

The officers from the individual divisions gave orders to pitch camp and sent reconnaissance patrols out into the surrounding countryside. One patrol rode up to the top of a small hill with a clear view southwards and saw the flickering of flames on the horizon.

'It's a fire!' the leader of the patrol suddenly exclaimed, 'Quickly! Let's go and take a look!'

'There's another one down there,' shouted another horseman.

'Over there as well! On the riverbank!' came an echo from another companion. The flames were rising everywhere.

'What can it be?'

Their leader turned his gaze towards the great glow of fire that now illuminated much of the sky over a large tract of the horizon. 'The Persians,' he replied. 'They're burning everything. Razed earth, so that we will find nothing of any use to us as we make our way through their land. They want us to die of starvation and exhaustion. Let's

go and check the situation,' and he spurred the horse on towards the fires.

They moved forwards, keeping the river on their right and soon they had confirmation of their fears – everywhere, across the plain and along the banks of the Euphrates, there were villages in flames. Some of them were situated on small rises of dried mud and they could be seen even more clearly as they were consumed by the fire, columns of smoke and sparks rising up against the night sky. Men on horseback were riding everywhere, torches and burning branches held aloft – it was a terrible sight.

'Let's go back,' ordered the leader. 'We've seen quite enough.' He pulled on his horse's reins and spurred it on in the direction of the camp. Soon he was with Nearchus and Hephaestion, reporting on what had happened, but now the light of the fires on the plain was so strong it could be seen from the camp; the horizon was burning red like some absurd southern sunset.

'The harvest has just been stored in the granaries and there won't be a grain of wheat left from here to Babylon. Alexander must be informed immediately!' exclaimed Hephaestion. He called a messenger and immediately sent him off in the direction of Tyre.

*

Alexander, in the meantime, had finished gathering provisions and equipment, had prepared the convoy of carts to transport them and was about to set off for the ford at Thapsacus. News of the imminent departure had spread and as usual the great entourage that always followed the army, setting up camp not far from the soldiers during

their stops, had assembled as well. It consisted of merchants plying all sorts of wares, male and female prostitutes, but also girls from poor families who had left home and had established long-term relationships with soldiers. Many of them were pregnant and some of them had already given birth to fine children with dark skin and blue eyes or blond hair.

That same day, as evening fell, a Macedonian ship moored at Tyre and unloaded shafts of ash and cornel wood for soldiers' spears, together with chests full of armour and spare parts for the war engines, but one particular member of the crew immediately disembarked and set off for the old town, asking where Callisthenes' lodgings were to be found.

He carried a bag over his shoulder and when he reached the door, which had been pointed out to him, he knocked discreetly.

'Who is it?' came Callisthenes' voice from inside. The man knocked again without replying and the historian opened the door. There before him was a rather stout man with a thick beard and black, curly hair who greeted him with a bow.

'My name is Hermocrates and I am a soldier in Antipater's guard. Aristotle has sent me.'

'Come in,' Callisthenes said, with a worried expression on his face. The man entered and looked around; he moved in that faltering way typical of those who have spent a long time at sea and he asked to be allowed to sit down. Callisthenes told him to make himself comfortable, but before doing so Hermocrates took the bag and placed it carefully on the table before them.

'Aristotle told me to give you this,' he said, taking a metal box from the bag. 'Together with this message.' The historian took the letter and continued to study the box with increasing apprehension.

'Why are you so late? This box should have arrived here much earlier. I do not know if now . . .'

He started reading the letter. It was certainly from Aristotle, but it was in code and had no heading. It read:

> This drug will bring about death at a distance of over ten days with symptoms similar to those of a serious illness. Destroy it when you have used it. And if you do not use it, destroy it anyway. Do not touch it for any reason and do not inhale its smell.

'All of this would have made sense a year ago,' said Callisthenes as he picked up the box gingerly.

'Unfortunately I encountered many problems on my journey. My ship was struck by a strong northern wind and was blown off course for days and days until it finally sank off the desert coast of Libya. My shipwrecked companions and I marched for months, eating fish and crabs until we reached the border with Egypt, where I was given news of the King's expedition to the sanctuary of Ammon. From there, still on foot, I reached a port on the Delta where I found a ship that had also been pushed off course by a northerly wind. They explained to me that they were heading for Tyre, where the King and his army and his companions were awaiting them, and they let me on board.'

'You are a brave and loyal man. Allow me to reward you,' said Callisthenes, reaching for his purse.

'I want no reward,' replied Hermocrates, 'but I will accept some money because I have none and I do not know how to return to Macedonia.'

'Do you wish to eat and drink?'

'I would gladly eat something. The food on the ship was terrible.'

Callisthenes placed the box he had been given in his personal chest, which he then locked. He then washed his hands in a basin and put bread, cheese, and some grilled fish and oil and salt on the table.

'How is my old uncle?'

'He is well,' replied the man as he bit into the bread after having dipped it in oil and salt.

'What was he up to last time you saw him?'

'He was leaving Mieza and heading towards Aegae. And with the bad weather on its way.'

'So his investigation continues,' said Callisthenes, almost to himself.

'What did you say?'

'Nothing . . . nothing,' said Callisthenes shaking his head. He sat for an instant observing his guest who was tucking into the food and then asked, 'Has there been any news regarding Philip's assassination? I mean, any rumours in Macedonia?'

Hermocrates stopped eating, swallowed what he had in his mouth and sat there in silence with his head bowed.

'You can trust me,' Callisthenes reassured him. 'Anything you may say will go no further.'

'They say it was Pausanias, that he was acting on his own initiative.'

It was clear to Callisthenes that the man did not want

to speak, and he also understood that his question had rattled him somewhat.

'I will give you a letter for my Uncle Aristotle. When are you setting off again?'

'With the first ship I find.'

'Good. I leave tomorrow with the King. You may stay here in this house until you find your ship.'

Callisthenes picked up his pen and began writing:

Callisthenes to Aristotle, Hail!

Only today, twenty-eighth day of the month of Boedromion in the first year of the hundred and twelfth Olympiad, have I received the thing I had asked you to send to Theophrastus. The motive behind my request no longer exists and therefore I will destroy this thing, so as not to create any pointless risks. Let me know, as soon as you are able, if you have discovered anything regarding the assassination of King Philip because not even Zeus Ammon wanted to answer this question. Now we are leaving the coast to march towards the interior and I do not know if I must say goodbye to the sea for the last time. I hope you are well.

He dusted the papyrus with ash, shook it, rolled it and handed it to Hermocrates. 'I leave at dawn tomorrow and so I will take my leave now. Travel well and safely and tell my uncle that I miss his advice and his wisdom very much.'

'I will do so,' replied the man.

*

The following day the army set off followed by the royal caravan with the women of Darius's harem, the Queen Mother and the concubines with their children. Barsine travelled with them and tried as best she could to help Sisygambis, now a very old woman.

East of the Vale of Orontes, before they reached the banks of the Euphrates, Hephaestion's messenger met them and asked to be taken immediately to Alexander.

'Sire,' he announced, 'we have constructed the floating bridge and we have taken the eastern bank of the Euphrates, but the Persians are torching all the villages along the road to Babylon.'

'Are you sure?'

'My own eyes have borne witness: as far as I could see everything was ablaze, even the stubble in the fields. The whole plain was like a sea of flames.'

'We must go then,' said the King. 'I am anxious to see what is happening.' He took two squadrons of cavalry and set off at a gallop together with his companions for the ford at Thapsacus.

9

THE FOLLOWING MORNING, before midday, Alexander crossed the floating bridge, followed by his companions and his cavalry. Hephaestion and Nearchus came to meet him.

'Have you spoken with our messenger?'

'I have. Is the situation truly so serious?'

'You may decide for yourself,' replied Nearchus, and he pointed to the columns of smoke rising everywhere around them.

'And to the east?'

'You mean off in that direction? As far as we know, there is nothing happening in that direction – no damage, no razed earth.'

'So Darius is waiting for us on the Tigris. These fires are clearer than any written message: the southern route is the same one Xenophon's ten thousand took seventy years ago, not without considerable difficulties in finding supplies. Now, with the villages and the harvest destroyed, it would be completely impossible. We have no choice but to take the second route, the one that leads to the ford across the Tigris and the King's Road.

'Darius will wait for us there and it is there that the final battle will take place. And to help us he has cleared the way, allowing us to replenish our supplies in the

villages which stand on the foothills of the Taurus Mountains.'

'And we will accept the invitation, is that not so, Alexander?' asked Perdiccas, stepping forward.

'Indeed, my friend. We must prepare ourselves now because from tomorrow our march begins – in six days' time we will be at the meeting point with the greatest army of all time.'

Parmenion was watching the columns of black smoke rising into the air above the horizon and he said nothing; soon he moved away in silence.

Ptolemy watched him as he went, 'The general does not seem to be so keen, does he?'

'He is getting on now,' said Craterus. 'He really ought to go home.'

Philotas was nearby and overheard these comments, 'My father may well be old, but he is worth more than the rest of you put together!'

'Hold on, calm down!' said Seleucus. 'Craterus was joking.'

'Well then he can joke about someone else, because next time . . .'

'Has anyone seen Eumolpus of Soloi?' Hephaestion asked, just to change the subject.

'I think he's behind us with the women's caravan,' replied Seleucus. 'Why, what do you want of him?'

'Nothing: I simply have to deliver a present. See you all soon,' and he leaped on to his horse and set off to where the women's camp was being pitched. He found Eumolpus sitting outside his own tent, being attended to by a pair of eunuchs – one was wafting him with a fan

while the other was serving a meal on a small well-laid table.

'I don't want to hear any stupid allusions to the sad events surrounding my imprisonment,' said the informer as soon as he saw Hephaestion dismount before him.

'Don't worry, I'm only here to deliver a present.'

'A present?'

'Yes, a present from an enemy. I was actually thinking of letting Alexander know about it. In my humble opinion if we were to squeeze your balls in an olive press then we might just hear some interesting stories from you.'

'Shut up, snot-nose, and let me see what this is all about.'

Hephaestion handed him the statuette. Eumolpus studied it carefully: 'An enemy you said? And who might this enemy be?'

'The Satrap of Babylonia – Mazaeus. He's a real bigwig, if I'm not mistaken.'

Eumolpus said nothing and continued scrutinizing the statuette and then, suddenly, he raised it above his head and struck it sharply against the edge of his table, shattering it into small pieces. Lying there was a small roll of papyrus, thickly covered with cuneiform lettering.

'Scheming with the enemy – things don't look good for you, Eumolpus.'

Eumolpus of Soloi rolled up the note, stood up and set off on foot towards the military camp.

'Hey! Where are you going?'

'To look for someone capable of thinking.'

'Mind you don't get your arse bitten off . . . Peritas is

around somewhere!' shouted Hephaestion. The informer did not even turn round, but his right hand instinctively moved to cover the area mentioned.

He found Eumenes in the commissariat tent, making an inventory of equipment, weapons and materials. With a gesture he let the Secretary know that he wanted to speak to him and Eumenes immediately left the registers to an assistant.

'What's new?'

'A message from Mazaeus.'

'The Satrap of Babylonia. By Zeus!'

'And the Great King's right-hand man.'

'What does he have to say?'

'He is willing . . . to help us on the battlefield, providing we agree to reconfirm him in his position as governor of Babylonia.'

'Do you have any means of replying?'

'Yes.'

'Tell him we agree.'

'But he will want some form of guarantee.'

'What kind of guarantee?'

'I don't know . . . a message from the King.'

'We can manage that. In the past I have written letters in Alexander's hand and with his seal. Drop by my tent tonight and I will give you everything you require – but take that wig off for Zeus's sake, if you want to keep your rear end intact. Peritas is around somewhere with Alexander.'

'I've already been warned about that,' replied Eumolpus as he regretfully relieved his bald head of its embellishment, placing the wig in his bag. 'He's already chewed

up a fur beret that was worth a small fortune. If he corners me I'll throw him the whole bag.'

He moved off and soon all that could be seen was his bald head shining under the sun as he walked away.

*

The army began moving eastwards the following day, keeping the mountains of Armenia to the left and the desert to the right. The officers leading the march had recruited some local guides because there were neither maps nor descriptions of the routes to be taken in crossing these lands. Indeed, as they advanced these officers made use of their own instruments and portable drawing boards to create maps that were as accurate as possible.

They travelled in six stages, each consisting of five parasangs, crossing over the Syrian Araxes after two days and then continuing through a burned, semi-desert area. Occasionally they came across herds of wild donkeys, of gazelles and antelopes, grazing among the few thorny bushes. A couple of times on the third night they heard the roar of a lion resound like thunder across the immense emptiness of the landscape.

The horses whinnied and began kicking, trying to free themselves of their shin straps, and Peritas woke up suddenly, barking furiously and trying to run off in the direction of the strong, penetrating smell of the beast.

Alexander calmed him down, 'There there, Peritas, good boy. We have no time now for hunting. Come on, go to sleep . . . sleep now,' he stroked and scratched the Molossian behind the ears until he lay down once again.

The following day they saw some ostriches, and even came across some nests with eggs in them – both ostrich eggs and bustard eggs. The cook held them up to the sunlight, saw that they were freshly laid, and gathered them all to use them for supper that evening. Alexander asked him to keep a few shells intact, so as to send them to Aristotle for his collection.

Hephaestion, however, was hankering after some fresh meat, and he organized an ostrich hunt together with Leonnatus and Perdiccas. They took twenty or so Agrianian and Triballian shock troops with them, armed with bows and arrows and javelins, but they soon realized it was no easy feat. The clumsy-looking birds in fact ran at incredible speeds, opening out their wings, holding them upwards and using them like sails to exploit the force of the wind. No horse could ever catch up with them.

As the hunters returned – tired, empty-handed and humiliated – Alexander greeted them and shook his head.

'Come on then, spit it out?' Hephaestion said angrily.

'If you had read the *March of the Ten Thousand*, as I have, then you would know exactly how one hunts an ostrich. Xenophon was a great hunter, do not forget this fact.'

'And what exactly was his technique?'

'In stages. One group follows the birds, driving them towards a certain area where other groups of horsemen are waiting in staggered groups. As the first horses tire the group stops and hands over the chase to the second group which sets off at full speed, then the third group and so on, until the ostriches, exhausted, slow down and then you simply surround them and finish them off.'

'We'll have another go tomorrow,' replied Hephaestion.

'In the meantime we can take some consolation in the eggs,' said Alexander. 'Apparently they are excellent both fried and hard-boiled, with salt and oil.'

'And then there are the feathers as well,' added Perdiccas. 'They'll look fine on my helmet. Just look at this! There are lots of them scattered all over the desert – it must be the moulting season.'

The following day and the day after that no ostriches came into sight, almost as though someone had warned them that the hunters had perfected a new system.

The army set off again without meeting a living soul, apart from the fifth evening when a couple of caravans from Arabia, carrying incense, camped at a respectful distance from the armies. Aristander asked the King to buy as much incense as possible because the gods would have to be honoured sufficiently, given the fact that the decisive battle was nigh.

On the evening of the sixth day, Alexander led Bucephalas to drink from the fast-flowing waters of the great River Tigris.

10

Even though twilight had descended, it was clear there was no one on the other side of the river. For as far as the eye could see there was no living soul and neither were there fires or any other signs of human presence. The air was completely still and a few herons glided lazily along the banks of the river in search of young fish and frogs.

Alexander let Peritas and Bucephalas drink, but occasionally he pulled on the horse's reins to stop him from filling his stomach too much. Then he gathered some water into his cupped hands and threw it over the horse's belly and his legs to refresh him slightly. Shortly afterwards all the cavalry battalions up- and downstream of the ford came to a halt and each horseman took his mount to the water to drink.

'I don't understand,' said Seleucus as he approached and looked across to the other side.

'I thought they'd all be lined up ready for battle on the opposite bank,' added Lysimachus as he took off his helmet and started unlacing his breastplate.

Ptolemy too had taken off his helmet, filled it from the river and was emptying it over his head, savouring the cool water, 'Ah! That's wonderful!'

'Well . . . if you like it that much . . . here you go!'

shouted Leonnatus as he prepared to fill his own helmet and throw its contents over Ptolemy, but all of a sudden he stopped and said, 'Hold on! Hold on! Here comes Mr Secretary General. Everyone ready for my signal, alright?'

Eumenes approached just at that moment in full combat dress, his helmet adorned with ostrich plumes.

'Alexander,' he began, 'listen to what I have to say. I have received news that—'

He didn't manage to finish the sentence because Leonnatus started shouting at the top of his voice, 'Ambush! Ambush!' and everyone let fly with helmetsful of water, soaking him from head to foot.

'I am sorry, Mr Secretary General,' said Alexander, struggling to stifle the laughter, 'but this was an ambush that took us all by surprise and even I wasn't able to prevent it.'

Eumenes was completely drenched and his ostrich feathers were in a sorry state. 'What a lovely joke,' he grumbled disconsolately as he took off his helmet and studied what was left of his fine plumage. 'Bunch of idiots, bastards and arseholes . . .'

'You must forgive them, Mr Secretary General,' Alexander sought to bring him round, 'they're just lads. But weren't you about to tell me something?'

'It matters not,' said Eumenes, 'I'll tell you some other time.'

'Come on, don't take it like that. I'll see you in my tent. And I'll see you lot as well!' he shouted at all the others. 'Hephaestion. Go and gather a team together to patrol the other side – I want news of their whereabouts before supper.'

He went off followed by Peritas towards the place where his men were pitching the royal tent, hammering in the pegs with mallets.

Eumenes arrived shortly afterwards wearing dry clothes and the King invited him to sit down with him while Leptine and the other women busied themselves preparing the tables and dining beds for supper.

'Well then, what is this news you spoke of?'

'It won't take long to explain. Eumolpus of Soloi has received a message. The Great King's army is about five parasangs from here towards the southeast, more or less on the road that leads to Babylonia, not far from a village by the name of Gaugamela.'

'That's a strange name.'

'It means "the house of the camel" and it derives from an old story. Apparently King Darius the Great, fleeing from an ambush astride a camel, reached safety thanks to the extraordinary speed of this particular animal. Out of gratitude, he had a stable built with every possible facility and awarded the animal the village's income for the rest of its life. That is how the village acquired its strange name.'

'A day's march away . . . strange. He could have nailed us on the riverbank and blocked us there for who knows how long.'

'It appears to be a deliberate strategy. Have you noticed what the terrain is like on both this and the other side of the Tigris?'

'Rolling, with potholes and the occasional rock protruding from the ground.'

'Exactly. It is not suitable ground for the scythed

chariots. The Great King is waiting for us on perfectly flat terrain,' he said, passing his hand over the smooth surface of the small table before him as he spoke. 'He has had all the potholes filled and the rocks cleared and flattened so that the chariots can reach maximum speed.'

'That may well be, but the fact is that no one has disturbed our approach, we have had no trouble finding supplies in the villages and now we could easily cross the Tigris.'

'Apart from the current.'

'Apart from the current – it must have rained up in the mountains.'

Just then the other friends arrived and Nearchus was with them as well.

'I see that Mr Secretary General is in a presentable state again,' said Leonnatus as he came in. 'What a metamorphosis! Only a few moments ago he looked like a drowned rat!'

'Enough!' said Alexander. 'Sit down. There are important matters to discuss.' Everyone sat down and even Peritas took up position at the King's feet, chewing on his sandals as he had done ever since he was a puppy.

'It appears that the Great King is waiting for us on a stretch of level ground a day's march from here.'

'Good!' exclaimed Perdiccas. 'Let's go then, I wouldn't like him to get bored.'

'The news, which reached us via Eumolpus of Soloi, comes from Persian sources, so we cannot exclude its being a trap for us.'

'Right! Let's not forget Issus,' moaned Leonnatus.

'That son of a bitch was about to sell us all out just to save his own arsehole!'

'Cut it out!' Perdiccas shut him up. 'I wonder what you would have done. What motive does he have to betray us? I trust Eumolpus.'

'So do I,' said Alexander, 'but this does not mean that we have to believe the information – it may well have been sent to draw us into a blind alley.'

'What do you plan on doing, then?' asked Lysimachus as he poured some wine into his companions' cups.

'Tonight Hephaestion will let us know if they are really so far from the river. Tomorrow we will ford the river, we will proceed in the direction of the enemy army and after two or three parasangs' march, we will send a group of reconnaissance soldiers to see how things stand. At that stage we will hold a war council and we will attack.'

'And the scythed chariots?' asked Ptolemy.

'We will put them out of action and then we will throw everything into the centre. Just as we did at Issus.'

'We win, they lose. Asia will be ours,' Nearchus gave his view succinctly.

'That's easy to say,' said Seleucus, 'but just try to imagine what things will be like when they set off with those chariots across that plain – the dust, the din of the wheels, the scythes glinting in the sun as they turn at such high speed. I think they will seek to take out our central units while the cavalry will attack our flanks.'

'Seleucus is right,' said Alexander, 'but there is no point in trying to lay out a battle plan now, before the

fact; as for the chariots, we will do just as the "ten thousand" did at Kunaxa. Remember? The heavy infantry opened up, creating corridors through which the chariots passed without causing any damage and then the archers turned and attacked the drivers and the charioteers from behind. I'm worried instead about the dust – if there is no wind then as soon as the battle starts there will be such a thick haze that we won't be able to see beyond our noses. We'll have to use the trumpets to keep the divisions in touch with one another. But let us eat and enjoy ourselves now – there is no reason for us to fret in this way, we have always won and we will win again this time.'

'Do you really think there will be a million men waiting for us down there?' asked Leonnatus, visibly worried. 'By Hercules, I can't even imagine it! But how many men are there in a million?'

'I'll tell you,' said Eumenes. 'It means that each one of us will have to kill twenty for us to win and they would still have some left over.'

'I don't believe it,' said Alexander. 'To feed a million men in constant movement is almost impossible, not to mention all the water and so on necessary for the horses. I think . . . I think there will be about half that number, just a few more than we faced at Issus. Anyway, as I said, we will wait and see how things really are when we make direct contact with the enemy.'

The servants began bringing the food and Alexander had some interesting 'companions' come in, freshly arrived from Greece, to cheer his friends up a little. Among them was an Athenian girl of truly striking

beauty, dark-haired and with burning eyes and a firm, solid body – a goddess.

'Look at that!' exclaimed Alexander as soon as she appeared. 'Is she not stupendous? Did you know that this girl posed nude before the great Protogenes, for a statue of Aphrodite? Her name is Tais and this year in Athens she has been declared the *callipygia*.'

'The finest pair of buttocks in the whole city, isn't that right?' laughed Leonnatus. 'But do you think we'll get a chance to see them?'

'Everything in its just time, my fiery young goat,' said the girl with a wicked smile.

Leonnatus turned to Eumenes with a puzzled look on his face, 'No woman has ever called me "fiery young goat" before. I don't know whether to take it as a compliment or an insult.'

'Don't expend too much energy thinking – you might do yourself an injury,' replied Eumenes. 'In any case, "fiery young goat" doesn't sound too bad to me. I think you've scored.'

Other 'companions' entered, all of them very attractive and they stretched out near the diners as supper was served. Ptolemy, in his role as leader of the symposium, had decided that the wine would be cut at a ratio of one to one, a decision that met with general approval.

When they had all finished eating and were all quite merry, Tais began dancing. She wore only a short *chiton* and was completely naked underneath – each time she turned she offered generous views of what she had been rewarded for back in Athens and what had led Protogenes to chose her as model for Aphrodite.

Suddenly she grabbed a flute from a table and began to play it, accompanying her own dance with the instrument, and the music seemed to dress her body which continued to turn and ripple ever more quickly before suddenly stopping in a cascade of sharp, almost strident notes. Tais crouched on the ground like a wild beast about to pounce – breathless and shining with sweat – and then she started to play again and her melody left the tent and travelled to the edge of the camp, reaching the guards standing motionless on their watch. The sweetest melody accompanied her more gentle, softer and sinuous movements now as she made gestures akin to more ardent lovemaking.

The men stopped laughing and joking and the King himself seemed to be transfixed by her movements as they picked up speed with the music, ever more rhythmic and incessant, drawing close to the climax. The small space in the tent seemed to be completely filled by the presence of Tais, impregnated with the smell of her skin and her hair with its blue sheen. It was as though her dancing had unleashed some irresistible energy, a powerful charm, and in a flash Alexander remembered another moment in his past life – the notes of the flute his mother Olympias played in the depths of a forest in Eordaea, instigating an orgiastic dance in the middle of the night, the *komos* of Dionysian pleasure.

When Tais fell exhausted and breathless, everyone's eyes were burning with desire, each expressing an irrepressible sexual drive, but no one dared move, waiting for the King to take his prerogative. The whinny of a horse and the noise of galloping suddenly broke the

tension of the moment – Hephaestion burst into the tent, covered in sweat and dust, 'Darius's army is half a day's march from here,' he said, struggling for breath. 'There are hundreds of thousands of them – their fires burn in the night like stars in the sky, their war horns call out in the night from one end of the plain to the other.'

Alexander stood up and looked around as though he had been abruptly wakened from a dream, and then he said, 'Go and rest now. Tomorrow we will ford the river, and tomorrow evening at sunset we will hold a war council within sight of the Persian army.'

11

THE TIGRIS FLOWED very quickly even at the ford, and the infantrymen who were the first to attempt the crossing soon found themselves in trouble: at the very centre of the river the water came up to their chests. Their shields were cumbersome and if they kept them low in the water then they caught too much of the current and were ripped from their arms; if they held them high then the soldiers themselves soon lost their balance and were dragged off downstream together with the shields.

Parmenion gave orders for two ropes to be tied between the two banks and for two double rows of soldiers to be lined up, without shields, across the river – one upstream of the ford, to break the flow, and one downstream of the ford, to catch those men who fell into the water and were carried away by it. The General had the rest of the heavy infantry pass through the sheltered corridor provided by the human barrier. The cavalry were the last to cross, followed by the carts with the supplies, baggage, the women and the children. It was early afternoon when the leading components came into sight of the enemy positions, but the tail end was still on the banks of the Tigris and it took what was left of that day for the last of them to join up with the rest of the army.

As planned, the King held a war council immediately after sunset with the two armies so close that from their side of the vast plain of Gaugamela the Macedonian guards could hear the calls of the Persian sentries.

As darkness fell and as the first night watch took up position, a lamp was lit in Alexander's tent and the Companions arrived with the generals of the high command: Koinos, Simmias, Meleager, and Polyperchon, led by Parmenion and Cleitus the Black. They all greeted the King and kissed him on the cheek, then they assembled together, standing around the table on which the officers had drawn a plan of the battlefield. The various infantry and cavalry divisions were represented by different coloured pawns from the King's games sets.

'Darius will almost certainly send his war chariots to attack us,' began Alexander, 'the idea being that they will overtake our ranks and send the phalanx into disarray; but we will advance obliquely to the enemy front line, which will certainly be extensive because of their overwhelming numerical superiority, and then we will try to move round to the other side of the area that the Great King has had flattened out for the chariot charges. As soon as you see them move, give the signal to the men to make as much noise as possible, beating their swords on their shields and shouting to frighten the horses. Then, when they are within range, the archers and the slingsmen will aim at the chariot drivers and try to take them out of action. This should take care of a great many of them, but the chariots which continue moving might still wreak considerable damage. At that point the commanders of each company will signal with their trumpets

to open up breaches in their lines, let the chariots through, and then attack from behind.

'When the chariot charge has been stopped, the phalanx will advance to the centre, preceded by the heavy cavalry and the *hetairoi* together with the Agrianian and Thracian assault troops, and I will lead the Vanguard across Darius's lines. We must break and cut off their entire left wing, converge on the centre and drive Darius and the Immortals of the Royal Guard on to the phalanx. Craterus's and Perdiccas's battalions will have to resist the impact and set up a counterattack. General Parmenion will remain in reserve at the bottom of our left flank with three battalions of *pezhetairoi* and the Thessalian cavalry, to be ready to deliver the final blow. The right wing of our line up will consist of the Greek allies and the mercenaries coordinated by the Black: their job will be to deal with any flanking manoeuvres from the Persian left wing, to give the Vanguard time to pummel the centre of the enemy lines. Are there any questions?'

'One,' said Seleucus. 'Why have we agreed to fight on terrain that has been chosen by our enemy?'

Alexander seemed uncertain as to whether he should reply, but then he moved closer and looked Seleucus in the eye, 'Do you know how many fortresses there are spread throughout Darius's empire from here to the Paropamisus Mountains? Do you have any idea how many fortified passes, how many strongholds and walled cities? To do otherwise would mean growing old in a vain and violent enterprise, we would lose all our forces in a slow death, dripping the lifeblood of our nation, depriving it of its youth and condemning it to an inevi-

table decline. Darius has been most skilful in drawing me here to this place and he now intends to annihilate me. I have had enough of the game. He does not realize that I have come here of my own free will and that at the very last I will defeat him anyway.'

'And with what?' asked Seleucus again, without lowering his eyes.

'You will see at dawn tomorrow,' replied Alexander. 'For now there is nothing more to say. Go to your men and try to rest because tomorrow I want you to fight to the last drop of sweat and to the last spark of energy. May fortune and the gods be with you.'

They all saluted and moved off. Alexander accompanied them to the door and, when they had all left, he went to Bucephalas to feed and water him. As the horse sank his nose into the bag full of oats, Alexander spoke, stroking his mane: 'My fine Bucephalas, my good friend . . . tomorrow will be your last battle, I promise you. After tomorrow you will appear only on parades; you will carry me whenever we enter in triumph into some city or when you and I alone ride through the hills of Media or along the banks of the Tigris and the Araxes. But first you must lead me to victory tomorrow, Bucephalas, you must carry me faster than the wind, faster than the Persian arrows and bolts – nothing will resist your speed.'

The animal lifted his proud head as he snorted and shook his mane.

'Do you understand, Bucephalas? You will crush underfoot the Median and Kissean, the Hyrcanian and the Khorasmian horsemen, you will breathe fire from

your nostrils like a chimera, in your vigour you will lead all your companions in the furious charge, yours will be the thunder that splits the mountains, and the five hundred steeds of the Vanguard will make the ground shake behind you.'

The stallion scraped the ground with his hoof and suddenly reared up, neighing forth with what seemed to be a challenge. Then he appeared to calm down and moved his muzzle near his master's chest, looking for a caress. He was trying to say that he was ready and that nothing in the world would halt his gallop.

Alexander kissed him and left, moving off in the direction of the tent of the Queen Mother, Sisygambis, which had been pitched underneath a clump of sycamores on the edge of the camp. He had himself announced by a eunuch who led him into the interior of the quarters, where she received him sitting on her throne.

Alexander waited for her to give him permission to sit down, as was customary at court, and then he began to speak:

'Great Mother, I have come to tell you that we are about to face Darius in a decisive battle, almost certainly the very last battle. By sunset tomorrow only one of us will have survived and I will do everything to make sure I win the day.'

'I know,' replied Sisygambis.

'This could mean that your son will die.'

The Queen nodded her head gravely.

'Or that I might die.'

Sisygambis lifted her eyes, moist with tears, and

sighed, 'In any case, for me it will be a sad day – however things may go, whatever may be the outcome of the battle. If you win, I will have lost my son and my homeland. If you lose or if you are killed then I will have lost a person I have learned to love. You have treated me as though you were my son and you have respected all members of my family as no other conqueror ever would have done. You too, my boy, have won a place in my heart. For this reason I can only suffer and I cannot even have the consolation of praying to Ahura Mazda for victory for my soldiers. Go, Alexander, and may you live to see tomorrow's sunset. This is the only blessing I can bestow upon you.'

The King bowed and left, setting off towards his own tent. The camp was buzzing with activity now in the hour before sleep: the soldiers, arranged on the ground in circles, were eating their suppers and trying to keep one another's spirits up with the final clash looming. They told tales of courage, they drank, they rolled dice, gambling with the money they now received in abundance from Eumenes' coffers, they ogled the prostitutes as they danced through the camp. Some others were spending that last evening in the merchants' camp, where many of them had regular girlfriends and sometimes even children to whom they became more attached with every day that passed. At such a juncture these deep ties of affection were a source of comfort while, at the same time, they were also a source of anxiety because no one knew exactly what awaited them on the following day. This imminent battle was one that might bring them glory and riches or death or, worse still, lifelong slavery.

Alexander came to his own tent after having crossed almost the entire camp. Leptine came to meet him and kissed his hands, 'My Lord, there has been a strange visit. A man came and brought some food for your supper. I have never seen him before, and I would not trust him if I were you – the food might be poisoned.'

'Have you thrown it away?'

'No, but—'

'Let me see it.'

Leptine led him into the banqueting area and showed him a dish which had been set on the royal table. Alexander smiled and shook his head, 'Skewered thrush.' And then he touched it, 'It's still hot. Where is he?'

'He went, but he left this for you,' and she showed him a tiny roll of papyrus. Alexander unrolled it, read it rapidly, then left straight away, calling to his shield-bearer as he did so, 'Quickly, prepare the Sarmatian bay.'

The shield-bearer ran towards the corral and immediately returned with the horse harnessed and ready. The King mounted and set off at a gallop, so quickly that his guards did not have time to realize what was happening. When they were ready to set off after him, he had already disappeared into the desert night.

12

ALEXANDER CAME TO A small village consisting of a few mud-brick and bitumen houses located halfway between his camp and the river they had crossed that very morning. He headed towards the well that was in the midst of a clump of palm trees, dismounted and waited.

The moon soon rose from behind a group of low hills bordering the eastern part of the plain and it spread its light over the expanse of stubble that surrounded the village like a golden ring and then over the desert which extended beyond that brief tract of cultivated land, in all directions. He left the horse to graze on the sparse tufts of grass growing here and there among the palms and waited until he saw a silhouette swaying its way along a track, little more than a pathway, which came from the south: Eumolpus of Soloi was approaching on a camel.

'You can dismount,' said Alexander, noticing his informer's worried air. 'Peritas is back at the camp.'

'Hail, O Great King and Lord of Asia,' began the informer, but Alexander had no time to spare and interrupted him:

'Have you managed to find out any more since you wrote that note?'

'I must tell you the truth – I already knew that Mazaeus was very disillusioned and was sure that the end

is nigh for the empire of Cyrus the Great, and I had asked Hephaestion to bring him over to our side if he ever met him on the ford across the Euphrates at Thapsacus. Hephaestion, however, refused to do it, he probably felt that to attempt to lead an opponent into desertion was somehow dishonourable conduct.'

'I feel the same way.'

'Let's say that he feels the same way as you.'

'If you prefer that.'

'Fine. But the goddess of fortune has come over to our side – she evidently has some sort of weakness for you, my King. You will find it hard to believe, but it was actually Hephaestion who unwittingly became our contact with Mazaeus. The Persian handed him a statuette to give me as a gift and he delivered it while I was near Thapsacus dealing with some business. The barbarian characters inscribed on the base read, 'break this statuette', which I promptly did. Inside there was a message from Mazaeus, which I had a courier communicate to you as you were approaching the ford on the Tigris with the army. However, I wanted to come here in person, to make sure that the message had reached you.'

'Quite. I saw your skewered thrush.'

'That was good, don't you think? My men caught a fair number of them this morning in their nets and so I had this idea of letting you have my password in a most original manner.'

'You certainly succeeded.'

'So, what exactly did the messenger tell you?'

'Mazaeus offers his aid on the battlefield and in

exchange he asks to be reconfirmed as Satrap of Babylonia. He says that he will be on the right wing of Darius's army and so I will be able to lighten my left wing to concentrate all my forces on the other side, where we risk being surrounded. Is that right?'

'That's it perfectly. Don't you think it's an honest proposal?'

'Would you trust a traitor?'

'Yes, if the traitor's proposal works for both parties, and it seems to me that in this case it does. Mazaeus is sure Darius cannot defeat you; he believes that you will emerge victorious and so he is offering you one thing in exchange for another. Fundamentally, you stand to gain and so does he.'

'Imagine for a moment that he is lying – I leave the left wing uncovered to reinforce the right wing in view of a possible surrounding manoeuvre by the Persian cavalry. Mazaeus instead leads a charge to my left and catches me from behind while I am about to launch an attack with the Vanguard. A disaster. The end in fact.'

'That is true, but if you do not take this risk in accepting Mazaeus's deal, then you may lose in any case because there are so many more of them than there are of you. What's more, you have accepted to do battle on terrain chosen by them. It really is a dilemma.'

'Yet I will soon return to my tent and I will sleep peacefully.'

Eumolpus sought to study Alexander's expression in the uncertain light of the moon, but he could see nothing that might reveal the King's true intentions. 'What must

I tell Mazaeus tonight?' he asked. 'As you can see, I am disguised as a Syrian merchant and I'll soon be with him to give him your answer.'

Alexander grabbed the reins of his horse and leaped astride it, 'Tell him I accept,' he said, as he made ready to set off.

'Wait!' Eumolpus stopped him. 'There is one last thing you might want to know – Barsine's son is in Darius's camp and he intends to take part in the battle tomorrow.'

Alexander sat motionless for a moment astride his steed, as though this news had somehow paralysed him, then he suddenly woke up and spurred the horse on, soon disappearing in a cloud of dust. Eumolpus shook his head and thought to himself for a moment about their conversation, then he had his reluctant camel kneel down and climbed up and sat astride it. He said something and the animal first of all lifted its rear end, almost making him fall forwards, then its front legs, almost making him fall backwards. Finally the animal gained some sort of balance and started trotting off towards the Persian camp, driven onwards by its rider's clumsy kicking.

Alexander saw a patrol of *hetairoi* from the royal guard, led by Hephaestion, coming towards him at a gallop. They stopped and the King asked, 'Where are you going?'

'Where are we going?' said Hephaestion in a rage. 'How can you ask us that? We're out here looking for you! You set off without saying anything to anyone, off into the night across land crawling with enemy patrols and this on the eve of a battle that will decide our destiny. Fortunately one of the sentries saw you and

made a report to his commander. We are half dead with fear and—'

Alexander stopped him with a simple gesture, 'It was something I had to deal with alone, but the fact that you are here is a good thing. Who is the commander of this division?'

A young man from the mountainous lands of Lyncestis moved forward, 'I am, Sire, and my name is Euphranor.'

'Listen to me, Euphranor: while we go back to the camp, you will go with your men to the village which lies ten stadia or so along this track and you will leave half of your men as a garrison there, led by someone you trust. You will take the other half to the banks of the Tigris and you will wait there until you hear someone call from the other side, "Where is the road to Babylon?" You will reply, "The road lies this way!" and then you will escort these people to the camp and consign them to Craterus.'

'Nothing else, Sire?'

'Nothing else, Euphranor. Carry out well the orders I have given you, for our army's safety depends on it.'

'You can count on us, Sire – we will keep a lookout and no one will pass between the ford and the village without asking permission from us. That is the way it must be, is it not?'

'That is exactly how it must be. Go now.'

'Who are we expecting?' asked Hephaestion as he turned his horse in the direction of the camp.

'You will see. And now we will turn back – we don't have long to rest before dawn breaks.'

They returned to the camp and went their separate ways – Hephaestion to his division of the Vanguard and Alexander to Barsine's tent. She came to him and kissed him, 'I heard tale that you had gone off on your own – I was worried.'

Alexander held her to himself without saying anything.

'You will lead your cavalry tomorrow, won't you?'

'Yes, I will.'

'Why do you expose yourself to such danger? If anything were to happen, your men would be leaderless.'

'A king has certain privileges, but he must also be ready to die first, every time his people face a danger. Listen to me Barsine: just eight or nine stadia in that direction lies the Persian camp, and your father Artabazos and . . . your son are both there.' Barsine's eyes suddenly filled with tears. 'If you wish to join them,' he continued, 'I will have you and Phraates escorted to the first Persian guard post.'

'Is this what you want?' Barsine asked.

'No. I want you, but I understand that your heart is rent by the conflict and for this reason you will never be happy.'

Barsine stroked his face and his hair and then she said, 'I am your woman, I will stay.'

'If you are my woman, then make me forget everything on this the eve of the battle, love me as you have never loved any man, give me all the pleasure you are capable of giving. All that may remain of me tomorrow is a handful of dust.' And without waiting for her answer he began kissing her neck and her breasts, caressing her body and her thighs, pulling her to himself with irresist-

ible force. Barsine felt the heat that came from his skin grow and grow until it became fever, she smelled the perfume of his hair and the intense musky fragrance that came from his groin and she let herself go on the rush of desire that ran just below her skin with the flow of her blood and her breath.

She undressed as he continued to caress and kiss her all over her body and then she undressed him, free of any inhibition now. She kissed his lips and his chest avidly and pulled him naked to the carpet. She caressed his belly and his thighs, she kissed him ever more passionately until the most burning of desires was unleashed in both of them. He took her with all his strength, as though this was the last time he would ever make love with her and he saw her eyes light up, her face transfigured by a pleasure that was ever more intense and moving, he felt her hands and her nails dig into his shoulders and his back and he heard her finally cry out in boundless pleasure, the pleasure that only the gods can give to mortal beings.

He let himself collapse on to the soft carpet as she continued to kiss him and caress him in total, passionate devotion, oblivious to everything else. Alexander responded to her kisses and then, with one last caress, he pulled away from her and stood up.

'Sleep here with me, I beg you,' Barsine said to him.

'I cannot. My men must find me tomorrow in the solitude that precedes the ultimate challenge. The sentries on the last watch must know that overnight they have stood guard over their King alone. Farewell, Barsine. If I should die in battle, do not cry for me: it is a privilege to

die on the field, thus avoiding old age and the decline of the mind and the body, the slow, inexorable extinguishing of the light in one's eyes. Return to your people and your children, and live your life happily, knowing that you have been loved as no other woman in the world has ever been loved.'

Barsine kissed him one last time before he disappeared through the door, and she did not have the courage to tell him that she was expecting his child.

13

It was General Parmenion who woke him up, entering the King's tent in person: 'Sire, it is time.' He was fully decked out in his battle armour and Alexander looked at him with the same admiration as ever. He was an elderly man now, but the old warrior was still as upright and solid as an oak. The King stood up and, naked as he was, gulped down the 'Nestor's cup' that Leptine had already prepared. While two attendants dressed him and helped put his armour on, another brought his shield and his shining helmet in the shape of a lion's head with gaping mouth.

'General,' began Alexander, 'this will be a day of great uncertainty, especially for our left wing. For this reason I have decided to give you command of that side of our lines. The Black will take the right side.

'We will move forward with our wings folded so that they are almost touching our flanks, like a hawk diving on to its prey. We will proceed until they decide to stop us and send their right wing on ahead. Then I will lead the charge and I will break their attacking front in two, but while I drive home the point into the enemy's centre, you will turn round with the flank out on the left. I know that you and your men will hold, that you will not give way for any reason.'

'I will not give way, Sire.'

Alexander shook his head, 'You are always so formal, and yet you held me on your knee when I was a child.'

Parmenion nodded, 'I will not give way, my boy, for as long as there is life left in me. May the gods be with us.'

As the King left he saw that at the centre of the camp Aristander was burning a sacrifice. The smoke rose slowly from the ground, twisting like a snake, struggling to find its way into the sky.

'What do your portents say, Seer?'

Aristander turned towards him with that characteristic movement which reminded him so much of Philip, his father, and said, 'It will be the hardest day of your life, Alexander, but you will win.'

'I hope to the gods that this is the truth,' replied the King as he took Bucephalas's reins from his groom. The camp was bustling with activity: everywhere orders were being shouted, squadrons of cavalry were taking up position, the infantry divisions were lining up in their marching formation. Alexander leaped on to Bucephalas and spurred him on to the very tip of the Vanguard, which was already lined up to perfection. Hephaestion took up position alongside. Just behind was Leonnatus – completely dressed in metal, his great cleaver held firmly in his hand – and at his side was Ptolemy. Behind them were Lysimachus, Seleucus and Philotas, coming before the rest of the squadron and the other divisions of the *hetairoi* cavalry. Ahead of everyone and out on the left flank the Thracians and Agrianians ran on foot, then

came the battalions of the phalanx and a division of shock troops led by their commanders: Koinos, at the head of the very first, then Perdiccas, Meleager, Simmias and Polyperchon. Craterus, last of all, was in command of the Thessalians. Out on the right the eight battalions of the Greek allies were already in marching formation, followed by a long tail of Thracian and Triballian foot soldiers, extending back as far as the royal tents and supplies.

The King raised his hand and the trumpets gave the signal for them to set off. The Vanguard started at a walk behind Alexander as he led them towards the far end of the field. Then came the sound of war horns and the Great King's army appeared – limitless, and with hundreds of standards and insignia going before it. At that moment the sun was rising so that from the midst of the cloud of dust they raised on their march there came the glinting of the metal of their weapons – like flashes of lightning coming from the depths of a dark storm cloud.

Leonnatus saw the immense line up, stretching from one side of the plain to the other, and he murmured to himself, 'Great Zeus!' But the King gave no sign of astonishment at this great spectacle and continued to advance at a walk, holding Bucephalas's reins to his chest while the horse arched his powerful, shining neck, snorting and champing at the bit.

Behind him the entire army started unfolding, squadron by squadron, battalion after battalion, to the rhythmic sound of the drums and the loud regular marching of the soldiers, the excited stamping of the horses. To

their left the vast levelled area opened up – all that separated them now from the Persian front line that continued its inexorable forward march.

Alexander began to turn towards the right, to reach a more irregular and rolling tract of land, but the enemy immediately realized what he was trying to do. The sombre, prolonged sound of the horns came once more and the entire Persian left wing, composed entirely of Scythian and Bactrian cavalry, set off on a counter manoeuvre. Alexander gave a signal and the Agrianian archers on horseback galloped towards the enemy as they approached and unleashed dense swarms of arrows; then he sent a squadron of *hetairoi* to slow down the enemy's thrust while he himself continued at the head of the Vanguard, at a walk, incredibly calm. Only those who were alongside him were able to perceive an occasional irregular blinking and the sweat on his temples.

The *hetairoi* spurred their mounts on, quickly devouring the space between themselves and the fast-approaching wave of the Asian horsemen. The impact was truly horrendous – hundreds of horses rolled to the ground, hundreds of horsemen on both sides fell with them and immediately, despite their injuries, they set to in mortal hand-to-hand combat in the midst of the hooves, in that inferno of dust, neighing and shouting that surrounded them on all sides. A thick cloud was raised, covering almost the entire field, so that it was no longer possible to make out what was happening and what might be the results of that first clash. Some of the Agrianians, having used up their arrows, had drawn their knives and thrown themselves into the ruck, driven on by their barbarian

fury, engaging in wild combat with the enemy horsemen who appeared like ghosts in the dense clouds.

Insistent trumpet blows echoed then from the left and Leonnatus touched Alexander on his shoulder, 'Gods above ... look! The chariots! The scythed chariots!' But the King did not respond at all.

From the centre of the Persian line up the frightful machines moved forwards, setting off towards the Macedonian left flank. Perdiccas, who had spotted them immediately, began shouting, 'Get ready, men! Carefully now! Get ready!'

However, at that very moment a group of enemy horsemen set off transversally across the field at full gallop, dragging behind them bundles of twigs which raised an impenetrable curtain of dust right before the Macedonian flank, hiding the chariots from view. All the Macedonians could see was occasional sinister glinting from the scythes as they revolved furiously on the hubs of the wheels or sliced through the air where they protruded from the car, the yokes and sides of the four-horse vehicles.

Perdiccas and the other commanders had the alarm trumpets sounded so that the marching foot soldiers might prepare themselves to open up as soon as the chariots appeared from the dust, but when they did appear they were less than half a stadium away and not all the soldiers managed to react in time to the signals which were raised on high pennants by their section leaders. At some points along the line the corridors were created and the chariots passed through without causing damage, but at other points they charged at full tilt into

the midst of the ranks, mowing down the soldiers like wheat, sending heads rolling, necks cut clean through, eyes still wide open in astonishment. Many soldiers' legs were caught by the scythes, and mutilated horrendously, others were caught head on by the horses, trampled and torn to pieces by the hooves and the spikes protruding from underneath the chariots, but the army continued to advance behind Alexander, maintaining its oblique line. Now they had covered more than a third of the vast area that Darius had cleared to allow an unhindered run for the chariots and the horses, and they continued to march in time to the constant beat of the drums.

Some of the second division of Agrianian archers set off like lightning towards the chariots, massacring their drivers, while others, on horseback, followed those who had passed through the lines to attack them from behind with their spears. In the meantime, however, at the most advanced point, the heavy Scythian and Bactrian cavalry – led by Bessus and at an advantage because of their numerical superiority – pushed back the *hetairoi* squadrons and began to spread out in a wide surrounding manoeuvre towards the far right, where the Greek allies were moving forward. As soon as the Greeks saw the barbarian horsemen advancing at full gallop towards them, they shouted: '*Alalalài!*' and proceeded to close ranks, tightening up the spaces between one another and arranging a barrier of shields and spears. In the confusion of shouting and neighing, Alexander pushed Bucephalas forward slightly more quickly now, almost trotting over the plain. To his side a standard-bearer held the Argead

flag, flame red with its golden star shining in the sun that was now high in the sky.

Other blows on the trumpet came from the left and another wave of Parthian, Hyrcanian and Median horsemen set off forwards at full tilt to separate the marching battalions of Perdiccas and Meleager and the tail-end battalions of Simmias and Parmenion. Mazaeus was leading them! They burst through the infantry lines and set off like a swollen river towards the Macedonian camp. Parmenion shouted to Craterus, 'Stop them! Set the Thessalians on them!' and Craterus obeyed. He signalled to the trumpeters and they immediately sounded the charge for the two squadrons of Thessalian cavalry who were moving forwards out on the extreme left, the last reserves. The Thessalians cut off Mazaeus's troops, engaging them in furious combat and Parmenion sent a unit of shieldsmen and shock troops in support.

'They're trying to free the royal family!' he shouted. 'Stop them at all costs!' At that point the far end of the left wing was a tangle of infantry and horses engaged in a gory and cruel battle with each side seeking to inflict more devastating wounds on the other, fighting furiously over every scrap of ground.

Alexander heard the desperate sound of the trumpets, but he did not turn round. He looked at the standard-bearer and signalled to him to raise the standard so that everyone might see it. He then let loose his war cry, so powerful and sharp as to penetrate through the din of the battle that was raging all around. Bucephalas stamped, neighed and then the King's shouting excited

him to the point where he set off in a furious charge, hammering the earth with his bronze shoes, snorting like a wild beast. And the Vanguard flew behind him in a wild gallop. Five squadrons of *hetairoi* opened up in a wedge shape behind them, eating up the ground leading to the point where the Persian centre was detached from its own right wing, engaged in its wide surrounding manoeuvre.

'Forward!' shouted Alexander. 'Forward!' and he unsheathed his sword, attacking the Immortals who were defending the imperial chariot. The entire Macedonian cavalry kept up with him, wiping out anyone who attempted to get in their way. Bucephalas was so heavy and so fast that anyone who touched him even marginally was immediately thrown to the ground by the impetus and the mass of the giant stallion, all bedecked in leather and bronze. Led by the King, the Vanguard made an about turn now, then lined up on a much wider front in four lines, flanked to the right and left by the *hetairoi* squadrons, and off they went like an avalanche of iron on the flanks and the back of the Persian centre.

In the meantime, however, the Macedonian camp seemed almost lost and Mazaeus's Kissean and Median horsemen galloped everywhere, setting fires, destroying, devastating everything, while another group set off towards the women's quarters. The Thessalians fought like lions, but, outnumbered, they began to give way to the force of the Hyrcanian outfits. Parmenion could no longer make out how the battle was going and he himself

fought wildly with his sword and his shield like a man in the full bloom of youth. Suddenly he saw an orderly passing nearby and shouted to him, 'Run! Run to Alexander and tell him we cannot hold . . . we need help! Now! Go! Run!' The man flew off on his horse. He jumped over upturned chariots and burning spears, passed by warriors still engaged in battle and reached the central area that was still relatively free, pushing his horse on towards the point in the distance where he could make out the Argead standard flying in the midst of the fury.

Darius's guard was supported by numerous Greek mercenaries and took the full impact from behind and on its flanks, but although they fought valiantly, they were soon crushed by the unstoppable drive of Alexander's troop. Hephaestion was at the King's side, wielding his massive ash-wood spear, running through all those who came towards them on horseback. Leonnatus swirled his heavy axe already dripping blood, and Ptolemy and Lysimachus let loose furious blows with their sword and Thracian sabre respectively, protecting Alexander's flanks and pushing back the continuous counterattack of the Greek mercenaries and the Immortals. No one wanted to give way, thinking that this really was the last chance to push back the enemy and save their lives and their homeland.

Out on the right wing, Bessus's cavalry had clashed with the great mass of the Greek heavy infantry, but they continued to launch attack after attack, rhythmically, like great waves breaking against the rocks. The divisions out

on the edge, having manoeuvred around the Greek lines, faced the Thracians defending the right-hand side of the camp, now in large part in enemy hands.

Indeed, out on the left wing the situation was desperate. Parmenion and his men were almost completely surrounded, but Perdiccas, Meleager and the others could offer no help because they had been ordered to charge with their spears lowered at the centre of Darius's line, while the King's cavalry maintained the pressure from behind and from the flank.

Mazaeus reached the Queen Mother's tent and kneeled before her, breathless, saying, 'Great Mother, quickly! You must follow me! It must be now, otherwise you will never be free and you will never hold power again. Let me lead you to your son, our King!'

The Queen made no move, however. She sat there on her throne, motionless, 'I cannot follow you. I am too old to mount a horse. Leave me here to wait for the outcome of this day, according to the will of Ahura Mazda. Go, and waste no more time with me! Take the royal concubines with you, and their children, if you can.'

Mazaeus tried once more, 'I implore you, Great Mother, I beg you!' – but it was all in vain. The Queen did not move at all.

At that moment not far away, a young warrior burst into another tent, the tent in which Barsine was waiting for the end of the frightful battle. He took his helmet off, freeing his shining locks and shouted, 'Mother! Quickly! I have come to free you! Quickly . . . let's go! Take a horse and follow me! Where is my brother?'

'Eteocles!' Barsine shouted, shocked at the sight of

him there in her tent. 'My son!' and she ran forwards to embrace him, but at that very same moment two Agrianians arrived brandishing their long knives – they had received orders not to allow anyone to touch Alexander's woman. Eteocles unsheathed his sword and took up position before them, trying to push them back, but he was just a boy and there was not enough strength in his blows. One of the Agrianians struck his arm and his weapon fell to the ground, while the other unleashed the mortal blow. Barsine threw herself forwards, shouting, 'No! He is my son!' and was caught in full by the blade – she fell to the ground instantly. Eteocles, although wounded, set about attacking one of the two soldiers, bravely wielding his dagger, but the Agrianian simply dodged the blow and replied with deadly precision. The boy fell on to the lifeless body of his mother and breathed his last breath over her.

The valiant Thessalians had been driven out of the camp by now and Mazaeus's troops were about to set off towards the centre of the battlefield to take the *pezhetairoi* and the Thracian infantry from behind, the units that were still putting up a fight against Bessus's cavalry. They thought they had already won the battle, but all of a sudden there came a trumpet blast and then the shouts of thousands of warriors: '*Alalalài!*'

At that moment, from the road leading from the river, there appeared three squadrons of newly recruited Thessalian and Macedonian cavalry who had crossed the ford during the night. Craterus, wounded in an arm and exhausted by the fighting, grabbed a standard and held it high as soon as he saw them, shouting, 'Men! Over here!'

Then he took the reins of a riderless horse as it passed by, leaped astride it and set off towards them. They had opened up across a wide front and were coming forwards at a charge. Craterus took up position at their head, leading them against the Medians and the Hyrcanians, against Mazaeus's Kisseans and Assyrians, engaging them in a new and brutal duel.

The progress of the battle began to alter now – Alexander moved ever more menacingly towards the enemy's centre and he could make out Darius atop his war chariot. The King of Macedon took a javelin from its holder and took aim. Protected by his companions, he let it fly with all his might, missing Darius, but striking the chariot driver and killing him instantly. The horses started galloping wildly towards the northern edge of the field and when Darius managed to grab the reins he continued to guide them at furious speed away from the battle. The Immortals, heedless of the King's retreat, continued to fight with unrelenting fury, fully aware that there was no escape for them; only late in the afternoon did they begin to give way, completely exhausted.

News spread that the Great King was in fact dead and many other divisions took flight. Bessus instead received news from a messenger that Darius had abandoned the battlefield and he immediately stopped all of the attacks against the Greeks on the left wing. Afraid that the emperor's rigid tiara might fall into Macedonian hands, he set off with his horsemen to look for the fleeing King, perhaps to protect him, perhaps, given the way events were moving, to take on the role of sole arbiter of Darius's destiny.

Mazaeus, who had been so close to victory, now found himself stuck between the Thessalian and the Macedonian reinforcements and the battalions of Perdiccas and Parmenion who had started counterattacking once again, and he surrendered.

14

Alexander rode through what was left of the Mace-
donian camp, amidst the fires and the devastation,
through the acrid smoke that hung in the thick, motion-
less air. He sought out Barsine's tent, but all that came
to him as he approached was the crying of a young
boy – Phraates was mourning over the bodies of his
mother and his brother, lying together in their final
embrace.

The King dismounted and approached, 'O gods above!'
he shouted, his eyes full of tears. 'Why? Why such a
bitter end for such blameless creatures?'

He knelt down alongside the two blood-covered bod-
ies and first laid out Eteocles as best he could manage,
covering the boy with his cloak. Then he approached
Barsine, freeing her face of her hair and gently caressing
her forehead. Her eyes still bore the sheen of her final
tears and they appeared to be staring towards some far
off point in the sky where the cries of the furore could
no longer reach her, the cries of the hatred and the
horror – these were eyes that seemed to have searched
long and hard for some cherished dream that had now
suddenly dissolved into nothing.

The unreal silence that had fallen on the devastated
camp made the boy's desolate crying even more harrow-

ing. Alexander turned towards the youngster who was sobbing away with his hands covering his face.

'Do not cry,' he said. 'Do not cry for you are the Son of Memnon of Rhodes. Take heart, little one, take heart.'

But Phraates continued to repeat through the tears: 'Why is my mother dead? Why is my brother dead?' And not even the most powerful king on earth could give him an answer; he simply asked, 'Who killed your mother, Phraates? Tell me and I will avenge her death. Tell me, I beg you.'

The boy sought to reply through the tears and pointed to a group of Agrianians who were stripping the body of a Persian horseman. Alexander understood. He realized that his own orders to protect Barsine at all costs had caused her death and the death of Eteocles.

A group of bearers escorted by a patrol of *pezhetairoi* came by at that moment to collect the dead and they approached to take Eteocles' body, but when they moved to take Barsine the King sent them away. He himself lifted her up in his arms and carried her into his tent which the fire had spared. He laid her down on his bed, arranged her hair, caressed her pale cheeks and gently kissed her bloodless lips. Finally he closed her eyes and whispered, 'Sleep now, my Love.' Then he took Phraates by the hand and went outside.

The soldiers had returned from the battlefield and their victory cries were resounding throughout the camp. The prisoners were all thrown into a stockade – the Greeks on one side, the Barbarians on the other. Hephaestion arrived and embraced him, 'I am sorry for her and her son – such a tragedy should have been

avoided. It is clear that Mazaeus had orders to break through our left side and then free Darius's family, and he came close to succeeding – Parmenion is wounded, as are Perdiccas and Craterus, and we have suffered many fatalities.'

At that moment the women of the Great King's harem with their children and the Queen Mother were being escorted towards a more peaceful spot where a new pavilion had been erected. Hephaestion saw Callisthenes in the group, followed by a pair of servants carrying his chests full of papyrus manuscripts and his personal effects.

Alexander acknowledged them with a nod and then turned again to his friend to ask, 'How many?'

'Very many. At least two thousand it seems, if not more, but the Persians too have suffered heavy losses. There are thousands and thousands of bodies scattered all over the plain and others are being killed as I speak by our cavalry who gave them chase.'

'And Darius?'

'He fled together with Bessus, probably towards Susa or Persepolis, I'm not sure. But we have taken Mazaeus.'

Alexander thought to himself for a moment and then asked, 'Is there news of Artabazos?'

'I think I saw him among the Persian notables who have been captured. He's with Mazaeus, if I'm not mistaken.'

'Take me to him.'

'But Alexander, the men are waiting to see you, to hear your victory speech . . . they fought like lions.'

'Take me to him, Hephaestion, and give orders to someone to take care of them,' he said, pointing to

Barsine and Eteocles; at that moment the bearers were laying the son alongside his mother. Then he turned to Phraates, 'Come with me.'

The Persian leaders – satraps, generals and relatives of the Great King – had all been gathered by Eumenes in a place far from the battlefield and quartered in the great tent of the war council. The Secretary had also given orders that all those in need of medical care should be treated by the army surgeons and physicians, who also had to take care of the hundreds of wounded crying out for help as they lay in the field.

Alexander entered and all the Persians bowed, but some of them went further, moving towards him, bending over to the point where their foreheads almost touched the ground, and then bringing their right hands to their lips to send him a kiss.

'What's this?' Alexander asked Eumenes.

'It's Persian protocol – a special kiss reserved only for the emperor himself. In Greek we call it *proskynesis*. It means that these men recognize you as their legitimate sovereign, the Great King, the King of Kings.'

Alexander in the meantime had not let go of Phraates' hand and he sought one particular face among all those present. Then he said, 'This boy is called Phraates and he is the son of Memnon of Rhodes and Barsine. The war has taken both parents from him, together with his brother Eteocles.' As he spoke he saw the eyes of an elderly dignitary at the back of the tent begin to fill with tears and he understood that this was the man he was looking for. 'My hope is,' he began again, 'that among you is his grandfather, the Satrap Artabazos, the last

member of his family left alive. My hope is that he will take care of Phraates.'

The old man stepped forward and said in Persian, 'I am the boy's grandfather. You may entrust him to me, if you so wish.'

As soon as the interpreter had finished translating, Alexander bent over Phraates who was drying his face with the sleeve of his tunic, 'Look, your grandfather is here. Go to him.'

The boy looked at Alexander with his eyes still full of tears and murmured, 'Thank you.' Then he ran to the old man who fell to his knees and held him tight. A hush fell on all those present and they moved aside, clearing a pathway between Alexander and the far end of the tent so that for a moment all that could be heard were the sobs of the boy and the quiet crying of the elderly satrap. Alexander himself felt much moved and turned to Eumenes and said, 'Leave them now to their grief, then arrange for Barsine's funeral according to her father's wishes and tell him that he will be reinstated as governor of Pamphylia. He will keep all his privileges and properties and he may educate the child as he thinks fit.'

Then another person attracted his attention – a seasoned warrior who was still wearing his armour and still carried signs of the battle on his body and on his face.

'That is Mazaeus,' Eumenes whispered in his ear. Alexander whispered something in return and left.

He went back to the centre of the camp and was welcomed by the ovation of the entire army, assembled on six lines and accompanied by all their officers, both infantry and cavalry. Parmenion, even though wounded,

gave the command for them to present arms and the *hetairoi* lifted their spears while the *pezhetairoi* presented their enormous *sarissae*, which all clanged together. His companions were there too, standing proudly to salute, and Craterus and Perdiccas displayed the wounds they had received on the battlefield.

The King rode Bucephalas over to a small rise and from this natural podium he turned to his army to thank them and to salute them: 'Men!' he shouted, and immediately a deep silence fell, broken only by the crackling of the last fires on the field. 'Men! Evening approaches and, as I promised, we are victorious!'

A great cheer exploded from one end of the camp to the other and a powerful rhythmic chant began, becoming progressively stronger and clearer in the midst of the din made by the clanging arms, reaching up to the sky: '*Aléxandre! Aléxandre! Aléxandre!*'

'I wish to thank our Thessalian friends and the other Macedonian horsemen who came to us from across the sea today, just in time to take part in the battle and turn it about. I was anxiously waiting for you, men!' The Thessalians and the Macedonians from the new squadrons replied with a cheer. 'And I also wish to thank our Greek allies who held firm out on the right – I know it wasn't easy!' The Greeks began beating their swords against their shields. 'Now,' he began again, 'all Asia is ours, with all its treasures and its wonders; there is no feat that is beyond us, there is no wonder we cannot work, there are no frontiers we cannot cross. I will lead you to the ends of the earth. Are you ready to follow me, men?'

'We are ready, King!' shouted the infantrymen and the horsemen, frenetically raising and lowering their spears.

'Then listen to me! Now we will enter Babylon and you will see the largest and most beautiful city in the world and you will enjoy your rest after so much effort. Then we will set off on our march again and we will not stop until we reach the banks of the world's final river, the River Oceanus.'

A slight breeze started blowing, gaining strength so that it lifted a light dust and made the crests on the warriors' helmets waver, a wind that seemed to come from far away, carrying weak, almost forgotten voices with it. The King felt the homesickness that was beginning to affect his men now as darkness approached; he felt just how taken aback they were by his words and he said, 'I understand you, I know that you have left your brides and your children and you want to see them, but the Great King is not yet fully defeated – he has simply retreated to the furthest corners of his empire and he thinks that perhaps we will not succeed in following him that far. But he is wrong! If there is anyone who wants to turn back, I have no criticism of him, but if you prefer to continue then I will be proud to lead men like you. From tomorrow onwards Eumenes will distribute three thousand silver drachmae to each of you and much more money when we conquer the other capitals which contain great treasures. We will stay in Babylon for thirty days and thus you will have time to think it over. Then Eumenes will read the roll call so that we know who is going back home and who wants to follow me in this new enterprise. Now dismiss, men, and prepare your-

selves, for tomorrow we set off on our march once more.'

The army exploded into a long, frenetic cheer, while Alexander spurred on Bucephalas with his heels as he rode once more through the ranks at a gallop. He signalled to his companions and they rode off with him towards the Persian camp, which was being kept under strict surveillance by the men of the Vanguard and a division of Agrianian assault troops.

It seemed impossible, but the royal pavilion was even more luxurious and sumptuous than the one he had seen at Issus, although there were fewer servants. They did find over two hundred talents in gold and silver coin that were to have been used to pay the wages of the mercenaries and the newly enlisted troops, and Eumenes immediately started preparing the inventory.

The King invited his friends to sit down with him and then ordered the servants to provide food, and he ate as well.

Leonnatus came out with a sort of loud groan and said, 'Lads, I really can't believe it, but I thought we'd had it today. There was that moment when they'd broken through on Parmenion's side, while Bessus was taking the Greeks out on the right, and we were right in the middle like a bunch of idiots.'

'So that's what the surprise was that you had in store,' said Seleucus. 'The reinforcements from Macedonia and Thessaly – but how did you know that they were going to arrive in time? Just one hour later and—'

'We'd all be out with stakes up us like skewers and the crows shitting on our heads, just waiting to tuck into

our eyes and our balls. That's exactly what they always start with . . . did you know that?' asked Leonnatus.

'Enough!' Alexander interrupted him. 'I have no wish to joke tonight.' Then, turning to Seleucus, 'General Antipater had prepared everything carefully and from Tyre onwards I was receiving news on the reinforcements' daily movements. I was sure they would make it. In any case we will soon know more – we are expecting visitors.'

'Nothing is ever sure, my young and resplendent God,' came a voice from the entrance to the tent. 'Just a little more rain up in the mountains last night and your Thessalians and Macedonians would have been stuck on the other side of the Tigris, waiting for the flow to recede or for Darius to cut you to pieces.'

'Come in, Eumolpus,' Alexander called out as he recognized the informer's voice. 'Perhaps I should have placed my trust in Mazaeus's promise? His was the most dangerous operation of them all and he very nearly managed to take us from behind.'

'Why don't you ask him?' said Eumolpus as he entered, accompanying the man Alexander had seen in the prisoners' tent. 'He is here. Just as you ordered.'

The satrap entered, walked directly towards Alexander and bowed so low that his forehead was directly above the ground, then he lifted his hands to his lips and sent a kiss.

'I see that you pay homage to me as your king,' said Alexander, 'but if I had believed in your word then the dogs and the birds would be picking my bones right now.'

The satrap stood up and said in perfect Greek, 'May I respond, Sire?'

'Of course. In fact, the pair of you ought to sit down because there are a number of things I'd like you to explain.'

15

THE DISCUSSION WENT on deep into the night and in the end Mazaeus confessed that he had wanted to honour the promise made to King Darius to bring his family back and that was why he had launched such a fierce attack on the Macedonian left wing. He pointed out, however, that he could have effected a much more damaging attack from the Macedonian camp, wiping out the supplies and even have wiped the phalanx units that were marching toward the Persian centre and thus had their backs exposed to him.

'And why didn't you?' Alexander asked.

'Because he couldn't,' Parmenion interrupted. 'We were still fighting and they couldn't get away without wiping us out first.'

'This is possible, but it would lead us into an endless discussion. So answer my question, Mazaeus.'

'I am a Babylonian, Great King, and the Babylonians are famed throughout the world for being able to read the messages written in the sky and in the movements of the constellations. Our magi have seen your star shining brighter than all the others in a dark sky, completely outshining Darius's star. I could not go against the signs written up there, the signs confirmed by Marduk, our

highest god, through his oracle in the temple of Esagila in Babylon.'

'I am not certain I fully understand your reasoning, Mazaeus,' replied Alexander, 'but I can tell you that as far as I know, and judging by what I saw, you fought valiantly in favour of your king and his family. This is why I intend to reward you, not for any pronouncement of obscure seers that may have stopped the charge of your horsemen at the last moment.

'Therefore you will be reconfirmed as satrap of Babylonia and you will have the support of the Macedonian garrison I will leave here to make sure your authority is respected.'

This was a skilful move in reconfirming a good local administrator under the direct surveillance of a Macedonian military authority, while at the same time showing himself to be magnanimous. Eumenes showed his approval with a nod of his head.

Mazaeus bent over in an even lower bow, 'Does this mean that I am free to return to Babylon?'

'To your palace, as satrap – right now, if you wish, with your personal escort.'

Mazaeus stood up and, lowering his eyes, said, 'There will be nothing from now on that can ever lead me to forsake the loyalty I swear here before you, before the gods and on my honour.'

'I thank you, Mazaeus, and now let us rest: this has been the hardest day and tomorrow we must see to the funerals of our fallen comrades.'

Everyone stood up, mounted their horses and rode off towards the camp. Alexander, however, took Bucephalas

by the bridle and started walking off on foot. Eumolpus of Soloi appeared behind him and asked, 'Do you mind if I walk some way with you?'

'Not at all. After a day like this, the best thing to do is to walk a while in the peace of the evening.'

'I have heard about Barsine and her boy – I am truly sorry. I told you he was in Darius's camp because I feared he might carry out some mad act.'

'Youngsters are like that,' replied Alexander, and his face, pale in the moonlight and framed by his long hair, seemed more than ever like a boy's. 'He did what he felt was the right thing – he died like a hero in the full bloom of his youth and we must not weep for him. No human being can lament being alive because no human being knows what tomorrow may bring. What awaits us may well be infinitely worse than death – disfiguring diseases, shameful mutilations, slavery, torture . . .'

Eumolpus kept up, trying to maintain the same slow pace as Bucephalas as he followed his master. Alexander ran his hand over the animal's mane, 'Poor Bucephalas – there hasn't even been time to have him washed and groomed.'

'Or perhaps you simply didn't want to separate yourself, not even for a moment, from a friend who helped you conquer the world today.'

'That's true,' agreed Alexander; and he said nothing else.

At that moment from far off they heard people moaning, accompanied by the mournful sound of flutes, and then they saw torches moving across the plain in a sort of procession. The King understood and took a short cut

to reach the end of the cortège that was moving in a wide circle towards a small rise surmounted by a stone tumulus. Eumolpus stopped and murmured, 'Go, my boy, accompany her to her final resting place.' And he moved off with his swaying gait towards the Macedonian camp. From the other side, beyond Darius's tent, came the first raucous sounds of the vultures and the other birds of prey as they descended to banquet on the limitless field of death.

The cortège reached the top of the hill and the pall bearers placed the litter on top of the stone tumulus that had been prepared – a 'tower of silence'. At the corners of the small construction they placed four censers, each of which released a light bluish cloud of incense, and then they left. Alexander, who up until that moment had stood quietly to one side, moved towards Barsine's body. Embalmed and perfumed, her appearance had not changed and her eyes looked as though they were closed lightly, giving the impression of sleep. They had dressed her in white with a blue stole and placed a crown of small yellow flowers from the desert around her head. Alexander stood alone before her and his memories came to him as in a flood of images. He saw her smile once more, together with her tears, and he felt her warm kisses over his body and it seemed impossible that it was all over and that her beauty, now lifeless, was destined to meet such destruction. He took his golden ribbon from his head and placed it in her hands, then he kissed her for the last time: 'Farewell, my Love. I will not forget you.'

In that extreme solitude, the din of the titanic battle

now behind him, together with the memory of her fragile voice and her beauty, neither of which would ever be anything more than memories now, all these things opened up a great void inside him, bringing a childlike fear of the darkness. For a moment he was overwhelmed by an infinite grief and melancholy and he fell to his knees and cried, his head leaning on the mound, calling out her name more than once.

Then he stood up to look upon her one last time and on seeing her there, still so beautiful, he found he could not accept the idea that her body would be torn apart by wild dogs and birds of prey. He returned to the camp and ordered Eumenes to have a stonework funeral sanctuary erected to protect her remains. Only when he saw that this had been completed did he agree to set off on the march again.

16

THEY SET OFF AFTER having buried the Greek and
Macedonian soldiers who had fallen in battle, for there
was not enough wood there to build sufficient funeral
pyres. The heat and humidity and the great number of
Persian bodies decomposing all over the field were poi-
soning the air and some soldiers had come down with
mysterious fevers for which no remedy could be found.

They came once again to the ford across the Tigris
and passed over to the western bank of the river before
beginning to move down towards Babylon.

On the fourth stage of this journey, while they were
crossing through a region called Adiabene, one of the
officers from Mazaeus's escort came to Alexander to tell
him that there was a remarkable natural phenomenon to
be seen – a naphtha spring!

'Naphtha?' the King asked. He recalled the occasion
back at Mieza when Aristotle had burned the naphtha he
had been sent from Asia in a flask, remembering the dense
smoke and the acrid smell; and he also remembered the
fireboat that the inhabitants of Tyre had launched against
him one night, setting fire to the assault towers, and how
the day after the air was still full of that same stink. So
he set off behind the officer who led him to the bottom
of a hollow where a fire burned continuously, releasing

a thick column of smoke into the air. All around there was a large, black and oily mass, like a swamp with strange iridescent reflections and from which there came that terrible smell. Callisthenes was already there and he was taking a sample of some of the liquid using a glass phial.

'I want to send some to Uncle Aristotle for his experiments.'

'But what is it exactly?' asked Alexander.

'Well . . . it's difficult to say. The taste is the most revolting you can possibly imagine – the smell and its appearance too. Perhaps it's a sort of humour, almost an exudate of this land that is so battered by the rays of the sun. As you know, however, it is combustible and generates incredible heat. Look!'

At that moment a group of soldiers, on orders from their officer, had filled some skins with the naphtha and were spreading two lines of it along the sides of the pathway that led to the camp. Then the officer took a lighted lamp from the hands of one of his men and ignited the ends of the lines – two walls of flame rose immediately and rushed as quick as thought itself towards the camp, leaving everyone with their mouths open in astonishment. The strange substance continued to burn along the pathway, accompanied by two curtains of dense, stinking smoke and an unbearable heat.

Alexander immediately took a bath to free himself of the smell which had impregnated even his hair, and while Leptine washed him, he spoke to Hephaestion, Ptolemy, Callisthenes, a new masseur who came from Athens and

whose name was Athenophanes, and his assistant, a boy by the name of Stephanus.

'From what I've seen,' said the King, 'this naphtha could be used as a weapon – just imagine the effect if we were to unleash it on our enemies!'

'I have heard that naphtha is not suitable for such applications,' said the masseur, who as a young boy had attended a few philosophy lessons. 'Indeed, the type of fire it produces is completely anomalous. Fire, as everyone knows, is an ethereal, celestial element, which is transmitted through the air spreading heat and light. Naphtha on the other hand comes from the earth and burns only on contact with a completely arid ground like sand or on earth that is too moist and rich like that of southern Babylonia. On a substance of some intermediate humour, such as a man might be considered to be, it would never catch fire – there is no doubt of this.'

'That seems a rather shaky hypothesis,' Callisthenes objected. 'It is difficult to apply intellectual categories to individual physical manifestations which are influenced by multiple and non-quantifiable components and what is more—'

'I am sure of what I am saying,' retorted Athenophanes as Alexander came out of his bath and Leptine began to dry him with a linen towel, 'and my assistant, Stephanus, has heard my teacher, the sophist Hermippus, expound this thesis.'

'Indeed, I am so sure that I am prepared to demonstrate it myself with an experiment, right here and now before all of you!' exclaimed the boy, perhaps simply to

attract attention and to ingratiate himself in some way with Alexander.

'I really don't think it's worth bothering about,' said the King. 'It's best just to forget it.'

The boy insisted, however, supported by Athenophanes who continued to spout his philosophical theories. No sooner said than done and a servant appeared with the naphtha which young Stephanus began spreading over his body very carefully, as though he were using olive oil.

'Now,' announced Athenophanes as he picked up a lamp, 'I will demonstrate that on a human body of medium humour naphtha cannot burn,' and he brought the lamp to the boy's skin. In the blink of an eye Stephanus's body was wrapped in a ferocious globe of flame that produced a terrible heat. His screams were heart-rending. Everyone grabbed buckets and any other container and threw the water from the bath over him, which fortunately was to hand, but even then it wasn't easy to put the flames out.

Alexander immediately called for Philip, who took care of the boy, spreading certain ointments over his skin for the burns. It took a great deal of effort on the physician's part, but he managed to save the boy's life. Stephanus, however, was seriously maimed and disfigured and his health remained poor for the rest of his life.

Callisthenes advised everyone to steer clear of the evil-smelling liquid until his Uncle Aristotle had completed his studies and discovered what its real characteristics

were. The following day they set off once more on their journey.

<div align="center">*</div>

As they advanced, the steppes gave way to an ever more fertile and rich land, irrigated by a great number of canals that linked the Tigris to the Euphrates. Throughout the countryside there were many villages whose peasants were busy getting the land ready for sowing.

Wherever they stopped the local chiefs offered them regional specialities – palm hearts in particular, which were very pleasant and refreshing. Palm wine, however, lay heavily on their stomachs and often caused headaches, but there were really no alternatives; normal wine, even the best wine, did not really keep well in that climate and the drinking water was often poor as well. The dates were excellent, as were the pomegranates that grew abundantly and were exceptionally tasty.

They also saw that vast stretches of the fields were flooded by the peasants themselves using a system of locks on the canals and Alexander found this practice rather strange. Callisthenes made enquiries and was told that in this way the land was gradually freed of the salt that formed on the surface because of the great heat and thus it preserved its fertility.

'What they are doing is reproducing artificially what happens naturally in Egypt with the flooding of the Nile,' said Ptolemy. 'This must be a peculiarity of very hot climates. What's surprising here, however, is that there are no crocodiles in the Tigris, and none in the Euphrates

either – perhaps these animals can only live in the waters of the Nile.'

Nearchus disagreed, 'Not at all. I have heard tale of a man from Massalia who sailed beyond the Pillars of Hercules, along the African coast, right to the estuary of a river called Chretes which was crawling with crocodiles.'

'Beyond the Pillars of Hercules . . .' sighed Alexander. 'A man's life is too short to allow him to see the entire world!' and he thought of Alexander of Epirus and his unavenged death in the lands of Hesperia.

Towards the end of the journey, their march became more and more of a parade because everywhere the local inhabitants came out of their homes and lined up along the road to acclaim their King. Then the spectacle went beyond all possible expectation and wonder when, there before them on the horizon, there appeared the walls, the towers, the pyramids and the gardens of the most celebrated city in the world – Babylon!

17

THE WELCOME BABYLON produced for the young conqueror was like something out of a fantastic tale. For ten stadia along the road leading to the city thousands of youngsters – girls and boys – had lined up and were throwing flowers before Alexander's horse. The majestic Ishtar gate, one hundred feet high and finished in enamelled tiles carrying figures of dragons and winged bulls, seemed to loom more and more as the King advanced with his companions and followed by his army in formation, his soldiers and his officers all dressed in their finest armour.

The inhabitants of the city had taken up position on the ramparts of the towers flanking the gate and along the gigantic walls – wide enough to allow the passage of two four-horse chariots side by side. They were anxious to see the new King who had defeated the Persians three times in less than two years and had forced many heavily fortified cities to surrender.

The priests and the dignitaries greeted Alexander and accompanied him to offer a sacrifice to the god Marduk whose shrine was at the top of the Esagila, the great stepped temple that stood towering over the wide sacred area. Before the immense crowd gathered in the great courtyard, Alexander, together with his companions and

his generals, climbed the steps which led from one terrace to another right up to the sanctuary on the summit which housed the god's bed of gold in this his earthly dwelling.

From up there the King was able to look upon and absorb the amazing spectacle of the majestic metropolis. Babylon extended before him at his feet with all its marvels, with its endless walls, the triple bulwark that protected the royal palace and the 'summer palace' located in the northern part of the city. He could see the smoke from the burning incense as it rose from the more than one thousand sanctuaries in the huge urban area – the wide, straight roads that met one another at right angles and all the main arteries, paved in terracotta tiles all bound together with asphalt. Each of the roads began and terminated with one of the twenty-five gates that provided access through the walls, with their colossal doors dressed in bronze, silver, and gold.

The city was split in two by the River Euphrates, shining like a ribbon of gold extending from one side of the walls to the other, flanked by gardens and exotic trees of all kinds in which flocks of multicoloured birds were roosting.

Beyond the river, connected to the western part of the city by massive stonework bridges, the royal palaces stood out because of their finish in polychrome enamel tiles, resplendent in the sun with images of fantastical creatures, storybook landscapes, scenes from the ancient mythology of the Land of the Two Rivers.

Not far from the royal palace stood the greatest structure in the entire city, considered to be one of the

most impressive wonders in the known world – the Hanging Gardens.

The typically Persian concept of the *pairidaeza* had taken shape here in a completely flat location whose climate was unsuitable for a large tree-filled park. Everything here was artificial, created with notable effort and ingenuity by the hand of man. The priests explained to Alexander that according to the story of the gardens' origin, a young Elamite queen, having arrived in Babylon as bride to King Nebuchadnezzar, suffered so much from homesickness for the wooded mountains of her homeland that the King gave orders for an artificial mountain to be created and covered with a shady wood and with the most beautiful flowers. That was why the architects had created a series of platforms, one above the other, reducing in size as they increased in height. Each was supported by hundreds of stonework pillars carefully covered in asphalt and linked by curved vaults, and the huge platforms which carried all the soil necessary to allow the bushes and the high trees to root and flourish were also asphalted. Many birds, even nocturnal species, started nesting in the trees and bushes while exotic species, such as peacocks and pheasants, were brought from the Caucasus and far off India. Fountains of all types were created with ingenious machines bringing the water from the Euphrates, which flowed past at the bottom of the wonder.

From the outside it looked like a hill covered with a flourishing wood, but here and there were signs of man's intervention – terraces and parapets hidden away among the climbing and trailing plants, all of them rich in flowers and fruits.

It moved Alexander to think that such a wonder had been ordered by a great king to ease the melancholy of his queen, a young woman born in the high, woody lands of Elam, and he thought of Barsine who slept now for ever on her 'tower of silence' in the arid desert of Gaugamela.

'Gods above!' he murmured as he looked around him. 'How many wonders there are here!' and his friends too, Ptolemy and Perdiccas, Leonnatus and Philotas, Lysimachus and Eumenes, Seleucus and Craterus, all looked in amazement at the city which for millennia had been considered the heart of the world and 'God's Gate', as its very name in the local language – Bab-El – actually meant. Vast green spaces opened up between the houses and the buildings, orchards and gardens with all sorts of fruit, and out on the river there were many boats moving agilely through the water. Some of these, made of bundles of reeds and driven by large square sails, came from the estuary areas where the oldest cities of Mesopotamian myth were located: Ur, Kish, Lagash. Others, round in shape, like large baskets and covered with tanned skins, came from the north and brought with them the fruits of those far off lands – produce from the green fields of Armenia, rich in wildfowl, animal skins, wood and precious stones.

The sky, the water and the earth all contributed towards the creation of a universe of harmonious perfection within the great city walls with their imposing crown of towers. Yet Alexander continued to look around in search of another marvel he had heard tale of since his

childhood. Indeed, his teacher, Leonidas, had been the first to mention the 'Tower of Babel', a mountain of stone and asphalt some three hundred feet high and as wide as that at its base. All the peoples of the world were said to have worked on its construction.

The priest pointed to a huge area that was completely abandoned and covered in weeds, 'That is where the sacred Etemenanki stood, the tower that touched the sky, destroyed by the Persians in their fury when the city rebelled, at the time of King Xerxes.'

'The same king who destroyed our temples when he invaded Greece,' said Alexander. 'I will rebuild the tower when I return to Babylon.'

That same evening the King celebrated with a sumptuous feast for hundreds and hundreds of guests. All the very best foods and wines and other inebriating drinks were served, and the most beautiful women of all the Orient danced that evening: Medians, Caucasians, Babylonians, Arabs, Hyrcanians, Syrians, Hebrews.

For thirty days behaviour at the banquets, the orgies, the binges was very much out of hand – nothing was denied the soldiers who had won at the Granicus, at Issus and at Gaugamela, the soldiers who had wiped out Miletus, Halicarnassus, Tyre and Gaza. For these same soldiers there was a new and difficult adventure in the offing, a troubled journey with all sorts of trials, ordeals and tribulations.

One evening Alexander had retired to the 'summer palace' to cool off a little when Perdiccas asked to see him.

He still had bandages around his torso, covering the

wounds he had received on the fateful day at Gaugamela, and in his eyes there was a strange expression that might have been either drunkenness or melancholy.

The King asked him, 'How are you, Perdiccas?'

'I am well, Alexander.'

'You asked to speak to me.'

'That's right.'

'And what do you have to say to me?'

'Your sister, Queen Cleopatra, has been a widow for more than a year now.'

'Unfortunately.'

'I love her. I have always loved her.'

'I know.'

'How do you know?' Perdiccas asked him, slightly embarrassed.

'I know and that's enough.'

'I have come to ask for her hand.'

Alexander remained silent.

'I have dared too much, have I not?' Perdiccas asked, his eyes liquid, almost completely lost. 'But I would never have found enough courage to ask you without first getting drunk.'

'Was it "Hercules' Cup"?'

'That's it,' nodded Perdiccas.

'The fact is that—'

'What?' asked Perdiccas, pathetically anxious, waiting for his reply with his mouth open.

'That Ptolemy has also asked for Cleopatra's hand.'

'Ah.'

'And Seleucus.'

'As well . . . no one else?'

'No one else, apart from Lysimachus, Hephaestion and . . . yourself, obviously.'

'By any chance Parmenion too?'

'No, he hasn't.'

'Just as well. In any case I don't have any hope.'

'If you want me to tell you the truth, I think you must be the only one to have asked to marry Cleopatra because she is the woman you love, rather than because she is Alexander's sister. However, this in itself is not enough. Still not enough time has passed since the death of Alexander of Epirus, and in any case the man who marries her will have to prove himself to be the worthiest, willing to face any risk, any sacrifice, and to bear ordeals and pains that not even you can imagine.'

Perdiccas had become sufficiently sober to feel like crying and he replied, 'But have I not already faced all these things for you?'

'No more than your companions. However, the most difficult part is yet to come, my friend. In twenty days' time we will set off on our march again to conquer this empire, to follow Darius to the farthest provinces, and then we will return to this city. It is when we return here that I will know who is the worthiest. Go now, get yourself a beautiful girl, there are so many of them, and have a good time because life is short.'

Perdiccas moved off and Alexander turned to the great flower-filled balcony that opened up over the city, out towards the river glowing with a thousand lights and towards the sky teeming with shining stars.

18

DURING HIS STAY IN Babylon, Alexander dedicated much time to the organization of the new provinces and the new administration, and the drawing up of his plan of action for the following year. One evening he summoned all his companions and the entire war council to the summer palace where the unbearable heat of these lowlands was slightly tempered by an occasional breath of wind, especially towards sunset.

'I want to let you know about my plans,' he began. 'During the first year of our campaign I decided to occupy all the ports, so as to exclude the Persian fleet from our seas and to render a counter-invasion of Macedonia impossible. Now we will take all of the capitals in the empire, so that it is clear that Darius's reign has come to an end and that all of his possessions are in our hands. Babylon is already ours and now we will take Susa, Ecbatana, Pasargadae and Persepolis. All that is left for Darius is to seek refuge in the far eastern regions, but we will follow him there until we capture him.

'And there is another reason for taking the capitals – money. Darius's treasures are all kept in his capitals and with this wealth we will send aid to General Antipater who has to fight in Greece against the Spartans, and who

has to deal with my mother on a daily basis, which is perhaps even more demanding.'

His companions all laughed and even Peritas, who was there with them, started barking loudly.

'Then we will be able to sign up more mercenaries and equip the new recruits who will soon be with us. General Parmenion will set off northwards with the Greek allies, three battalions of the phalanx, one squadron of the *hetairoi*, the supplies and the assault engines. He will reach the Royal Road and proceed along it to Persepolis. With the rest of our forces we will move up into the mountains to take the passes and to free the territory of the final Persian garrisons. It will not be easy because the snow is already falling up in the mountains.

'So enjoy yourselves now while you can, but make sure you gather all your strength because this will be no laughing matter.'

After they had all left, Eumolpus of Soloi came in and Alexander took hold of Peritas by the collar because he immediately started growling.

'I have done everything as you requested, Sire,' began Eumolpus. 'I have made arrangements for one of my men to go to Susa to make sure that the royal treasure does not disappear. As far as I know it's worth thirty thousand talents in coin and ingots, as well as all the precious objects that adorn the palace. The young man's name is Aristoxenus and he knows what he is doing. If he should ever need to contact you he'll use the usual password.'

'Skewered thrush,' repeated Alexander, shaking his head. 'Listen, this might be the right time to change it.

At the moment there are no imminent dangers that might justify such an absurd password.'

'Too late, Sire. Aristoxenus is already on his way. We'll change it next time.'

Alexander sighed and held Peritas while Eumolpus, light footed as usual, dissolved into thin air through the corridors of the palace.

Shortly before leaving, Eumenes took some money from the royal coffers, leaving it in the hands of one of his Macedonian collaborators – Harpalus, a man who had never fought in any battle because he was crippled. Throughout the campaign he had earned a reputation as being very well versed in economic management. Alexander knew him well because as a boy he had spent time at the palace in Pella even although he had not been able to take part in military exercises because of his disability.

'He ought to do a good job,' said Alexander. 'I think he has his wits about him.'

'I think so too,' replied Eumenes. 'He has always been a good lad.'

*

They set off again towards the end of the summer, after having reconfirmed Mazaeus as Satrap of Babylon and leaving a Macedonian garrison to safeguard the defence and the safety of the province. They proceeded up the Pasitigris, a tributary of the Tigris which flowed down through the Elam mountains. The landscape was beautiful – rich in green pastures with many flocks of sheep and herds of cows grazing, and in that area there grew all types of fruit trees, including the wonderful *persica*

with its velvet skin and its incredibly juicy and tasty flesh. There was also plenty of sun-dried fruit such as figs and prunes.

It took the army six days' march to come within sight of Susa, and Alexander recalled the enthusiastic description of the Persian guests who had been visiting Pella many years before, when he was still just a boy. The city stood on a flat area, with the Elam mountain chain as a backdrop, the high peaks already covered with snow, their slopes green with firs and cedars. It was huge, surrounded by walls and towers decorated in shining tiles and with its battlements all decorated in silver- and gold-plated studs.

As soon as the army began approaching, the gates opened and a troop of splendidly dressed horsemen appeared, escort to a dignitary who wore a soft tiara on his head and an *akinake* at his side.

'This is most certainly Abulites,' Eumenes said to Alexander. 'He is the Satrap of Susiana and he intends to surrender. Aristoxenus, Eumolpus's man, told me last night. By all accounts all of the treasure – or at least most of it – is still held in the city.'

The Satrap came nearer, dismounted and bowed before Alexander in the traditional Persian show of homage: 'The city of Susa welcomes you in peace and opens its gates to the man Ahura Mazda has chosen as successor to Cyrus the Great.'

Alexander graciously bowed his head and signalled to the Satrap to mount his horse and to continue alongside him.

'I don't like these barbarians at all,' said Leonnatus to

Seleucus. 'See what they're up to? They surrender without fighting, betraying their own sovereign, and Alexander leaves them with the same position they had before, while we're still here on horseback riding day and night. Will we ever reach the other side of this damn country?'

'Alexander's right,' replied Seleucus. 'He leaves the old governors in their places so that the people don't feel they're being ruled over by foreigners, but the tax officials and the military leaders are all Macedonian. It's not at all as you imagine. Isn't it better this way? The cities open up their gates to us and we haven't assembled the siege engines since we left the coast. Perhaps you'd prefer to see some blood spilled, just like Halicarnassus and Tyre?'

'Not at all, but—'

'In that case just be thankful for the way things are now.'

'Yes, but . . . I really don't like these barbarians being so close to Alexander – eating with him and all the rest of it. I simply don't like it, that's all.'

'Don't worry, nothing's going to happen. Alexander knows full well what he's up to.'

The city of Susa – immense and almost three thousand years old – had four hills at its four corners and on one of them stood the royal palace which at that very moment was fully illuminated by the rays of the setting sun. The entrance was a majestic temple-style *pronaos*, consisting of large stone columns with capitals in the form of winged bulls supporting the ceiling. Then came an atrium paved with marble of all colours and partly covered by magnificent carpets. There were also other

columns supporting the ceiling, these in cedar wood painted red and yellow. Through a corridor and across another atrium, Alexander was led into the *apadana*, the great audience chamber, while the dignitaries, the eunuchs and the chamberlains all retreated to the sides of the great hall, lowering their heads until they were almost touching the floor.

The King, followed by his Companions and his generals, came to the throne of the Achaemenid emperors and took his place, but he soon found himself somewhat embarrassed. He was so short that his feet failed to touch the ground and actually dangled in a not very regal manner. Leonnatus, who was endowed with a militaristic sensibility with regard to such things, spotted a piece of furniture made of cedar wood nearby and pushed it over so that Alexander could rest his feet on it, as though it were a stool, and begin speaking to the onlookers.

'Friends, what seemed to be an impossible dream not so long ago, has now become a reality. Two of the greatest capitals in the world – Babylon and Susa – are now in our hands and soon we will take possession of others as well—' No sooner had Alexander begun his speech than it was interrupted by the noise of someone quietly crying. The King looked around and complete silence fell in the great hall, making the sobbing of one of the eunuchs, who was standing with his head against the wall, stand out even more. Everyone moved out of the way because they realized that the King wanted to see him, and the poor soul was then left standing tearfully alone under Alexander's gaze.

'Why are you crying?' Alexander asked. The man

shielded his face as he dried his tears. 'Come now, speak freely.'

'These castrated specimens,' whispered Leonnatus to Seleucus, 'they burst into tears for nothing, just like girls, but apparently they're better than any woman in bed.'

'There are eunuchs and then there are eunuchs,' replied Seleucus. 'This one, for example, doesn't look up to much.'

'Come along now, speak,' insisted Alexander.

The eunuch then moved forward and it was clear to everyone that he was staring intently at the stool under the King's feet.

'I am a eunuch,' he began, 'and by nature I am loyal to my master, whoever he may be. Before I was loyal to my Lord, King Darius, and now I am loyal to you, my new King. Despite this, I cannot help but cry when I consider how rapid the reverses of fate can be. The piece of furniture you are using as a stool,' and at this point Alexander began to realize why the eunuch was crying, 'was Darius's dining table, the table on which he ate his meals, and therefore for us it was a sacred object, worthy of veneration. Now you are using it as a footrest . . .'

Alexander blushed and was about to get up, having perceived that he had committed an act of unpardonable vulgarity, but Aristander stopped him: 'Do not move your feet from that table. Does it not strike you that there is a message in this apparently coincidental event? The gods wanted this to happen so that everyone will know that they have laid the power of the Persian empire at your feet.'

So it was that Darius's table remained where it was, a footstool for the new King.

The audience in the throne room came to an end and everyone dispersed throughout the palace. The chamberlain, another eunuch, led Alexander, alone, into the imperial harem where there were many enchanting young women – all of them beautiful, all of them dressed in their national costumes, and they welcomed him with excited giggling. Some were dark in complexion, while others had fair skin and blue eyes – there was even an Ethiopian girl and to the King, with her proud bearing, she looked like one of Lysippus's bronze statues.

'If you want to play with them,' said the eunuch, 'they'll be pleased to do all they can for you, even this very night.'

'Thank them for me and tell them that I will soon come to enjoy their company.'

Then he moved into another room of the great palace and suddenly noticed his friends all lined up looking at a monument and he too stopped to observe – a statuary group in bronze representing two young men with their daggers raised, as though about to strike someone.

'Harmodius and Aristogiton,' explained Ptolemy. 'It's the monument to the men who killed Hipparchus, Hippias's brother, friend of the Persians and traitor to the Greek cause. King Xerxes took it in Athens as war booty before torching the city. It has been here for one hundred and fifty years, testimony to that humiliation.'

'I have heard that these two did not in fact kill Hipparchus to free the city of a tyrant, but rather it was

a question of jealousy because both Hipparchus and Aristogiton had fallen in love with Harmodius,' said Leonnatus.

'That changes nothing,' said Callisthenes as he looked on the famous monument in admiration. 'Whatever happened, these two men brought democracy back to Athens.'

There was a certain embarrassment in the air at these words – everyone recalled Demosthenes' vehement speeches in favour of democracy in Athens and against the 'tyrant' Philip. It seemed that as each day passed Alexander was forgetting the democratic education he had received from Aristotle, and perhaps even the letters of advice that came from the philosopher were having no effect. The King's spirit was increasingly attracted by the imperial grandeur surrounding him in Persia.

'Make arrangements for the monument to be sent to Athens as my personal gift for the city,' said Alexander who had somehow understood what everyone was thinking and no one dared say. 'I hope they will understand that Macedonian swords have obtained a result that a thousand speeches by their orators could never even describe.'

The Queen Mother, Sisygambis, together with the King's concubines and their children were once again allowed to settle into the apartments they had left such a long time previously. They were all much moved to be in these familiar surroundings once again; they wept into the pillows on the beds in which they had made love and in which they had given birth, they crossed the thresholds leading into their bed chambers, rendered sacred by the

presence of the Great King. In truth, however, things were no longer as they had been – the corridors and the halls of the palace contained the same objects and items, but the palace resounded to the sound of a hostile, incomprehensible language and the future looked dark and worrying. Only the Queen Mother seemed calm, completely immersed in the mysterious serenity of her wisdom. She had asked for and had been granted custody of Phraates, Barsine's youngest son who, if anything were to happen to his grandfather, Satrap Artabazos, would be the only survivor of the family.

Alexander often visited the royal harem, sometimes alone and sometimes together with Hephaestion, and the young women grew to love the King and his friend together, satisfying their every desire and sleeping with them in the same bed through the fragrant nights of that warm summer, as they listened to the singing and the music of their companions and the great voices of the metropolis, once joyous but now dampened by the fear of the unknown.

Every day he was in the city he visited the Queen Mother's apartments, talking with her for a long time with the aid of an interpreter. On the eve of their departure he spoke to her once again, just as he had done on the night before the battle at Gaugamela. 'Mother,' he said, 'tomorrow I will leave to pursue your son into the farthest reaches of his empire. I believe in my destiny and I believe that my conquests have come about with the help of the gods, and for this reason I will never leave my work incomplete, but I promise you that as far as I am able I will never inflict any harm on Darius and I will

try to save his life. I have also arranged for you to be taught Greek by the best teachers, because I want to hear my language one day on your lips and I want to listen to you without any interpreter coming between our thoughts.'

The Queen Mother looked him in the eyes and murmured something that the interpreter failed to catch, because she had spoken in a secret, mysterious language, the tongue which only her god could understand.

19

THE TRUMPETS SOUNDED the signal for departure one morning early in autumn, while the city was still in shadow and the Elam mountain tops were just being touched by the first rays of the rising sun. The army was split into two: Parmenion led the majority of the forces, the carts with the unassembled war engines and the supplies along the Royal Road, while Alexander was with the light forces, the shock troops and the Agrianians, and they took the mountain path that led across the Elams to Persepolis, the capital founded by Darius the Great.

Led by guides from Susa, he moved along the river as it became ever narrower and then climbed up towards the pass which led through to the highlands that were home to an indomitable people of wild and primitive shepherds – the Ouxians. Although they were nominally under the control of the Great King, in fact they were independent and when Alexander asked them, with the help of an interpreter, to allow him to cross their land, they replied, 'You may cross if you pay, just as the Great King always did when he wanted to take the shortest road from Susa to Persepolis.'

Alexander replied, 'The Great King no longer governs his empire and my behaviour will not be his behaviour.

Therefore I will cross your land, whether you like it or not.'

The Ouxians were frightful to look at – bristling all over with hair; dressed in goat- and sheepskins, they stank just like their animals. It was clear that they were not easily scared and they were not prepared to concede anything. They had every faith in the difficult, steep nature of their land, its narrow valleys, its steep pathways where only a few people at a time could climb up. They had no idea that the foreign King was accompanied by warriors who were even wilder and more primitive than themselves, and who were used to moving agilely over even more challenging terrain, capable of withstanding cold and hunger, pain and exhaustion: bold and ferocious, bloodthirsty and eager to fight, blindly obedient to the hand that fed them – the Agrianians!

Alexander united the leaders and the guides from Susa so that they could explain the layout of the two main pathways that led to the Ouxians' highlands. It was decided that Craterus, with the shock troops, would follow the less steep of the two paths which ran directly to the passes that led to Persis, while Alexander, with the Agrianians and two battalions of shieldsmen, took on the more difficult route that led straight to the terrain held by the enemy warriors.

Craterus waited for the King to begin climbing up the steep slope with his troops, attracting the majority of the Ouxian forces, and then he made his move, shielded by the thick vegetation, along the pathway that led towards the passes.

The Ouxians who took on Alexander let fly with

arrows, with stones fired from slings, with large rocks rolled by hand down the slope, but the Agrianians were extremely agile and took shelter behind every available outcrop and then moved forward briskly across open terrain and hid once again behind tree trunks and rocks. When they finally came into contact with the first Ouxians, they attacked them with such savage ferocity the defenders had no chance of stopping them. Many fell to the ground with their throats slit open, others collapsed holding their guts as they spilled out of long belly wounds. The Agrianians were relentless – they struck to kill and to kill alone, to wipe out the enemy completely and to terrorize them with wounds that were horrific to look upon.

Immediately behind the Agrianians came the shieldsmen who took up their regular formation again and set off at a run towards the villages of stone and brick where the Ouxians lived together with their animals in some form of primitive symbiosis. Alexander gave orders for incendiary arrows to be used and soon the straw and hay roofs of the huts were transformed into blazing infernos and the animals fled in terror every which way.

The Ouxians had never even imagined the possibility of such an invasion and they fled towards the passes where they felt they might be able to organize a more effective defence, but these had already been occupied by Craterus and his assault troops. A rain of arrows greeted the highland people and many of them were killed instantly.

Now the Ouxians were caught between Alexander's and Craterus's troops and they surrendered, but the King

inflicted a terrible punishment on them – they were to be torn completely from their lands and deported to the plain, so that they would never again be able to block the passage between Susa and Persis.

As soon as they heard from the interpreters about the fate that awaited them, they threw themselves at the King's feet, imploring him and crying, shouting out in despair. The women and children joined in these laments, but Alexander was resolute – he said that they should have accepted his initial proposal and that in this way they would learn that he never issued empty threats and that no force in the world could ever stop him.

One of the guides from Susa, however, suggested to the Ouxians that they should appeal to Queen Mother Sisygambis, the only person who might have some influence over the implacable conqueror; they took this advice and in secret sent two of their leaders through the Macedonian lines. Four days later, when the cavalry had already reached the highlands along the easier of the two paths, the Ouxian leaders returned with a letter from the Queen Mother written in Greek which pleaded with Alexander to allow these poor folk to remain on their lands:

Sisygambis hails Alexander!

Representatives of the Ouxian people have come to ask me to intercede with you on their behalf. I know they have insulted and mocked you, but the punishment you wish to inflict upon them is the most terrible – worse than death itself. Indeed, there is nothing more painful than being torn from the land on which

one has lived since childhood, from the waters that have slaked one's thirst, from the fields that have provided nourishment, from the sight of the sun that rises and sets behind the horizons of our mountains.

Many times you have called me mother, that most sweet of names, that name destined only for Olympias who gave birth to you in the palace at Pella. Now, on the grounds of the name with which you honour me, I ask you to listen to me as you would listen to your mother – spare this people the ordeal of being torn from their homeland.

Remember your own homeland and the love you have left there! These wretches have done nothing more than defend their land and their homes.

Be merciful!

The letter moved Alexander and quenched his rage – the Ouxians were allowed to remain in their highland homes, paying an annual tribute of five hundred horses, two thousand pack mares and common livestock. They accepted willingly, thinking that this angry young man and his savage warriors would never come back to claim their goats and their oxen and that it was in any case a request they could not refuse.

With the highlands dealt with, Alexander set off again towards the highest pass – a narrow throughway known as the 'Persian Gates', across which the Satrap Ariobarzanes had built a defensive wall very high up, impregnable by virtue of its position. The army set off on its march before dawn one freezing morning, across the wind-beaten plateau, while from the grey sky above the first flakes of snow were beginning to fall.

20

THE VALLEY LEADING to the Persian Gates grew progressively narrower, to the point where it became a rocky gorge, both sides of which rose steeply. It took considerable effort to move forwards though the deep snow and across the sheets of ice with the horses and the mules slipping and hurting themselves, sometimes even breaking legs. It took almost the whole day for the leading troops to reach the first buttresses of the ramps that led up to the great wall protecting the pass.

Then, as Alexander was assembling the leaders of the Thracians and the Agrianians in order to study some means of climbing over the steep banks and the wall itself under cover of darkness, a series of loud crashing noises shook them all – from the top of the walls the Persian soldiers had started rolling down enormous rocks which set off great landslides of rubble that came crashing down towards the bottom.

Everyone started shouting, 'Out of the way! Move clear!' – but the rocks moved faster than the men and the result was a massacre. Alexander himself, caught in an avalanche of pebbles, was injured in several places, although fortunately no bones were broken. He immediately gave orders for the men to retreat, but in the meantime the enemy soldiers had taken up their bows

and, despite the thickening snow and the decreasing visibility, they fired into the crowd below without ever missing the mark.

'The shields!' shouted Lysimachus, in command of the assault troops. 'Put the shields over your heads!'

The men obeyed, but the Persians were running along the sides of the gorge now, firing arrows at the rearguard who had still not understood what was happening. Only darkness brought the massacre to an end and with great effort Alexander managed to gather his army together in a wider space where they could set up camp. They were all deeply discouraged, not only by the great number of fatal casualties, but also by the cries of their wounded – unable to bear the pain of limbs that had been cut and torn open, the pain of crushed bones.

Philip and his surgeons set to work in the lamplight, closing wounds, pulling out arrow- and javelin heads from the living flesh of the warriors, setting fractures, immobilizing limbs with splints and bandages, even making use of arrows and spear shafts when they had no other material available.

One by one the Companions came to the King's tent for a meeting of the council. There were no fires nor embers with which they could warm themselves, but the lamp hanging from the main pole spread some light and with it a slight sense of warmth. They were all painfully aware of the incredible and dramatic change in fortune their lives had undergone in the space of a few days – from the luxury and the indulgence of the palaces in Babylon and Susa to the ice and the hardships of this desperate undertaking.

'How many of them do you think there are?' asked Seleucus.

'I don't know,' replied Ptolemy, 'several thousand in my opinion. If Ariobarzanes has decided to hold the pass then they cannot hope to do so with just a few poorly armed soldiers. They must have considerable numbers of crack troops.' At that moment Eumenes came in, blue with cold, his teeth chattering. His papyrus carrying case was over his shoulder, containing the sheets, the pen and the ink with which he wrote the expedition journal every evening.

'Have you counted our losses?' Alexander asked him.

'They are very heavy,' replied the Secretary as he ran through a sheet of hastily compiled notes, 'at least three hundred dead and a hundred wounded.'

'What do we do now?' asked Leonnatus.

'We cannot leave them out there for the wolves,' replied Alexander. 'We have to bring them back.'

'But that will mean even more losses,' said Lysimachus.

'If we go out there now we'll come to grief on the rocks in the dark; if we go out in daylight tomorrow they'll be able to pick us off from the top of the gorge.'

'I'm going now,' said the King. 'I cannot leave our boys out there unburied. If you're afraid, you don't need to follow me.'

'I'll come with you,' said Hephaestion, getting to his feet to show his willingness.

'You know perfectly well it's not a matter of fear,' said Lysimachus, stung into replying.

'Oh no? Well what is the problem then?'

'There's no point arguing,' said Ptolemy. 'That's no solution to anything. Let's try to give it some thought.'

'I . . . I think I might have a solution,' said Eumenes.

Everyone turned to look at the Secretary General and Leonnatus shook his head, thinking to himself that this little Greek specimen always had the answer to everything.

'A solution?' asked Alexander. 'And what might that be?'

'Just one moment,' replied Eumenes. 'I'll be back straight away.' He left and returned shortly afterwards with one of the local guides who had accompanied them up to that point.

'Speak freely,' said the Secretary. 'The King and his friends will listen to you.'

The man bowed to Alexander and his companions and began speaking in reasonably understandable Greek, with an accent that sounded slightly Cypriot.

'Where are you from?' Alexander asked him.

'I am Lycian from the Patara area. I was given into slavery as a young man in order to pay a debt of my father's with his Persian landlord, a man by the name of Arsaces who took me with him when he returned, and gave me his animals to look after while they grazed in this area. For that reason I know these mountains like the back of my hand.'

All those present held their breath as they realized that this poor wretch might have the fate of the entire army in his hands.

'If you go back into that gorge,' he continued, 'the Persians will wipe you out before you reach the bottom

of the wall – only small units can operate down there. I know a path, however, an hour's march from here, that leads up through a forest. It's a goat track and men can only move along it in single file, but four or five hours ought to be enough to reach the top and take the Persians from behind.'

'It seems to me we have no other choice,' said Seleucus, 'if we really want to move forwards.'

'I think so too,' said Alexander, 'but there is a problem – if the pathway is so very narrow then we won't be able to get enough of our men up to the top to be able to withstand a counterattack from the Persians. Someone will, in any case, have to engage them head on at the wall.'

'I will take care of that,' said Lysimachus.

'No, you will come with me along the path. Craterus will go with the Agrianians, the Thracians and a battalion of the assault troops, trying to keep losses to a minimum. We will attack at the same time – our men from above, and Craterus from below. A simultaneous attack of this kind ought to throw the Persians into a panic.'

'We'll need a signal,' said Craterus, 'but what can it be? The gorge is too deep for light signals and the distance between our units might be too much for noises or shouts.'

'There is a way,' said the Lycian shepherd. 'There is a place near the wall where the echo bounces across the walls of the gorge – a trumpet blow carries a long distance. I've experimented with it many times with my horn to wile away the time when I was out with the sheep.'

Alexander looked at him, 'What's your name, Lycian?'

'My master used to call me Ochus, which in Persian means 'bastard', but my real name is Rhedas.'

'Listen, Rhedas, if you have told us the truth and you can lead us up behind the Persians, I will make you a rich man – you'll be able to live in luxury for the rest of your days, return to your home town, buy the finest house there with servants, women, animals – everything and anything you wish.'

The man replied without lowering his eyes, 'I would do it for nothing, Sire. The Persians kept me as a slave, they beat me and punished me thousands and thousands of times for no reason. I am ready to set off whenever you say.'

Leonnatus put his head outside, 'The snow is easing off.'

'Excellent,' said Alexander. 'Let's have supper served and give some wine to all those who have to go with Craterus. Make sure you offer an incentive to all those who volunteer because they'll have to set off immediately after supper – the Persians will never imagine we're so mad as to try again so early on. We will follow Rhedas after the first watch.'

The King ate with his friends in the tent, the same military rations that were distributed to the soldiers, and then they each went off to get ready for the night expedition. Craterus set off first with his men, then Alexander, as he had announced, after the first watch, with the majority of the army.

Rhedas led them to the beginning of the path and then up towards the pass through a thick wood. It was a

narrow, difficult throughway, cut into the side of the mountain not by the hand of man, but by the centuries-old passage of shepherds and travellers searching for a shortcut on their journey towards Persis. There were moments when the path went alongside precipices and they had to blinker the horses to keep them from bolting in terror; on other occasions it was interrupted by a landslide or made slippery by the ice, and the men had to hold on to one another or tie themselves together with ropes so as not to fall down below and end up smashed to pieces on the rocks.

The guide moved forward sure-footedly, despite the darkness, and it was clear that he could have made the journey even blindfolded. Some warriors, however, actually fell down into the chasm and it was impossible to recover their bodies. Alexander walked behind Rhedas, but he often stopped to help those who were struggling – more than once he risked his own life to save those of soldiers who were in danger.

Before dawn the temperature dropped further and the men found the going even harder, their limbs stiff and already tired by the long ordeal of the night march, but the glow of the sun began to filter through the dense clouds on the horizon and gave them heart – at least now they could better make out the landscape around them and the thinning vegetation told them they were evidently approaching the summit.

When they finally reached the top, the wind fell and Alexander gave orders for the leading troops to stay put until at least a part of those following on behind had caught up with them. Then they set off on a silent

march, trying to make use of such vegetation as there was to keep themselves out of sight of the Persians for as long as possible.

The guide then indicated a rise in the land there before them, a sort of rocky outcrop which extended out towards the gorge, and he said, 'This is where the echo works. On the other side of the rise we will come into sight of the fortified wall which controls access to the Persian Gates. We have reached our destination.'

Ptolemy stepped forward, 'Do you think Craterus will already be in position?'

'Certainly, as long as everything has gone according to plan,' replied Alexander, 'and even if he has encountered some difficulty, we have no choice now. Line up the men and have the signal sounded – we will attack the Persian positions.'

Ptolemy ordered his soldiers into three lines – first of all a squadron of cavalry, then the light infantry with the archers and javelin throwers, then the shock troops and the shieldsmen under Lysimachus. At that point he signalled to a trumpeter who immediately took up position on the rocky outcrop above the gorge. The trumpet blast rose as sharply as the call of a cockerel, piercing the still air of dawn, and immediately there came the echo from the wall before them and it rolled repeatedly across the hills all around until it was finally extinguished across the vast immaculate expanse of snow.

There followed a silence as heavy as the leaden sky as it loomed over the assembled army and they all listened out, waiting for a reply. Suddenly, there came the sound of another trumpet and then another, multiplied many

times by the echo, and then the wild cries of the warriors as they threw themselves into the attack.

'Craterus has unleashed the Agrianians!' shouted Alexander. 'Forward, men! Let's show them how we've survived the cold!'

He leaped on to his horse and took up position at the centre of his squadron, riding up to the rise which overlooked the Persian garrison, while the infantry followed at a run so as not to lose contact with them. Then, as soon as the Persian positions came into view, he led the assault, spurring on his mount and shouting the war cry.

All the trumpets sounded in unison, all the infantrymen set off, their weapons ready, while the horsemen galloped forward to clash with the enemy who now found themselves having to divide their forces on two fronts. Alexander's cavalry charged over the dyke which protected the garrison and the infantry followed on immediately behind, engaging the defenders in mortal hand-to-hand combat.

The Persians quickly realized the situation they were in and sounded their alarm, but in responding they had to leave parts of the battlements uncovered and the Agrianians climbed up, using their daggers in the cracks of the wall, flattening themselves against it every time the enemy threw rocks or fired arrows at them. Soon the first of them reached the top and while some of them engaged the Persians, others helped their companions climb up more easily by throwing ropes down to them. Although there were fewer of them, the Macedonians and their allies got the better of the enemy, perhaps

because many of them had been taken by surprise in their sleep and were still unarmed.

Ariobarzanes had only just managed to move out of his quarters, sword in hand, when he found himself immediately surrounded by a group of Macedonian cavalry threatening him with the points of their spears. He was forced to order a general surrender and then watched helplessly as Alexander's army marched through the freed pass which was supposed to have protected Persepolis. The city was now at the mercy of the enemy.

21

ALEXANDER WAITED UNTIL all the rest of his army had climbed up and then gave orders for them to begin the descent down towards the highlands of Persis. Before setting off, however, he summoned the Lycian shepherd who had guided them up to the fortified pass.

'Your assistance was crucial,' he said. 'You have helped Alexander conquer an empire, perhaps even change the course of history. No one can say whether this is a good or a bad thing, but I am in any case most grateful to you.' He was about to add, 'Tell me whatever it is you wish in reward and it will be yours,' but then he remembered the occasion when he had said this unfortunate phrase to Diogenes, the old philosopher, as he lay naked in the fading light of sunset, and he finished by saying simply, 'Thank you, my friend.'

The shepherd had tears in his eyes as he watched the King mount his horse and move off down the hill, but he came to himself when he heard another voice behind him. It was Eumenes: 'The King has told me that you may have whatever you want, just as he promised you. All you have to do is let me know.'

Rhedas replied, 'If I were younger, I would like to travel with him, to see what will happen next, but I have to think about my life as an old man – I would like to

buy back my father's field and the house I was born in, on the coast. I haven't seen the sea in such a long time . . .'

'You will see it again, shepherd, and you will have your house and your field. You will also be able to start a family, if you so wish; and if you have children and grandchildren, you will tell them of the night on which you led King Alexander to his destiny; and if they don't believe you, you will show them this.'

'What is it?'

Eumenes placed a small pendant in his hand, 'It's the golden star of the Argeads. Only the King's closest friends have them.'

He also gave him a leather document holder: 'In here is a letter from the King to the governor of Lycia, ordering him to give you everything you wish. It is worth more than any sum in gold or in silver. Make sure you do not lose it. Farewell, shepherd, and good luck.'

*

They came down to the foothills of the mountains during the course of the following evening and found themselves with the highlands of Persis spread before them, the river banks edged with long lines of poplars and dotted with villages consisting of rough brickwork homes.

They came to the Royal Road on the banks of the Araxes and Alexander set up camp to wait for Parmenion with the rest of the army, but they had just served the supper when a *hetairoi* of the royal guard entered and announced a visitor, 'Sire, there is a man who wants to

speak to you. He has crossed the river in a boat and appears to be in a great hurry.'

'Have him come in then.'

The soldier introduced a man dressed in the Persian manner, his trousers tied above his ankles and a linen drape wrapped around his head and tied round his neck.

'Who are you?' asked Alexander.

'I come on behalf of the Satrap Abulites, he who commands the fort at Persepolis. He is ready to surrender the city to you and has asked me to tell you to set off straight away, if you want to find the Great King's treasure still intact. If you waste any time, then those who are calling for the city to be defended to the bitter end might win the day. There are yet others who are calling for the treasure to be hidden so as to finance King Darius's return. What must I tell my master?'

Alexander thought in silence for a few moments, then replied, 'Tell him that I will be within sight of Persepolis in two days' time, at sunset, with my cavalry.'

The man left and was accompanied straight away to his boat. The King immediately summoned Diades of Larissa, his chief engineer.

'I must have a bridge built across the Araxes by tomorrow evening,' he said, before he had even sat down.

Diades, who by now was used to being asked the impossible with impossible deadlines, did not bat an eyelid. 'How wide do you want it?' he asked.

'As wide as possible . . . we must get the cavalry through as quickly as we can.'

'Five cubits?'

'Ten.'

'Ten cubits it will be then. Very well.'

'Do you think you can manage it?'

'Have I ever let you down, Sire?'

'No.'

'But I will have to begin the works right now.'

'As you wish. You may give orders to anyone, even the Generals, you have all my authority.'

Diades left, gathered up ten teams of men, equipped with axes, saws, cables and ladders, together with mules and horses, and sent them out to cut fir trees in a wood nearby. Some of the trunks were cleaned, their ends carved to a point and flame-hardened, while others were cut into planks. Three hundred people worked all through the night and by dawn the material was all piled on the riverbank, ready to be assembled.

Diades took the pointed stakes and began by driving them into the riverbed with sledgehammers, two at a time, some ten cubits apart. Then he connected them length- and breadth-wise with nailed boards, creating a lateral rib and a horizontal deck for the crossing. The bridge advanced segment by segment towards the middle of the river where the stakes were reinforced with great rocks, which helped break the force of the flow.

At sunset Alexander lined up the army in battle formation, waited for the last plank to be nailed to the supports and then set off on Bucephalas at a gallop, followed by his companions and four squadrons of *hetairoi*. Behind them came the infantry, led by Craterus.

They rode all through the night and only stopped to rest around the third watch, before sunrise. Alexander,

completely exhausted by events of recent days and by his many sleepless nights, fell into a deep sleep. The thin highland air, the light eastern breeze and the shady wood of mountain planes and maples gave them all a sense of peace and deep tranquillity. The horses grazed freely along the banks of a stream, the waters of which ran clear and clean, its banks lined by willows and cornels. Bucephalas trotted among them, followed by Peritas, snapping happily at the horse's hocks. There was no hint of what was about to happen.

One of the scout patrols pushed on towards the west in the direction of the Royal Road to check that there were no surprises waiting for them in that direction. They could not believe their eyes when they saw a long column of men moving forward towards them, red standards flying in the wind – Parmenion's army!

They galloped to them and immediately identified themselves. 'I am Euthydemus, commander of the eighth company of the third squadron of the *hetairoi*,' said their chief to the leading officer of the column. 'Take me to General Parmenion.'

'General Parmenion is down at the end of the column, with the rearguard, because there have been some skirmishes with the Median cavalry on the highlands. I will summon General Cleitus for you.'

The Black arrived shortly after; the highland sun had darkened his complexion even more, to the extent that he could almost have passed as an Ethiopian. 'What's up, Commander?' he asked. 'Where are you all?'

'Less than twenty stadia from here, General; we managed to break through the Persian Gates and we haven't

slept for two nights, but as soon as the sun rises above the horizon we'll be ready to set off for Persepolis. You may continue at your own pace while we go on as quickly as possible – I'm sure the King will explain everything when the time comes.'

'That's fine,' replied the Black. 'Salute the King for me and tell him we have met no serious difficulties. I will inform General Parmenion. Is his son Philotas well?'

'He is in good shape and took part in the battle at the pass without suffering any injury.' He turned his horse and started back, together with his men.

The contingent was ready to move off behind Alexander who was astride Bucephalas and was about to give the signal. The sun was rising just at that moment, giving a pinkish tint to the peaks of the Elam mountains which rose up out of the dark green of the woods below and the yellow stubble of the fields that spread as far as the eye could see across the plateau. Caravans of camels passed by with their loads. There were peasants astride donkeys on their way to market, pulling small carts full of all sorts of poor wares; women dressed in brightly coloured clothes on their way to the stream to get water; others already on their way back with brimming containers balanced on a pad on their heads. It was like any other day, but instead it was the day on which the largest and most powerful empire in the world would be struck at its very heart.

The trumpet sounded and the squadrons set off at a trot along the bridleway, lifting up a dense curtain of dust. As they advanced the appearance of the landscape around them altered profoundly – not only in terms of

its physical features with tree-filled parks, orchards and gardens, but also in the behaviour of its inhabitants. As the mounted army passed by, the doors of the houses closed, the roads cleared of people, the marketplaces were suddenly deserted – news of the young *yauna* conqueror, with all the associated legends of terror, must have reached the people here.

Suddenly, around midday, the King came upon a strange, worrying sight as he rode at the head of the army, flanked by Hephaestion and Ptolemy: a strange group of limping people came towards them along the road, all clad in rags and all waving their hands, or their stumps in the case of those who had no hands, as though trying to attract attention.

'But who are these people?' the King asked Eumenes, who was following behind.

The Secretary drew up alongside to take a better look: 'I have no idea, but we will soon find out.'

He dismounted and moved off on foot towards the wretches. As he approached he realized that there seemed to be many more of them than there had first appeared to be. Alexander also dismounted and started walking, but as he got nearer he found himself increasingly disturbed by a deep sense of anguish. When he was close enough he heard that they were talking to Eumenes in Greek.

He continued forward and saw that they all bore the most terrible mutilations – some of them had had both hands amputated, others a leg or even both legs, while others still had not only lost limbs, but their skin was

ridged with deep scars, typical of someone who has been sprayed with a boiling liquid.

'Oil,' explained one of the wretches as he felt Alexander's gaze on his maimed body.

'Who are you?' asked the King.

'Heratosthenes of Methone, *Heghemón*, third *syssitia* eighth battalion, Spartan.'

'Spartan? But . . . how old are you?'

'Fifty-eight, *Heghemón*. I was taken prisoner by the Persians during the second campaign of King Agesilaos, when I was twenty-seven years old. They cut my foot off because they knew that a Spartan warrior would never accept the idea of being held prisoner – he would rather be killed.'

Eumenes shook his head, 'Times have changed, my friend.'

'I tried to commit suicide anyway, and my master threw boiling oil on me. Then I resigned myself to my fate and accepted captivity, but when I heard that Alexander was on his way—'

'We spread the word so that we could all come to meet him,' piped up another, waving his two stumps, his forearms having been chopped off just below his elbows.

'Why did they do that to you?' asked the King, his voice trembling in anger and emotion.

'I was serving in the Athenian army during the war of the satraps, a rower on the *Krysea*, a beautiful trireme, a new vessel, just out of the yard. We fell into an ambush, I was taken prisoner and they said that I would never row on an Athenian ship again.'

Alexander saw another whose eyes sockets were empty and dried up like those of a skull. 'What happened to you?' he asked.

'They cut off my eyelids, covered my eyes with honey and then tied me to the ground near an anthill. I also served in the Athenian navy – they wanted to know where the rest of the fleet was hidden, but I refused and . . .'

Yet others came forward, displaying their mutilations, their miseries, their white hair, their scalped skulls, their hands devoured by scabies.

'*Heghemón,*' said the Spartan once more, 'tell us where we may find Alexander so that we can pay homage to him and thank him for having freed us. All of us here are testimony to the price paid over the years by the Greeks in the battle against the barbarians.'

'I am Alexander,' replied the King, pale with rage, 'and I have come to avenge the wrong done to you.'

22

ALEXANDER TURNED ROUND and called out loudly to his companions, 'Ptolemy! Hephaestion! Perdiccas!'

'Ready, Sire!'

'Surround the royal palace, the treasury and the harem and make sure no one dares set foot there.'

'As you wish,' they replied, setting off at a gallop to the head of their divisions.

'Leonnatus, Lysimachus, Philotas, Seleucus!'

'Ready, Sire!'

Alexander pointed to the great city that stood there before them up on the hill, shining in gold, bronze and enamel under the sun.

'Lead the army into the city – Persepolis is yours, do what you will with it!'

He turned back to the *hetairoi* who were waiting motionless on their horses – 'Have you understood what I have just said? Persepolis is yours! What are you waiting for? Take it!'

There came a great cry from the squadrons of cavalry and they set off at a gallop towards the capital, which at that moment was just preparing to open its gates. They mowed down the group of delegates that Abulites had sent to meet them and burst into the richest and greatest city in the world with all the fury of a herd of wild bulls.

Eumenes made no move and looked at Alexander in amazement, 'You cannot give such orders, gods above! Call them back, call them back while there's still time. You cannot do this.'

Callisthenes approached, 'Of course he can, and unfortunately he already has.'

The group of mutilated Greeks who had come to meet them pulled back in confusion now, as though realizing that without wanting to they had caused a disaster of inhuman proportions. The King saw how upset they were and nodded to Eumenes.

'Tell them they will have three thousand silver drachmae each and safe conduct for any of them who wishes to return home to his family. If they prefer to remain here they will have a home, servants, and plenty of land and livestock. Take care of it all.'

The Secretary communicated these arrangements, but as he spoke it was difficult for him to think because already the sounds of the looting and the desperate cries of the city's inhabitants at the mercy of the military had reached his ears.

In the meantime the infantry units arrived and ran in their turn towards the city gates, afraid they were too late to find much loot. Some messengers reached Parmenion's army, now just a few stadia away, and announced that the King had left the capital to the soldiers. Discipline quickly gave way to complete disorder as the men broke ranks and headed off towards Persepolis, from which columns of smoke and tongues of flame began to rise.

Parmenion spurred his horse on at full speed, followed

by the Black and Nearchus and came to Alexander who was sitting astride Bucephalas, contemplating the slaughter from a hilltop, as motionless as a monument in stone.

The old General leaped to the ground and moved closer with anguish written all over his face, 'Why, Sire? Why? Why destroy what is already yours?'

Alexander did not even turn to look at him, but Parmenion could see the darkness of death and destruction in his left eye. Callisthenes also looked at him and murmured, certain that he would not be heard, 'Ask no more, General, I am sure that at this moment his mother Olympias is engaged in some bloody rite in some secret place and is in complete control of his spirit. Oh, if only Aristotle were here now to take care of this nightmare!'

Parmenion shook his head, stared at the Black and Nearchus with an expression of amazement, then mounted his horse and left.

Only towards sunset did the King move, as though waking up from a deep sleep, and he proceeded to ride Bucephalas through the gates of the city. One of the most beautiful and beguiling places in the world, the highest expression of universal harmony according to Achaemenid ideals, was now at the complete mercy of a horde of drunken savages – the Agrianians were raping young maids and boys, tearing them from the arms of their parents; the Thracians were on the rampage, full of wine and covered with blood, showing off the severed heads of the Persian warriors who had attempted resistance; the Macedonians, the Thessalians and the Greek auxiliaries were no less brutal – running like madmen, loaded down with loot, with containers full of precious

stones, wonderful candelabra, fine cloth, armour in gold and silver. Here and there they met up with companions who still had had no success in their looting and fights broke out, with blood being spilled and throats cut in the middle of the streets, all sense of humanity having been abandoned. At other moments, on seeing some companions who had requisitioned particularly beautiful women, they sought to take them by dint of force, and when they succeeded they took turns at raping them there and then on the ground sodden with the blood of the victims' relatives.

The King and Bucephalas walked through all that shouting and all that blood, through all those horrors, but his face gave away no emotion, as though it had been sculpted in Lysippus's cold marble. His ears seemed not to hear the heart-wrenching cries of the infants being grabbed from their mothers' arms, of the women invoking the names of sons and daughters as they cried over the maimed bodies of their husbands who had been slaughtered mercilessly outside their own homes. It was as though all he heard was the slow clopping of Bucephalas's shoes on the stone of the road.

He stared straight ahead, feasting his eyes on the endless extent of the royal palace, the divine *apadana*, surrounded by its marvellous gardens with their towering cypresses, silver poplars, and plane trees reddish in the glowing rays of the last sun. He took in the splendid atria with their gigantic columns, with winged bulls, griffins, and images of the Great King who had built and decorated this wonder. Alexander, the little *yauna*, lord of a small realm of peasants and shepherds, once a vassal, had

now come as far as to pierce the giant's heart, and the giant lay moribund at his feet.

He climbed up the huge stairway on horseback and there, in the stone on both sides, he saw representations of the processions of the kings and the chief vassals bearing gifts for the feast of the new year. Medians and Kisseans, Ionians, Indians and Ethiopians, Assyrians and Babylonians, Egyptians, Libyans, Phoenicians and Bactrians, Gedrosians, Karmanians, Dahae – many nations all advancing solemnly towards the gold baldachin over the throne of Darius, the King, the Great King, the King of Kings, Light of the Aryans and Lord of the Four Corners of the Earth.

Here was the throne now, here before him. Made of fragrant cedar wood and ivory, encrusted with precious stones, held by two griffins with eyes of rubies. Behind, on the wall, King Darius I was represented – gigantic and in all the splendour of his ceremonial robes, while he fought with a winged monster, the incarnation of Ahriman, genius of evil and of darkness.

The great hall was empty and silent, but outside the waves of an ocean of grief were breaking cruelly on the walls of that paradise. Philip's courageous, loyal soldiers had become a horde of beasts fighting over scraps of prey left in the streets, shouting obscenities from their foul mouths, setting fire to the gardens and the palaces, devastating the sanctuaries of Ahura Mazda, god of great Persepolis.

Alexander dismounted, moved towards the throne, climbed the steps and sat down, resting his hands on the polished marble armrests. He relaxed, let the backrest

take his weight and sighed deeply, then suddenly he saw dark silhouettes appear in the doorway and heard confused, hurried steps.

'Who goes there?' he asked, without moving.

'It's us, Sire!' said a voice. It was one of the Greek slaves who had come to meet him along the road to Persepolis.

'What do you want?'

The man did not reply, but moved to one side and let two of his companions through; they were carrying an infirm, elderly man.

'His name is Leocares,' explained the man. 'He is one of Xenophon's "ten thousand", the last survivor, I believe. He is almost ninety years old and has spent seventy-two in captivity and slavery.'

Alexander struggled to hide his emotion, 'What do you want, old man?' he asked. 'What can I do for a hero of the "ten thousand"?'

The old man whispered something the King could not catch.

'He wants nothing. He says that all those Greeks who have died before this day have missed the greatest joy possible, the joy of seeing you sitting on that throne. He says that he can die a happy man now.'

The old man was so moved and there were so many tears streaming down his sunken cheeks that he could say no more, but the expression on his face painted more than a thousand words.

Alexander nodded and continued to look at him, almost incredulously, while he shuffled away, supported by his companions. Then the King came down from the

throne and walked towards Bucephalas who was waiting in the atrium, but as he took the bridle he saw a Persian warrior there before him, like something out of a dream, splendidly clad in the dress uniform of the Immortals and astride a sorrel horse decked in golden tack. He seemed to be looking at Alexander.

Alexander gripped the hilt of his sword, but he did not move; at that very moment the dark sky was rent by a blinding bolt of lightning followed immediately by a thunderclap that shook the entire palace.

He recognized the Immortal in an instant of awareness – the warrior who on that far off day had saved him from the lion's claws, the Persian he had saved from certain death on the battlefield at Issus.

The man pushed his horse forward a few steps and spat on the ground before Alexander; then he turned, spurring the animal on with his heels and set off at full gallop across the vast deserted yard.

23

'It was founded by King Darius I – Darius the Great – in the very heart of Persis, and it was to be the most glorious capital of all time – fifty thousand people from thirty-five different nations worked on it for fifteen years. Entire woods on Mount Lebanon were cut down, their trunks used for ceilings and doors while marble and other stone was quarried from throughout the empire, precious lapis lazuli was brought from the mines of Bactriana, gold was transported by camel from Nubia and India, precious stones from the Paropamisus Mountains and the deserts of Gedrosia, silver from Iberia and copper from Cyprus. Thousands of Syrian, Greek and Egyptian sculptors created the images that you now admire here on these walls and on the doors of the palace and the goldsmiths added decoration in precious metals and gemstones. The best weavers were called to make the carpets, the drapes and the tapestries that you see on the floors and on the walls. Persian and Indian painters worked on the frescoes. The Great King's intention was that this city would constitute a harmonious, total expression of the civilization that made up his limitless empire.'

Callisthenes stopped speaking and let his gaze run silently over the death throes of the great capital – rare plants brought to the *pairidaeza* from remote provinces

burning now like torches, the porticoes and the buildings all blackened with smoke. He looked on the roads full of soldiers drunk with looting and raping and all kinds of unspeakable excess, the fountains that continued to gurgle although they were now full of bodies, the blood-red water overflowing into the streets. The historian beheld the broken statues, the columns, the profaned sanctuaries; he turned to Eumenes and saw in his eyes the same expression of terror and confusion.

'This sublime palace,' he continued in the same voice, 'was called the "Palace of the New Year" because the Great King came here to celebrate the first day of each year, on the morning of the summer solstice, so as to receive on his forehead the first ray of clear light that rose from the east, illuminating his countenance, and he reflected it, almost as though the King himself were a new sun.

'Throughout the eve of that dawn, until morning, the priests' prayers rose up, insistently, towards the stars, invoking light for the Great King, for he who was the living terrestrial symbol of Ahura Mazda. Everything here is a symbol, the entire city is a symbol and so are all the images and the reliefs we see around us in this building.'

'We are burning a . . . symbol,' stammered Eumenes.

'A symbol, and much more than that. The city was designed the day following a total eclipse of the sun that took place seventy years and six months ago: it was to be a monument to this people's faith, the faith according to which the world would never again be the dominion of the powers of darkness. Look here, and you see the lion tearing into the bull, the light defeating the darkness,

the light of their supreme god Ahura Mazda who for them was incarnate in their King.

'As dawn broke, while the palace was still in shadow, hundreds of delegations waited in religious silence until the light spread through the halls of purple and gold, through the huge courtyards. Then began the grand procession of which Ctesias and other Greek and barbarian authors who were lucky enough to have witnessed it have written; many of the reliefs that adorn the terraces and the stairways depict this procession too.

'And now . . . now this people is bearing witness to an abomination, the ultimate and most atrocious of all sacrileges – fire, which for them is sacred, consumes their capital and burns their corpses.'

'And yet they too, in their time, have carried out all sorts of bloody deeds,' replied Eumenes. 'You saw those poor souls, you have heard them tell of the inhuman tortures inflicted on them. Those who built this wonder, the Great Kings Darius and Xerxes, were the same kings who invaded our land – razing and torching it, decapitating and crucifying the maimed body of King Leonidas at the Thermopylae pass, burning the temples of our gods after having besmirched them in every way imaginable.'

'Certainly, and do you know why? Look here,' he said, pointing to an inscription on one of the walls. 'Do you know what this says? "I have burned the temples of the *daiwa*", the temples of the demons. That's the explanation – our gods, for them, were manifestations of the demons that their evil god, Ahriman, unleashed on the earth to bring about disaster. They believed they were carrying out an act of piety. All of the world's peoples

see evil in others, in foreigners and in their gods, and I fear there is no remedy for this. Thus they destroyed the most beautiful expressions of our civilization. Thus we destroy the most beautiful expressions of theirs.'

He stopped because he had nothing more to say now and their silence was soon filled with the cries and the laments of the dying city.

*

The Queen Mother heard of the devastation of Persepolis three days later, from a horseman of the Immortals who had crossed the snow-covered passes without ever stopping. She burst into tears as he gave her a few details of the massacre of the defenceless city, the destruction of such beautiful works of art.

The warrior wept as he prostrated himself before her, 'Great Mother,' he said, 'kill me because I deserve death. I know the little *yauna* demon and I am responsible for everything. Many years ago I was the one who saved his life during a lion hunt in Macedonia, and when he saved my life on the battlefield at Issus and set me free, I did not understand that this is how the demons conceal their true, ferocious nature. Instead of plunging my dagger into his throat, I thanked him, I showed him all my gratitude. Now this is the result. Have me killed, Great Mother, and perhaps my death will appease the gods and will bring them to take our side, to lead us out of the darkness of humiliation and defeat.'

The Queen sat motionless on the throne, her cheeks wet with tears. She looked at him, her expression full of compassion, and said, 'Stand up, my loyal friend. Stand

up and do not lay the blame on your generosity and your courage. What happened was inevitable. When Cyrus took the city of Sardis and torched it, what did the Lydians think in their misery? And what did the Babylonians think when he changed the course of the Euphrates and took control of the capital, putting their King in chains? We too have burned and pillaged, we have drowned many revolts in blood, we have burned temples and sanctuaries. King Cambises killed the bull Apis in Egypt, committing the most heinous of sacrileges in the eyes of that people. King Xerxes torched the temples of the Acropolis in Athens and razed the city to the ground – all the inhabitants abandoned their city and fled to a small island from which they watched the glow of the flames in the night sky as they consumed their homes. I was told this by those who keep the books of our history.

'Now the same fate has touched us and our wonderful cities, our sanctuaries, but not because Alexander is evil. I know him, I know his feelings, I know the tenderness and the concern of which he is capable and had I been present I am sure I would have succeeded in obtaining clemency from him, in illuminating him with the light of Ahura Mazda against the darkness of Ahriman. Have you ever looked into his eyes?'

'Yes, my Lady, and I was afraid.'

The Queen Mother was silent for a few moments, then she lifted her head and asked, 'Where will you go now?'

'North, to Ecbatana, to King Darius and I will fight alongside him, I will die for him if necessary; but please give me your blessing, Great Mother, for it will keep me

warm in the snow and the cold, it will help me bear the hunger, the thirst, the ordeals, the pain.'

He knelt down and bowed his head. The Queen Mother raised her trembling hand and placed it on his head, 'I bless you, my boy. Tell my troubled son that I am praying for him.'

'I will tell him,' replied the Immortal. He then begged leave to be allowed to go, and left.

24

It was not until the following day that Alexander himself visited Darius's palace. He had got up early and had looked around him with a strange expression, almost as though waking up from a nightmare. His Companions were already in formation alongside the throne, armed and ready for his orders.

'Where is Parmenion?' he asked.

'He's outside the city, in his camp together with those of his men who did not take part in yesterday's events,' replied Seleucus.

'And the Black?'

'The same. He says he feels unwell and asks if you will excuse him for not being present.'

'They've left me on my own,' murmured the King as though thinking to himself.

'But we are with you, Alexander!' exclaimed Hephaestion. 'Whatever you may do and whatever may happen. Isn't that right?' he asked as he turned to their companions.

'Exactly,' they all replied.

'Enough now,' said Alexander. 'Take some patrols of assault troops and cross the city with a proclamation. All soldiers – Greeks, Macedonians, Thessalians, Thracians and Agrianians, all of them with no exceptions – must

leave Persepolis and move back to the camps outside the city walls. Only the Vanguard and my guards will remain here.'

The companions left to carry out the orders they had just received.

Alexander, Eumenes and Callisthenes, accompanied by an interpreter and a group of still terrified eunuchs, began their tour of the palace. They went from the *apadana* to the throne room true and proper. It was huge, more than two hundred feet wide and equally long, supported by one hundred columns in cedar wood, its walls painted in gold and purple with the capitals and the ceilings adorned with engravings and paintings. The throne was of wood with inlays in ivory and behind it, propped up against the wall, were the parasol and the ostrich-feather fans operated by servants in full dress on audience days.

From there they moved directly to the treasury, opened up for them by the four eunuchs who kept the keys. The massive bronze doors moved slowly on their hinges and the enormous room appeared before its new master. There were no windows at all, however, and Alexander could only see that part of the interior illuminated by the light that came through the door they had just opened, but what he was able to see left him amazed – thousands of gold and silver ingots bearing the seal of the Achaemenid monarchy – the effigy of King Darius I firing an arrow from his bow. That same effigy also appeared on the coins which for this reason were known as 'darics'. There were many buckets filled to the brim with these coins, some of them lined up on shelves along the walls.

The eunuchs brought lanterns and the reflections of the thousands and thousands of polished surfaces glimmered in the half-darkness of the room as they moved.

The King, Eumenes and Callisthenes set off along the corridor that ran through the middle of the room and their wonder grew with each step they took. Not only was there metal in coin and ingots, there was even an area that functioned as a store for the precious objects accumulated over two hundred years of conquests and domination of a territory that extended from the Indus to the Ister. There were jewels in unbelievable quantities, chests full of precious stones of every shape and colour, white and black pearls, bronzes and pendants, candelabra, statues and votive images from ancient sanctuaries, weapons of all kinds, both parade and battle types – spears and swords, helmets adorned with the most impressive plumes, jewelled daggers with straight and curved and even snake-shaped blades, bronze shields covered with silver- or gold-leaf, or even wooden shields decorated with ivory and silver, greaves and sword-belts in gold chain mail with buckles adorned with lapis lazuli and coral, gold and silver enamelled tiles, masks of ebony and ivory, Indian, Assyrian and Egyptian neck- and chestpieces in gold and silver. And then crowns and diadems that had adorned the heads of Egyptian Pharaohs, Greek Tyrants, Scythian chiefs, Indian Rajahs, sceptres and command staffs of ebony, ivory, gold, bronze, silver and electrum, all wonderfully decorated.

And fabrics – Egyptian linen, Syrian byssus, Ionian wool, Phoenician purple cloth, and even more cloths of incredible splendour in the most varied and rarest

of colours. They all came from a far off country, it was explained, beyond the central deserts and beyond the Paropamisus range. Then again there were pieces of another type of fabric produced in India, as cool as linen, equally easy to dye, but infinitely lighter: 'Wearing this material,' said the eunuch, 'is like wearing nothing at all.'

As they proceeded the eunuch repeated the list of the inventory in a monotonous voice: 'Twelve buckets of one talent each of gold darics minted by His Majesty King Darius I, twenty talents of silver ingots with the seal of His Majesty King Xerxes, a turtle breastplate inlaid with ivory and coral which belonged to the Rajah of Taxila, a dress sabre which once belonged to the Scythian King Kurban II . . .'

Alexander realized that it would take a whole month to listen to the description of all those wonders, but he simply could not tear his gaze from the gleaming items, from these dazzling splendours, from those forms and those wonderful ornaments.

'How much does it all come to, in coin and ingots?' Eumenes suddenly asked.

The eunuch looked first at Alexander, as though expecting from him the permission to provide an answer and then, as soon as he had some indication of agreement, said in a low voice, 'One hundred and twenty thousand talents.'

Eumenes went pale, 'Did you say one hundred . . . one hundred and twenty thousand?'

'That is exactly what I said,' replied the eunuch impassively.

Thus, still astonished, they left the greatest accumulation of precious objects that existed on the earth and Eumenes continued repeating to himself, 'I cannot believe it, by the gods on Olympus, I simply cannot believe it. If we consider that just a little more than three years ago we didn't have enough money to buy hay for the horses and wheat for our men . . .'

'Have ten minae distributed to each of them,' Alexander ordered.

'Did you say ten minae to each of our soldiers?'

'That is what I said. They deserve it. I will also give an extra talent to the officers, five to the commanders of the bigger infantry and cavalry units, and ten to the generals. Let me know how much it all comes to.'

'This will be the richest army on earth,' grumbled Eumenes, 'but I don't know if it will still be the most valiant. Are you sure this is the right thing to do?'

'I have never been more sure of anything. In any case, they are not going to have enough time to spend all that money.'

'Why? Are we setting off again?'

'As soon as possible.'

Instead, however, they stayed on in Persepolis for months. The imperial archives and chancellery were here and Eumenes explained to Alexander that before pushing on further it was necessary to consolidate what had been won already, and organize the road and communications systems, so vital for supplies. They had to instruct all the Satraps and administrators of those provinces which had already been subdued, and guide relations with Macedonia and with the regent Antipater. Eumenes also hunted for

any document that might constitute proof of the Persian court's involvement in the assassination of King Philip, or traces of any contact with Prince Amyntas of Lyncestis who, on the King's orders, was still under surveillance following the accusations of his having colluded with Darius when the army was still in Anatolia. The archival material was all in cuneiform characters and, given the scarcity of capable translators, the work involved in studying it all carefully would have taken years.

As Eumenes had predicted, however, the inertia and the free availability of money was radically changing the behaviour of the soldiers and Alexander's own Companions given that they all lived now in the most beautiful palaces of the city, cleaned and restored, and they lived like kings. He continued to invite them for rides on horseback and often organized ball games to keep them in some sort of physical shape. His friends went to these without much enthusiasm, simply to keep him happy, but once they actually started playing they found that they enjoyed themselves just as they had done when they were boys.

Thus in those days the porticoes of the palace rang to shouts and laughter just as the palace at Pella had done many years previously.

'Pass me the ball! Pass me the ball, by Hercules!' shouted Alexander.

'You lost it last time I gave it to you!' replied Ptolemy, shouting even louder.

'Shoot instead of chatting. Are you sleeping or what?' shouted Leonnatus.

The one who always asked for a break first was

Eumenes because he had had neither the education nor the training of a warrior, 'Lads, that's enough, my heart is about to burst.'

'What heart? You've got books in place of a heart!' said Craterus, the most skilful and the fastest of them all.

However, these moments of relief gradually became fewer and farther between. Once the game was over, the influence of power and riches fell over them once more.

One day Eumenes wanted to speak to Alexander in private and went to him in his apartments in the imperial palace.

'With every day that passes it gets worse,' he began.

'What do you mean?'

'I mean they've all changed. Ptolemy has girls brought from as far away as Cyprus and Arabia, Leonnatus only trains for his wrestling if he has the finest Libyan sand and he has it sent by camel. Lysimachus has had a urinal made of solid gold and encrusted with precious jewels. A urinal, would you credit it? Seleucus has one woman slave to do up his sandals, another to comb him, another to perfume him, and one who . . . well, let's leave it at that. As for Perdiccas . . .'

'Perdiccas too?' Alexander asked, incredulous.

'Yes, even Perdiccas. He's had purple sheets made up for his bed. And then there's Philotas – he has always been on the arrogant and presumptuous side, but now he's worse; rumour has it that he—'

But the King interrupted him, 'Enough!' he shouted. 'Enough! Call a herald immediately!'

'What are you going to do?'

'Did you hear me? I told you to call a herald!'

Eumenes left and returned shortly afterwards with an orderly.

'You will proceed without delay,' said the King, 'to the homes of Ptolemy, Perdiccas, Craterus, Leonnatus, Lysimachus, Hephaestion, Seleucus and Philotas to tell each of them to come here immediately to see me.'

The orderly ran outside, leaped on to his horse and set off to deliver his message to the King's Companions. Some were not at home and he left word with the servants, indicating not only the bare message, but also an idea of the King's mood so that the servants soon set about looking for their masters.

'It must be another game,' Leonnatus suggested to Perdiccas as they climbed the stairs together.

'I doubt it. Have you ever seen him use an orderly from the assault cavalry to invite people to a ball game?'

'I reckon we're off to war again,' said Lysimachus who appeared just at that moment.

'War? What war?' said Seleucus, as he arrived in a rush.

Eumenes met them all in the antechamber with a deadpan expression on his face, saying only, 'He's through there.'

'Aren't you coming in?' asked Ptolemy.

'Me? No . . . this doesn't regard me,' he said as he opened the door, had them enter and closed it behind them before immediately getting into position to listen in. Alexander was soon shouting so loudly that he had to move his ear away from the lock.

'Purple sheets!' he cried. 'Solid gold urinals! Sand from Libya for wrestling! Of course there's no sand here, right?

Or perhaps it's just not fine enough for your delicate backside?' and he grimaced as he approached Leonnatus. 'You're a bunch of spineless imbeciles! That's what you've become! Do you think I brought you all this way to see you reduced to this?'

Ptolemy tried to calm him down, 'Alexander, listen—'

'What right do you have to speak? I hear you have your whores brought all the way from Cyprus and Arabia! I brought you this far to change the world, not to soften you up in luxury. Perhaps we engaged in this war simply to pick up the way of life of those we defeated? Is this the reason why we marched and suffered through heat and cold, through hunger and all sorts of ordeals? To lower ourselves to the same level as those we conquered? Don't you understand that this is exactly why the Persians lost? Because they lived just as you are living now?'

'In that case then why—' Perdiccas began and had he been able to finish he would have added, 'why leave all the Persian governors in their previous posts?' but the King cut him short:

'Silence! From tomorrow onwards you will all be billeted out in the camp, under canvas as before. Each one of you will groom his own horse and will polish his own armour. And the day after tomorrow you will all come with me on a lion hunt up in the mountains, and if you end up being mauled to death because your rear ends have grown too fat to let you move, then I won't be lifting a finger to save you. Do you all understand?'

'We understand, Sire!' they all shouted.

'Then clear off out of here, the lot of you!'

Everyone rushed to the door and disappeared down

the stairs. At that moment the herald arrived and explained that he had not been able to find Philotas and that he had left messages for him. Eumenes nodded and was about to leave after the Companions when Alexander called him back.

'Yes, Sire?' he said as he entered Alexander's rooms once again.

'Philotas was not here,' said the King immediately.

'The orderly couldn't find him. Do you want him to keep looking?'

'No, it doesn't matter. I'm sure he'll hear tale of all this anyway. And you?' he asked. 'What are you doing with all the gold you've received?'

'I'm living comfortably, but without overdoing it. I'm putting what's left to one side for my old age.'

'Well done,' replied Alexander. 'You can never tell. If one day I find myself in need of a loan, I'll know who to turn to.'

'May I go now?'

'Yes, of course,' and Eumenes headed for the door. 'Just a moment.'

'What's wrong?'

'The order, of course, applies to you as well.'

'What order?'

'The one about sleeping in the camp, under canvas.'

'Of course,' retorted Eumenes, and then he left.

*

Some days later Alexander summoned Eumenes to tell him that, when they eventually started marching northwards, he intended to transfer all the treasure of Persepolis to

Ecbatana. Eumenes was amazed by this decision, which to him seemed completely useless, senseless even, but it was clear the King would not be moved in any way.

Such an operation would last more than two weeks, and require a caravan of five thousand pairs of mules and ten thousand camels, because the mountain paths of Media made transportation by carts virtually impossible.

Eumenes failed to comprehend the reasoning behind the decision – to him it seemed strange and even risky, but any time he tried to obtain an explanation from Alexander he received vague and evasive replies. In the end he gave up asking, but his heart remained heavy with some sort of dark presentiment, a sombre portent of some dramatic event.

25

FOR SOME TIME THE Companions respected the orders
and lived in the camp, but then Hephaestion asked to be
allowed to return to the palace because he wanted to be
near Alexander, and the King did not know how to deny
his friend this request. Having made this concession to
Hephaestion, he could do nothing to stop the others,
who with a variety of excuses obtained permission to
move back into their residences in the city. They all
swore most solemnly of course to live simple, frugal
lives. Spring was almost over now and the more serious
wounds of the devastated city were slowly beginning to
heal, but it was clear Persepolis would never be as it once
had been. In the meantime, from the still independent
northern provinces of the empire, there came news that
Darius was assembling another army and that he was
ready to stand ground on the Caucasus Mountains, on
the Caspian Sea, and Alexander decided that it was time
to move. He organized a party and a banquet to bring
their period of rest to an end, celebrations which indeed
proved to be memorable events.

All the rooms of the immense palace were brightly
illuminated by hundreds of lamps; the royal cooks set to
work to prepare the finest dishes; the finest looking
eunuchs and girls of the palace were chosen to serve at

table in states of semi-undress, after the Greek fashion. At the centre of the dining hall great vases of solid gold taken from the imperial treasure were positioned and used as craters for wine and aromatic and spiced drinks made according to oriental recipes.

Cups of gold and silver from the royal collection were placed on the tables, while everywhere there were vases full of roses and lilies – cut from the palace gardens, the only gardens to have survived in the whole city.

The feast began immediately after sunset and Eumenes realized that Hephaestion had been nominated 'leader of the symposium' and that as such it was he who had decreed that the wine should be served in the Thracian manner – straight.

'Are you not celebrating with us?' Callisthenes asked as he suddenly appeared behind Eumenes.

'I'm not hungry,' replied Eumenes, 'and it's my job to oversee everything and to make sure it all goes well.'

'Or is it that you'd rather stay sober just to make sure you enjoy the spectacle?'

'What spectacle?'

'Well ... I don't know, but something's bound to happen. This feast makes no sense. It's grotesque. I arrived from the Western Gate, and believe me the palace so full of light is a terrible and dramatic contrast with the devastation and the darkness of the city. We've been here for months and Alexander hasn't ordered the reconstruction of even one single house.'

'But he hasn't stopped anyone from rebuilding.'

'No, that's true; but he hasn't done anything to stop the nobility and the landowners leaving. Only the poorest

people remain, and that means the city is effectively condemned to death. And with the city—'

Eumenes lifted his hand as though to chase away some nightmarish vision, 'I don't want to hear about it.'

'Where is Parmenion?' Callisthenes asked, apparently changing the subject.

'He's not here.'

'And that doesn't mean anything to you, I imagine. And the Black?'

'I haven't seen him.'

'Exactly. Anyway, I don't believe he was ever on the guest list – but just look at who *has* turned up.'

Eumenes turned and saw Tais coming along a corridor towards them – the beautiful Athenian, barefoot and with a most daring gown on, similar to the one she had worn when she first danced before the King.

'I think she's been sleeping with Alexander,' said Callisthenes, 'and I don't think there's anything good about that.'

'I think I agree with you,' replied Eumenes, 'but things don't necessarily have to get any worse.'

Callisthenes made no comment and went off towards the door named after Xerxes that led out on to the rear portico. From there he could see the tombs cut into the side of the mountain that towered over the palace, lit by the votive lamps burning for the Achaemenid sovereigns. Among them was the as yet unfinished tomb of Darius III. From inside the palace came the ever louder shouting and laughing of the banqueters, increasingly boisterous as they celebrated.

Suddenly he heard some music, which for a moment dominated the din made by the revellers, rhythmic music

accompanied by drums and apparently suited to some orgiastic dance. Callisthenes lifted his eyes to the skies and murmured to himself, 'Where are you, Aristotle?'

Eumenes in the meantime had looked in on the great hall of the *apadana* and had realized that the banquet was beginning to degenerate. Tais was almost naked now and was dancing wildly, her movements accompanied by the sound of tiny metallic cymbals attached to her fingers. With each pirouette she made her short *chiton* revealed her statuesque legs in full, together with her marble-smooth buttocks and her sex, while the onlookers shouted all sorts of filth at her.

Suddenly the girl twisted violently and stopped, standing on the points of her toes, and then she crouched down slowly, with all the sensual movements of a cat, still accompanied by the music that somehow seemed to follow the development of her movements. When she got back to her feet she was holding a *thyrsus*, a staff just like the one held by the maenads, covered in ivy and bearing a pine cone at its tip; she held it aloft and shouted loudly, like a woman possessed, '*Komos!*'

She moved through the columns in the hall like a maenad through the trunks of a great forest and called everyone to take part in the orgiastic dance. Alexander was the first to reply, in his turn shouting, '*Komos!*'

Everyone joined in with him. With her other hand Tais grabbed a torch from a holder on the wall and started leading the frenetic dance through the audience chamber, the corridors, the bedchambers of the wonderful royal apartments, followed by the revellers – the men

all with erections, the women half-undressed or even completely naked, doing their utmost to excite the men even more with their sensual movements.

'Dionysius is with us!' shouted Tais, her gaze burning bright in the light of the torch she held in her hand.

Everyone replied, '*Euoè*!'

'Dionysius wants revenge on these barbarians!'

'*Euoè*!' all the men and women shouted again in their delirium of wine and desire.

'We will avenge our soldiers, those who died in battle, and our destroyed temples, our burned cities!' the girl shouted once more, and right before Alexander's eyes she threw the torch against a purple drape that hung alongside a doorway.

'Yes! Revenge!' shouted Alexander and he threw another torch under a large piece of furniture in cedar wood. He was completely out of his mind. Eumenes watched on, witnessing events without being able to do anything about it, and with his eyes he searched for someone who might put an end to the madness, but there was no one in the midst of that cauldron of men and women in heat whose gaze showed any sign of reason.

The flames took hold and the room crackled as it was illuminated as bright as daylight with the vermilion light of the fire. As though possessed by demons, the revellers spread out through the chambers, shouting as they went, setting fire to everything.

The wonderful palace was soon enveloped in a whirlwind of flame. The hundreds of columns made from

cedars of Lebanon burned like torches, the fire licked the ceilings and spread to the beams and the joists that groaned and split with the violence of the blaze.

The heat became unbearable and everyone ran outside towards the great entrance courtyard, continuing their dance down there, their songs and their mating. Eumenes came out of a side door, clearly in shock, and as he moved away down the external stairway he saw Tais lying completely naked on a carpet in the atrium, Alexander and Hephaestion both taking her as she writhed and turned in ecstasy.

The people who had remained among the ruins of Persepolis ran out of their slums to bear witness to the disaster – the palace of the Great King was exploding now, devoured by fire, collapsing in an inferno of sparks, in a vortex of black smoke that blotted out the stars and the moon. They looked on motionless, petrified, all of them in tears.

*

On the following morning, what had once been the finest palace in the entire world was simply a pile of smoking debris, in some places four or even five cubits deep, out of which protruded only columns with their capitals in the shape of winged bulls. The portals remained, together with the podium and the foundations and the stairways with the images of the great new year procession and the Immortals of the imperial guard for future millennia, mute witnesses to the disaster.

Towards morning Alexander reached his pavilion in

the camp and dropped on to a bed there, falling into a deep, troubled sleep.

*

Parmenion came shortly after dawn and the *pezhetairoi* of the guard tried in vain to stop him by crossing their spears before the entrance. The old General roared like a lion: 'Out of my way, by Zeus! Let me through, I must see the King!'

Leptine came towards him with her hands raised as though she too were trying to stop him, but he pushed her out of the way and silenced the growling Peritas with a fierce look and a simple, 'Get to bed!'

Alexander jumped up, holding his bursting head and shouting, 'Who dares . . .'

'I do!' shouted Parmenion, no less loudly.

Alexander calmed down, as though Philip himself had come into the tent. He moved over to the basin to put his head in the cold water. Then, completely naked, he moved towards his unexpected guest, 'What's wrong, General?'

'Why did you do it? Why did you destroy that wonder? Is this what Aristotle taught you? This is moderation? This is respect for the beautiful and the noble? Before the world you have shown yourself to be an uncultivated and primitive savage, an arrogant and presumptuous man who believes he can behave like a god! I have dedicated my life to your family, I have sacrificed a son to this enterprise, I have led your army through all its battles. I have every right to expect a reply from you!'

'If anyone else ever dared say and do these things, these things that you have said and done, General, they would be dead already, but I will answer you. I will tell you why I did this. I permitted the sack of Persepolis because in this way the Greeks know that I am the real avenger, I am the one they can identify with, the only one who has succeeded in bringing a centuries-old duel to an end. And I wanted it to be a young Athenian woman who torched the palace of Darius and Xerxes. Given that the city was already destroyed, what point would there have been in keeping the palace? I left it standing for just the time that was necessary to transfer the treasure and the archival documents to Ecbatana and Susa.'

'But—'

'We are about to set off, Parmenion, to follow Darius into the farthest provinces of his empire. That palace, if I had left it intact with its treasure, would have been too strong a temptation for anyone, even for one of my Macedonian governors – the atmosphere there, the luxury of those halls, those scenes sculpted everywhere with memories of Achaemenid greatness and then that throne . . . empty! The gold heaped up in unbelievable quantities under those vaults would have made any man the richest man on earth. No end of Persian nobles would have tried to take it at any cost. They would have been willing to spill any amount of blood to sit on that throne, to hold that sceptre in their hands, and all of this would have sparked off new wars – bloody, exhausting, endless. Is this what I should have allowed to happen?

'I had no choice, General, I had no choice, don't you

understand? If you don't want the stork to return then you have to destroy the nest.

'It is true, I have destroyed one of the wonders of the world, but who is to prevent me, when the moment comes, from building an even grander and more wonderful building? In doing this I have destroyed the symbol of Persia and her kings, I have shown the Greeks and the barbarians of the whole world who exactly is the new master – I have shown that the past is dead, the past is ashes, and a new era is being born now. It was beautiful, General, too beautiful, and for this reason it was too dangerous to be left standing.'

Parmenion lowered his head – the orgy, the dancing, the shouting for the god Dionysius, the state of possession that Eumenes and Callisthenes had told him of just a short time before ... it had all been planned, all been constructed. The production had certainly been a most realistic one, but it was still acting! Alexander was capable even of this, he was better and more consummate than Thessalus, his favourite actor. And the reasoning behind his defence of his actions was faultless, from the political, military and ideological point of view. That boy thought and acted now as though he were Lord of the entire world!

The King took a scroll from his library and handed it to Parmenion: 'Read it, it arrived last night. Antipater tells me that the war against the Spartans has been won. King Agis fell in battle at Megalopolis and now there is no one in Greece who opposes my position as supreme leader of the pan-Hellenic league. As for me, I have done what had to be done – I have kept my promise of

defeating the centuries-old enemy of the Greeks, and the destruction of the palace also represents this fact. Now all I have on my mind is to follow my destiny.'

Parmenion read through Antipater's letter with some difficulty because his sight was not what it used to be, but he understood what his King was telling him.

Alexander put a hand on his shoulder and looked at him with a mixture of gruff affection and military severity: 'Prepare yourself, General,' he ordered. 'Assemble the army, restore the strictest discipline. We are about to set off again.'

26

THE ARMY STARTED moving towards the end of spring and headed north, climbing up to the centre of the highlands with the desert on their right and the snow-covered Elam Mountains on their left. They travelled in four stages for a total of twenty parasangs and as evening fell they reached Pasargadae, the ancestral capital of Cyrus the Great, the founder of the Achaemenid dynasty. It was a small city, inhabited predominantly by shepherds and peasants but at its centre stood the first *pairidaeza* that had ever been built – the breathtaking grounds surrounding Cyrus's old palace. A complex system of irrigation took water from a spring at the base of the hills and kept all the plants fresh and green – the grass, the roses, the cypresses and the tamarinds, the fragrant gorse, the yews and the junipers.

To one side, to the west, lay the tomb of the founder. It was extremely simple in form, like the quadrangular tent of skins with a double-sided sloping roof, typical of the nomads of the steppe, the four-centuries-old ancestors of the Persians. Initially these people had been vassals of the Medians and their King Astyages, then they themselves became conquerors of vast territories. This simple construction was placed on an impressive foundation of seven steps, like a Mesopotamian tower, and it was

surrounded by a colonnade that enclosed a garden with yew trees that were well looked after and pruned.

The tomb itself was still cared for by a group of magi and by a priest who officiated every day at the ceremonies in honour of the great King. Alexander's approach frightened them because they had heard of what he had done in Persepolis, but the King soon allayed their fears. 'What has been done has been done,' he said, 'and it will not happen again. Show me this monument, I beg you. I simply wish to pay homage to the memory of Cyrus.'

The priest opened the door to the sacellum and let the young King through. He looked around in silence, a ray of sun coming in through the door to illuminate the rough-hewn sarcophagus on which there was but one inscription:

> I AM CYRUS, KING OF THE PERSIANS
> DO NO HARM TO THIS MY TOMB

At the bottom, hanging on a hook, was the great conqueror's armour – a breastplate of iron scales, a cone-shaped helmet, a round shield and a pure iron sword with an ivory hilt, the only precious material in the entire panoply.

There was a deep silence across the entire plateau, the only sound being the light whistle of the wind as it blew over the imposing solitary tomb. At that moment there came to Alexander a sharp feeling of a sense of the evanescent nature of human destiny, of the ephemeral procession of events. Empires grew and collapsed to make way for others that in their turn would become

great and powerful and then dissolve into oblivion. Was immortality simply a dream? He felt his mother's presence, so strong it was as though he could virtually touch her, all he had to do was stretch out his hand towards the dark wall of the sanctuary. And he thought he heard her voice saying, 'You will not die, *Aléxandre* . . .'

He turned, went out on to the terrace at the top of the steps, breathed the dry, fragrant air of the great plateau and felt himself being flooded by that most clear of lights. When he lowered his gaze to start moving down once more, he saw Aristander who appeared to be waiting for him.

'What are you doing here, Aristander?' he asked.

'I have heard a voice.'

'So have I, my mother's voice.'

'Be careful, *Aléxandre*, remember what happened to Achilles,' Aristander warned him, and he moved off, the wind making his cape flap and snap like a flag.

On the following day they crossed the territory of a tribe who were vassals to the Great King and they quashed them, but a little further on, while they climbed up even higher towards the Median highlands, a message arrived from Eumolpus of Soloi:

King Darius is in Ecbatana, from where he is trying to assemble an army of Scythians and Kadusians, paying them with the treasure from the royal palace. He has sent the harem to the east through the Caspian Gates. It is urgent that you reach the city as soon as possible, otherwise you will have to engage in a tough battle the outcome of which is most uncertain – the Scythians

and the Kadusians are indefatigable horsemen and are truly formidable opponents. They never attack frontally, but carry out incursions and make use of decoying techniques, disorientating the enemy and tiring them out with continual attacks and retreats. Remember that Cyrus and Darius the Great were also defeated by the Scythians.

On reading the message Alexander decided to set off immediately with the cavalry and the infantry ready for battle, entrusting the convoy with the supplies and all the treasure to Parmenion who had only three battalions of *pezhetairoi* and one of light Thracian and Triballian infantry. There was just one capital left to conquer now.

Thus they began climbing up through the mountains at double-quick pace, moving along the valleys and the rivers when possible, which made their passage easier. The landscape was increasingly dramatic due to the violent colours, the mountainous outcrops as black as basalt and the snowy peaks that shone like sapphires under the sun. Down below was the golden tawny colour of the desert, unfolding into the distance and dotted here and there with green splashes, like islands – oases with their villages of peasants and shepherds. Other villages stood on the sides of the valleys, close to the springs and the brooks from which the purest water flowed, and when the army passed the people came out of their houses and their huts to look at the foreigners on horseback without trousers and with wide-brimmed hats on their heads.

Here and there large stone towers standing on terraces

rose up out of the highland plains – towers of silence on which the inhabitants of those lands had exposed their dead to let them dissolve into nature, contaminating neither soil nor fire – and Alexander thought of Barsine, placed on a rough tumulus out in the harsh desert of Gaugamela. He thought of young Phraates who had returned to Pamphylia with his grandfather, their family's only survivors. What was going through the adolescent boy's mind at that moment? Dreams? The will to vengeance? Or the simple melancholy of an orphan?

It took ten days' march along increasingly narrow valleys before they came into sight of the splendour of Ecbatana, surrounded by a crown of snow-capped mountains and a green valley. The upper edge of the walls and the battlements, decorated with blue tiles and with gold leaf, shone like a pendant on a queen's forehead while the pinnacles and the spires of the palaces and the sanctuaries, all dressed in pure gold, glittered brightly. Alexander recalled his conversation with the Persian guest in the palace at Pella as though it had taken place just the previous day. For him back then, when little more than a child, it had all seemed like some tale of fantasy: he had looked into the man's deep black eyes, studied his black, curly beard, his ceremonial solid-gold sword and he had seemed to be an unreal being, a messenger from some realm of stories. Now, here, that legendary city lay before him.

With him was Oxhatres, son of Mazaeus, the Satrap of Babylonia, and the King's cousin on his mother's side, a young and ambitious man who burned with the desire to prove himself in the eyes of the new Lord. He spurred

on his horse, approached the walls and exchanged a few words with the sentries. Then he turned to Alexander to tell him in his uncertain, but now comprehensible Greek: 'Great King Darius gone. He no fight, he run with treasure and with army.'

'Which way?'

'That way,' replied the young man, pointing northwards. 'Satrap surrenders.'

Alexander nodded and gave the signal to the army to follow him to the gates of the city which were opening at that very moment. Everyone followed in perfect order because by this time the stiffest discipline had been re-established and the slightest violations were punished with the whip or even worse.

Parmenion, with his troops and the caravan, arrived two days later, as evening was falling, but it took five days and five nights for him to enter, unload and then leave through the other side with the twenty thousand beasts of burden which had carried the one hundred and twenty thousand talents of the royal treasure – on average seven talents each, a terrible weight which had slowed down the march of the animals considerably.

When the operation was completed and the troops billeted in the camp outside the city, Alexander invited the old general to supper. It was a very light meal, frugal even, and at table there was no wine, only water. He must be doing penance for the excesses of Persepolis, Parmenion thought to himself as he bit into a piece of Persian bread that had been baked in the embers of a fire.

'What can you tell me of my cousin, Prince Amyntas?'

Alexander began. 'I wonder if I can trust him now, or whether I should still keep him under surveillance.'

'Has nothing turned up in the royal archives?'

'It will take months, if not years, to check the royal archives. Up to now, as far as I know, Eumenes has not found anything regarding the assassination of my father, or any possible collusion between Amyntas and Darius. I think in any case that it makes sense to tread carefully and to keep the surveillance in place.'

Alexander took a sip of water, then began again, changing subject now: 'I am sorry that we have not always seen eye to eye . . .'

'I have always told you what I think, Sire, just as I used to do with your father.'

'I know, but now I want you to listen,' said Alexander as the cook served beans, greens and cups of curdled milk which had an acid taste. 'I will pursue Darius until I find him and I will force him into the final battle, after which this empire will be ours completely.

'To do this I need someone here, in Ecbatana, someone who will watch my back and guarantee contact with Macedonia – supplies, reinforcements, and all the rest, as well as guarding over the royal treasure. You are that man, General, the only man I can trust. As for administration, I will give that job to Harpalus. He is a good man and Eumenes holds him in high esteem. Well then, what do you say?'

'I understand. I am too old and you no longer want me on the battlefield; you're putting me out to grass and—'

'Of course you're old, General,' replied Alexander with

a strange smile, and then, almost shouting, 'Given that today is your seventieth birthday!'

At those words a rowdy chorus of male voices resounded from behind the tent:

> The silly old soldier's off to the war
> And falls to the floor, falls to the floor!

And all Alexander's Companions, together with Philotas, Eumenes and his assistant Harpalus burst into the tent, carrying a roast calf on their shoulders, an enormous crater full of wine, a skewer of partridges and two of pheasants, chickens and geese, and great quantities of other food of all types. Even Parmenion's second son, Nicanor, had been invited.

Leonnatus threw the beans and the curdled milk to the floor as he shouted, 'Enough of this rubbish! Let's eat, give everybody eat!'

Parmenion was much moved to see that they had prepared such a feast for him and turned discreetly to dry his eyes. Alexander came to him holding a sealed roll of papyrus sheets in his hand: 'This is my birthday present for you, General,' and he handed it to him with a smile.

Parmenion opened and read it without any difficulty because it had all been written in block letters – the King had made him a present of a beautiful palace at Susa, another in Babylon and a third one in Ecbatana, and besides this there were gifts of huge estates in Macedonia, Lyncestis and Eordaea, and a life pension of five hundred talents. The next sheet bore the nomination of his son Philotas as commander of all the cavalry. Then came the

royal seal with the countersignature, 'Eumenes of Cardia, Secretary General'.

'Sire, I . . .' began Parmenion, his voice trembling, but the King stopped him. 'Don't say another word, General. All this is so much less than you deserve, and we all hope that you will be with us to enjoy it all until you are over a hundred years old. As for your role, it is the most important and crucial position east of the Straits and you are the only person I can fully trust.'

Parmenion passed the sheet bearing the nomination as commander of the cavalry to his son Philotas and said, 'Look at this, my son, just look at this. Come now, show it to your brother.'

The King embraced the General while all the companions applauded and the party went on into the night. It was getting on towards the second watch by the time they all reached their beds, every one of them drunk, including Parmenion.

27

ALEXANDER WANTED THEIR stay in Ecbatana to be as brief as possible and to set off immediately on the chase for Darius, but there were so many things to sort out and so many letters to write: to his mother who continued to complain about how she was treated by Antipater, to Antipater who had won the war with Sparta but was still very critical of Olympias, and then to all his satraps and governors.

'How do you intend to solve this problem between the Regent and your mother?' Eumenes asked him as he sealed the letter. 'You cannot carry on pretending there's nothing wrong.'

'No, I cannot, but Antipater has to realize that one of my mother's tears is worth more than a thousand of his letters.'

'This simply isn't fair,' replied Eumenes. 'The Regent bears the greatest of responsibilities and he needs peace of mind.'

'He holds all the power and my mother, in the end, is the Queen of Macedonia: you have to consider her position as well.'

Eumenes shook his head as he realized there was nothing to be done. Indeed, the King hadn't seen his mother now for four years and it was understandable

that he only remembered her good points. He also missed his sister Cleopatra a great deal, and often wrote to her.

When they had finished with the correspondence, Alexander said, 'I have decided to dismiss the Greek allies.'

'Why?' asked Eumenes.

'The pan-Hellenic league is once again firmly in our hands and we have enough money here to sign up any army we may need. Furthermore, the Greeks, once they reach home, will recount everything they have seen and done and this will greatly influence the people, much more than the *History* that Callisthenes is writing.'

'But they are excellent soldiers and—'

'They are tired, Eumenes, and the march that lies ahead is a long one. There may come a moment in which they feel themselves to be too far from home and they may find themselves taking some unwise decision at the wrong moment. I would rather avoid all of this. Have them fall in at dawn just outside the camp.'

*

Many things led the Greeks to realize that something important was in the offing – the early hour, the order to prepare their baggage and the transport carts and to wear their armour brightly polished.

Alexander appeared astride Bucephalas, armed to the teeth and flanked by his guards. He waited until the first rays of the sun made the Hoplites' armour shine and then he began to speak:

'Allies! Your contribution to our victory has been most

important, in some cases crucial: none of us will forget that it was the Greek infantry at Gaugamela that held the right wing against the continuous assaults of Bessus and his Median horsemen. You have been valiant, bold, loyal to your oath of allegiance to the pan-Hellenic league and its supreme command. You have accomplished something that no Greek, not even those who took part in the Trojan War, ever succeeded in doing – conquering Babylon, Persepolis, Ecbatana.

'The moment has come for you to enjoy the fruits of your efforts: I free you now from your oath of allegiance and I dismiss you. Each of your officers will receive one talent, each soldier thirty silver minae, and, on top of that, money to pay your travelling expenses from here to Greece. I thank you; return now to your families, to your children, to your cities!'

Alexander expected an explosion of joy and applause, but instead there came a slight murmur that soon grew into the noise of animated discussion among all the soldiers and officers.

'What is wrong, men?' he shouted in surprise. 'Have I not paid you enough? Are you not happy to be returning?'

An officer of about forty years of age, by the name of Heliodorus of Eghion, moved forwards and said, 'King, we thank you for everything and we are happy that our assistance has been important for you, but we do not wish to leave you.'

Alexander looked at him in disbelief, and Heliodorus continued, 'As we fought by your side we learned things

which no one else could ever have taught us, we have accomplished feats that no soldier would ever dream of undertaking. Many of us wonder what you will do now, which lands you will conquer, which far off territories will those who serve under your standard live to see? Of course, many will accept your offer and will return to their homes, joyously in one sense, but deep in sadness in another, because in all this time they have learned to admire and to love you.

'Others still have no families, or if they do have families they think that for them it is more important to follow you and to fight honourably in your service, risking their lives if necessary. If you want them, these men would rather stay with you.'

Heliodorus had finished his speech and he now moved back into the ranks alongside his soldiers.

'There are few men like you,' Alexander replied, 'and I am greatly honoured by anyone who chooses to remain, but whoever chooses to stay will be with us on a private basis rather than an ally sent by his city. He will be a professional soldier. I will give such men payment of six hundred drachmae for the entire campaign and, should any of you die in battle this will be the sum that will go to your families. Those who wish to remain will take three steps past the front line, the others are free to go whenever they wish with my gratitude, my friendship and my affection.'

The men beat their spears on their shields and shouted the King's name, just like Macedonian soldiers. Then those who wanted to remain took their three steps over

the line and Alexander saw that they constituted almost half of his Greek allies.

*

The Greeks who had chosen to return home set off that very same day, marching through the two wings of the infantry and the cavalry lined up for the final salute, while the trumpets sounded the signal for the army to fall out; and when Parmenion himself ordered, 'Present arms!' many of these men, inured to all dangers and all of life's excesses, had their eyes full of tears.

As soon as they had disappeared round the first bend in the road and the sound of the drums that marked their steps had faded away, Alexander had the trumpets sound once more, and his army turned and set off in pursuit of the Great King. Oxhatres knew all the short cuts and offered to go on ahead with two of his Scythian mercenaries and set off at a gallop.

The army advanced over a vast plateau on which small antelopes and wild goats were grazing, and every now and again at night they could hear lions roaring. The pace of their march was almost unbearable – many of the infantrymen had to stop because of sores on their feet and more than a few beasts of burden collapsed under the weight of their loads – but Alexander rejected all suggestions that they should slow down and instead demanded that they move ever more quickly, sleeping only for a few hours each night without pitching their tents, all of this to keep up the pressure on Darius.

He reminded all the veterans how they had once marched to Thebes from the banks of the River Ister in

just thirteen days, and he too slept out in the open at night, covered only by his military cloak. Occasionally they were able to find some shelter in the caravanserai along the road leading to the eastern provinces, but these structures were rather limited in size, places designed for people who were ill or those who really were struggling along their journey.

The air was becoming thinner and sharper, especially towards evening, and Eumenes had started wearing trousers again, which made him feel much better. For six days of the march eastwards they followed the edge of an impressive mountain chain dominated by the highest peak any of them had ever seen, its top covered with snow. Then they came to a narrow passage that took the name of the Caspian Gates. This was a gorge at the bottom of which flowed a torrent, flanked by walls so steep that even the Agrianians would find it almost impossible to scale them.

'If they ambush us here,' said the Black, 'they'll tear us to pieces.' And indeed it seemed unlikely that Darius would not seek to make the most of this natural advantage.

Alexander looked up the almost vertical walls and watched the slow gliding of an eagle, 'Do you think there might be anyone up there?'

'There is only one way to find out.'

'The Agrianians.'

'I'll send them up immediately.'

Shortly afterwards the soldiers, at a halt on the bottom of the gorge, turned their faces skywards and watched the acrobatics of the Agrianian assault troops as they

climbed up the rocky faces, chipping away at times with their picks, creating passageways so as to be able to move through crevasses and then continue upwards, indefatigably agile. One of them, shortly before reaching the summit, lost his handhold as he was trying to reach out to an outcrop, fell and was smashed to pieces on the rocks below. His companions continued climbing, but another group set off from the bottom of the gorge up to the point where the battered body had become stuck between two rocks. They took it and at great danger to themselves dragged it down to the bottom where they prepared a stretcher, laid him out on it and covered him with a cloak before waiting to start the march again.

In the meantime the others had reached the top and blew a horn to give the signal to advance. The army moved forward and there were no signs of any of the Great King's soldiers offering any resistance. At the first stop the Agrianians celebrated their companion's funeral; they put him on a pyre of pine branches and cremated him while together they sang a mournful dirge. Then, after burying his ashes in an urn, together with his weapons and the buckle of his cloak, they got drunk and revelled together for the rest of the night.

28

It was just before the end of the fourth watch when Alexander, half asleep, became aware of Peritas growling.

'What's up? What can you hear? Good boy, good boy . . . it must be a wolf, a lynx perhaps.' He raised his eyes to the sky and saw the bonfires the Agrianians had lit on the sides of the gorge to show that the coast was clear, for the moment. Then he heard the noise of shuffling feet and confused whispers.

'What's up?' he repeated, louder this time.

Hephaestion moved forward, 'Oxhatres has come back with his Scythians – he wants to speak to you.'

'Oxhatres? Let him through.'

From the bottom of the gorge three horsemen advanced, armed with bows across their shoulders, all completely covered with dust. Oxhatres, exhausted, dropped to the ground and walked forwards, swaying slightly. He had probably lost all feeling in his legs after having ridden beyond the limit. 'King Darius deposed and made prisoner by Bessus,' he gasped, 'Satrap of Bactriana.'

'The son of a bitch who very nearly took us from behind on the right at Gaugamela,' said Leonnatus.

Oxhatres asked for help from an interpreter to be sure he would be understood and continued, 'The King

had left Ecbatana with six thousand horsemen, twenty thousand infantrymen and seven thousand talents of the royal treasure with the intention of razing the earth behind him and waiting for you at the Caspian Gates, but his soldiers ended up demoralized due to all their retreating; it was common knowledge that neither the Scythians nor the Kadusians would be sending any reinforcements. Many of them had begun to desert, and indeed we actually met some who gave us this information. They would abandon the encampment at night and spread out in the mountains and through the desert, while the scouts brought back news of the approach of your leading soldiers. At that point Bessus, supported by other Satraps – Satibarzanes, Barsaentes and Nabarzanes – arrested the King, had him put in chains and locked him up in a cart which is now on its way at top speed towards the farthest eastern provinces.'

'Where are they now?' asked Alexander. In the meantime his Companions had dressed and put on their weapons – someone had added wood to the fire and they all stood around it, feeling in their bones that they would soon be going into action.

'Somewhere between us and the city of Hecatompylos, the capital of the Medians, but the gorge is free, and if you rush now with the cavalry you will manage to capture them. It is terrible that this ambitious traitor is enjoying the fruits of his treachery. If you are thinking of pursuing him, then I will come with you and I will be your guide.'

'I don't think you're up to riding any more,' replied Alexander. 'You're exhausted.'

'Give me time to eat something and stretch my legs a little and you'll see.'

Leptine appeared just then with a jug of 'Nestor's Cup' and Alexander nodded to her to serve some for Oxhatres, 'Try this,' he said, 'it's strong enough to bring people back from the dead.' Then, turning to his companions, 'All cavalry units prepare to move immediately.'

This was exactly the order they had all been waiting for. The trumpets blared out the signal to fall in, and immediately afterwards Alexander leaped on to his horse and set off at a gallop along the bottom of the gorge, beside Oxhatres, followed by Hephaestion, Ptolemy, Perdiccas, Craterus and all the others. The *hetairoi* divisions set off as they became ready and as the space cleared down at the bottom of the narrow gorge.

They rode for hours, stopping only to let the horses get their breath back. The gorge was now opening up towards the valley, which led down towards the city, and the sun was just beginning to show from behind the snowy peaks of the Hyrcanian Mountains. Suddenly Oxhatres shouted, 'Halt!' and tugged on his horse's reins. The animal snorted heavily and pulled up, shining with sweat, and Alexander and his men stopped too, arranging themselves in a wide circle and preparing their weapons. The King unsheathed his sword, Leonnatus unhooked his cleaver and everyone turned to the Persian Prince who was pointing to an object off at a distance of some two stadia.

'It's a carriage from the royal stables,' he said. 'Perhaps they abandoned it so as to be able to speed up.'

'Let's move forward and keep our wits about us,'

Alexander ordered. 'It might be a trap. Hephaestion on that side, Ptolemy over there. You, Perdiccas, move forward along the road and see what the situation is just beyond that bend. Be careful.'

Oxhatres spurred his horse on towards the carriage and Alexander followed him, together with Leonnatus and Craterus.

The royal carriage was there in the middle of the road, apparently intact, its doors closed.

'Wait,' said Leonnatus. 'Let me go first.' He dismounted and wielded his axe as he opened the door and looked inside: 'Oh, by Zeus . . .'

Alexander also approached – King Darius lay there on the floor, dressed in his country clothes and completely lacking in any sign of his regal status, apart from his majestic head: his long hair, his beard bedecked with rings and his thick black moustache which contrasted greatly with the deathly pallor of his skin. A wide red stain covered his chest, his clothes were soaked in blood right down to his belt, and his hands were bound together. Out of contempt they had used a gold chain for this job.

'Bastards!' Alexander swore indignantly.

'Quickly, let's pull him out!' exclaimed Ptolemy. 'Perhaps he's still alive. Call Philip, quickly!'

Two soldiers delicately lifted the Great King's body and placed it on the ground on a blanket. Philip arrived in a rush and knelt down by Darius, placing his ear on his chest to listen for a heartbeat.

'Is he dead?' Leonnatus asked.

Philip gestured for him to be quiet and continued to listen, 'It's incredible . . .' he said. 'He is still breathing.'

Everyone looked at one another. Alexander knelt close to Philip, 'Is there anything you can do for him?'

The physician shook his head, then he began undoing the chain around Darius's wrists, 'This is all I can do – let him die as a free man. It's a matter of moments now.'

'Look!' exclaimed Craterus. 'He's moving his lips . . .'

Oxhatres too knelt down and tended his ear towards the King's lips for an instant, then he stood up with his eyes full of tears.

'He is dead now,' he said, his voice trembling with emotion. 'Great King Darius III is dead.'

Alexander moved closer: 'Did he say anything?' he asked. 'Did you manage to hear his words?'

'He said, "revenge"!' he replied.

Alexander looked on his enemy, at the glassy eyes that had once stared at him for an instant on the battlefield at Issus, and he felt a deep sense of pity for this man who up until a few months before had sat on the highest throne on the earth, revered as a god by millions of subjects and who now, betrayed and murdered by his own friends, lay abandoned on a dusty road. There came to his mind the lines of the *Fall of Ilium* which describe the lifeless body of Priam, killed by Neoptolemus:

Here lies the King of Asia, the powerful lord of armies
Like a tree felled by lightning
An abandoned trunk, a body without a name.

He murmured, 'I will be the one to avenge your death. I swear it,' and he closed Darius's eyelids.

29

Alexander to Sisygambis, Great Queen Mother, Hail!
Your son Darius is dead. He died not by my hand, nor
at the hands of my men, but was killed by his own
friends: they assassinated him and abandoned his body
by the side of the road to Hecatompylos.

He was still breathing when I found him, but we
were unable to do anything to help, apart from
swearing to avenge the ignominy of his death. His last
thoughts were certainly for you, just as my thoughts
are with you now. This death is for me a great offence,
just as it was for him because it has deprived us both
of a fair match, face-to-face, which would have left us
with a winner and would anyway have left the loser
with some honour.

I will send him to you now, so that you may
embrace him for one last time and weep for him as
you accompany him to his final resting place. His body
has been prepared so that it might survive this last,
long journey to the ruins of Persepolis where the tomb
that had been dug alongside the other Kings is ready
to welcome him.

Arrange a fine funeral for him. As for me, I will not
rest until I find the assassins and avenge his death. For
a mother there is no greater grief than the loss of a
child, but I beg you not to hate me – the gods at least

have given you the possibility of mourning him and burying him, in keeping with your ancestral customs. My mother, who has been waiting for me for years, will perhaps not even be granted this concession.

Sisygambis closed the letter and cried for a long time in the intimacy of her own room, then she called the eunuchs and ordered them to prepare her small carriage and the horses, their mourning dress and the funeral offerings. She set off the following day across the land of the Ouxians, the people on whose behalf she had interceded with Alexander to stop him clearing them out of their own lands.

When word spread that the Queen Mother was travelling up to Persepolis to bury her son, all the people gathered along the road – men, women, the elderly and children together greeted the old grief-stricken Queen in silence and escorted her to the frontiers of their lands, to the edge of the highlands from which the ruins of the burned capital could now be made out – the columns of the luminous Palace of the Solstice, petrified trunks in a forest devoured by fire.

She stopped at the gates of the destroyed city and had her tent pitched there and she fasted for days until she saw, way down on the road leading from Ecbatana, the carriage pulled by four horses bearing her son's body.

<p style="text-align:center">*</p>

Alexander immediately set off once more in pursuit of Bessus and his accomplices. On the following day they came to the city called Hecatompylos, where the Persian

commander surrendered without any resistance and from there they moved on to Zadracarta, the city of the Hyrcanians. Before them now lay the limitless extent of the Caspian Sea.

The King dismounted and began walking barefoot over the wet pebbles on the seashore, and his companions, surprised and somewhat puzzled, followed him along the watery frontier that marked the extreme point of their march.

'Whereabouts in the world are we exactly, do you think?' Leonnatus asked Callisthenes when they found themselves there before the sea.

'Give me your spear,' replied the historian.

Leonnatus gave it to him with a puzzled look on his face. Callisthenes stuck it into the beach as straight and as deep as he could manage and then carefully measured its shadow.

'More or less at the same level as Tyre, but I have no idea how far from Tyre we are.'

'And where does this sea end?'

Callisthenes sent his gaze out across the great liquid expanse that was just beginning to turn red in the sunset and then he turned to Nearchus who at that moment was approaching and perhaps had an answer to this question. The navarch bent over, picked up a pebble and threw it with all his strength as far as he could. The stone fell into the sea and produced a series of concentric ripples that moved through the water and died on the shore. He replied:

'No one knows, but if I could build a fleet I would like to sail over that horizon, over there towards the

north. That way we would discover whether this is a gulf of the northern Ocean, as many say, or whether it is a lake.'

As they spoke, they heard voices coming from the encampment, growing in excitement until they became cries of joy and songs of exultation.

Alexander turned to look back: 'What's happening at the camp?'

'I don't know,' replied Leonnatus, picking up his spear again.

'Go and find out then.'

Leonnatus leaped on to his horse, set off at a gallop towards the camp and, as he approached, heard increasingly loud and distinct shouting and singing. Then he realized what it was that had generated all these celebrations – the soldiers had heard of Darius's death and thought the war had finished, and rumours were spreading that they were finally returning home. They danced and drank and shouted for joy, singing old Macedonian songs that had almost seemed forgotten and some even started preparing their baggage for the long journey.

Leonnatus jumped to the ground and stopped the first soldier who passed before him, an infantryman of the *pezhetairoi*: 'What's happening here, by Hercules?'

'We're going home! Haven't you heard? The war's over!'

'It's over? Who told you it's over?'

'Everyone says it's over – Darius is dead and the war's over. We're going home! We're going home!'

'You fool!' Leonnatus shouted into his face. 'Tell all these imbeciles to calm down and stop this din. There is

one man and one man alone who will tell us when the war is over – Alexander! Understand? Alexander! And he has said nothing, I can assure you of that.' He left the soldier standing there like a halfwit in the middle of the camp and the deafening racket of the groundless celebration and returned quickly to the King.

'Well then?' Alexander asked.

'It's difficult to—'

'By Hercules, speak, man! What's happening in my encampment?'

'Nobody knows how, but a rumour has started that the war is over and that we're all going home ... ever since you told the Greeks they could return our men have been sure that it was their turn next, and since Darius is dead now ... they're all celebrating wildly and—'

Alexander leaped astride his horse and galloped to the camp. As soon as he entered, he called the trumpeters and had them twice sound the signal to fall in. The racket subsided, mutating into a suffused buzz of voices, then the men, in groups, in divisions or one by one, gathered in the middle of the camp around the assembly podium. Alexander, surrounded by his Companions, stood upright at the very centre, his face thunderous. He lifted his hand to ask for silence and began:

'Men! What are you doing? Come on, I want an answer! Send me your commanders and tell me what you are doing!'

The buzz grew in volume again and it was clear they were all shocked by this sudden dampening of their

celebrations. One by one the commanders of the various units moved forwards, conferred for a moment among themselves at the base of the podium and then their spokesman said, 'Sire, after you dismissed our Greek allies, news spread that you were about to dismiss the Thessalians as well, and they started preparing their baggage. At that point, when news reached us that Darius is dead, we all thought the war was over and that you would send us home too. The men started celebrating – they all want to return to their wives and their children who they haven't seen for four years.'

'This is true,' replied Alexander. 'I intend to dismiss the Thessalians just as I have already dismissed the Greeks. They are our allies in the pan-Hellenic League and their task is complete now. We had promised freedom for the Greek cities of Asia and defeat for the long-standing enemy of the Greeks and we have kept those promises. We have conquered the four capitals, the Great King is dead, but our own task is not yet over.' The buzz of disappointment grew at these last words. 'No, men! My veterans of so many battles! My friends! To the east, the rebel Satraps are preparing a counterattack; they have assembled a new army of thousands and thousands of warriors and they are simply waiting for us to turn our backs to them.

'They will attack us from every possible direction with their fast horses; they will not relent for one moment, neither by day nor by night; they will poison the wells along our path; they will burn the crops; they will destroy the villages where we might seek shelter from the harsh

winter. Our return journey, after having accomplished such glorious feats, will be transformed into a catastrophe. Is this what you want?'

The answer to the King's question was a silence full of despondency and disappointment. These men who had always fought with such formidable courage, who had faced up to every danger without ever worrying about their own lives, were now full of doubt and uncertainty. What they saw stretching before them were completely unknown lands and seas; even the positions of the very constellations in the skies seemed to be changing and they had no idea of where they were. Suddenly they felt they were too far away from their homes. For the first time they felt sure that Alexander himself had absolutely no intention of returning home, that he simply wanted to move forwards, forwards into eternity. Their fear now was that they would never return.

The King spoke once more: 'We must move onwards! We have to seek them out, defeat them and establish our authority over all the empire that belonged to the Persians. If we fail to do this then all we have done so far will be wasted, all we have built will collapse, none of us will ever be sure of being able to return home. Men! Have I ever betrayed your trust? Have I ever deceived you? Have I not paid you generously for your labours, and don't you think I will do even more for you when we bring this enterprise to its conclusion? I know, you are tired, but I also know that you are the best soldiers in the world, you have no equals in terms of bravery and daring. I have no wish to force you, no one knows more than I do just how much you deserve your rest and your

recompense. So I will not detain you any longer – those who wish to leave may leave now, with honour and with my gratitude, but you must know that even if you should all abandon me now to return to Macedonia, I will go forward anyway with my Companions until my undertaking is complete, and if necessary . . . I will do it alone!' He fell silent as he crossed his arms on his chest. There followed another interminable moment of silence.

Alexander's Companions, those who years before had travelled through the snows of Illyria to join him in his exile and who at that moment stood behind him, took a step forward as though obeying some command, lining up alongside him with their hands on the hilts of their swords, and together with them Philotas and Cleitus the Black also stepped forward.

On seeing this, one of the men of the Vanguard, who had been ready for the off and was standing in the middle of the field, let his bundle of possessions fall at his feet as he unsheathed his sword and beat it against his shield so that it resounded like a thunderclap in the silence. Everyone turned towards him and another soldier replied immediately with a similar noise. A third joined in and then a fourth and soon all the horsemen of the Vanguard, wherever they were, near the gates or the fence or in the middle of the field or busy preparing their baggage, they all unsheathed their swords and one by one started beating them against their shields as they gradually approached the podium until they were standing there before the King, and they continued, incessantly, rhythmically, to make the deafening din of bronze on iron. After them came other soldiers – cavalrymen and infantrymen, assault

troops and scouts, Thracians and Agrianians – they all lined up in ranks and joined in with the horsemen of the Vanguard in beating their swords on their shields. Then the standard-bearer of the first battalion lifted the red flag with the Argead star and everyone stopped and stood stock still where he was. The standard-bearer took a step forward, dipped the flag and shouted, 'Your orders, Sire!'

Alexander, visibly moved, came forwards and lifted his arms to the sky to thank his soldiers for not abandoning him. Ptolemy, who was standing very close by, saw that his eyes were full of tears. He stood there for what seemed like a long time while the entire army shouted his name in a voice of thunder: *Aléxandre! Aléxandre! Aléxandre!*

Then, flanked by his Companions, the King came down from the podium, crossed the field between two arrays of shining spears, and came to Bucephalas. The great horse stood waiting, stamping impatiently.

30

THE ARMY MOVED on to Zadracarta, the capital of the Hyrcanians, and there Alexander found the court of Darius III, which Bessus had abandoned in his retreat towards the farthest provinces of the empire. At this point the King discharged the Thessalian cavalry, giving the horsemen the possibility of remaining as mercenaries, and then ordered his army to prepare for the long march eastwards. They were to depart as soon as the new contingents they were waiting for arrived from Macedonia, reinforcements which Parmenion was to send on to them as quickly as possible.

The members of Darius's court were all staying in one particular area of the city under the surveillance of the eunuchs and Alexander gave orders for them all to be put under the protection of his army. Indeed, he requested precise information regarding which members of the royal family were still part of the court.

The master of ceremonies – a man of about sixty, his body completely hairless and his head shaven – came before the King to report.

'All the King's concubines are here with their children, as is the Royal Princess Stateira.'

'Stateira?'

'Yes, my Lord.'

Alexander recalled the letter in which Darius had offered him dominion over Asia west of the Euphrates and the hand of his daughter in marriage, and he recalled how he had rejected this offer, going against Parmenion's wishes.

'I want you to arrange an audience with the Princess for me,' he said. The eunuch took his leave and in the early afternoon sent a messenger to announce that the Princess would be expecting him after sunset in her apartments in the palace that had belonged to the Satrap of Parthia.

He arrived for the audience dressed in a very plain Greek *chiton*, white and ankle-length, together with a blue cloak held in place by a gold buckle.

The eunuch was at the door, 'The Princess is in mourning, my Lord, and begs your pardon for not having been able to adorn herself in a mode befitting your presence, but she is glad to receive your visit because she has heard that you are a man of noble spirit and sentiment.'

'Does she speak Greek?'

The eunuch nodded, 'When King Darius offered you her hand in marriage, he had her instructed in your language, but then—'

'Would you care to have me announced now?'

'You may enter straight away,' replied the eunuch. 'The Princess is expecting you.'

Alexander entered and found himself in a small atrium decorated with floral motifs and festoons of fruit, and there before him was another door, framed in sculpted

stone with a lintel supported by two griffins. The door opened and a handmaid showed him in before she herself left, closing the door behind her.

Princess Stateira stood before him, alongside a small reading table on which there were some rolls of papyrus and a bronze statuette representing a horseman of the steppes. She was dressed in an ivory-coloured tunic of coarse wool, tied round her waist with a leather belt and leather slippers decorated with stylish embroidery in blue wool. She wore no jewellery, apart from a small pendant of silver representing the god Ahura Mazda. She was not made up, but her strong and graceful features gave emphasis to her countenance – proud and delicate at one and the same time. She had her father's dark, deep eyes and marked eyebrows, while her soft, moist and full lips must have come from her mother together with the slender neck, the firm and proud breasts, and the legs, which were certainly long and shapely.

Alexander moved forward until they were face to face, close enough to smell the delicate perfume of cassia and nard, close enough to feel himself being enveloped in the spell that he had now learned to recognize as characteristic of oriental women.

'Stateira,' he said, lowering his head. 'I am deeply sorry for the death of your father, the King, and I have come to tell you . . .'

The young woman returned his bow with a sad smile and extended her hand, which Alexander held for a moment in his own.

'Would you not care to sit down, my Lord?' the girl

asked, and the Greek language came from her lips with a strange but intensely musical lilt that reminded him very much of Barsine.

He felt his own heartbeat suddenly increase as he sat before her and began talking once again, 'I wanted to tell you that Darius will receive the highest honours and he will be buried in his tomb in the rock at Persepolis.'

'I thank you,' replied the young woman.

'I have also sworn to capture the assassin, the Satrap Bessus, who has fled toward Bactriana, and I will inflict on him the punishment that Persian law reserves for one who betrays and kills his own King.'

Stateira lowered her head with a light, graceful movement – a sign of approval, but she said nothing. In the meantime one of the handmaids entered with a tray and two cups full of snow and freshly squeezed pomegranate juice, brilliant pink in colour. The Princess handed one cup to her guest, but she herself did not drink, in observance of the strict laws of mourning, and she watched him in silence – it seemed to her impossible that this young man whose features were so very perfect and whose bearing was so direct and noble could possibly be the inexorable exterminator who had crushed the most powerful armies on earth, the demon who had burned the palace of Persepolis and abandoned the city to looting and pillage. At that moment he seemed to her to be the kind young man who had treated all the Persian women he had taken prisoner with respect, the conqueror who had honoured his opponents and even won the affection of the Queen Mother.

'How is my grandmother?' she asked, completely

naturally, but then she immediately corrected herself, 'I mean, the Great Queen Mother.'

'She is well enough. She is a noble and strong woman who bears fate's blows with great dignity. And you, Princess, how are you?'

'I, too, am well enough, my Lord, under the circumstances.'

Alexander caressed her hand once again, 'You are beautiful, Stateira, and most charming. Your father must have been proud of you.'

Tears came to her eyes, 'He was, poor Father. He would have been fifty years old today. But thank you for your kind words.'

'They are sincerely felt words,' replied Alexander.

Stateira bowed her head, 'It is strange to hear that from the young man who refused my hand in marriage.'

'I didn't know you.'

'Would that have changed anything?'

'Perhaps. One glance can change the destiny of a man.'

'Or a woman,' she replied, staring at him intensely with her shining, liquid eyes. 'Why have you come here? Why did you leave your land? Is it not a beautiful land?'

'Oh yes,' replied Alexander. 'It is indeed. There are mountains covered with snow, red in the light of the sunset and silver in the moonlight, there are lakes as pure and clear as the eyes of young maids and meadows covered with flowers and woods of blue spruce.'

'Don't you have a mother, a sister? Don't you think of them?'

'Every evening. And every time the wind blows

towards the west I entrust it with words that come from my heart and I pray that it might carry them to Pella, to the palace where I was born, and to Buthrotum, where my sister lives, like a swallow, in a stone nest high above the sea.'

'So why this enterprise?'

Alexander hesitated, as though afraid he might be about to reveal his very soul to this young stranger, and he let his gaze wander far away, beyond the walls, out across the landscape of wooded mountains and green pastures. At that moment from the road below there came voices – the sound of men selling wares, and women chattering as they spun wool and then came the gruff call of the Bactrian camels as they walked along in their caravans.

'It is difficult to answer,' he said suddenly, as though having just woken up. 'I have always dreamed of going beyond the horizon that presented itself there before my eyes, of going to the very ends of the earth, to the waves of the Ocean . . .'

'And then? What will you do when you have conquered the entire world? Do you think you will be happy then? Will you have achieved everything that you really want? Or perhaps you will find yourself in the grip of an even stronger, deeper anxiety – invincible this time?'

'Perhaps, but I will never know these things until I reach the limits that the gods have assigned to human beings.'

Stateira looked at him in silence and for a moment she had the feeling, on looking into his eyes, that she was gazing into a mysterious, unknown world, into a desert

inhabited by demons and ghosts. She felt a sense of vertigo, but together with it came an all-consuming sense of attraction and instinctively she closed her eyes. Alexander kissed her and she felt the caress of his hair over her face and her neck.

When she opened her eyes again, he was no longer there.

On the following day Eumenes, the Secretary General, came to her and asked for her hand in marriage for his King.

31

THE WEDDING TOOK place according to Macedonian
tradition – the bridegroom cut a loaf of bread with his
sword and offered some to the bride who then ate it
together with him. It was a simple and yet evocative rite
that Stateira enjoyed. The celebration following the
ceremony was also conducted after the Macedonian fash-
ion with great libations, an interminable feast, singing,
shows and dancing. Stateira did not take part because she
was still in mourning for her father's death, and she
waited for her husband in her bed chamber, a cedar
wood pavilion at the top of the palace, equipped with
wide drapes in Egyptian linen and illuminated by lamps.

When Alexander came to her the bawdy songs of his
soldiers down in the courtyard could still be heard, but
as soon as their din faded there came a solitary song
through the night, a gentle air that flew like the nightin-
gale's song above the canopies of the trees all covered in
blossom.

'What's that?' the King asked.

Stateira moved towards him dressed in a light Indian
gown and put her head on his shoulder, 'It is one of our
love songs – do you know the story of Abrocome and
Anthia?'

Alexander put his arm around her waist and pulled

her to him, 'Of course I know it, in Greek. One of our authors described it in a work entitled *The Education of Cyrus*, but it is beautiful to hear it in Persian, even though I do not understand your language. It is a wonderful story.'

'It is the story of a love that goes beyond death,' said Stateira, her voice trembling.

Alexander undid her gown and looked at her there, naked before him, then he lifted her up in his arms as though she were a child and laid her on the bed. He loved her with such intense tenderness, almost as though repaying her for everything that had been taken away from her – her homeland, her father, her carefree youth. She responded with passion and ardour, guided by her instinct as a young, intact woman and by the instruction in the ageless acts of love imparted by her handmaids so that she would not disappoint her husband in their wedding bed.

While he held her in his arms, kissing her breasts, her soft belly and her slender, supple thighs, her moans of pleasure blended with the ancient song of Abrocome and Anthia, the lost lovers, sounding through the fragrant air like the sweetest, most harrowing of hymns.

He took her more than once, consummating their union with potent tenderness. Then he let himself relax by her side while she curled up next to him, caressing his arms and chest until she fell asleep, and the song, too, faded away into the night. The sound of some unknown instrument, smoother and more harmonious than a lyre, lingered in the air and then nothing more.

<p style="text-align:center">*</p>

The first light of the sun stirred Alexander at dawn. He started to get up and was about to call Leptine, as he usually did, when he saw that there before him was a long procession of people – men and women, all neatly lined up and evidently having waited for some time for his awakening.

In the partial awareness of being half awake, Alexander's first instinct was to reach for his sword, but he stopped himself. He sat up in bed and rested his back against the headboard before asking, more in amazement than in anger, 'Who are you?'

'We are your personal servants,' replied a eunuch, 'and I am in charge of your morning ceremony.'

Alexander shook Stateira who was still asleep and she too sat up, covering herself with a robe. 'What do I have to do now?' he whispered to her.

'Nothing, My Lord. They will take care of everything. That's what they're here for.'

Indeed, immediately afterwards the eunuch signalled to him to follow through to the bath chamber where two handmaids and another semi-naked eunuch washed, massaged and perfumed him, while Stateira was taken care of by her own maids.

Immediately afterwards the young and handsome eunuch approached and dried him gently, lingering diligently on the most sensitive areas of his body. Then it was time for them to dress him; one by one, on the supervising eunuch's signal, the maids came forward, each of them bearing one item of clothing which they slipped on with the most expert and delicate of movements – first of all underwear, which Alexander had

never used up to that moment, and then the trousers of embroidered byssus. He rejected them with a movement of his hand.

The eunuch shook his head and exchanged puzzled looks with the wardrobe supervisor.

'I don't wear trousers,' explained the King. 'Give me my *chiton*.'

'But, My Lord . . .' said the wardrobe chief, for whom it seemed absurd that someone might put on underwear without actually putting on the top layer as well.

'I don't wear trousers,' Alexander repeated categorically and, even though the man did not understand Greek, he understood the King's tone and his gesture perfectly. The maids struggled to stifle their laughter. The eunuch and the wardrobe attendant exchanged looks and then they sent a servant to fetch his Greek *chiton* and put it on him. At that point, however, they were not sure how to proceed with dressing him. The young and handsome eunuch then decided to take the initiative and had a handmaid give him a *kandys*, the splendid royal over-gown with its wide pleated sleeves, and handed it to Alexander to put on. He looked at it, then looked at the wardrobe attendant who continued to stare at him in ever greater surprise, and then with some reluctance he put it on. They then brought him the veil and draped it around his forehead and his neck, letting it fall in many rich folds over his shoulders.

Other servants sprayed perfume over him and the young eunuch brought a mirror so that he might look at himself and said to him in Greek, 'You look wonderful, my Lord.'

Alexander was surprised that this youngster spoke Greek so well and asked him, 'What is your name?'

'My name is Bagoas. I was King Darius's personal servant and I was his favourite. No one knew how to please him as I did. Now I am yours, if you want me,' and he said these words with a voice so suave and sensual that the King was taken aback. He did not answer as he looked at the image reflected in the sheet of polished silver and felt a sort of ingenuous satisfaction, feeling that the clothes actually suited him. He was about to go to Stateira to be admired, when the corridor suddenly resounded with the clacking of Macedonian studded shoes and immediately afterwards the Black appeared, armed to the teeth and visibly shaken. He began speaking before he even entered the room, 'Sire, there is important news from—' But, as soon as he saw Alexander, he stopped and his expression changed until he burst out laughing, 'By Zeus! But who are all these people? All these women and all these ball-less wonders! And then . . . what on earth are you wearing?'

Alexander did not laugh at all and indeed was clearly irritated and resentful when he replied, 'Stop it immediately! I must remind you that I am the King!'

'The King?' continued the Black. 'What King? I barely recognized you, you look like—'

'One more word and I'll have you stripped of your weapons and thrown into custody. Then we'll see if you find so much to laugh about.'

The Black lowered his head.

'What had you come to tell me?'

'News has arrived that Bessus is in Bactriana, where

he has proclaimed himself Great King, with the name Artaxerxes IV.'

'Anything else?'

'The reinforcements from Macedonia have been spotted on the road from Ecbatana, about seven thousand men and the squires are with them too. They'll be here by evening.'

'Good. I will meet them myself, at sunset. Have the army fall in.'

The Black left, biting his lip to stop himself saying anything else, but it was not long before the rumour was doing the rounds in the camp that Alexander was dressed up like a Persian and was surrounded by women and eunuchs.

'It can't be true!' exclaimed Philotas when he heard. 'My father could never bear even to cast his eyes upon such a shameful spectacle.'

'I can well believe it,' replied Craterus. 'Wasn't it Alexander himself who warned us, when we were in Persepolis, that he hadn't brought us all this distance to see us behaving like those we have defeated?'

'I don't think there's anything strange in it,' said Hephaestion. 'You've already seen Alexander in Egypt dressed like a Pharaoh. Why when we're in Persia shouldn't he dress like the Great King? He has married the Great King's daughter and has inherited his realm.'

'Whatever Alexander does or says, for you it's always alright,' Philotas retorted, 'but King Philip would be horrified to see such a thing and—'

'Cut it out!' Hephaestion interrupted him. 'He is King and he has every right to do whatever he wishes. And

you are the ones who ought to be ashamed – you too, Black, for your behaviour. When he heaped favours on you, when he filled your tents with Persian gold, you all took it gladly, didn't you? You, Philotas, you were pleased when he nominated you supreme commander of the cavalry, no? And now you're all indignant about a few Persian rags. You make me laugh!'

'I make you laugh? I'll soon cure you of that!' shouted the Black who was already in a terrible mood, and he lifted his fist, ready to strike.

Ptolemy immediately stepped in to separate them and Seleucus backed him up: 'Stop right there! Have you gone mad? That's enough! Cut it out!'

The two of them moved apart, but continued staring at each other; Craterus moved over to Cleitus's side, as though to let him know that he was supporting him.

'Listen,' said Seleucus. 'It's idiotic to come to blows for these things. Alexander might well be dressed up in Persian clothes to please Stateira, or out of simple curiosity. We have always got on and we have to continue getting on together. We're right in the heart of a territory that is for the most part hostile. If we start arguing among ourselves then we're lost, don't you understand that?'

'These things aren't trifles,' came a familiar voice from behind him. Seleucus turned, 'Callisthenes—'

'I repeat, these things are not trifles. Alexander left Greece as leader of the pan-Hellenic League with the task of destroying the Greeks' age-old enemy. This is his only true purpose, the one he solemnly swore to pursue at Corinth.'

'He razed Persepolis to the ground,' said Eumenes, who up until then had remained silent. 'Isn't that enough? He sacrificed the most beautiful palace in the world on the altar of the pan-Hellenic idea.'

'You're wrong,' retorted Callisthenes. 'He did it because he had no choice, and I tell you this because I have it from the most reliable source. Greece and the Greeks no longer meant anything to him at that point, just as, I fear, they mean nothing to him now.'

At that moment the trumpets sounded and a division of *hetairoi* in parade dress came out of the western gate of the camp at a gallop, lining up in two rows along the sides of the access road. Shortly afterwards there came the rhythmical sound of the drums and the regular march of an army moving closer.

'The reinforcements are here!' exclaimed Ptolemy. 'Alexander will arrive at any moment. Let's get ready, instead of standing here talking.'

Callisthenes shook his head as if to express his forbearance and moved off. The others went with greater or lesser haste to put on their armour so that they could line up with the rest of the army which was preparing to welcome the companions who had just arrived from Macedonia.

The new arrivals marched in perfect order across the field, saluted by shrill trumpet blasts and by the *hetairoi* division which presented arms, and then went to line up before the podium which stood alongside the royal tent. Behind them were the ranks of the massed army. The squires, the young sons of the finest Macedonian nobility, stood out more than all the others because of their white

capes and their red *chitons*. They had come here to serve King Alexander just as Perdiccas, Ptolemy, Lysimachus and the other Companions had come to serve King Philip in the palace at Pella.

Then came the sound of yet more trumpet blasts and this time they all turned towards the eastern gate because they had been told that the King would make his entrance there.

'Oh by the gods,' said Ptolemy under his breath as he raised one hand to his forehead. 'He's still wearing the Persian clothes.'

'This way they'll all know how to behave,' said Seleucus impassibly. 'It's the best thing, believe me.'

Alexander arrived at a gallop astride Bucephalas and his Persian clothes made of the finest byssus flew in the wind like veils. The scarf that framed his face and moved down to cross his chest and then his shoulders gave him an unusual look, but one that nevertheless was strangely attractive.

He leaped to the ground before the podium and slowly climbed the steps leading up to the platform, then, dressed as he was, he turned and faced the Macedonian army with its veterans and its new recruits, before the astonished eyes of everyone, from the companions to the very last soldier – even the young men lined up directly under the stage stared at him as though they could not believe what they were seeing.

'I wanted to come in person,' he began, 'to welcome these our recent recruits who have been sent to us by the regent Antipater and to welcome the young men that the nobles of Macedonia have sent to us so that they will

grow in the service of their King and learn to become valiant and loyal warriors. I read the astonishment in your eyes, as though a ghost had appeared here before you, but I know what the reason is – it is this coat I am wearing, a *kandys*, and this cloth I am wearing around my head. This in fact is Persian dress that I am wearing over my Greek warrior's *chiton*, and I want you to know that I have done this deliberately because now I am no longer simply the King of Macedon. I am also Pharaoh of Egypt, King of the Babylonians and Great King of the Persians. Darius is dead and I have married the Princess Stateira, and therefore I am his successor. As such I claim authority over the whole empire that was his and intend to make use of this authority by pursuing the usurper Bessus wherever he may be hiding. We will get him. And we will inflict on him the punishment he deserves.

'Now I will distribute gifts to the new arrivals and this evening you will all have a special supper with plenty of good wine. I want you to enjoy yourselves and I want you to be in good spirits because before long we will set off once again and we will not stop until we have achieved our goal!'

There was some lukewarm applause, but Alexander did nothing to provoke any warmer, more enthusiastic reaction. He was aware of what was going through the minds of his men and his companions, and he realized just how puzzled were the young men, the squires who had just arrived from Macedonia; for them he was already a living legend, and here they found themselves before a man dressed in the clothes of the recently defeated barbarians, clothes which had a definite feminine feel

about them. And that was not all – what he was about to say was even worse.

He waited until there was silence and then began speaking again: 'The enterprise we are about to undertake is no less difficult than the feats we have accomplished up to now, and the fresh troops who have just arrived from Macedonia are not enough – we will have to pit ourselves against enemies we have never seen nor fought against before, we will have to impose garrisons in so many cities and fortresses, clash with armies still more numerous than those we defeated at Issus and at Gaugamela.' Total silence now fell on the camp and all the warriors' eyes were fixed on Alexander, their ears poised so as not to miss a single word. 'It is for this reason that I have taken a decision you may not approve of, but it is absolutely necessary – we cannot use up the lifeblood of our homeland with the continual calling up of young men, neither can we leave its defences unmanned. I have therefore arranged to recruit thirty thousand Persians and to train them in Macedonian military techniques. Training will begin immediately – by tomorrow the military leaders of all the Satrapies of the empire will receive precise instructions.'

No one applauded, no one asked to speak, no one made a sound. In that stony silence, the King was alone as he never had been before. Only Hephaestion moved closer and held the bridle while Alexander leaped astride Bucephalas and immediately disappeared at a gallop.

32

Eumenes rolled up the document and looked Callisthenes in the eye, 'So this, for you, is Alexander?'

'Perhaps I should say, "This is what Alexander should be,"' replied Callisthenes with a puzzled expression in his eyes.

'The historian's role ought to be that of recounting the facts as they happen, after having witnessed them himself or after having consulted reliable eye witnesses,' replied the Secretary as though reciting some memorized formula.

'You think I'm not aware of what a historian's task is? But I also have to try to interpret Alexander's soul and his thoughts and render them understandable for those who will read my work. I allowed you to read what I have written up to now because I need your support and because you write the expedition's journal every day, but especially because—'

'Because he is moving beyond the margins of your page, beyond the confines you had marked out for him in your work?'

'Perhaps.'

'Then you have to put your mind at rest – Alexander is no longer the person we knew; perhaps in truth he never was that person.'

'He took an oath before all the Greeks to lead a pan-Hellenic expedition against Persia, the age-old enemy.'

'He has done that. And he won. He is the leader of all the Greeks.'

Callisthenes started and got to his feet, evidently irritated, 'Yes, but now he is becoming one of them – he dresses like them, he is surrounded by eunuchs and concubines, he is having them instructed in our combat techniques; apparently he's even having Persian lessons, they say that . . . yesterday, during one of his wild parties, he actually kissed that . . . that Bagoas on the mouth in public.'

'He has decided to scandalize all those who look at these things in the same way you do,' retorted Eumenes. 'He wants to show you that we have reached a point where there is no turning back. As for the parties, I don't believe ours were any less barbaric. We have to learn to accept that which is and that which always has been, believe me, and we have to forget the image we had created because it gave us peace of mind.'

'Peace of mind?'

'Yes. The image you provide in your *History* is a reassuring one, easy to understand and love for a well-educated Greek with reasonably moderate ideas – but Alexander is something quite different.'

'Oh, there is no doubt about that, and with every day that passes he misses no opportunity to remind us of the fact. The men are worried, the new recruits and the young squires who have just arrived from Macedonia are shocked. They thought they were coming here to serve a hero, a conqueror, heir to Achilles and Hercules, but

instead they see a man dressed like a woman who introduces barbaric customs and contemptible, shameful habits.'

'Customs that are simply different from those we are used to, Callisthenes. He has led us into territory that no Greek had ever crossed before, under another sky, across deserts and highlands; he has led us beyond the Nile, the Tigris and the Euphrates and he is dreaming of the Indus. Nothing could remain as it was, don't you understand?'

'I understand it, but I will never accept it.'

'Have you told him?'

'Certainly.'

'And what did he say?'

'He said, "Write whatever you like, Callisthenes." Nothing means anything to him any more, he doesn't care.'

Eumenes said nothing else; he was aware that Callisthenes was so disillusioned that nothing now could shift him from the conviction and the ideas that had formed in his mind. It was late, and he stood up to leave, but before crossing the threshold he turned because he felt he still had something to say to Callisthenes and some advice to give him, 'Alexander changes continually because his curiosity is insatiable and his vital force is inexhaustible. He is like the halcyon, the bird they say never lands on earth during its life and which even sleeps as it flies, being carried along by the wind. If you do not feel up to following him, Callisthenes, then go now, turn back while there is still time.'

Eumenes left, leaving the historian to meditate over these words and to read through the lines of his *History*

of Alexander's Expedition in the lamplight. A servant's voice broke into his concentration some time later, 'Lord, there is a man here who arrived with the reinforcements and who has been looking for you for some time. He says he must speak to you.'

'Show him through and pour something to drink for us.'

The man entered and introduced himself: his name was Evonymous, a native of Byzantium, but he lived near Neapolis, in Thrace. A great wise man of Stagira had entrusted him with a message to be delivered to Callisthenes, paying him for his trouble and guaranteeing that the recipient would give him more money.

'I am Callisthenes,' he said, reaching for his purse, 'and here are two bright staters for your kindness. May I have the message now?'

The man handed over the missive, pocketed the money, drank a glass of wine and left.

The message read:

Aristotle to his nephew Callisthenes, Hail!

I hope this finds you in good health. Unfortunately I have a pain in my shoulder that torments me and means I have no rest, not even at night. I wonder where you will be when this letter reaches you and I hope you are in good spirits. For some time now I have been receiving a certain number of rare plants and animals from Alexander for my collections, which indicates that you are moving increasingly far away towards remote, unknown lands.

For my part, whenever I am free from my commit-

ments at the Academy, I return to Macedon and Thrace to continue my investigations. The man who said his name was Nicander and claimed to have been Pausanias's accomplice in Philip's assassination, in truth is called Eupithos, and, as I told you in a previous letter, he has a daughter whom he kept hidden away in a temple to Artemis in Thrace, near Salmydessus. I found this girl with the help of one of Antipater's officers and I had her taken into custody in a place where her father might see her and thus come round to the idea that he would have to speak if he wanted her back.

I think he has told me all he knows, which is that Pausanias was killed by one of the Epirote guards who was actually working with the assassins and that he, Eupithos, was given the job of finding a hiding place for that guard and making sure he disappeared without trace. All the clues seem to confirm our suspicions of the Queen Mother, but it makes sense to continue to reason things out with as few prejudices as possible until everything has been clarified.

This man is still alive and he is hidden away in a village in Phocis, not far from Haliartus. I intend to go there, just as soon as the weather, terrible now, improves slightly and when this pain in my shoulder relents.

Take good care.

Callisthenes closed the letter, put out the lamp and lay down on his bed, trying to think of something that might send him to sleep.

The march began again a few days later and on the evening before their departure, all Alexander's Companions

and the commanders of the great divisions of the pha-
lanx and the *hetairoi* cavalry received silver tack for their
horses, after the Persian fashion, together with cloaks of
purple cloth. No one dared refuse them, not even Cleitus
the Black, but neither he nor Philotas made use of them.
Stateira was sent back to Ecbatana with her ladies in
waiting and from there she was to go to visit her father's
tomb in the rock at Persepolis. Alexander was very sorry
to part from her.

'Will you think of me?' the girl asked him as her
handmaids prepared her for the journey.

'Always, even in the midst of battle, even when I am
so far away that our familiar constellations will appear in
the sky low down on the horizon. And you too must
think of me, my sweet bride.'

'Will you take Bagoas with you?' Stateira asked with
just the slightest hint of malice.

'Yes,' replied Alexander. 'I find him amusing and he
manages to pull me up even when I am oppressed by
troubles and cares. He dances and sings enchantingly.'

'And he is also very handsome,' said Stateira. 'His hips
are perfect, the envy of even the most graceful of maids,
and his skin is as smooth and soft as a rose petal. I
suppose you can consider him as my gift to you because
I was the one who gave him to my father.'

Alexander held her in a long embrace and then he
helped her climb into her carriage, 'If you should realize
that you are pregnant, let me know immediately, wher-
ever I may be, with the fastest messenger in the city. I
have written to Harpalus, my treasurer, telling him to
put all you need at your disposal.'

'What I need is you,' replied the girl, 'but one cannot have everything. Be careful, do not always be the first to put your life in danger. I could never bear losing you,' and she kissed him again on the lips, while the sun rose from behind the high peaks of the Hyrcanian Mountains.

At that moment there came the sound of thousands of hooves, the shouting of mule drivers and a great squeaking of wheels. Alexander turned and saw an interminable line of carriages similar to the one on which Stateira was about to set off, and this convoy was manoeuvring to tag on immediately after the last divisions of the army, escorted by armed Persian horsemen.

'But . . . who are they?' the King asked the Persian officer who was leading the escort.

'Your concubines, my beloved husband,' replied Stateira before the officer even managed to open his mouth. 'Three hundred and sixty-five – one for each day of the year, each with her own entourage, naturally.'

'My concubines? But I am off to war and—'

'You cannot travel without them. Each of them is the daughter of a king who is our ally or of some powerful leader of the tribes of the steppes. You must not make enemies of them, for this would force them into an alliance with Bessus.'

'No,' replied Alexander with concern in his voice. 'Certainly not.'

33

THE ARMY SET OFF eastwards not long after, proceeding over rolling highlands covered with rich vegetation. The news that the entire Persian court, apart from Princess Stateira, was now following the expedition soon spread throughout all the divisions. The reactions ranged from sarcasm to worry and even derision in some cases. More than once Hephaestion found himself about to unsheathe his sword to defend his King's honour, but Ptolemy and Seleucus had positioned themselves by his side and immediately calmed any challenges and fights that could easily have degenerated into much worse trouble.

After twenty days' march, while the guides were about to head north towards Bactriana where Bessus had taken refuge, news came that Satibarzanes and Barsaentes, satraps of the provinces of Aria and Arachosia, had rebelled and were preparing an army to take the invaders from behind.

Alexander immediately called a war council and appeared at it dressed in Greek armour, but no one failed to notice that as well as the ring with the Argead star, he also wore one with the Persian royal seal.

'Friends,' he began, 'you will have heard that our march must now change direction – we have to head south to quash the rebellion of Satibarzanes and Barsaen-

tes. This is what we will do: while Craterus follows with the infantry, I will set off with the cavalry. Philotas, Hephaestion, Ptolemy, Lysimachus and Leonnatus will all follow me. Perdiccas and Seleucus will remain with Craterus. We will attack the rebels as quickly as we possibly can, before they realize that we have changed route, and we will wipe them out. Craterus will provide us with support as soon as he arrives, if we need it. If anyone has any better idea, please let me hear it now.'

No one spoke, no one laughed or joked or made any wisecrack as they normally did. There was a strained atmosphere of discontent and embarrassment. Everyone had heard how the King had treated Cleitus at Zadracarta when he had criticized him for his clothes. Everyone was thinking, without saying anything, about how much work was involved in escorting the enormous entourage of concubines, servants and eunuchs who slowed up the march pointlessly. Everyone had tales to tell of continual episodes of friction and mutual intolerance between Macedonian and Persian troops.

Alexander searched their faces one by one, for expressions of friendship or of understanding, but they all lowered their eyes, almost ashamed to make any display of the positive feelings they had nourished for him over so many years.

'You don't seem very enthusiastic,' he said in a deliberately humble tone. 'Have I perhaps treated you badly? Have I disappointed you in some way? Come now, speak!'

Hephaestion piped up, 'They're too frightened to say it, but they're afraid. Look at them! Now they are rich

and they hope to enjoy life, they're afraid. They are critical of you because you dress too luxuriantly, because you have this following of Persian soldiers and all those girls, but they would like to do the same things, perhaps comfortably billeted in some fine palace located between here and the Phoenician coast. They have forgotten the promises they made to follow you wherever, even to the ends of the earth. Isn't that so, men? Isn't that it? Come along, say something . . . or has the proverbial cat got your tongues?'

'That's enough, Hephaestion,' Craterus said. 'I am ready to give my life for the King, here, right now, and all our companions are ready to do the same thing. It is not only a matter of clothes or concubines: the men need to know when this war will finish. They need to know where it will end and how much time is required to reach that point. They cannot continue discovering day by day, at the very last moment, that there is to be yet another stage, and then another again. Northwards . . . no, southwards . . . or perhaps we shall head westwards now? They need to see something familiar in you, Alexander, to know that you are still their King. They are willing to follow you, but they can no longer live in such conditions of uncertainty, living day by day without hope, without any sort of security.'

Alexander nodded without saying anything, as though taking in a situation that he could not even have imagined just a month previously. Hephaestion spoke once more at that point: 'But what have you all told your men? You, Philotas, you are now commander-in-chief of the cavalry, what have you told your *hetairoi*? Are you

still telling them that Alexander would never have suc-
ceeded in doing anything without the help of you and
your father? That he has become spineless? That every
night his only concern is to watch his concubines parade
naked before him and to choose the one who will look
after his dick? That he no longer reads, that he's no
longer worried about his men and their fate?'

'These are all lies!' shouted Philotas, his temper flaring.
'I never said anything of the kind!'

'Whatever,' replied Hephaestion, 'but these are the
rumours one hears and they were already doing the
rounds in Cilicia after the Battle of Issus, and in Egypt
following our return from the Oasis of Ammon.'

'It's all untrue! Lies! Bring me the person who said
these words, find just one person to support openly what
I have been accused of, if you have the courage. Yester-
day came news that my brother Nicanor was wounded
at Zadracarta, struck by an arrow during a patrol on the
Hyrcanian mountains, and no physician has as yet been
able to cure him: I ask you now if anyone has bothered
to ask after him? Has it occurred to anyone that my
father, having already lost his youngest son, now runs
the risk of losing another one? Have any of you heard
me ask for leave to stay with him and help him?'

'You are commander-in-chief of the cavalry and this
role is important enough in itself to make you forget all
about poor Nicanor,' Hephaestion retorted sarcastically.

Philotas stood up and made a move as though about
to attack Alexander's friend, but Ptolemy blocked him
and then turned to look Hephaestion straight in the eyes,
'Stop it!' he shouted. 'It is not right to speak of Philotas

in this way. Nicanor is dying, I had news just a short time ago from a messenger, before this council started. He might already be . . .'

A grave silence fell over the council tent and for one endless moment all that could be heard was the whistling of the wind across the highland – the disconcerting voice of an infinite solitude – together with the flapping of the royal standard against its flagpole. Philotas covered his face with his hands; Hephaestion had lowered his eyes and knew not what to say now. Seleucus and Ptolemy exchanged worried looks, each looking in vain in the other's eyes for some idea of how to unblock the unbearable tension. Peritas, who had curled up at Alexander's feet, lifted his nose towards his master and whined. It was as though he felt the weight lying on Alexander's soul.

Alexander stroked him, then he stood up and said, 'I am sincerely sorry for Nicanor, but I must know if I can count on all of you.'

Craterus looked at his companions, then he stood up in his turn and walked towards Alexander, 'How can you doubt us? Have we not always been with you? Haven't we always fought to the very last, haven't we received all sorts of wounds in our battles? All we wish to know is what you want from us, but above all else what you want from the men who have followed you this far.'

'I want to be understood,' replied Alexander, 'because I have not changed. What I do are things that must be done.'

'May I speak?' Leonnatus asked him at that point.

'Of course.'

'The men are afraid that you want to become a sort of Great King, that you want to force them to behave like Persians and force the Persians to behave like them.'

'If I had wanted to become like the Great King, do you think I would have burned the palace at Persepolis and the throne room there? Tomorrow we set off on our march once again: Eumolpus of Soloi has informed me that Satibarzanes is now at Artacoanta. We leave at dawn. Whoever feels he doesn't want to continue may leave now with his men.'

'But Alexander, we . . .' Leonnatus sought to reply, but the King simply stood up and left.

Philotas raised his head and looked around at his companions, 'He has no right to treat us in this manner. He has no right.'

Alexander in the meantime reached his tent and entered. Eumolpus of Soloi was waiting for him.

'Is there any more news of Satibarzanes?' he asked, sitting down on a chair.

'He is preparing for battle, but his troops are disheartened: I don't think they will fight to the bitter end. How did the council go?'

Alexander shrugged his shoulders.

'Don't let it get to you. They simply have to come round to the novelty of the situation. They are all very much attached to their own traditions and in my opinion they're also jealous – they're afraid that you are somehow moving away from them, that they are no longer as close to you as they once were.'

'You seem to know them very well.'

'Well enough.'

'What do you mean by that?'

'I mean that after Issus, when I started working for you again, I took an interest in your friends as well. Who do you think put the girls in their beds?'

'You. But I didn't . . .'

'Ah! Nonsense! If a job's worth doing . . . and then pillow talk is my speciality. You know that men are inclined to talk much more freely after a good fuck? Interesting point, don't you think?'

'Stop it.'

'And the girls told me everything.'

'My friends would never betray me.'

'Perhaps not. But some might be more easily led into temptation than others. Philotas, for example, your commander-in-chief of the cavalry – a man with an important role.'

Alexander was suddenly much more alert: 'What have you heard about Philotas?'

'Not much – but back then he was telling everyone that you were simply a presumptuous little boy, that without him and his father you would never have won any battle – neither at the Granicus, nor at Issus – and that you treated them unfairly.'

'Why didn't you tell me about this immediately?'

'Because you wouldn't have listened.'

'And why should I listen now?'

'Because you are in danger. You are about to cross through completely unknown lands, to face savage peoples. You have to know who you can count on and who you can't count on. Be careful of your cousin Amyntas as well.'

'I have had him kept under discreet surveillance ever since that first episode when I had him arrested in Anatolia. He has always behaved valiantly and has always been loyal.'

'Indeed – a loyal and valiant prince. If you should ever fall out of favour with your men, to whom would they turn?'

Alexander stared at him in silence and it was Eumolpus who gave verbal expression to the answer he read in the King's eyes, 'To the only survivor of the Argead dynasty. May the gods grant you a peaceful night's sleep.'

He stood up, nodded gently and then, having made sure that Peritas was not following, set off towards his own tent.

34

ALL ASIA UNFOLDED before Alexander's army, and its landscapes became ever harsher and more desolate; these now were rocky terrains, realm of scorpions and snakes, rendered arid by the sun as it shone relentlessly. Here and there thorny bushes grew in dried-up riverbeds and ponds, all bordered with vast expanses of salt deposits. For days on end the soldiers marched in silence without any relief, without a single breath of wind bringing any freshness to the suffocating heat.

The very sky itself was empty and incandescent, as dazzling in its brightness as a polished bronze shield, and whenever they spotted the slow movement of wings off in the distance, the birds always proved to be vultures drawing circles around pack animals that had lost their way or had already given up in the battle against death and were now laid out for the scavengers among the deserted rocks.

Not even the journey to the Oasis of Ammon had been as anguish-ridden as this because the dunes of the desert had their own majestic beauty with their sharp crests, their clear contrasts of shadow and light – the purity of their graceful, changing shapes, sculpted by the wind. Like some golden ocean that had suddenly been left motionless by a gesture from some god's hand, the

dunes had been a grand and solemn setting for an imminent epiphany.

These rock-strewn lands, however, inspired thoughts of nothing but death, of empty solitude, of immutable desolation, and in his heart each of the men nurtured some deep nostalgia, a harrowing desire to return home. There was no objective, no meaning that gave any sense to their endless fatigue, and they took each step with growing reluctance, overwhelmed by the dread of that limitless, featureless landscape in which their local guides' only certainty appeared to be knowledge of some destination beyond the shimmering horizon. The most glorious days of their enterprise now seemed so very far away, and many of the men appeared to regret having responded positively to the King's call. None of them could understand what he was looking for so far inland, in these wastelands that provided sustenance only to occasional villages with homes made of mud bricks covered with camel or sheep dung.

Then, gradually, the landscape began to change and the very air became fresher and sharper. Highlands appeared, watered occasionally by the rains and covered by a light green veil of vegetation, nourishing here and there a solitary tree or small herds of shaggy dromedaries or bristly-haired horses. They approached a river valley and then the banks of a huge lake on whose waters they finally saw a reflection of the walls and towers of Artacoana, the capital of the Arians, the fortress of Satibarzanes.

The army did not even have enough time to spread out before the doors of the fortress were flung open and

a squadron of horsemen rushed out to attack, shouting loudly and lifting a cloud of red dust that billowed up over the plain. Philotas and Craterus had the alarm trumpets sounded and the *hetairoi* spurred on their tired and thirst-stricken horses.

Immediately after the initial clash they seemed to be having the worst of it. Their opponents were rested and fresh. Nevertheless they fought valiantly as they moved in measured retreat, always seeking support from their comrades who ran forward in waves to join them as the trumpets sounded.

Alexander then sent the Persian soldiers into the attack. Up until that moment he had kept them in reserve to protect the carriages and the entourage of courtiers and concubines. Their Parthian horses, more inured to bear the heat and the fatigue, threw themselves into a gallop with just as much impetus as their adversaries. The Median and Hyrcanian warriors, together with the last remaining Immortals, keen to make a good impression before the King, drove into the enemy ranks, opening up breaches and spreading confusion as they went. Dressed in similar fashion to the enemy, they did not stand out and this was a great advantage as they struck with devastating force during that first charge.

The intensity of the battle gradually lessened, the front fragmented into smaller clusters of furious fighting and the horsemen of the Vanguard, who up until that point had not taken to the field, mounted their steeds and rushed towards the enemy's flank, led by the King in person. Satibarzanes' men were hit hard and pushed backwards, enough of a shock to leave them suddenly

disheartened, and at that point Perdiccas unleashed the Agrianian foot soldiers, armed with their knives and their long, sharp hooks. The thick dust protected them as they moved like ghosts, singling out their victims and striking with precision so that none of their blows was wasted.

On seeing that his attack had failed, Satibarzanes had the horns sounded for their retreat and his troops turned back, not without more losses, through the walls and into the city. Soon a wind rose up, sweeping away the dust and revealing hundreds of bodies scattered over the field, many of them already fatal casualties, but some of them wounded, crying out for help in their pain.

The Agrianians moved from man to man, cutting the throats of all the enemy soldiers and stripping them of their weapons and ornaments – all of this under the eyes of the women who looked on from the top of the walls, tearing their hair and crying out heart-wrenchingly to the sky.

Eumenes had given orders to set up camp and to build defences all around it in the form of a trench and a dyke. As he supervised the works he could hear the soldiers' grumbling about the King's decision to use the Persians in the attack on Satibarzanes' army.

'Why did he need to use those barbarians?' they asked. 'We could have managed perfectly on our own. Our infantry wasn't even deployed.'

'That's right,' someone agreed. 'The King was obviously out to humiliate us and this simply isn't right, after all the hard work we have put in and all the dangers we have faced.'

'But what can we do?' commented another. 'He's one

of them now, surrounded by Persian guards, taking his bath with that eunuch who gives him massages and who knows what else, and then he drags around all those concubines while we're left to stand guard . . .'

Eumenes listened on in silence because these were words that hurt.

Eumolpus of Soloi listened too; even though he stood to one side and spent most of his time sitting under his tent, he had many ears and eyes and very little, if anything, escaped his notice. Despite all of this information, however, Eumolpus had no idea that for the first time in his life events were about to surprise him.

The camp was set up now and everyone was getting ready to rest for the night. As the sun descended behind the ochre walls of Artacoana, the long, plaintive sound of a horn rose into the air. Oxhatres, who had been the King's guide on the road to Ecbatana and Zadracarta, drew close to Alexander and said in his rapidly-improving Greek, 'This is a herald. One of Satibarzanes' heralds.'

'Go to them, Oxhatres, perhaps they want to negotiate . . . to surrender.'

Oxhatres mounted his horse and rode towards the city walls while a lone emissary came towards him. They soon met up and exchanged a few words before they both returned to their respective camps.

In the meantime the King's Companions had all gathered around him to report on their losses in the battle and to make their proposals for the following day's action. Oxhatres appeared just then and made his own report: 'Satibarzanes challenges the strongest of you to a

duel. If he wins, you leave; if he loses, you take the city.'

The blood immediately rushed to Alexander's head as his mind filled with all the scenes of duels between Homeric champions that had populated his childhood imagination. 'I will go,' he said, without hesitating.

'No,' replied Ptolemy immediately. 'No King of Macedon will stoop to fight a satrap. Choose someone to represent you.'

Oxhatres intervened at this point, 'Satibarzanes is big and strong,' and he lifted up his arms to suggest the imposing mass of their opponent.

'I will go,' said Leonnatus. 'I too am big enough and strong enough.'

Alexander looked him up and down and nodded, as though reassuring himself and his Companions. Then he clapped a hand on his friend's back. 'I agree. Tear him apart, Leonnatus.'

*

The two champions faced each other at dawn the following day on a flat, open space and the two armies, with almost everyone present, lined up in semicircular formation on each side to watch the duel. Word had spread quickly among the Macedonian soldiers and with the news came febrile excitement. They all knew of Leonnatus's strength and his impressive physical ability and had had plenty of opportunity to admire it during their many decisive battles; they broke into cheers of encouragement as soon as they saw him appear, armed from head to

foot, bearing his great shield with its silver star on his left arm, wielding his shining steel sword in his right hand, and sporting a red-crested helmet.

When the Persian lines opened up to let Leonnatus's opponent through, however, many of the Macedonians were stunned into silence: Satibarzanes was truly gigantic in stature and moved forwards with slow, heavy steps. In his right hand he held a long, curved sabre, its blade obviously extremely sharp. His shield was of wood, covered with highly polished scales of iron, and his helmet was of the Assyrian type. Attached to it was a studded leather neck covering that reached his shoulders, together with a chain-mail throat band. His thick raked moustache and his black eyebrows, united across the bridge of his nose, all combined to grant him a fierce and daunting air.

Soon they were facing each other and looking into each other's eyes without saying a word, simply waiting for the signal from the two heralds – one Macedonian, the other Persian. The interpreter translated: 'The noble Satibarzanes proposes a fight to the death with no fixed rules – strength and valour alone will win this day.'

'Tell him I agree,' replied Leonnatus, gripping his sword tightly and readying himself for the first blows.

The heralds gave the signal for the duel to begin, the duel that could now only finish with the death of one of the two warriors.

Leonnatus moved closer, seeking out some opening in his opponent's defences, while the Persian managed to cover himself almost completely with his shield and held his sabre low, as though not in the least worried. But

when Leonnatus attacked, Satibarzanes unleashed a swiping blow that caught him full on the helmet, making him rock and sway in confusion.

'Back!' shouted Alexander, clearly rattled. 'Leonnatus, move back! Cover yourself . . . keep your guard up!' His instinct was to run to his friend's aid, but he had given his word as King that no one at all would intervene in the clash.

Satibarzanes struck again and again, while Leonnatus tried to fend off the blows with his shield before him as he moved backwards on his shaking legs. The whole army watched, impotent observers of the rain of terrible blows crashing down on their champion. On the other side the Persians shouted encouragement to their giant who advanced inexorably, seeking out a chance to inflict the mortal blow. Leonnatus, still unable to react, fell to his knees and another swipe from his adversary first caught the silver star on his shield, a frightful omen for the Macedonian soldiers, and then tore the flesh from his shoulder, sending up a spray of blood.

At the sight of this an anguished cry of disappointment ran through the ranks of the *pezhetairoi* and tears came to many of their eyes as they waited for the fatal blow to be unleashed by the Persian, but the pain, as sharp and as startling as the lash of a whip, brought Leonnatus his second wind. The Macedonian champion started to his feet with remarkable energy and in one deft movement tore his dented helmet from his head and hurled it away. At the same moment he caught sight of his own wound, spurting blood, and realized instantly that he did not have much time before his strength abandoned him

completely: he rushed forward with a wild cry, crashing into his opponent's shield with his own.

Satibarzanes was taken by surprise and was visibly shocked by this new aggression as he lost his balance. Leonnatus made the most of this momentary advantage and struck out once, twice, three times with his sword while the Persian tried to parry the blows with his own weapon. Satibarzanes fell backwards and Leonnatus let fly with even greater strength, but the blade of his sword snapped in two against the higher quality of the satrap's metal.

The Persian reacted, soon regaining his balance, and then moved forward towards his unarmed enemy. He raised his sabre on high and it glinted menacingly in the rising sun, but just as he was about to strike, Lysimachus shouted, 'Catch, Leonnatus!' as he threw his double headed axe. Leonnatus caught it cleanly and in a flash, before Satibarzanes let fly with his sabre, he chopped the Persian's arm clean off; his opponent stood motionless, petrified by the pain, and another blow from Leonnatus cut straight through the Persian's neck and his head rolled across the ground, its big black eyes still wide open in astonishment.

A great cry of exultation rose up from the Macedonian ranks and immediately the attendants ran to offer help to their champion, pale now as a result of his labours and the loss of blood. They carried him to Philip's tent so that the physician might save his life.

The Persians gathered round the dismembered body of their leader, forming a barrier to hide the terrible spectacle from the assembled ranks of their enemy and

only when Satibarzanes' body was recomposed and placed on a litter did they set off towards the city at a slow funeral march, leaving long streaks of blood on the ground behind them.

Artacoana surrendered before sunset that day.

35

ALEXANDER RENAMED THE city Alexandria of Aria when news came from Egypt that his first Alexandria, the one designed for him by the architect Dinocrates and built on the shore, was flourishing. Its trade was burgeoning and its population was growing day by day as new inhabitants came from all over to buy homes, land and gardens, so that it was enjoying great and tumultuous growth.

Alexander left a Macedonian governor at Alexandria of Aria, together with a small garrison of mercenaries to whom he assigned an income, properties, slaves and women. The idea was that they might set up families and thus come to feel themselves tied in some way to that remote, forgotten place, and perhaps their homesickness would never become too acute.

He waited until Leonnatus was fully recovered from the injuries sustained in the duel with Satibarzanes, then he gave orders for the army to set off northwards, along the green valley of a river that had many tributaries crisscrossing it continually, creating thousands of small green islands, which shone like emeralds, in a silver net. They were to march towards a chain of the highest mountains, which they'd been told made any other peak in the world seem like a small hill. This formidable barrier was called Paropamisus and it separ-

ated Bactriana from the limitless plains of Scythia, as vast as the ocean.

Leonnatus, his left shoulder still strapped up, had the servants prepare his baggage while Callisthenes, who seemed to be in an increasingly dark mood, looked on. The Macedonian champion asked him, 'Can it be that those mountains are actually higher than Olympus?'

'We are approaching places that none of us have ever seen before,' replied Callisthenes, 'we will meet peoples none of us knows. It is possible that those mountains mark the farthest ends of the earth and for this reason they are higher than any others we know. We are now in a land where everything and anything is possible, and everything and anything is absurd at the same time.'

'What do you mean?'

The historian lowered his head without replying and Leonnatus said nothing else. The great joy of his victory had soon soured with the discontent he felt spreading through the army, with the atmosphere of suspicion he sensed even among their leaders and officers. The only men who seemed truly enthusiastic about their achievements were the youngsters who had come from Macedonia to serve as squires to the King. They cast their eyes around in continual wonderment as they took in the majestic, stupendous landscape with its bright colours at sunset, the intense blue of its skies, suspended between the immaculate snow of the mountaintops, in the incredible splendour of the myriad stars in the clear nights.

Even nature itself amazed them with its continual changes – plants they had never seen before and animals they had only ever heard tale of. Someone spotted the

striped coat of a tiger down by the river – it was crossing over at dawn to hunt deer and gazelles or great curly-horned buffaloes that grazed on the other side.

The duties of the young squires often brought them to the royal residence alongside Alexander, as well as to the other residences of the King's Companions and the higher officers of the army. It was in this way that one of them, a slender, graceful and blond boy of fifteen by the name of Cebalinus, came to hear a terrible secret – a plot to kill the King!

He recounted the story to a slightly older friend of his, a youngster by the name of Aghirios who sometimes protected him against bullies, and had his bunk nearby in the dormitory tent. Cebalinus woke him up when all the others were sound asleep and the older lad rubbed his eyes as he sat on the edge of the bed and listened on, incredulous.

'If you're not absolutely sure of these things you have told me then say nothing to anyone,' was Aghirios's advice.

'I am sure. There is no doubt,' replied Cebalinus. 'I heard two officers of the phalanx discussing how, where and when.'

Aghirios shook his head, 'We've been here for just a matter of days and already we're involved in something like this. It's frightening.'

'What do you think I should do? Should I speak to the King?'

'No . . . you must be out of your mind. Not the King. We could never manage to speak to him directly, especially now that court protocol has become so compli-

cated. You might be able to speak to one of his Companions – Philotas, for example, he's supreme commander of the *hetairoi* cavalry and from tomorrow we'll be assigned to him as his attendants. He'll make sure the King is warned.'

'I think you're right,' replied Cebalinus. 'That's good advice.'

'Sleep now,' said Aghirios. 'Tomorrow our commander is going to wake us up at dawn for horseback training.'

The young man tried to get to sleep, but the enormity of the secret he now bore was too great and he lay there on his back for a long time, his eyes wide open in the darkness, tormented by this bloody regicidal nightmare. At the same time he was deeply excited as he sensed the great merit that might come his way with his revelation of the plot, as he thought that Alexander III of Macedon in person, the conqueror of Memphis, Babylon and Susa, might owe his life to him, Cebalinus, the smallest of the squires, the one who always bore the brunt of the others' scorn and practical jokes.

He got dressed before the morning trumpet was sounded and took breakfast in silence with the other squires, sitting next to Aghirios.

'Hey! The cat has got Cebalinus's tongue!' said a companion.

'Leave him alone!' Aghirios shut him up. 'You're all so good at picking on those smaller than you.'

'Well . . . do you want me to start on you, by any chance?'

Aghirios ignored the provocation and finished eating,

then they all followed the commander who led them towards the horse stockades for their daily training.

Cebalinus was so preoccupied he fell several times during training, acquiring a considerable number of bruises, but no one thought anything of it, putting it down to his usual ineptitude.

That evening, before supper, he was admitted, together with his friend, to Philotas's quarters in order to help the General take off his armour and to help him look after his weapons – shine his breastplate and greaves, check the straps on his shield, sharpen his sword and spear. They set about their work enthusiastically and Cebalinus anxiously waited for the right moment to speak to Philotas, but he could not quite pluck up enough courage.

So it was that he said nothing, neither that day nor the day after.

Aghirios encouraged him to speak up: 'The General will surely praise you for telling him of the conspiracy. You mustn't be afraid. Time is slipping by and any moment now the conspirators might decide to kill the King. Come on, what are you waiting for?'

The young man made up his mind and the following evening, when Philotas was about to go out, he finally managed to speak, 'Commander . . .'

Philotas turned, 'What is it, lad?'

'I must speak with you, Sire.'

'I have no time now. What is it about?'

'It is about a most important matter. It regards the King's life.'

Philotas froze suddenly on the threshold, shocked as

though struck by a bolt of lightning, but he did not turn round to face Cebalinus.

'What do you mean by that?'

'I mean his life is in grave danger. Someone wants to kill him and—'

Philotas closed the door abruptly and turned, 'Madmen!' he hissed through his teeth, 'They simply wouldn't listen to me . . .' The youngster moved backwards, frightened by this reaction, but then Philotas gave him a look of encouragement, 'What is your name, boy?'

'My name is Cebalinus.'

'Fine. Sit down here and tell me what you know. We'll sort everything out, you'll see.'

36

THE DAY DESIGNATED for their departure was drawing closer and Alexander had Princess Stateira come from Zadracarta, so that he could spend some time with her before what would be a long separation. He met her as she came along the road and as soon as she saw him she alighted from the carriage and ran to him like a young girl rushing to the arms of her first love. He too dismounted and held her to himself as she wrapped her arms around his neck. He was completely enamoured of her fresh ingenuousness, her docile and accommodating nature, and the fact that she made no demands on him, not even in the letters she wrote.

Then they set off on foot, talking like old friends, in the direction of the King's residence in Alexandria of Aria and Stateira noticed all the building sites that would make a Greek city of old Artacoana: the gods' temples on the highest level, the gymnasium to one side of the square for the young warriors' training, the theatre for dramatic productions.

'What moves me most of all,' said the King, 'is to think that in this place so far away from Athens, from Corinth and from Pella, the poetry of Euripides and Sophocles will soon be heard. Have you ever seen one of our tragedies?'

'No,' replied Stateira, 'but I have heard tale of them. A story is told, there are actors who recite, a chorus that dances and sings, is that not how it is? My tutor told me how he had once seen a tragedy in one of the *yauna* cities on the coast.'

'That's more or less how it works,' replied Alexander, 'but actually to witness these dramas is quite another thing – in this way the emotions and the passions of the ancient heroes and their women are relived, just as though they were alive and real once again.'

Stateira squeezed his arm to let him know how moved and excited she was by his words.

'I would like to wait for the theatre to be completed, but there is no time. The usurper Bessus is about to cross the Paropamisus to join up with the Scythian tribes of the great plains. I must reach him and dispense justice, and therefore I have arranged for the drama to be performed tomorrow on a wooden stage with wooden terraces. I will depart the day after.'

'May I sleep with you this evening?' Stateira asked him. Then she whispered, 'Believe me when I tell you I have travelled seventy parasangs on this carriage for this and no other reason.'

Alexander smiled, 'I hope I am worth such a sacrifice. In the meantime I will make sure suitable accommodation is found for you.' They had now reached his residence, the palace that had been Satibarzanes', and the women took care of the Princess and led her to her rooms.

The King visited her that evening, coming from the camp where he had spent the afternoon checking on the

preparations for their departure. The sun had slipped below the horizon and the last golden rays gilded the occasional clouds that floated slowly across the sky, but looking eastwards the heavens were already dark and it was in that direction that Alexander noticed the flames of a solitary fire.

'Who is that down there?' he asked his guards.

'Perhaps it is a shepherd preparing his meal before going to sleep,' came the answer, but when they moved closer, they saw a white cloak flapping in the evening breeze.

'Aristander,' the King murmured as he urged his horse on towards the fire. The guards made ready to follow him, but he nodded to them to stay where they were and they had to obey.

The seer stood before a pile of stones on which the fire was burning, his gaze fixed on the flickering flames as they consumed the acacia twigs and branches. He did not seem to have heard the noise of the horse's hooves, but he started at the sound of Alexander's voice:

'So you heard my call?' he asked, his voice somehow altered now.

'I saw your fire.'

'You are in danger.'

'I have always been in danger. My body is covered with scars that prove this fact.'

Only now did the seer's eyes seem to register Alexander's presence and as he stared at him he said, 'It is strange, only your face has been spared. It is said that your father instead was disfigured when he died.'

'Have you perhaps received some premonition of my

death, Aristander? I want to realize my dream and I would like very much to have a child ... before ...'

The seer interrupted him, 'You will survive, but listen out carefully for a boy's voice. A boy's voice,' he repeated. 'I can say no more, I cannot ...' and his eyes were moist.

'And your nightmare? Do you still see that naked man being burned alive on a funeral pyre?'

'I see him all the time,' and he pointed to the fire burning there before him. 'And his silence troubles me greatly. His silence, do you understand?'

Alexander moved away on foot, holding his horse by its bridle as he set off along the path to where his guards were waiting. He had a vision of his father falling, run through by the sword of one of his men and he waved them off, 'Go now. I have no need of any guards. My men love me, as do my Companions. Go now I tell you.'

*

Philotas left his quarters after nightfall and walked quickly towards the higher part of the city, to a large building made of mud bricks that had been assigned to the officers of the *hetairoi* cavalry. There was no moon, but the sky was nevertheless brimming with a myriad of incredibly large, bright stars and the shimmering ribbon of the galaxy was spread out against the celestial vault like a long sigh of light.

He was wearing a dark cloak and a hood covered his head and face so that no one would recognize him. He only revealed himself to the guard at the entrance, who immediately lowered his spear in salute. He entered and

found himself standing before Simmias, one of the battalion commanders of the *pezhetairoi*.

'Where are the others?' he asked.

'I don't know,' replied the officer.

'Of course you know. You know as well as I do where they are. I will not leave here until I have seen them all, every one of them, otherwise I will inform the King.'

Simmias turned pale and said, 'Wait here. Some of them are in the turret of the eastern bastion, others in the guard house of the central courtyard.' He exited through a side door and Philotas was left to pace up and down, wringing his hands as he waited.

They arrived in dribs and drabs and Philotas looked them up and down as though inspecting a division of troops, but with an expression of disgust on his face: Simmias of Neapolis, commander of the third battalion of *pezhetairoi*, Agesander of Leucopedion, deputy commander of the fifth squadron of *hetairoi*, Limnos of Calestra, commander of the first company of the Vanguard, Polemon and Attalus, brothers of Amyntas, commanders of the shock troops, and Aristarchus of Poliakmon, deputy of the shieldsmen.

He started his lecture without even giving them time to open their mouths.

'Have you gone mad? What is this story about your having decided to kill the King?'

'Listen, you've got it wrong,' Simmias sought to reply.

'Enough!' Philotas shut him up. 'Who do you think you're speaking to? I want you now to tell me who took this decision and when exactly you intend to act, but above all else I want to know why.'

'You know why,' replied Polemon. 'Alexander is no longer our King, he is a barbarian king, he dresses like a barbarian and he is surrounded by barbarians. And what of us? We who have conquered an empire for him and are now required to wait in humiliation in antechambers when we need to speak to him.'

'And as if that were not enough,' Simmias intervened, 'there are his crazy plans to conquer the world. Understand? Conquer the world. But what world? Do any of us know where the world ends? And what if it never does end? Does that mean we have to drag ourselves through deserts, across mountains and desolate prairies just to conquer the occasional miserable little village like this Artacoana?'

'And that's not everything,' said Limnos of Calestra. 'He's founding colonies now, but have you noticed where? Not on the coast, in suitable locations like the one chosen for the first Alexandria. Now he's creating cities in desert places, among barbarous peoples and at great distances from the sea. He's forcing thousands of poor wretches to set up home in frightful places and to mate with barbarian women to spawn a generation of unhappy bastard children.'

'All the Greeks of the colonies have mated with barbarian women,' said Philotas. 'This is no reason for killing him.'

'Don't be such a hypocrite,' replied Simmias. 'You have always agreed with us, the only one among his friends, on the fact that we cannot continue in this manner. You are the only one who understands our men and their suffering, their fears, their desire to return

home, and now you pretend to be surprised by something you already knew.'

'This is not true!' Philotas retorted. 'Our understanding was completely different. We had decided that our divisions would act when the right moment presented itself, and that we would make him change his plans.'

'With force if necessary,' Aristarchus offered some detail.

'But not with blood,' Philotas replied, even more decidedly now. 'If your mad plan succeeds now the army will be left leaderless in the midst of a foreign land and the throne will be left without a king.'

'This is not so,' said Polemon. 'We have a king.'

'Amyntas IV,' said Simmias. 'The legitimate son of the legitimate King, Amyntas III.'

Philotas shook his head. 'This is impossible. Amyntas is loyal to Alexander.'

'So you think,' said Simmias. 'Just wait until he has the crown of Macedon on his head.'

Philotas sat down heavily on a chair and fell into silence. Simmias began speaking again after a few moments. 'You are the supreme commander of the *hetairoi* cavalry and the new King will have to be able to count upon your support. We must know where you stand.'

Philotas sighed, 'Listen . . . I think, indeed I am certain, it is not necessary for us to stain our hands with Alexander's blood; we all owe so much to him.'

'He's the one who owes *us* so much,' Aristarchus interrupted. 'And then, when he is dead, there is no reason why we cannot grant him great honours, build

statues and monuments and celebrate him throughout the world with inscriptions in stone . . . this is the done thing. As for Amyntas, the throne means he will be in our debt and he will listen to us.'

Philotas continued as though Aristarchus had said nothing, 'I don't want to kill him. Neither will you assassinate him. I will tell you how to act and when.' He spoke with such decision that no one dared contradict. Then he covered his head once again with his hood and left the building.

Simmias waited until the sound of Philotas's footsteps had died away and then he turned to his fellow conspirators, 'Who told him?'

They all shook their heads.

'Philotas knew of our decision, so someone told him.'

'I said nothing, I promise,' Limnos assured him.

'And neither did we,' the others echoed.

'Our lives are on the line here,' said Simmias. 'Not a word of this to anyone, neither to lovers nor friends nor brothers. In any case Philotas has come to know, and in the same way others might know as well, anyone might learn of our plans.'

'This is true,' said Aristarchus. 'What do you think we should do now?'

'We must act immediately.'

'You mean . . . kill the King . . . now?'

'As soon as possible. If he hears tale that Philotas has learned of our plot, all is lost. Have you ever witnessed a Macedonian trial for high treason? I have. And the execution as well. The traitors are torn to pieces by the army . . . slowly.'

'When do we strike?' asked Polemon.

'Tomorrow,' replied Simmias, 'before any other qualms worm their way into Philotas's mind. Once Alexander is dead, he won't be able to back out and he'll assume his full responsibilities in all this. As for Perdiccas, Ptolemy, Seleucus and the others, they will all look at the situation rationally. They are almost all reasonable men. Listen to me carefully now because the slightest error might give us away and expose us to some terrible fate.' He unsheathed his sword and began drawing on the beaten earth floor. 'Tomorrow the King inaugurates the new theatre – he wants Stateira to see Thessalus's performance in the *Suppliants*. He will set off from Satibarzanes' palace and will come along this road through the spice merchants' quarter. When he reaches this point he will take the road that leads to the theatre; it will be lined with two rows of *pezhetairoi* from the phalanx and they will offer him their salute and protect him from the crowd. That will be our moment.'

He drove his sword firmly into the ground and looked his fellow conspirators in the eyes, one by one.

37

CEBALINUS HAD MANAGED to push his way through almost to the front row, together with his friend Aghirios. On the one side he anxiously watched the approach of the King, surrounded by his friends, while from the other direction came the commanding officers of the combat units together with Prince Amyntas.

'I cannot see Commander Philotas,' he said, after having searched for him in vain among the men in Alexander's entourage.

'Do you think he has informed the King?' Aghirios asked him.

'I'm sure he has,' replied Cebalinus. 'He listened to me carefully and told me not to worry, that it would all be sorted out.'

'But when do you think they'll do it?'

'I don't know. There was a lot of noise outside while I was listening, so I didn't catch everything they said. I imagine they'll strike before the army sets off on the march to Bactriana.'

'Look,' said Aghirios as he pointed to the leaders of the procession as it came towards them. 'There's the King with Princess Stateira and his companions. I can't see Commander Philotas either.'

'Perhaps he was busy today; I've heard that the other

satrap, Barsaentes, is prowling around the foothills with bands of armed Saka and Gedrosian warriors. Perhaps he has received orders to deal with them.'

'Perhaps . . .'

The King was coming closer now and Cebalinus felt himself suddenly gripped by the strangest sensation, all his limbs started trembling for no apparent reason.

'What's wrong?' Aghirios asked him. 'You don't look well.'

At that very moment his young friend had remembered a word he had heard from the lips of one of the generals, a word that at the time had seemed meaningless, but now resounded in his mind with awesome significance – *Xsayarsa gadir*, 'Xerxes' Gate'. And there they were! There behind him and up in the turret three bowmen had appeared and were now taking aim. Cebalinus rushed forward through the barrier of *pezhetairoi* and shouted, 'They're about to assassinate the King! They're killing the King! Save him!'

The arrows came raining down at that very instant, but already Ptolemy's and Leonnatus's shields were in position, protecting the King's exposed chest. Perdiccas shouted with all the breath he had in him, 'Arrest those men!' and he sent a group of assault troops off in the direction of Xerxes' Gate.

All these words echoed through Alexander's mind, amplified by a memory that reawakened a nightmare – the image of his father Philip as he fell into a pool of blood with a Celtic dagger in his ribs. He heard Stateira's voice as she shouted curt orders in her own language, and then came the metallic clangour of weapons, the

hammering gallop of horses, but all he could see was blood and yet more blood and the deathly pallor of Philip as he lay dying.

It was Ptolemy's voice that brought him round: 'This is the boy who saved your life. He is a young, courageous and devoted squire, his name is Cebalinus.'

Alexander looked at him intently – fine features, almost graceful limbs, large, fair eyes. He was still shaking and kept his eyes to the ground to hide his emotions. The King asked him, 'Where are you from, boy?'

'I am from Eunostos, a village in Lyncestis, Sire,' the young man managed to stammer.

'You have saved my life. Thank you. I will give orders that you be rewarded for your loyalty. But tell me, how did you know that someone wanted to kill me?'

'Sire, I had spoken of this with General Philotas, who will certainly have told you that—' he stopped suddenly and looked around, somewhat lost, seeing the expression of surprise on the King's face and on the face of all the King's companions.

The Secretary General was also there, Eumenes of Cardia, and he came forward and clapped Cebalinus on the back, 'Come, my boy, let's go. You must explain everything to us, from the very beginning.'

Upset and also excited by his role as saviour of the King, Cebalinus recounted every detail of the conspiracy and how he had warned Philotas who had promised to inform the King immediately.

When he had finished, Eumenes clapped him on the back once more and said, 'A fine lad, you have served us all well. King Alexander grants you with immediate effect

the title of Commander of the Royal Squires, with all the income and the honours the rank brings with it. He also wishes to make a gift of one talent of silver, which you may keep or send, in part or completely, to your family. Go now, go and rest – this has been a most trying day for all of us.'

The boy was still excited as he took his leave and ran immediately to his friend Aghirios to give him the news, already experiencing a taste of the pleasure he would draw from giving orders and inflicting punishments on all those companions who had previously made fun of him and bullied him.

Alexander immediately signed arrest orders for the commanders Simmias of Neapolis, Limnos of Calestra, Polemon and Attalus of Andromenes, Aristarchus of Poliakmon, Agesander of Leucopedion and also for Philotas, General of the *Hetairoi*, as well as for Prince Amyntas of Lyncestis. Then he went to his rooms in the palace and gave orders that he was not to be disturbed by anyone.

Seleucus, Ptolemy and Eumenes decided to speak to Hephaestion, the only person Alexander might receive at such a dramatic moment, and they went to see him that evening, in his quarters.

'Try to find out what his intentions are,' said Eumenes.

'Especially with regard to Philotas,' added Seleucus.

'I'll try to speak to him. I have never seen him in such a state, not even when we were in exile and we risked dying of starvation and exposure every day.' He was just about to set off when an orderly knocked at the door and handed him an immediate summons from Alexander.

'Never mind,' said Eumenes, 'he's one step ahead of us.' All four of them left Hephaestion's rooms together.

'What do you think he'll ask us?' said Hephaestion.

'It's obvious,' replied Eumenes. 'He'll ask us what we think of the conspiracy and above all else he'll ask us what we think he should do with Philotas.'

'And what will we say to that?' Seleucus asked gravely and quietly, as though asking himself.

Perdiccas arrived on horseback at that moment and immediately, on seeing his friends, he dismounted and joined them, leading his horse by its bridle. 'I would rather take on a lion with my bare hands than say what I think of this affair. Have you all thought about it?'

His friends looked at him and in their eyes Perdiccas read all the anguish and the suffering and the uncertainty that were certainly visible in his own. He shook his head, 'So you don't know what to say to him either, am I right?'

They were close to the Governor's Palace now, guarded by a patrol of *pezhetairoi* together with four Immortals of the Imperial Guard. From the opposite direction Leonnatus approached, his shoulder still strapped up, together with Cleitus the Black and Lysimachus.

'Only Craterus is missing,' said Ptolemy.

'And Philotas,' said Eumenes, lowering his eyes.

'Quite,' said Ptolemy. They looked at one another without saying anything. They knew that before long they would have to tell the King whether in their opinion one of them – one of the troop with whom they had shared food and hunger, sleep and sleeplessness, joys and

dangers, hope and despair – whether one of them should live or die.

Leonnatus broke the silence: 'I never did like Philotas – he's conceited and full of himself, but the idea of seeing him cut to pieces in a military execution is a terrible one. Let's go now, I can't bear this uncertainty any longer.'

They entered the palace and went to the council room where Alexander was waiting for them, sitting on his throne – pale, with all the signs of a sleepless night on his face. Peritas was curled up at his feet, occasionally lifting his muzzle, hoping to be stroked.

He did not even wait for them to sit down but began immediately: 'You were all present at the assassination of my father.'

'That is true,' said Eumenes, who still carried the event gaping like an open, painful wound to his soul, 'but it would be a grave mistake to judge these events under the influence of those bloody images. It is not the same thing, it is not the same situation and—'

'No?' Alexander suddenly shouted. 'I was the one who pulled the dagger from his body . . . I was the one whose clothes were stained with his blood . . . I was the one who heard his death rattle. I was the one . . . understand? Me!'

Eumenes realized that there was nothing he could do or say. It was obvious that Alexander was obsessed by the idea of regicide and that he had spent the hours of darkness tormented by the nightmare of Philip's violent death. At that moment Craterus entered, he too in the darkest of moods.

'If you have already made your decision,' said Ptolemy at that point, 'why have you summoned us here?'

Alexander seemed to calm down somewhat. 'I have taken no decision as yet, nor will I. It will be the assembled army that will judge, in accordance with ancient custom.'

'And therefore,' said Seleucus, 'we cannot be of much use—'

Alexander interrupted him, 'If you wish, you may leave, I will detain you no further. I had called you here to listen to your advice and draw comfort from your presence. Six of our most valiant officers, and with them one of our most intimate friends, almost a brother, have conspired to kill me. You were all present, you all saw and heard the squire's testimony.'

The Black, silent up to this point, now spoke: 'Be careful, Alexander. You have no proof against Philotas apart from the boy's testimony.'

'The boy who saved my life and who in all other matters has told the truth. The three bowmen have confessed under torture and have confirmed Cebalinus's story. The interrogations were carried out separately, but they all said the same thing.'

'What do we know of Philotas?' the Black asked once more.

'He most certainly knew, yet he said nothing. Do you understand, Black? If it had been up to him then I would be dead already, run through with arrows, my body lying out there in a pool of blood.' Alexander's eyes were full of tears as he spoke these words and they all understood

that it was not the thought of the weapons destined to enter his flesh that made him cry. It was, rather, the thought that a friend to whom he had entrusted the most important rank in their army after his own, making him the virtual custodian of Alexander's very person, the thought that this friend had schemed and conspired against him, that this friend had been ruthless enough to envisage the arrows tearing through his flesh, leaving him to die in spasms of agony. At that moment no one failed to notice the pain in his gaze, the tremor in his voice, his hands as they gripped the arms of the throne spasmodically.

'What have I done to you to deserve this?' he asked, almost crying. 'What have I done?'

'Alexander, we do not—' Ptolemy sought to reply.

'You are defending him!' he shouted.

'No,' retorted Seleucus. 'We simply cannot believe it, even though all the evidence goes against him.'

With the evening shadows a deep silence fell in the room and no one managed to break it, not even Peritas who sat motionless, looking up at his master with his large watery eyes. They all felt too much alone and too far from the happy times of their friendship and their adolescence. Suddenly the days of their dreams and their heroism were so remote and now it was doubt and anguish that kept them company. Now their task was to find some way out of the coils of intrigue, of falsity and suspicion in which they were caught.

'What do we know of Prince Amyntas?' the Black asked.

'He was to be the new King following my death,'

Alexander replied gravely. Then, an instant later, he asked, 'What do you all think I should do?'

The Black spoke for them all: 'We have no choice. These are officers of the King's army, and the King's army must judge them.'

There was nothing more to say and they all left, one after the other, leaving Alexander alone with his ghosts. Not even Hephaestion was brave enough to stay.

38

EUMENES AND CALLISTHENES went to Alexander before dawn and found him sitting on a plain stool, covered only by a rough Macedonian *chlamys*. It was clear that he had not slept at all.

'Has he confessed to his treason?' he asked, without even lifting his head.

'He bore the torture with incredible courage. He is a great soldier,' replied Eumenes.

'I know,' said Alexander darkly.

'Don't you want to know what he said?' asked Callisthenes. The King slowly nodded his head.

'At the height of his suffering he shouted, "Ask Alexander what he wants me to say and let's be done with it!"'

'A cut above all things,' said the King, 'like a true Macedonian noble. Disdainful as always.'

'How is it you have no doubts in this matter?' asked Callisthenes.

'There is no doubt,' replied Alexander. 'The evidence is overwhelming, and it is confirmed by the killers themselves.'

'And Amyntas?' asked Eumenes. 'Spare him at least. There are no accusations against him.'

'He has come under suspicion before. And he was

to be King following my assassination. Is that not enough?'

'No!' exclaimed Callisthenes with a courage and conviction he had never shown before now. 'No! It is not enough! Do you want to know why? Do you remember the letter from Darius promising two thousand talents? It was false! It was all false – the letter, the messenger, the conspiracy ... or rather there certainly was a conspiracy, but it was your mother who organized it, together with Sisines the Egyptian, and their aim was to eliminate Amyntas.'

'You are lying!' shouted Alexander. 'Sisines was a spy employed by Darius and for this reason he was executed following Issus.'

'Yes, but I was the last person to speak to him; he sought to buy me and to buy Ptolemy. I pretended to accept the offer – fifteen talents for myself and twenty for Ptolemy so that we would keep quiet and corroborate his innocence. I told you nothing and I kept this secret so as not to cause you more anguish and so as not to put you into a situation of conflict with your mother. Olympias has always been obsessed by your succession – it was she who arranged for Eurydice's young son to be strangled in his cradle, or have you forgotten?'

Alexander shivered as an image of Eurydice covered in bruises came into his eyes, her face scratched, her hair dirty as she clasped her baby's body to her breast.

'A child born of your same bloodline,' Callisthenes continued, implacable, 'or perhaps you really do believe yourself to be the son of a god?'

Alexander jumped to his feet as though lashed by a

whip and he rushed at the historian with his sword unsheathed, shouting, 'You have gone too far!'

Callisthenes turned pale as he suddenly realized he had provoked a rage the consequences of which he was incapable of managing, but Eumenes swiftly took up position between the two and the King stopped short at the very last moment. 'Callisthenes has spoken his thoughts. Do you want to kill him for this? If you want adulators and courtiers who always tell you only those things you want to hear then you have no need of us.' Then the Secretary General turned to the historian, who was deathly pale and trembling like a leaf, and said, 'Come, Callisthenes, let's go; the King is out of sorts today.'

They left and Alexander sat heavily on his stool, bringing his hands to his head as though to contain the stabbing pains in his temples.

'It's a nasty business, I agree,' said a voice behind him, 'but unfortunately you have no way out. You must strike without any hesitation, even if you have doubts. Perhaps Philotas did not want to kill you, perhaps he wanted to have you kept in custody or to force you to act according to his wishes, putting his trust in his position and in that of his father, but he was certainly involved in the conspiracy and that in itself is enough.' Eumolpus of Soloi crossed the almost dark room and sat on another stool opposite the King.

'Did you listen to the other things that Callisthenes had to say?'

'The story of Amyntas? Yes, but in this case too, can you really be sure? Who was present at the interrogation that preceded the execution of Sisines? No one, as far as

I know, apart from Callisthenes himself, and therefore his story cannot be corroborated. Objectively, Amyntas is a threat; in the Persian court he would have been eliminated immediately. Remember that you are now King of the Persians. You are the King of Kings. However, I don't really think you will have to stick your neck out: the court will certainly find him guilty. All you will have to do is refuse clemency if anyone should ask for a pardon for him.'

An attendant entered, flanked by two squires carrying the King's weapons. 'Sire,' he said, 'it is time.'

*

The military trial held before the assembled army was an ancient and most awesome rite, conceived by the forebears to inflict the maximum of pain and shame on the traitors: it was chaired by the King and was celebrated in the presence of all the soldiers, the generals of the cavalry, the infantry and the auxiliaries. The members of the court, ten in all, were drawn by lots from among the officers of the highest rank and the oldest soldiers.

The army lined up on the desert plain before dawn, called by a high, prolonged trumpet blast, piercing in its single note, as cutting as a blade. The *pezhetairoi* were arranged in seven rows, armed to the teeth, their *sarissae* held firmly in their hands. Before them was the *hetairoi* cavalry. Out at the far reaches of the flanks, almost closing the two long lines in a rectangular form, the light infantry assault troops were lined up, together with the shock troops and the shieldsmen, leaving only a small entrance way on the eastern side, through which the

King, together with the judges and the prisoners, was to enter. Neither the mercenary Greeks of the infantry nor the Thracians and the Agrianians were admitted, because only Macedonians could judge Macedonians.

At the centre of the *hetairoi* line-up was a low podium with the King's throne together with chairs for the rest of the court.

The sun was rising from behind the mountains and its rays struck the points of the *sarissae* first of all, making them shine with a sinister gleaming and then the light moved down gradually to illuminate the men, motionless in their metal armour, sculpting their stony faces, marked by the sun, by the wind and by the ice.

Three trumpet blasts announced the King's arrival and shortly afterwards came the judges, followed by the prisoners in chains. Philotas stood out among them, much maimed by the torture, and then came Amyntas, who walked forward apparently impassible.

When the King and the members of the court had taken their positions on the podium, the eldest member read the charges out loud. The witnesses were then lined up and a herald repeated each and every statement they made, so that the entire assembly could hear. Then the members of the court voted and the verdict was unanimous for all of the accused – guilty.

'Now,' shouted the herald as he repeated the words of the eldest judge, 'may the assembly vote. Your votes are to be cast for each of the accused individually. Those who do not agree with the verdict will place their swords on the ground. All of you will then take ten paces backwards so that their weapons may be counted.'

The eldest judge called the names of the accused one by one and each time he did a certain number of warriors placed their swords on the ground and stepped back. The accused looked this way and that, first towards the infantry lines, then towards the cavalry, in the residual hope that their fellow soldiers might try to save them, but every time they did so there were too few swords left shining there on the ground. When it came to Philotas's turn there were more swords, especially from the *hetairoi*, but not enough to overturn the verdict. His haughtiness and his inability to familiarize with the men, particularly with the foot soldiers, cost him dear, and in any case the testimony of Cebalinus the squire, which everyone had heard now, lay heavily against him.

Unlike the other prisoners, Philotas did not turn his gaze groundwards; instead he continued to stare at Alexander, gritting his teeth to stifle his groans of pain. He was still staring at the King when they put him before the stake for his execution. He pushed back the executioners who wanted to tie his wrists and his ankles and he stood erect in all his pride, presenting his chest to the troop of archers who were to carry out the sentence. The officer in command moved closer to the podium, as custom dictated, to hear whether the King wanted to grant a reprieve.

Alexander issued his orders curtly: 'The heart. First time round. I don't want him to suffer an instant more than necessary.'

The officer nodded, went to his unit and exchanged a few words briefly with his men. Then he shouted an order and the bowmen notched their arrows and took

aim. The camp was brimming with soldiers, but now a leaden silence fell around and the horsemen kept their gaze on Philotas's body for they knew that even at this extreme moment, even though already on his last legs because of the torture, he would teach them how a commander of the *hetairoi* should die.

The officer gave the order to fire, but Philotas, before the arrows sped through his heart, had the time to open his mouth and shout: '*Alalalài!*'

He fell to the dust, and a pool of blood expanded around him.

Prince Amyntas was executed last of all, and many of those present found it impossible not to cry when they saw what a pathetic end such a noble, valiant young man had come to. Fate had deprived him first of his throne and then of his life in his prime.

Alexander returned to his palace, more upset than he ever had been before in his life, filled with anguish because he had lost a childhood companion, not on the battlefield but before an execution squad. He was still unable to conceive of the fact that a young man of his same age, who had always participated gladly in his enterprises, to whom he had entrusted the highest of responsibilities, could have suddenly come to such a point of rejection and refusal as to turn his back on him completely and to conspire against him.

The season of deceit and blood was not yet over – now an even more terrible decision had to be taken.

He convened a council of his Companions after sunset, under a tented cover that stood alone in the midst of the countryside. Eumenes was present, but not Cleitus the

Black, who had been given the job of burying the executed men. There were no guards at the entrance, nor were there any chairs, tables or carpets under the cover, only the bare earth. They stood to discuss matters by the light of a single lamp. No one had eaten supper and only bitterness and dismay could be read on each of their faces.

'This is unlike you,' began Alexander. 'No one said anything to save Philotas from death.'

'I am Greek,' said Eumenes immediately, 'I had no right to say anything.'

'I know,' replied Alexander, 'otherwise you would have spoken in his favour in public, just as you had done in private, but at this point the judgement has been handed down, approved by the assembly and the sentence carried out. What's done is done.'

'So why have you summoned us here?' asked Leonnatus.

'Because it's not over yet. Am I right?' said Eumenes. 'When one starts something, it must be carried on to the bitter end.'

'Have you discovered there are other conspirators?' asked Ptolemy anxiously.

The King turned to him for an instant with a lost expression, as though he now had to face the most difficult, the most repugnant of tasks, and then he began, his voice very quiet, 'Today, when I came back to my quarters after the executions, I sat at my table and I began writing to General Parmenion . . .'

The very mention of the name was enough to evoke the enormity of the tragedy that was now unfolding and

they all realized the nature of the terrible decision that had to be taken.

'I started writing to him personally to give him the news that his son Philotas had been condemned to death and the sentence had been carried out according to the wishes of the assembled army. I wanted to tell him that as King I had to accept that verdict, but that as a man I would rather die than have to inflict such terrible pain on him.' Eumenes looked and saw tears were streaming down his cheeks as he spoke; at that moment Alexander's suffering was the same as the old General's. 'However, my hand soon stopped writing. A deeply troubling thought prevented me from continuing and led me to summon you all here. None of us will leave this until a decision is reached.'

'How will Parmenion react? This is the thought that torments you, is it not?' Eumenes once again provided an answer with a question.

'That's right,' said Alexander.

'He had already given you two of his sons,' said Eumenes. 'Hector, who drowned in the Nile, and Nicanor, struck down by a fatal blow. And now you have had his third son, his firstborn, the son he was most proud of, tortured and executed.'

'Not me!' shouted Alexander. 'I had granted him the highest rank after myself. He was judged for his actions,' and he lowered his head for one long, interminable instant before beginning again in a softer voice:

'We are alone, stuck here in the midst of a limitless, unknown land, and we are about to embark once more on the enterprise we swore to bring to a conclusion. The

slightest error on our part might ruin everything, might grant new strength to an enemy who is still not completely quashed, and who as I speak is preparing to fight to the last; an error might spell the collapse of our entire expedition. Do you want to see our comrades scattered to the winds or made prisoners, tortured and killed, or sold like slaves into far off lands, deprived forever of the hope of returning home one day? Do you want our land to be invaded, our families annihilated, our homes burned by these implacable enemies? Don't you realize that if Alexander falls, the known world will be thrown into tremendous turmoil? Is this what you want, Eumenes of Cardia? Is this what you all want? I had no choice but to strike without hesitation, suppressing all scruples, all emotion, all . . . mercy.'

His eyes burned with tears as he spoke, his voice cracked with the passions that lashed his soul and his Companions were aware of all this. They felt now the overwhelming force that in some way they had almost forgotten. It was as though Alexander's breath had penetrated their breasts, as though his tears were running down their cheeks, as though his doubts and his anguish were troubling their souls.

The King looked straight into their eyes one by one, before saying, 'And the worst is yet to be done.'

'To kill Parmenion?' Eumenes asked, his voice trembling.

Alexander nodded. 'We have no way of knowing what he will do when he hears of Philotas's death, but should he decide to avenge it, then we are all in trouble – he has all the money for our supplies, he controls the roads

and all our contacts with Macedonia for the reinforcements we need constantly – he has it in his power to close the gate behind us and leave us to our destiny, or he might even ally with Bessus or someone else and wipe us out completely. Can we run this risk?'

'Just one thing,' said Craterus. 'Do you believe that Parmenion knew of the conspiracy, or that he was involved in it? Philotas was his son – it is reasonable to assume that he might have informed him.'

'I don't believe so, but I have to bear the possibility in mind. I am the King and no one can help me in this – I stand alone while I take such terrible decisions. The only comfort for such anguish comes from friendship – without you, I do not know if I would find the strength, the will, the meaning of all this. Listen to me now – I have no wish to inflict upon you the burden of my remorse, a burden that I alone should bear, but if you think that all this is madness, if you think that I have gone beyond every reasonable limit, if you believe that what I am about to do is the action of a heinous tyrant, then kill me. Now. At your hands, death will not be so terrible for me. Then to take my place elect the best among you, for I have no children; strike some agreement with Parmenion and turn back home.' He undid his breastplate and let it fall to the ground, leaving his chest unprotected.

Hephaestion was the first to speak. 'I swore I would follow you to the farthest limit, and I meant this in every sense, even beyond the frontier that lies between good and evil.' Then, turning to his companions, he said, 'If anyone wishes to kill Alexander then he must kill me as well.'

Hephaestion undid his own breastplate and let it fall as he took up position alongside Alexander.

There were tears in all of their eyes and some of them hid their faces in their hands. At that moment Craterus remembered a far off day when they had travelled through a blizzard in an icebound pass in Illyria to join Alexander, just to let their exiled Prince know they would never abandon him for any reason in the world, and he called out, his voice hoarse, 'Alexander's troop!'

'Present, Sire!' they all replied.

39

EUMOLPUS OF SOLOI entered the old armoury of the Satrap's Palace. At the sound of his footsteps the man who had been waiting there turned suddenly.

'Who are you?' the spy asked him. 'And which division are you from?'

'My name is Demetrius,' replied the man. 'Fifth division of the third battalion of assault troops.'

'I have orders for you from the King,' said Eumolpus, showing him a small tablet with the Argead star embossed on it. 'Do you recognize this?'

'It's the royal seal.'

'Indeed, and it is with this authority that the orders you are about to receive from me come directly from Alexander. This task is a difficult one and brings with it much responsibility, but we know that you are no stranger to such duties and you have always acted with great speed and precision.'

'Who must I kill?'

Eumolpus looked him straight in the eye, 'General Parmenion.' The man's reaction was barely perceptible – the slightest quaver of his eyelashes. Eumolpus continued, still watching him carefully, 'The order is transmitted by word of mouth and only you know of it. No one, not even the King, knows that you have been

chosen for this mission. You will have two completely trustworthy local guides and you will use dromedaries from Satibarzanes' stables – the fastest and strongest animals hereabouts. You must reach him before news of Philotas's death arrives in Ecbatana.' He handed Demetrius a roll of papyrus, 'This is the documentation with your credentials as royal messenger, but in order to gain access to Parmenion with a verbal message you must know the password used by the King and Parmenion.'

'What is this password?'

'It's an old Macedonian rhyme, sung by children. Perhaps you know it, it goes like this: 'The silly old soldier's off to the war . . .'

The killer evidently took some pleasure in the irony as he nodded and completed the verse:

'*He falls to the floor!*'

'Exactly,' confirmed Eumolpus, without displaying any emotion whatsoever.

He continued, 'There is no remuneration for this mission, but you will receive a talent of silver from my own pocket.'

'There's no need,' replied the man.

'It will be useful. Use a dagger and strike at his chest. Macedonia's greatest soldier must not die from a wound inflicted in his back.'

Demetrius nodded, 'Is there anything else?'

'You must take him by surprise. If he realizes what is happening, you're lost. Don't be lulled into a false sense of security because he's seventy years of age. A lion is still a lion, even when long in the tooth.'

'I'll be careful.'

'Go now, then. There is no time to lose. Your guides await you in the stables with the dromedaries. The money is already in Ecbatana at the temple of Eshmun of the Chaldaeans, just outside the southern gate. You must leave immediately afterwards, never to return.'

The man left by a side door that was pointed out to him, went down the stairs to the stables and set off immediately in the direction of the setting sun. From the heights of a tower Alexander stood pale and motionless, watching the killer until he disappeared from sight over the undulating profile of the desert.

It took Demetrius six days and five nights to reach Zadracarta, sleeping only for a few hours each night and eating and drinking while still astride his animals. Together with the guides he changed mounts when possible so as to maintain a constant speed – it was incredible just how far they could travel in a short space of time with this system. They reached Ecbatana around sunset of the thirteenth day and Demetrius went immediately to the entrance of the Governor's Palace.

'Who are you? What is your business?' asked the sentry.

Demetrius showed him the document with the royal seal. 'The King's messenger with a most urgent mission – to deliver a verbal communication to General Parmenion.'

'Do you have a password?'

'Of course.'

'Wait then,' replied the sentry. He entered the guard house and spoke with his commander who came out

almost immediately and spoke directly to Demetrius, 'Follow me.'

They entered a huge colonnaded courtyard at the centre of which was a well from which servants were drawing water for guests and for animals, and they crossed it from one side to the other. On the western side of the portico, in shadow now, they took a stairway leading to the upper floor. Then they turned into a corridor guarded by a couple of *pezhetairoi* and walked down to an unguarded door at the bottom of it. The officer knocked and waited. Shortly afterwards there came the sound of footsteps and a voice that asked, 'Who is it?'

'Guards,' replied the officer. 'A courier has arrived from the King, he has an urgent message, a verbal one, and he says he has a password.'

The door opened and there appeared a man of about fifty years of age, almost bald, bearing a slate under his left arm and a stylus in his right hand. He introduced himself, 'I am his correspondence secretary. Follow me, the General will see you immediately. He has just finished replying to a series of letters and was preparing to wash before supper. I hope you bring him good news. He still suffers greatly for the loss of Nicanor and he is increasingly anxious about the King and his last surviving son, poor man.' As he spoke he peered at the killer's stony face, trying somehow to guess the nature of the news he was about to give his General and in truth he could see no sign at all of it being good.

They stopped before another door and the secretary

said, 'Wait here – there is a formality to be dealt with before being admitted into the General's presence.'

Demetrius was afraid he might be searched and gripped the hilt of his dagger under his cloak. Some moments passed in silence until, finally, the secretary reappeared with a tray on which there was a slice of bread, a bowl of salt and a cup of wine.

'General Parmenion wants all those who enter his quarters to enjoy his hospitality. He says it brings good luck,' he added, a half smile on his lips. 'Please, help yourself.'

The killer let go of his dagger and stretched out his hand towards the tray. He took the bread, dipped it in the salt and ate. Then he washed it down with some wine.

'Thank the General for me,' he said, wiping his mouth with the back of his hand.

The secretary nodded, placed the tray on a table, then led Demetrius to the door that led into Parmenion's study and asked him to wait just a few moments more. He heard their voices through the door that was slightly ajar. Then the secretary came out and nodded to indicate that Parmenion was ready. Demetrius entered and closed the door behind him.

Parmenion was sitting at his desk and behind him was a shelf full of rolls of papyrus, each one bearing a small card with a label, while to one side was an easel with a map representing the provinces of the Persian empire east of the Halys river. As soon as he saw the messenger enter, Parmenion stood up to greet him. He wore only

his military *chiton* which covered his legs to his knees and his Macedonian boots came halfway up his calves. He was of extraordinarily robust constitution and his iron and leather armour that hung now on a stand before the left-hand wall must have weighed, together with his shield, almost one talent. He was unarmed. His sword, with an antique blade, hung from its bandolier on the same stand.

He pointed to a chair. 'Sit down, soldier.'

'I am not tired,' replied the killer.

'No? It looks to me as though you've been to hell and back,' replied Parmenion. 'You look terrible. Come on, sit down.'

Demetrius obeyed, so as not to raise suspicion and decided he would wait for the General to move nearer, but as he sat the hilt of his dagger stuck out from his cloak, sufficiently for it to be noticed. Parmenion moved back instinctively towards his armour and weapons, 'Who are you?' he asked as he reached out for his sword. 'You said you had a password.'

Demetrius stood up, 'The silly old soldier's off to the war . . .' he said as he put his hand to the hilt of the dagger once more. At those words Parmenion let go of his sword and moved towards him with an expression of pained stupor on his face, 'The King . . .' he mumbled, '. . . but how can this be?'

The killer swiftly drove the dagger into Parmenion's heart and watched as he fell without a sound, a large pool of blood spreading out over the floor. He watched him die and saw neither hatred nor rebellion in his eyes

as the life ebbed from them. Only tears. And it seemed to him that the general's lips whispered something with his last breath . . . perhaps . . . perhaps that password.

He left by another door on the wall to the right and disappeared into the corridors of the great palace. Shortly afterwards the peace and tranquillity of sunset was torn asunder by a long cry of horror.

*

Thirteen days later Alexander heard that Parmenion had been assassinated, and even though he himself had given the orders, the news was a cruel blow, as though he had somehow hoped that some god might have dictated a different fate. He closed himself away in his tent and in his anguish for days, without seeing anyone, without food or water. Leptine went to him more than once, but each time she came out in tears and then sat down on the ground outside the tent, crying through sun and rain as she waited for the King to let her in. Every now and then his friends would come to the tent to see if there was any sign of life and all they could hear was his hoarse, monotonous voice as it repeated again and again an old Macedonian children's rhyme, and they left shaking their heads.

Eumenes finished the fourth book of his *Journal* with this paragraph:

On the seventh day of the month of Pyanopsion General Parmenion was killed on the King's orders, even though he was guilty of nothing. He was a valiant man, who always went into combat with

honour, fighting like a youngster even though he had reached a great age. There is no stain on his memory, nor will there ever be any: he will live for ever in our hearts.

40

THE DAY FINALLY came when Alexander returned to the palace alone and on foot, unshaven, his hair matted and dirty. He had lost much weight and there was a hazy, ambiguous look in his eyes. Stateira welcomed him into her arms and sought to ease his pain as each night she sat at his feet, singing and playing her own accompaniment on the Babylonian harp.

Summer was already coming to an end when the King ordered the army to assemble and fixed a date for their departure. The officers leading the march spoke with the guides; those in charge of the supplies prepared the carts and the pack animals; the commanders of the various battalions lined up all their divisions and led them on training marches lasting days at a time, all this to get them used to the trials and hardships that awaited them through the gorges of the Paropamisus range. This resumption of military activity caused much excitement throughout the camp; the soldiers could barely wait to leave this terrible place that had brought such harrowing events and they all wanted nothing more than to put behind them the days of idleness and blood they had lived along the banks of this lifeless lake, there in the shadow of the crumbling walls of Artacoana, which now bore the name Alexandria of Aria.

Princess Stateira discovered she was pregnant and this news seemed to provide some relief for the King and even brought him some happiness. His friends were pleased as well, thinking that before long there would be a new, smaller Alexander among them. The march northwards was too arduous for a woman in this delicate condition and Alexander asked her to turn back and settle for the duration of her confinement in one of his palaces. Stateira obeyed and set off towards Zadracarta, with the intention of joining up with her mother at Ecbatana or Susa.

The trumpets sounded the signal for the departure one clear autumn morning and the King took up position at the head of his army, dressed in his splendid armour astride Bucephalas, just as things had been back in the days of his most glorious feats. Riding by his side were Hephaestion, Perdiccas, Ptolemy, Seleucus, Leonnatus, Lysimachus and Craterus – all decked in metal and with their helmet crests waving in the sun.

For days they travelled up the valley down which flowed the river of a thousand tributaries, passing through village after village and nothing happened. The Persian nobles who were following them with their own troops spoke to the people who lived in these places and explained that the shining young man astride the gigantic black horse was the new King of Kings and occasionally someone would appear shaking a branch of willow in salute. The night sky was increasingly clear and the twinkling up there seemed to grow wildly, almost as though the very stars were being born by the thousands in the great curved vault, like flowers in a spring field.

Callisthenes explained that the air, at this height, was much clearer because there were no fumes and vapours to thicken it and this was why the stars were so much easier to see, but many soldiers felt that the sky was changing with the changes they were seeing in the land around them and in any case nothing could surprise them any longer in those remote lands.

They set up camp every evening at sunset along the riverbank, and when they lit their fires, the great multitude of soldiers – together with their entourage of women, merchants, servants, bearers, shepherds and herdsmen with their livestock – looked like an entire city on the move.

One day, the valley of the river of the thousand tributaries widened out into a vast plain, surrounded for the most part by a grand series of ridges of extremely high mountains all capped with snow and shining in the sun, standing out wonderfully against the sky.

'The Paropamisus!' shouted Eumenes, much moved at the sight of such natural beauty.

Callisthenes, however, was less impressed: 'I have exchanged a series of messages with my uncle Aristotle of late and in his opinion the mountains in this area must be the last extensions of the chain of the Caucasians, the highest chain in the world.'

'And we're supposed to march up there?' Leonnatus asked, pointing to the passes up near the peaks, suspended between heaven and earth.

'Exactly,' replied Ptolemy. 'There's no doubt now that Bessus is on the other side, with an army of Bactrians,

Sogdians and Scythians; Alexander is determined to take him on, whatever the cost.'

Leonnatus brought his hand up to his forehead to shield his eyes and looked once more at the imposing mountain chain, blinding up there with its shroud of ice and snow, then he shook his head and moved on.

Callisthenes' geographical theory was endorsed by the King and over the following days he identified in the wide fertile valley an ideal place to found a new city, to have a part of the great entourage that moved with his army settled there. He called it Alexandria of the Caucasus and garrisoned it with thousands of people, together with some two hundred mercenaries who opted to stay rather than face the vertiginous climb up through the mountains.

In the clear air under the brilliant blue of that sky, out on those emerald meadows, all framed by the silver ribbons of the river and its tributaries, the ghosts of Artacoana seemed to fade away for a short time, but Parmenion's blood-stained shadow continued to appear during Alexander's nights. One day, at sunset, oppressed by his dread of the onset of darkness, he appeared at Aristander's tent and said, 'Get a horse and follow me.'

The seer obeyed and soon, having slipped past the surveillance of the guards, they were moving swiftly through the darkness that was already descending from the mountains and they began their ascent up the slopes of the great ridges.

'What have we come here for?' asked Aristander.

'I want you to summon the ghost of Parmenion for

me,' replied the King, staring at him with a feverish look in his eyes. 'Can you do this for me, Aristander?'

The seer nodded. 'If he is still roaming around these lands, I will have him come to you, but if he has already descended into Hades, then I know not if I can reach him without putting my own life in danger.'

'I dreamt I saw him a few nights ago, alone and on foot, somewhere near that pass over there. He walked with his back bent, as though carrying some heavy burden, and his white hair merged in with the whiteness of the snow. Now and then he waved to me to follow him . . . his great warrior's calloused hand. Suddenly he turned towards me and I saw the wound he bore on his chest, but in his eyes there was neither hatred nor resentment. Simply an infinite melancholy. Call him for me, Aristander, I beg you!'

'Do you remember where exactly on the mountain you think you saw him?'

'Up there,' replied the King, pointing to a place where a stony path disappeared into the snow.

'Take me there, then, before night falls and surprises us, leaving no trace of the road we must take.'

They set off first on horseback and then dismounted when the path became narrower and more difficult. Before midnight they reached the snowline and stopped there before the white field that ran all the way up to the high peaks.

'Are you ready?' asked Aristander.

'I am ready,' replied the King.

'For what?'

'For everything.'

'Even death?'

'Yes.'

'In that case undress now.'

Alexander obeyed.

'Lie down in the snow.'

Alexander lay down on his back in the snowy shroud and shivered as he watched Aristander kneel down near him and begin rocking backwards and forwards on his heels, singing a strange lullaby, syncopated now and then by short cries in an incomprehensible barbarian tongue. As Aristander's song climbed up towards the remote and freezing sky, Alexander's body seemed to fall deeper into the snow, to the point where it was almost submerged.

He felt his skin pierced by thousands of icy needles that seemed to reach his heart and the pain was growing with each instant that passed and was quickly becoming unbearable. At a certain point he realized that he himself was emitting a series of rhythmic shouts in the same barbarian tongue used by Aristander, and then he noticed that the seer's eyes were all white now and expressionless, like those of a marble statue washed colourless by the rain.

He tried to speak, but nothing came; he tried to get up, but he felt that he was not strong enough. He tried to shout again, but now he had no voice at all. He was falling deeper and deeper into the snow, or perhaps he was floating in the freezing, limpid air above the mountain peaks . . . he saw himself as a child, as though in a dream, running through the rooms of the palace while old Artemisia breathlessly tried to keep up with him. Then, suddenly, he found himself in the great council hall, in the armoury where the generals of the realm used

to sit by his father's side, and he stood there speechless before the majestic warriors all enclosed in their shining armour. At that point he saw an impressive-looking man come out of a side corridor, his white mane flowing behind him – the most important soldier of the realm, General Parmenion!

The old soldier stared at him and said as he smiled, 'How does that rhyme go, Little Prince, what was it again? Aren't you going to sing it again for your silly old soldier who's off to the war?'

Alexander tried to sing it, the rhyme that made everyone laugh, but he couldn't because a great lump had shut his throat tight. He turned to move back into his room, but before him he saw the landscape all covered with snow and he saw Aristander once more, on his knees, his eyes still white. He desperately tried to summon his last energies to reach out and touch the cloak he had abandoned just a short time before on the snow, but as he made the tremendous effort to turn his head in that direction he was suddenly paralysed by the shock of seeing Parmenion there before him, pale in the moonlight, encased in his armour with his magnificent sword hanging at his side.

His eyes filled with tears as he managed to murmur, 'Old . . . brave . . . soldier . . . forgive me.'

Parmenion raised his lips slightly in a sad smile and replied, 'I am with my boys now. We are together. Farewell, *Aléxandre*. You shall have my forgiveness when we next see each other. And that moment will not be long in coming.' He moved off slowly across the virgin snow and disappeared into the shadow.

Right then Alexander suddenly jerked back into consciousness and there in front of him was Aristander, holding out his cloak and saying, 'Quickly! Cover yourself! Cover up! You have been very close to death.'

Alexander managed to lift himself up and wrap himself in his cloak and the warmth of the wool slowly brought life back into his body.

'What happened?' Aristander asked. 'I used up all the power I had in my soul, but I remember nothing.'

'I saw Parmenion. He was dressed in his armour, but he bore no wounds and he smiled at me,' and as he spoke he lowered his head. 'But it was probably just an illusion.'

'An illusion?' said the seer. 'Perhaps not. Look.'

Alexander turned and saw a row of footprints in the snow that ended just a stone's throw from them, as though whoever had walked in that direction had dissolved into thin air. He knelt down and touched them with his fingertips and then he turned towards Aristander with his gaze full of wonder, 'Macedonian boots . . . studded. Oh, by Zeus, is it possible?'

The seer stared out towards the horizon, 'Let us return now,' he said. 'It is late. The stars that have protected us this far will soon disappear in the morning light.'

41

ALEXANDER CELEBRATED THE birth of his new city with solemn rites and sacrifices, after which he announced athletics, games and a poetry competition with elaborate stage settings. The best tragic actors who had acted in all the most demanding roles now sought to compete with the legendary Thessalus. The highland air, however, seemed to confer even grander timbre and power to the great actor's voice.

The high point of the cycle of tragedies came with a production of *Seven against Thebes* in which a young actor from Mylasa acted with striking realism the part of Tydeus, sinking his teeth into the skull of Melanippus. However, the prize for the best interpretation was won yet again by Thessalus for his majestic performance as the protagonist of *Agamemnon*.

The celebrations lasted seven days. On the eighth day, the army set off on its march behind a patrol of local guides in the direction of the pass. After just two stops, they found themselves advancing through deep snow across a land that appeared to be completely deserted. Because the access paths were all extremely steep and difficult to climb up, the pack animals had all been loaded with half of the weight they normally carried, so that the expedition's autonomy was much limited.

The guides explained that there were villages up there and there were provisions to be found, but the snow hid them all so well there was no trace whatsoever. The only way to find out where these settlements were was to wait until evening when the inhabitants lit their fires to cook their supper and the smoke gave their precise location away. In this way the soldiers filled their bellies, but the inhabitants of those poor villages were deprived of all they needed to survive and had to leave their mountain homes and move down towards lower lands where they fought over food with other poor wretches.

The march continued, but it was so strenuous it began to take its toll, with many men suffering from the effects of snow blindness.

Alexander summoned Philip the physician to his tent after sunset and showed him a passage from *The March of the Ten Thousand*. 'Xenophon recounts that he had the same problem with his men in the snows of Armenia – he says that a fair number of them even lost their sight.'

'I have given orders for the soldiers to bandage their eyes, leaving only slits for them to see out just as much as is necessary,' replied Philip. 'This measure ought to help save their sight. I cannot do any more than this – we do not have enough medicines for everyone, but I do remember that my old teacher, Nicomachus, the man who delivered you, made use of snow to cure irritations of the tissues as well as for stemming or stopping haemorrhages. I have carried out some trials with our soldiers and the results are encouraging. In this case we really can say that the cure is to be found in the offending substance.'

Then, noticing that Alexander looked strained, 'And how do you feel in yourself, Sire?'

'My pains are of a type that are beyond your cures, my good Philip, only wine sometimes helps assuage them . . . never until now had I understood what my father meant when he said that a king stands alone.'

'Are you managing to sleep?'

'Yes . . . occasionally.'

'Then go now and rest. May the gods grant you a decent night.'

'And to you too, *iatré*.'

Philip smiled for the King used his full medical title only when he was particularly pleased with some element of his work as a physician. He saluted Alexander with a slight nod of the head and went out into the starry night.

In the course of the following day they came within sight of an enormous rock – high and craggy. Callisthenes studied it for a long time and then had himself accompanied to its base by a patrol of Agrianians. He had noticed a vaguely semicircular projection on one side, reminiscent of a gigantic nest, while on the other side, exactly halfway up the rock face, were some rust-coloured, ring-shaped stains and then a depression that made one think of the shape of a human body of enormous proportions. He immediately sent for Aristander.

'Look,' he said, 'it's extraordinary! We have found the rock that Prometheus was bound to! That thing there,' he said, pointing to the projection, 'might well be the nest of the eagle that ate his liver and those,' pointing now to the rust stains, 'are from the chains that held the Titan prisoner. And that is the mark left by his body . . .

if my uncle Aristotle is right, as I believe he is, and this is the Caucasus, then this might well be Prometheus's rock.'

The news spread quickly among the ranks of the army. A fair number of the soldiers left their positions to go and see it and the more they looked at it the more they were convinced of the truth in what Callisthenes had said. Thessalus too came, and, inspired by the grandiose nature of the landscape around them, he began reciting verse from Aeschylus's *Prometheus* – the lament of the Titan, chained to the Scythian rock. His stentorian voice, echoed by the high peaks, sent the words of the poet resounding through that barbarous and remote land, perennially gripped by ice:

> O you bright sky of heaven, you swift-winged breezes, you river-waters, and infinite laughter of the waves of ocean, O universal mother Earth, and you, all-seeing orb of the sun, to you I call! See what I, a god, endure from the gods.

The King also stood still and listened to those sublime words, but then Callisthenes replied to Thessalus with the words of Hephaestus, forced to put the Titan in chains:

> Therefore on this joyless rock you must stand sentinel, erect, sleepless, your knee unbent. And many a groan and unavailing lament you shall utter; for the heart of Zeus is hard, and everyone is harsh whose power is new.*

* Aeschylus, *Prometheus Bound*, (lines 88–90, 31–35), translated by Herbert Weir Smyth.

These words cut Alexander to the quick, almost as though they had been spoken for him and him alone.

At that very moment an eagle took to the skies from one of the higher peaks and sent its raucous, strident call through the immense space above them as it hovered slowly over the icy desert, as though Zeus himself were replying, offended by the insolent mortals and their puny words.

Callisthenes turned and saw the King's preoccupied gaze: 'Are these verses not splendid?'

'They are,' replied Alexander, and he began walking once more.

*

It took sixteen days' marching for the army to cross the great mountain chain from one side to the other, going through all sorts of trials and ordeals before they came down towards the Scythian plain. Some of the animals had to be put down in order to get past the last part of that formidable barrier, but in the end Alexander was able to cast his gaze over a new province of his immense dominion.

From the last mountain pass he looked out over an endless steppe and once again the men were overwhelmed at the sight of such a uniform, endless landscape, but above all they were amazed that the eternal ice and snow should almost border on such semi-desert lands, baked by the sun.

Being once again part of Alexander's enterprise made them feel as though they had been sucked up in some vertiginous current, by an invincible and irresistible force.

They felt that they were once again engaged in an incomparable adventure that no one else in the world would ever live through; no one except them had had the fortune of encountering such a man, assuming he was a man. Indeed, many of those who followed the army, used to seeing him from far away, shining in his silver breastplate alongside the red standard with the golden star, had now come to think of him as some superhuman being.

As soon as they reached the plain, they set off towards the capital of the region, a city by the name of Bactra, which stood at the centre of a verdant oasis where they would finally find refreshment. The city surrendered without a fight and Alexander confirmed the existing satrap, Artaozos, in his position. He was the one who welcomed the King to the place and informed him that Bessus had retreated, razing the earth in his wake.

'He never imagined that you would reach us so quickly, that you would have crossed the mountains in a matter of days, overcoming snow and hunger. He wasn't able to assemble a sufficiently large army to face you on the open field, so he has crossed the River Oxus, one of the largest of those that flow down from our mountains, and he is now in the midst of those cities which are his allies, and he has destroyed all the bridges behind him.'

On hearing this news the King decided not to waste any time and set off again on their march with the intention of crossing the river where he could. When they reached the banks, he called Diades, his chief engineer, and pointed to the other side, 'How long will it take you to build a bridge?' he asked.

Diades took a javelin from one of the guards and drove it as deep as he could into the riverbed, but the flow immediately tilted it until it was almost lying flat on the water. 'Sand!' he exclaimed. 'It's just sand!'

'What does that mean?' asked the King.

'It means that no supports will hold, just as the shaft of that javelin failed to hold.' He looked around before speaking once again, 'What's more, there are not enough trees nearby.'

'I will send men back to the mountains to cut fir trees.'

Diades shook his head, 'Sire, you well know that nothing has ever stopped me, that there has never been any enterprise that I have ever felt was impossible, but this river is five stadia wide, its flow is very strong and its bed is pure sand. There are no supports that can hold and without supports there can be no bridge. I advise you to look for a ford.'

Oxhatres moved forward and in his uncertain Greek said, 'No ford.'

Alexander started walking up and down the bank in silence, under the gaze of the entire army, as well as his puzzled Companions. Then his attention was drawn by the work of some peasants who were busy in the fields alongside the river. They were separating the straw from the chaff, making the most of the windy day as they threw it all up into the air with shovels and forks. The straw fell not far from them while the chaff, lighter as it was, fluttered in the wind and was carried to the edges of the threshing floor. It was beautiful to watch – a sort

of golden vortex of thousands of shining golden strips fluttering in the air.

As the handsome young man approached them, the peasants stopped their work and looked at him keenly in wonder as he bent over to gather a handful of chaff.

He turned back towards Diades who in the meantime had stuck other poles into the riverbed, not far downstream and was watching them despondently as they were flattened by the current.

'I have found a way,' said Alexander.

'A way of crossing? How?' asked the engineer as he opened up his arms in disbelief.

The King raised his hand and let the chaff he was holding fall to the ground. 'With this,' he said.

'With the chaff from the straw?'

'Exactly. I've seen it done on the Ister. They fill cattle-skins with chaff, then they sew them up and put them in the water. The air trapped in the chaff will make these leather bags float for long enough to let us cross the river.'

'But we don't have enough skins for all our men,' said the engineer.

'No, but we have enough to build a walkway. We can use the skins from the tents . . . what do you think?'

Diades looked at him incredulously. 'It's an ingenious idea. We can grease them with tallow to make them more waterproof.'

A council of the Companions was called and everyone's duties were specified: Hephaestion was to collect the chaff, Leonnatus to gather up all the skins normally used for the tents and to requisition those of the locals as

well. The boards for the floors of the war engines were to be used for the walkway, and stones with ropes tied to them were to be the anchors.

The material was ready as evening fell and Alexander inspected the army, but when he found himself there before the veterans, exhausted after their long crossing of the mountains, he looked on them with compassion as though seeing them for the first time. Many were almost sixty years old. Others were even older and they all bore the signs of the ordeals they had been through – the battles, the wounds, the various hardships. He knew that they would follow him anyway, but he saw in their eyes their awe at the sight of that enormous river that they were attempting to cross with sacks of straw and beyond it the empty vastness of the desert plain.

So he called Craterus and ordered him to assemble all the veterans in front of his tent immediately after sunset because he wanted to dismiss them. Craterus obeyed, and when the old soldiers were all gathered at the centre of the camp, Alexander climbed up on to a podium and began speaking.

'Veterans! You have served your King and your army with honour, overcoming every difficulty and every trial without ever sparing yourselves. You have conquered the greatest empire that has ever existed and you have now reached an age at which it is right that a man should enjoy the rest and privilege that he has earned in honourable combat. I free you of all your bonds and I send you back to your homes. You will each have two hundred silver staters as my personal gift and your salary will be paid until you reach Macedonia. Greet our homeland for

me and live there happily for the rest of your days. You deserve this.'

He was quiet now, expecting an ovation, but instead there was only a buzz through the ranks, the noise of subdued chattering, then an elderly division commander stepped forward and said, 'Why do you no longer want us, Sire?'

'What is your name, Commander?' Alexander asked.

'My name is Antenor.'

'Do you not want to see your family?'

'I want to see them . . . yes, of course.'

'And don't you want to see your home once more and spend some time there eating and drinking and being looked after?'

'Indeed.'

'Then you may all leave now happily and let the youngsters who are about to join us take your places. You have done your job.'

The man did not move.

'What else is there, Commander?'

'I am thinking to myself that the first day will of course be wonderful – I will see my wife and my children, a few of my friends, our house. I will buy new clothes and plenty of food, but the day after that frightens me, Sire. Do you see what I mean?'

'I understand, Commander. The day after that frightens everyone, myself included. This is precisely why I cannot bring myself to stop . . . ever. I must rush to reach it, to go beyond it.'

The veteran nodded even though he had not understood and said, 'You're right, Sire. You are young and

we are old. It is time for us to return home. But at
least—'

'What?'

'At least ... may I embrace you for all of my
companions?'

Alexander held him fast like an old friend and then the
men broke out in an ovation because the veterans, from
the first to the last, felt that the King was embracing
them all and that he was much moved, and they all felt
the tears come into their eyes.

That night Callisthenes wrote a long letter to his uncle
Aristotle and gave it to one of the departing veterans
who lived near Stagira. In payment he received a golden
stater, the first one minted by Philip and bearing Alex-
ander's image, an Alexander who for Callisthenes no
longer existed and who had not existed for some time
now. The veterans left at dawn, saluting with all arms
presented and great trumpet blasts as they moved off
towards the west, following the line of the mountains in
the direction of Zadracarta.

The echo of the drums that marked their march could
still be heard when Diades set about assembling their
bridge as quickly as possible and then, immediately
afterwards, the crossing began: first the *hetairoi* on foot,
leading their horses by the bridle, and then the infantry.

The entire contingent were on the other side by
afternoon and the engineers continued to work until after
nightfall to recover the material on the northern bank of
the river. While the men were setting up the tents,
Oxhatres and his horsemen carried out a far-reaching
reconnaissance mission and then returned to Alexandria

to report that they had found many horse tracks and that these must have come from the army accompanying Bessus the usurper.

The King immediately called a council of his Companions, Cleitus the Black and some battalion commanders who had performed particularly well during all their recent operations. He also admitted Oxhatres and some Persian cavalry officers and this was received very coolly by Cleitus and his commanders.

'Our Persian friends have provided us with precious help,' he began, 'in putting us on our enemy's trail. Now we know where Bessus is going and we know what must be done. We have to catch him now or we never will. Ptolemy will take command of the Vanguard, together with a squadron of *hetairoi* and two of light assault troops and he will give chase as rapidly as possible. Oxhatres will accompany you with his division.' At this point Ptolemy gave a slight sign of irritation that Alexander did not fail to notice. 'Any objections, Ptolemy?'

'None whatsoever,' came his prompt reply.

'So that is settled then. You will leave immediately. Your guides know the way even through the darkness.'

Ptolemy put on his helmet and left, followed by all the other members of the council. Only the Black remained.

'Was it strictly necessary to send those barbarians with Ptolemy?' he asked. 'Haven't we always managed on our own?'

Alexander looked firmly into his eyes. 'Yes, it was necessary, and for two reasons, Black. The first is that they know these lands like no one else, the second is that

they will soon be part of our army at the same level as our cavalry and infantry.'

Cleitus lowered his head as though having received some terrible blow. 'You are making a terrible mistake, Alexander.'

'Why?'

'Because sooner or later you will have to choose . . . us or them,' and he left without saying goodbye. Not long after, Ptolemy's trumpets sounded the signal for his army to fall in.

42

OXHATRES IMMEDIATELY PROVED to be indispensable. He sported Scythian leather trousers and a bodice of reinforced leather with metal plates, his bow and quiver over his shoulder and a long Hyrcanian sabre hanging by his side. He rode a horse typical of the steppes – small and with a long-haired coat, but very strong.

He made sure they all had torches, then he lit his own and stared into Ptolemy's eyes with an eloquent expression, as though to say, 'Let's just see if you're as tough as you make out you are.' He then set off at a gallop, the flaming torch held on high to illuminate the path and to be as visible as possible to the troops following on behind. As they advanced, the tracks they were following appeared progressively fresh and evident, a sign that they were gaining ground.

Ptolemy noted that the Asian horsemen never stopped at all, even urinating while still astride their mounts. When he finally gave the order to stop, to give the animals some rest and a few hours' sleep to the men, Oxhatres shook his head to manifest his disagreement, then he let himself fall forward on to his horse's neck and dozed for a while, as did his Hyrcanian and Bactrian horsemen. The others had just settled on the ground, wrapped up in their cloaks, when the barbarian straightened his

back once more and grabbed the bridle, saying, 'It's late, Bessus will not be expecting us now.' He lit a second torch from the smoking remains of his first and set off at a gallop, followed by his men. He came to a halt just before dawn, dismounted, gathered up some horse dung and showed it to Ptolemy. 'It's fresh . . . we'll have them tomorrow.'

'If we haven't died of exhaustion before then,' replied one of the officers of the Vanguard.

Ptolemy, who did not wish to appear any less valiant, shouted, 'To your horses, men! Show them what you're made of!'

Pride and self-respect were enough to awaken some residue of energy in the tired horsemen's limbs, but Ptolemy noted that some of them were bleeding from wounds on the inside of their thighs.

'Perhaps you understand now why they wear trousers? Let's move, let's go now!'

The sun rose shortly afterwards and in its clear light their shadows lengthened along the completely deserted steppes of the plain. All the colours of this apparently godforsaken land were called up out of the darkness and at that moment of pure peace and quiet, the landscape was truly lovely. There were the small yellow flowers of the wild daisies, tufts of purple thistles and occasional silver-coloured bushes that shone like jewels on the ochre of the sandy earth. At a certain point they met a long caravan of gigantic camels – hairy and with two humps and called 'Bactrians' – filling the morning silence with strange, mournful bellows.

'They are on their way to Smyrna,' Oxhatres explained, laughing. 'Do you want to go with them?'

Ptolemy shook his head and nodded to the barbarian to continue. His eyes were burning now because of the fatigue and he had blisters everywhere, but he would rather have died than ask to rest. Some of his men, however, had already stopped or had simply collapsed out of exhaustion. He abandoned them there where they fell, thinking he would pick them up again on the way back.

The sun had now risen high in the sky and the heat was almost unbearable. Swarms of flies arrived from who knows where and buzzed around their eyes, keen to suck up the humour, while hundreds of horseflies tormented their steeds, which stomped and neighed in pain. Ptolemy noticed that the Persian horses were impervious to these insects thanks to their thick, bristly hair and their tails that reached almost to the ground, long enough to scare off any of the parasites that approached. He thought that perhaps Alexander was right, up to a certain point, regarding the barbarians' abilities and their knowledge of these lands and the people who inhabited them.

As he was lost in these thoughts, Oxhatres' voice broke in as he said, 'There's the city,' and pointed to a great wall in mud brickwork surrounding a grey-coloured settlement of low buildings, with just one structure that was high and imposing enough to single it out as the residence of the chief. Ptolemy nodded and the cavalry took up formation in an arc so as to surround the city in a sort of ring, so that no one could enter nor exit.

Oxhatres negotiated with the enemy leader and after some time he came back to report to Ptolemy: 'They are surprised to see us here and they have lost heart. Two satraps will hand him over to us, providing we let them go free.'

'Who are they?'

'Spitamenes and Datafernes.'

'Where are they now?'

'In the city. Bessus is with them.'

Ptolemy considered this for a moment while the flocks of sheep, that were returning now with the shepherds, found their way to the city blocked and started gathering outside the lines of soldiers, who in their turn were all covered in the dust raised by the animals. Then came Ptolemy's decision. 'We accept. Get them to tell you where they will hand him over. We will leave most of the army here to avoid any surprises and we will go to the appointment.'

Oxhatres went back and spoke again for some time with the negotiators, then he signalled to Ptolemy that they had reached an agreement and so the flocks of sheep were allowed through. Together with their shepherds the animals rushed through the open gates. Soon afterwards the ramparts of the walls were teeming with people – men and women, the old and the young, all of whom wanted to see the *daiwa*, all decked in metal and with their helmets crested, on those enormous horses with their shining coats. They pointed them all out to one another and then they pointed to the sunset-red mountains as if to say that these men had swooped down from there like birds of prey.

Oxhatres reported the terms of the arrangement – Bessus would be handed over in a place some three stadia away from the city, at nightfall. As soon as it was dark, a group of their Sogdian horsemen would deliver the prisoner, while Spitamenes and Datafernes would retreat through the eastern gate that was to be left free for this very reason.

'Tell him we agree,' replied Ptolemy, thinking that he had received orders to capture Bessus and not to take the other two satraps, and so he allowed his men to eat and drink as they sat there on the ground. Then he gave orders for the eastern gate to be left free as soon as night fell.

'Who guarantees that they will keep to the pact?' he asked, rather worried, while they moved towards the appointed place.

Oxhatres replied, 'I left a group of my men at the eastern gate; they all know Bessus and they will realize if he passes through that way.'

He stopped when he came within sight of an old, dried up acacia tree by the side of a pathway, and he turned to Ptolemy and said, 'They will bring him here. All we have to do is wait.'

With nightfall the vast plain had been swallowed up by the silence, but as time slipped by the call of the crickets came ever louder, adding to the long drawn-out call of the jackals that seemed to come from nowhere and disappeared into nowhere. Perhaps an hour went by and there came first the barking of a dog and then the stamping of hooves. Oxhatres stirred and was the first to speak, 'They're on their way.' Suddenly he tensed up,

like a predator waiting to strike. A group of shadows appeared from the steppes – some ten or so Sogdian horsemen led by a Persian officer and with a prisoner in chains. Oxhatres blew on the glowing stump of a torch he was carrying and the flame came back to life. He held it up to the face of the prisoner, recognized it and his own features lit up in a most sinister, wolf-like grin. The horsemen who had accompanied Bessus slipped away, immediately disappearing from sight.

Oxhatres nodded to one of his men to hold the torch and to another two to hold the prisoner still.

'What are you doing?' shouted Ptolemy. 'He is Alexander's prisoner!'

'He's mine before he's his!' replied the Persian, with such a ferocious look in his eyes that Ptolemy did not have the courage to react. Then he slipped his dagger off his belt, its blade razor sharp, and moved towards the prisoner who clenched his jaws in preparation for all the pain that a man who has fallen into the hands of his worst enemy might expect.

Oxhatres cut all of the fastenings off his clothes and left him completely naked – there was nothing more humiliating than this for a Persian. Then he grabbed him by the hair and sliced off first his nose and then his ears. Bessus bore these horrendous mutilations with truly heroic courage, without crying or shouting, his disfigured, bloody face sitting atop his still impressive, sculpture-like body which was graced with a dramatic, frightful dignity.

'Enough!' shouted Ptolemy, horrified at what he had seen. 'I won't stand for this!' and he jumped to the

ground and pushed Oxhatres out of the way, calling a surgeon and ordering him to bandage the prisoner's wounds so that he didn't lose too much blood.

There was no other way for the physicians to stem the blood apart from wrapping a bandage round the prisoner's face. Bessus was then forced to set off on foot, naked and barefoot as he was, along the pathway littered with sharp flints. Ptolemy watched him as his enemies dragged him along by a rope tied round his neck and this pathetic scene seemed to him to be a grotesque parody of a passage from *Oedipus Rex*, a tragedy that he had seen as a young man performed by a travelling company in his native town. Oedipus had appeared like that, a bloody bandage round his head, after having driven the point of his buckle into his eyeballs.

They walked all through the night and all of the next day. On the third day they met Alexander with the rest of the army. The King came forward, surrounded by his friends and by a group of Persian officers and stared at his enemy, the would-be Artaxerxes IV. Those Persians present who had been loyal to King Darius sent him a rain of spit, punches and other blows on his still open wounds, reducing his face to a bloody mask.

Alexander said nothing because at that moment he was avenging Darius's death and he felt himself to be truly the only and legitimate successor to the King of Kings. He waited until they had given vent to all their hatred, then he called Oxhatres. 'That's enough,' he said. 'Have him taken back to Bactra and tell them to set up a trial for my return. Up until then no harm at all must befall him.'

Then he turned to Ptolemy. 'You have accomplished an extraordinary feat. I have been told that you managed ten day's march in three days. Will you dine with me this evening?'

'I will,' replied Ptolemy.

Night was falling and Alexander returned to his tent where Leptine was preparing his bath. Just as he was getting into the tub a visit from Philip, his physician, was announced.

'Come in,' he said. 'I was about to take a bath. Is someone not well by any chance?'

'No, Sire. Everyone's well enough, but I have some sad news for you – Princess Stateira has miscarried.'

Alexander lowered his head, 'Was it . . . a boy?' he asked, his voice quavering.

'As far as I have been told, it seems so,' replied Philip. The King asked nothing more and not even the physician managed to say much more because a huge lump was now blocking his throat. He added only, 'I'm sorry . . . I am truly sorry.' And then he left.

43

THE ENTOURAGE FOLLOWING the King's army grew in number all the time. Sometimes it encamped as far as a few days' walk from the military and in effect it constituted a moving city with its own courts for administering justice, travelling theatres that put on local popular dramas as well as comedies or tragedies from the Greek repertory, and emporia that bought and sold all types of merchandise.

As the entourage grew, so too did the numbers of relationships between Macedonian soldiers and local girls, with the subsequent birth of many mixed race children. For all these people the young King was now a god in every respect – because of his appearance, because of his invincibility and because of his ability to overcome all natural obstacles, from the highest of mountains to the widest and fastest-flowing of rivers.

However, Alexander was perfectly aware that this entourage would eventually cripple the army, impeding its ability to move and slowing down its reactions in case of attack. He therefore decided to send back part of the army with Craterus, to the banks of the Oxus, to found there a new Alexandria. He settled a few hundred people in the city, together with four hundred soldiers, those who had set up families with the women of their

entourage, and this community was organized with all the institutions of Greek cities, with elected assemblies and magistrates.

Then the King set off once more on his march northwards, through land that for the most part was completely arid, until he reached the banks of a tributary of the Oxus that the locals called 'The Most Honourable', and thus the Greeks decided to call it by the same name – Polytimetus. A fine city overlooked the river – Samarkand, frequented by both Sogdians and Asian Scythians who came from the limitless territories beyond the river and who brought their goods to market there: skins, livestock, gemstones, gold-dust and occasionally slaves plundered from far off lands. The caravans that came across the mountain passes from India also travelled through the city.

From here Alexander moved eastwards to the farthest point ever reached in that direction by the Persians. It was a city founded on the River Jaxartes by Cyrus the Great in person and it bore the name Kurushkkat, which means Cyropolis. At that moment it was the stronghold of a group of rebels, friends of the two satraps, Spitamenes and Datafernes, who had handed Bessus over to Ptolemy, and were still intent on leading the resistance of their people against the new sovereign.

The city was protected by an old bastion of rough stonework, much eroded by the rain and the wind and surmounted by some lookout turrets made of wood. Surrounding it were another seven smaller cities. It took less than a month to bring them all under control, one

by one, and they were all forced to accept a Macedonian garrison.

*

Alexander chose to celebrate his victory with a banquet and he sent a personal invitation to all his Companions and higher officers.

The King welcomed them all at the door, kissed them on the cheek one by one and then had them enter where the symposium had been arranged with a crater, cups and ladles. When they had all taken their places, the other guests arrived and everyone turned to watch them as they entered; Oxhatres and his nobles, dressed in their fine national costumes, took the places that had been assigned to them. They had acquitted themselves admirably in the attacks on the rebel cities and the King had decided to honour them by inviting them to his table.

The other guests watched in amazement and then looked at one another – speechless all of them. Alexander was the first to speak in the general embarrassment. 'We have taken Bessus, my friends, and we have occupied the rebel cities thanks to the extraordinary speed of Ptolemy's division and thanks to the help of our Persian friends. Now I must make an important announcement – tomorrow I intend to dismiss the allied cavalry of the Thessalian veterans. I will keep only the youngest, those who came with the latest reinforcements.'

'You want to dismiss the Thessalians?' Cleitus asked in amazement. 'But the Thessalians saved us from defeat at Gaugamela . . . have you forgotten that?'

The Thessalian commander, who had evidently already been informed about this decision by the King himself, said nothing at all.

'I have no wish to send them away, but many of them are tired, some want to join their families after all these years of war, others again do not feel that they can risk an expedition against the Scythians.'

'Against the Scythians?' asked Craterus. 'Are we going after the Scythians? But no one has ever succeeded in defeating them – Cyrus the Great lost his life, Darius's army was annihilated . . . no one knows exactly how many of them there are, where they are, and no one knows where their territory ends. It's like advancing into . . . the unknown, into the void.'

'That may be,' replied Alexander calmly, 'and in any case this is exactly what I wish to discover.'

'I am with you,' said Hephaestion. Craterus had nothing to add and he began to eat, reluctantly, the mutton roast that was being served at the table.

Some moments of silence passed by, interrupted only by the chattering of the Persians as they spoke quietly among themselves.

It was Cleitus who piped up first, with a question: 'And how will you substitute the three magnificent battalions of Thessalian cavalry?'

'There are two thousand Persian horsemen on their way – all of them trained in the Macedonian manner,' replied the King, staring him straight in the eyes. 'I have called them the Successors.'

The words left the Black paralysed and his eyes grew

moist with anger. He stood up and said, 'So it seems you no longer have any need of us.' Then he wrapped himself up in his cloak and made for the door.

'Stop, Black! Stop! Do not defy me in this way, Black!' shouted the King.

But Cleitus did not even turn as he left. Others stood up, leaving the food on the tables – the commander of the Thessalians, then the battalion chiefs Meleager and Polyperchon, followed by almost all the commanding officers of the *hetairoi* cavalry.

'Do you wish to leave as well?' asked Alexander, turning to his friends.

Seleucus, usually the coolest of them all, sometimes apparently the most cynical, said, 'Do not be upset by this, none of it is worth worrying about. We are the ones – those of us who are left here now – we are the ones who swore we would follow you to the ends of the earth. The others are free to do what they will, we have no need of them.'

'That's it!' shouted Leonnatus, who in all truth just a short time before had not seemed at all sure of this. 'And then these Scythians can only be made of flesh and bones . . . I have seen them, did you know that? In Athens they are paid to maintain public order and they patrol the city holding great wooden clubs and their bows slung across their chests. They didn't look like anything special to me.'

Ptolemy approached and ruffled his hair. 'Well done, Leonnatus, you're quite right; but bear in mind that these Scythians out here are made of sterner stuff. What

Craterus has told you is the simple truth: Cyrus ended up biting the dust when he tackled them and they brought Darius to his knees. Entire armies have ventured into the Scythians' limitless lands with all memory of them being lost forever.'

44

ALL SORTS OF GIFTS were heaped on the Thessalians
when they left, and, as with the other veterans, they also
received a generous payment to cover the expenses of
their journey home; all of which helped considerably in
minimizing their feelings of resentment towards Alex-
ander. In fact many of them were much moved when
they took their leave. One veteran who had fought in all
the battles, from the Granicus to Artacoana, told him
simply, 'I have heard that you will have the barbarians
fighting alongside your troops and allow some of their
officers to form part of the high command. I do not
believe this is a good decision on your part, and yet I
have to admit that every time we have grumbled and
complained about you and your policies and the fact that
it all seemed like so much madness to us, in the end you
have always been right.

'What we want is to be with our families once more,
to see our cities again and our villages and in all honesty
we are not keen on the idea of running after Scythians
across an endless prairie where no olives or vines grow
and where we are told there are no houses to be seen for
a hundred days' march. And yet, and here I speak on
behalf of most of my companions, we are sorry to leave
you, Sire. We will lose sleep thinking of you out there in

that deserted land, surrounded by barbarians on all sides, but nothing, I fear, will ever change your destiny. It has been a magnificent experience, fighting by your side. Take good care, *Aléxandre*, and farewell.'

Alexander, astride Bucephalas, inspected them, sending a smile or a salute to every soldier, and he shook the hands of all those he recognized or had seen fighting valiantly in the field. The tears that ran down his face were sincere as he watched them all set off at a walk in rows of eight against the sun as it descended red towards the western horizon.

The following day saw the arrival of the first Persian horsemen, combat-trained and equipped after the Macedonian fashion. The only difference, apart from their physical appearance with their thick moustaches and their elaborate hairstyles, was the fact that they used trousers, although another striking feature was their custom of approaching the King using the same ceremonial protocol they had always used with Darius – bending forwards and sending a kiss from a distance. The Macedonians and the Greeks called this gesture *proskynesis* – 'prostration' – and they dismissed it contemptuously as a barbaric custom, more suited to slaves than to men; but Alexander accepted it, thus demonstrating that he now considered himself to be the legitimate successor of the Achaemenid emperors.

Just beyond Cyropolis was the great Jaxartes river, the Persians' northern border, and Alexander reached it in a single day's march, setting up camp on its banks. Groups of Scythian horsemen soon made their appearance on the other side, splendidly dressed and armed, shouting defi-

antly, making threatening gestures and even firing arrows.

One man, who must have been their leader, stood out from the others because of his size and his long hair held in place by a ribbon of red cloth. He wore a long-sleeved tunic and cloth trousers in the same colour with a band of gold down the sides. His chest was protected by a scaled breastplate and the lower part of his legs by metal greaves after the Greek fashion. There was a sword hanging from his belt, a bow across his shoulders and his quiver hung from his horse's bridle. All the horses wore forehead pieces in embossed metal and the bundles of leather protecting the base of their necks were adorned with magnificent gold leaf ornament.

'What are they saying?' Alexander asked his interpreter.

'They are saying,' said Oxhatres who understood them, 'that you are a coward and a cur and that you must leave immediately after having left them a tribute. They suggest one hundred talents of silver.'

This infuriated Alexander and he rode Bucephalas to the edge of the riverbank, heedless of the rain of arrows the Scythians fired against him; Leonnatus and Ptolemy sought to protect him with their shields. He shouted, 'I am not afraid of you! I will cross the river and I will follow you everywhere, even if it means to the shore of the northern Ocean!'

'Do you think they've understood?' asked Seleucus with his usual irony.

'Perhaps not,' replied Alexander, 'but they soon will. Tell Lysimachus to take all the catapults to the riverbank

and keep them under constant fire. Tomorrow we will cross to the other side and we will found another city – the farthest Alexandria.'

*

Lysimachus had twenty catapults lined up in two rows almost at the water's edge and began firing. As one row let fly with a salvo of harpoons, the other reloaded, so that the rain of projectiles was uninterrupted and deadly. The Scythians fell in swathes and those who did not suffer direct hits fled, terrorized by these machines they had never seen before. At this point Alexander sent the Agrianians in with orders to swim across the river; the assault troops then quickly established a bridgehead on the other bank which was secured before midday. Diades of Larissa then began launching a series of rafts on the skin bags filled with straw and chaff, just as he had done previously on the Oxus.

The Vanguard were on the other side by sunset and Alexander decided to pitch camp on the northern bank even although Aristander had received several negative omens while making sacrifices to the gods.

The seer appeared after nightfall and was in such a bad mood that he chose not to take supper in the royal tent. In the meantime, by torchlight, the rest of the army continued to cross the river: the *hetairoi* and a squadron of Persian cavalry made up above all else of Medians, Hyrcanians and Bactrians. The few locals who were still on the other side witnessed an extraordinary spectacle – an endless line of horses and horsemen weaving its way

across the plain, as it went by illuminating first the fields of grain and then the shining surface of the river.

On the following day, while the engineers were busy marking out the limits of Alexandria-the-Farthest, thousands and thousands of horsemen appeared suddenly on the northern horizon, all lined up across the widest imaginable front.

'The Scythians!' shouted Leonnatus. 'Alarm! Alarm!'

The trumpets sounded, and while the heavy infantry took up position in a square formation around the freshly marked limits of the new city, the cavalry assembled in the space just before them.

'What can we do?' asked Craterus.

One of the Thracian commanders, a man who had battle experience under Philip, stepped forward and asked Alexander, 'May I speak?'

'Of course,' replied the King, without taking his eye off the approaching menace of the Scythian line as it advanced across the plain.

'I fought against the Scythians on the Ister together with your father and I remember it well. Anyone who enters Scythian territory and moves too far from his own base is in big trouble. Just look at that plain – it extends uninterrupted, apart from the big rivers, as far as the Ister, as far as the border with Macedonia, and those men,' he continued, pointing now to the shining warriors in their scaled metal breastplates, 'move across the plain like fish in water. Their sense of direction is such that they can keep to a route and travel thousands of stadia without seeing even a tree or a hut. Now they are lined

up frontally, but this is not how they will attack us. As soon as we move they will charge in a circle around us, without ever coming within the range of our arrows, yet from that distance they will send a hail of their own upon us. Hundreds of our men will be wounded, many of them not seriously, but enough to put them out of action.

'The attack will naturally provoke a reaction, but they will not engage us immediately and they will pretend to retreat, so as to draw us farther away until they suddenly reappear, like ghosts, and give chase again, letting fly with swarms of arrows to weaken us even more. Only then will they unleash the frontal assault, wiping out all survivors. When all of their enemies are dead they start stripping the bodies of anything of value, cutting off heads to exhibit them as trophies, or simply scalping them to decorate their spears and the handles of their battle axes with the hair of their defeated enemies.'

'An interesting custom,' said Seleucus, running his hands through his hair.

Alexander looked around and saw the Black off at some distance, watching over his men as they pitched tents. He was keeping out of the King's way since he had left his table at Cyropolis and spoke to him as little as possible, but on this occasion there was no way out when Alexander called him over with a gesture.

'At your command, Sire!' he responded, using the impersonal formula of military protocol as soon as he reached Alexander.

'I have no orders for you,' replied Alexander. 'I would

like you to listen to the words of this friend who fought against the Scythians on the Ister.'

'I fought there too,' said Cleitus.

'What do you suggest then?'

'I suggest we turn back.'

Alexander looked again at the huge enemy line that was now immobile in the midst of the steppe, 'You are free to do so, even though I am now in need of your experience and your valour more than ever, but I have never retreated before an enemy lined up against me in the open field.'

'I think I have a useful suggestion,' said the Thracian.

'What?' asked the Black, unable to help himself being drawn into the urgent discussion.

'Let's send quite a strong group forwards – a thousand or so men. We'll have them move out to the right as though aiming to drive towards the interior of Scythian territory and we'll keep an eye on the enemies' movements using a relay system, perhaps one horseman every five stadia. If they make no move then we'll send out a second contingent with another line of communication . . .'

'I understand,' said Alexander. 'As soon as they decide to attack the news reaches us and we take them from behind with the forces we have left here.'

'And as quickly as possible,' added the Thracian. 'What's more, given the situation we're in, these men will be precious,' he said, pointing to the Persian contingent.

The Black grimaced, but said nothing.

'Well . . . Black, are you with us?' asked Perdiccas.

'Where can I go if I'm not with you?'

'Who's going to be the first off then?' asked Alexander.

'To be the bait? That's a job for me, since I'm the hardest to chew here,' replied Cleitus. He had the fall in sounded for his squadron and then gave orders for them to advance at a walk. Lined up in rows of four, the *hetairoi* formed an ordered and glinting dark mass in the midst of the green plain, moving compact and united to the rhythmic roll of the drums. Gradually they disappeared as they moved into the distance, but at least one relay horseman remained in sight, while the Scythian cavalry, taken by surprise by this manoeuvre, seemed unsure of what to do.

'They're not moving ... they're not biting...' said Ptolemy, shaking his head.

'Let's send a second squadron,' ordered Alexander. 'Perdiccas, you go, and move as quickly as you can – the sooner you join up with the Black the better – and take them with you,' he added, pointing to the Persian contingent, still awaiting orders at the edge of the field. Oxhatres nodded to indicate he had understood and as soon as the trumpets sounded and Perdiccas's division moved forward, he too lined up with his horsemen of the steppes.

The Scythians appeared not to react this time either, then, as though obeying some sudden signal, they turned about and disappeared over a rise in the rolling terrain.

Alexander gave orders for all the rest of the forces to be lined up and waited for any sign that something was about to happen.

In the meantime the sky had filled with a strange mist

that filtered the sun's rays into a diaphanous and milky glow, wiping out even further the sense of distance and depth.

'Look!' exclaimed Leonnatus all of a sudden. 'Signals from our messengers! They're attacking.'

45

ALEXANDER ASSEMBLED ALL the remaining horsemen, gave command of the auxiliary divisions and squadrons to Ptolemy and the others, and set off at a gallop together with Oxhatres' second division, which consisted of a hundred or so Scythians who for some time had fought as mercenaries in the imperial army.

He chose not to come within sight of the enemy as he advanced, maintaining contact through the messengers until he received confirmation that the Scythians had engaged in battle with Perdiccas and Cleitus.

'What formation have they adopted?' the King asked.

'It's not a formation in the true sense – they are circling around our divisions, firing thick swarms of arrows. Up to now our men have used their shields to protect themselves, but I don't know how long they can hold out.'

'Indeed, it is time to put an end to this,' replied Alexander. He called his Companions and said to them, 'We will now move forward at a moderate speed until we make contact with them. As soon as we come within sight, the trumpets will sound the signal: Cleitus and Perdiccas will break out of the circle surrounding them, immediately fanning out and turning back towards us as we take the Scythians from behind in a pincer move.

There will be no way out for them, not even on the open sides. Take no prisoners unless they surrender. And now, to your mounts!'

Alexander was astride his Sarmatian bay, the standard-bearer alongside him and all the others followed, spread out over a huge front along the flat plain, four rows deep.

As soon as the Scythians appeared with their bright costumes and their scaled armour, the King had the trumpets sound the agreed signal. Almost immediately Cleitus and Perdiccas arranged their men in a wedge shape and charged forward, breaking out of the circle and galloping in a straight line until the last of their men had come out of it. Then they split into two halves, each of which made a wide turn, and united once more into a single front; then they turned around, charging compactly with their spears held low, ready for battle.

At the same moment Alexander appeared from the other side with all his squadrons already speeding forward at a charge. Taken by surprise there in the middle, the Scythians were forced into hand-to-hand combat in a space that was too cramped and with no opportunity of finding escape laterally. They were furious at having been trapped in this way in the very midst of their ocean-like plain, like fish in a net, and they sought to break out in any way possible, but the terrain was so flat and regular that the Macedonian cavalry was able to maintain their front completely intact and to make the most of the advantage of their heavier weapons.

The Scythians fought bitterly, suffering terrible losses, and it was towards afternoon, when they realized they

were facing a massacre that they made one final effort, grouping together and driving through a small gap that had formed in the enemy front; led by their commander, they managed to push through into open terrain and slip away.

The Macedonian soldiers cried out in victory, raising the points of their spears to the sky, but the King soon stopped them. 'It is not over yet,' he said. 'Now we must follow them to their villages and we will make sure they will remember for all time Alexander and his *hetairoi*.' But just as he was about to give orders for them all to leave, some messengers arrived from the camp with a message from the infantry commanders.

'Sire, the Satrap Spitamenes has incited the Sogdians and the Bactrians and they are now attacking Samarkand. The commanders want to know what they should do.'

'Leave a garrison in the new city and then turn back towards Samarkand. I will reach you there as soon as I have finished my incursion here.'

The messengers left and Alexander began the march across the plain once more, led by Oxhatres. They proceeded at a walk now, following the tracks of the Scythian horsemen who had escaped the battle, and the immense vastness of the plain filled them with wonder and awe: there was not even a tree to be seen, no rocks or stones, not a hill or a rise in the land while behind them the mountains of the Paropamisus were pinkish red as the rays of the setting sun fell on the snow-covered peaks.

Ptolemy said, as though speaking to himself, 'On the island of Euboea, the cities of Chalcis and Eretria fought

fiercely for fifty years for control of a plain some thirty-five stadia long.'

'Quite,' Perdiccas said in agreement, 'and here our gaze reaches the horizon with no obstacles at all and no sign of any human presence.'

'Yet they cannot have disappeared into nothing,' said Hephaestion. 'They are not ghosts.'

'They are nomads,' explained Oxhatres who was riding behind them. 'They live in carts drawn by oxen and inside are their families – wives, the elderly, children. Their nourishment comes from milk and meat and they can travel for days and nights without ever stopping because their horses have incredible stamina.'

'How far does their land extend?' asked Alexander, remembering his father's tales of his battles against the Scythians beyond the Ister.

'No one knows,' replied the Persian.

'According to some people,' said Seleucus, 'they border to the north with the Hyperboreans and to the east with the Issedonians whose diet consists of nothing but horse milk.'

'What if we get lost?' Leonnatus asked, looking out over the flat, stepped land.

'Impossible,' Seleucus reassured him. 'We have the mountains behind us and the Jaxartes to our left. In any case I would turn back, given what is happening now at Samarkand.'

Alexander continued riding in silence – this was his way of putting them to the test, of seeing just how strong their loyalty, their friendship and their determination to face the unknown still were. Then the Scythian tracks

disappeared all of a sudden, as though their horses had grown wings and taken to the skies.

'By Zeus!' exclaimed Perdiccas.

Oxhatres dismounted and examined the ground. 'They've wrapped up the horses' hooves so they leave almost no trace on this dry grass, but my Scythians ought to be able to make something out.'

'Let's go on then,' ordered the King.

The march began once more until darkness fell and not even Oxhatres' Scythian scouts were able to see anything. Alexander had the trumpets signal a halt and everyone placed their cloaks on the ground, took a little bread and dried meat from their satchels together with their water bottles and sat to eat the most frugal supper they had had for some considerable time. Yet there was a great sense of peace everywhere – the moon was almost full and it was rising now from behind the mountains, illuminating the great plain and making the waters of the rivers shine. The brightest constellations appeared one after the other in the clear night sky that was completely free of cloud. Only far off, towards the east and over the mountain crests, were there some flashes of lightning to be seen; apart from this the world was fully immersed in the peace and quiet of the evening. The Asian warriors had formed their own circle and had managed to light a fire.

'How do they do that?' Hephaestion asked, beginning to feel quite cold. 'I haven't seen any trace of a bush or anything for a hundred stadia.'

'Dung,' replied Oxhatres in his uncertain Greek, and with an expression of profound contempt.

'Dung?' asked Seleucus, raising his eyebrows.

'Sheep dung, horse dung, goat dung. They collect it all in a sack and when it's dry, they burn it.'

'Ah!'

'For us it's a form of sacrilege – the profanation of fire. In Persia it is punishable by death, but they are . . .' and he pronounced a word that in Persian meant 'barbarians'.

'Don't you think this is a tasty meal despite it all?' asked Alexander, changing the subject.

'When hunger bites . . .' said Hephaestion in approval.

'And this place . . . I have never seen anything like it. Not even a single habitation between us and the horizon in all directions.' Then he turned to Oxhatres, 'What do you think? Will Alexandria-the-Farthest survive and thrive?'

'It will thrive,' replied the Persian warrior. 'When the soldiers leave, the merchants will arrive and the city will fill up with people, with livestock, with life. It will thrive.'

They slept that night guarded by a double ring of sentries on horseback who watched over the moonlit plain. They were up at dawn and set off on the chase immediately. After three days they came across wheel tracks and soon they came within sight of the movable village of the Scythian leader who had fled from the battle – three rings of vehicles, all of them covered with tanned hides.

Oxhatres recognized the standard flying from the leading carriage: a wooden shaft with two bronze ibexes engaged in a clash of horns. 'He is a King,' he said. 'Perhaps the one with the red band around his head . . .

and now he has no way out. At this moment he will be thinking, "How did you find me here in the middle of my plain, how did you find your way across a landscape with no recognizable features?"'

Alexander signalled to his Companions and each of them lined up his own division so that together they surrounded the small city on wheels. The horsemen sat upright on their mounts, the long shafts of their spears held firmly in their hands. They looked like superhuman beings in that solitary place, expressing a sense of irresistible power in the shining muscles of their steeds, in the sharp points of their weapons, in the flashing brightness of their polished helmets, the crests waving in the first breeze of daybreak.

In the unreal silence of the early hour suddenly there came the sound of a horn that faded out across the immensity of the plain. Then the Scythian king appeared, astride a splendid dappled stallion, very different from the small, bristly horses ridden by his men – perhaps a gift from some neighbouring king, or loot from a raid somewhere. He was still wearing his battledress – his scarlet ribbon, the scaled armour of his breastplate. His wife followed him on foot, sporting a high headdress in gold, decorated with parallel bands, a long red veil and a crimson tunic adorned with small plaques of gold sheet on its edges, together with a long dress that reached her feet and almost covered her shoes of embroidered wool. She led by the hand a young girl of about twelve years of age, certainly her daughter, judging by how closely they resembled each other.

The chief looked around, almost as though inspecting

the great line up of armoured warriors who had appeared from nowhere, then he advanced confidently towards Alexander and began talking. Oxhatres had had one of his Scythian mercenaries accompany him and as this man translated, the Persian translated in his turn for Alexander.

'No one in our memory, has ever dared push this far into Scythian territory. No one has ever managed to defeat the Scythians and to surprise them in the heart of their land. Also I have heard that you defeated the King of the Persians and took his realm from him. So you are either a god, or you have a god on your side. Fighting against you I lost my best warriors and I struggled to save my own life. I have come to offer you peace and as part of my pledge I offer you my daughter as your bride.'

At these words the Queen pushed the reluctant girl forward and Alexander saw that her eyes were full of tears under her long, black eyelashes.

He dismounted, looked at the girl and tears came to his own eyes as he thought of his sister Cleopatra and how young she had looked when he had left for Mieza and his long period of study under the guidance of Aristotle . . . how long ago was that now?

'Your daughter still needs the love and the care of her mother and I have no wish to take her away,' he replied. 'To seal a pact between Kings all that is required is an oath made on the sky, which sits above all men, and on the earth, which one day will welcome us within itself. And a handshake.'

He waited until the interpreter had finished translating, then he offered his hand to the Scythian king who

shook it firmly, raising his other hand first towards the sky and then extending it, palm downwards, towards the ground.

'My name is Dravas,' said the leader, fixing his eyes on those of the young golden-haired stranger, 'and what is your name?'

'Aléxandros,' came the reply, 'and I can return here at any moment and from any place I may be.' He said this in such a tone and with such a look that the Scythian leader had no doubt at all, not even for a moment, that he was telling the simple truth.

46

ON THE FOLLOWING morning they set off again, westwards now towards the Jaxartes, but the terrain here was completely arid and burned by the sun, so that the men soon finished their supplies of water. The soldiers of the light cavalry who had borne the brunt of the hardest work in the long-distance reconnaissance missions and the watches were the first to run out, and Alexander gave orders for his personal supplies to be given to them. In this way they continued forward for one more day, but then their thirst became unbearable. The King drank from a puddle of water in a hollow and before nightfall he found himself the victim of terrible pains in his abdomen, soon accompanied by high fever and dysentery.

Hephaestion had a stretcher made and so he was carried, delirious, for another two days. The King lay burning up with fever and thirst, soiled by his own excrement which for lack of water could not be cleaned off, and tormented by swarms of flies.

'If we do not reach the ford soon, he may die,' said Oxhatres. 'I will go on ahead to look for it. Follow my tracks. If you manage to catch any wild game, eat the meat raw. No one must drink anything that the Scythian mercenaries refuse to drink – they know about these things.'

He disappeared off towards the west, together with a group of Sogdian horsemen, the most resistant to the heat and the thirst, while the column of men continued to advance at a walk under the relentless sun. He returned after nightfall and immediately asked of the King, 'How is he?'

Hephaestion shook his head without replying. Alexander lay on the ground in his own filth, his lips cracked and dried, his breath rattling.

'I have found the ford,' said the Persian, 'and I have brought water for drinking, but not for washing.'

Alexander drank as did all those whose thirst had brought them closest to death, then they set off once more on the march to the Jaxartes after dark. The river came in sight with the first light of dawn. The King's Companions immediately immersed him in the cold waters and kept him there until his body temperature fell. He regained consciousness slowly and asked, 'Where am I?'

'At the ford,' explained Oxhatres. 'We have fresh fish here and wood for cooking.'

'Your Greek is getting better,' Alexander had the strength to reply.

*

They joined up with the rest of the army near Samarkand, where a nasty surprise was awaiting them. The commanders of the *pezhetairoi* had launched an ill-considered attack on Spitamenes' troops on the Polytimetus river and had been soundly defeated. Almost a thousand soldiers had fallen and several hundred were left

wounded; the funeral pyres burned for days and days, the sky dark and gloomy.

Leptine cried in despair when she saw the King in such a terrible state. She washed him, dressed him in clean clothes and had men with feather fans keep him cool day and night. Philip was soon at his bedside and realized that the fever was still very high – every evening, at sunset, Alexander became delirious. The physician recalled some of the teaching of his master, Nicomachus, and so sent for Hyrcanian horsemen and instructed them to collect snow on the mountains, and he covered the King's body with it every time the fever began rising while Leptine continued to change the cold cloths on his forehead all through the night. Then he began feeding him with dry bread and sharp apples until his diarrhoea calmed.

'Perhaps you'll scrape through this time as well,' he said to him when he saw him gain some colour, his temperature finally normal, 'but if you carry on behaving in this way then not even Asclepius himself, who they say can revive the dead, will be able to save you.'

'I am convinced that you are better than Asclepius, iatré,' the royal patient managed to reply before falling asleep again.

As soon as he was able to give orders, Alexander prohibited all the survivors of the battle of the Polytimetus to speak of it with anyone, so as to avoid discouraging any of the men. Then he sent Perdiccas, Craterus and Hephaestion to counterattack Spitamenes' forces, driving the rebels back towards the mountains. At that stage, however, autumn was already on its way and it would have been madness to set off through the mountains

after them. He decided to return to Bactra, where Bessus was being held prisoner, marching westwards along the northern limits of the empire, to affirm his authority in that area and to see if Scythian territory also extended in that direction for such a distance.

They crossed the Oxus again on the bridge of tent-skins and ventured into an area that was deserted for the most part – vast and completely flat, it extended north-wards and disappeared into the foggy horizon. Occasionally they met long caravans of Bactrian camels heading westwards, at other times they found themselves being followed at a distance by groups of Scythian horsemen, recognizable by means of their clothes and their deco-rated trousers, and their characteristic scaled armour. One day, around sunset, just as they were preparing to pitch camp, a member of the advance guard came back with some startling news: 'Amazons!'

Seleucus grinned, 'I didn't realize that one of the solutions to all the drought we've been experiencing had been to give undiluted wine to the troops.'

'I am not drunk, Commander,' replied the soldier in all seriousness. 'Right now there are female warriors lined up on that hill opposite us.'

'I don't fight women,' said Leonnatus solemnly, 'unless that is—'

'But they are not looking for a fight,' said the soldier. 'They smiled at us and the one who looks like their leader is beautiful and . . .' At this point he turned to show the King where the meeting had taken place and saw that she was now right behind them, less than half a stadium away, escorted by four of her companions.

'Let them come forward,' ordered Alexander and instinctively he ran his hand through his hair, as though to tidy it up a little. 'Perhaps we really are in the land of the Amazons.'

In the meantime the beautiful warrior had come nearer and dismounted, and her companions followed suit. Some distance away others could be seen pitching a tent. One single tent in the midst of that immense expanse of land.

The King moved forward to meet her, flanked by Hephaestion and Craterus, while from behind them came a buzz of amazement as the news ran through the ranks of the soldiers and among all the people in the King's entourage. Word reached Callisthenes and he elbowed his way through; even Leptine had moved up close, intrigued by this strange event.

The warrior Queen and the King were now face to face and she took off her headdress – a sort of conical helmet made of leather with cheek protectors – and thus she revealed her stunning hair, black and shining, gathered into a long plait that almost reached her waist.

She seemed to be about twenty years of age and was very different from the images of the Amazons they all knew, which they had seen represented gloriously naked in the reliefs sculpted by Bryaxis and Scopas in the Mausoleum at Halicarnassus or painted by the brushes of Zeuxis and Parrhasius in the 'Decorated Portico' of Athens. Apart from her fine olive-coloured face, no part of her body was visible. She wore trousers of blue wool embroidered in red and above it all a strange leather tunic, tight at her waist and wide below her knees. She

had a sword hanging from her waist together with a water bottle and a bow and arrows across her shoulders, weapons considered traditional for the Amazons, but she was not carrying the half-moon-shaped shield.

She looked at him with her big dark eyes and said something that no one understood.

Alexander turned to Oxhatres. 'Did that mean anything to you?'

The Persian shook his head.

'And you Scythians?'

Oxhatres exchanged a few words with them, but they too explained that they had not understood anything.

'I do not understand you,' said Alexander with a smile and he was deeply sorry to find himself there before one of the mythological creatures who had peopled his childhood dreams without being able to say a single sentence that she might understand.

The young woman spoke again, returned his smile and tried to help with some gestures, but to no avail.

'I understand her,' came a voice suddenly from behind Alexander.

The King turned in surprise because it was a woman's voice – 'Leptine!'

The girl moved forward, and to everyone's amazement she began speaking with the young woman warrior.

'How can this be?' Callisthenes asked, astonished by this remarkable event. Alexander, however, recalling a far off winter's evening he had spent with Leptine at Aegae, in the ancient palace of his ancestors, remembered that she had spoken in a strange, incomprehensible tongue and there had been that tattoo on her shoulder, identical to

the image on the golden pendant on the Amazon's necklace – a crouching stag with its long branch-like horns.

'Such things happen,' said Philip the physician. 'Xenophon recounts of a similar episode he came across in Armenia, when a slave suddenly recognized the language of the Calybeans, a people he did not know at all.'

Leptine was speaking in the meantime, initially somewhat hesitantly, and then with greater confidence, even though her words seemed to come out reluctantly, one by one, as though emerging from some great abyss in her memory. Alexander moved towards her and uncovered the tattoo on her shoulder, showing it to the young Amazon Queen. 'Do you recognize this?' he asked.

The woman's astonished expression showed clearly that not only did she recognize it, but the image had some extraordinary significance for her.

The two women spoke once more in their mysterious language, and the Amazon held Leptine's hands as she stared into the eyes of the young King from far away. Then she moved back towards her tent.

'What did she say to you?' Alexander asked as soon as she had moved away. 'You are one of them, aren't you?'

'Yes,' replied Leptine, 'I am one of them. I was taken by a group of Cimmerian warriors when I was nine years old, and they must have sold me to a slave merchant in some emporium in the Pontus. My mother was Queen of a tribe of these women warriors and my father was a noble from among the Scythians who live along the Jaxartes.'

'A Princess,' murmured Alexander as he now held her hands. 'That is what you are.'

'That is what I was,' Leptine corrected him. 'Those days are gone now, for ever.'

'This is not true. Now you may return among your people, you may take up the position that is yours by rights. You are free and I will grant you a rich dowry – gold, livestock, horses.'

'My position by rights is at your side, my Lord. I have no one else in the world and for me those women are nothing but foreigners. I will go with them only if you reject me and force me to.'

'I will not force you to do anything you do not wish to do, and I will keep you with me for the rest of my days, if this is what you want. But tell me, why did that young woman come here? Why has she pitched her tent down there?'

Leptine lowered her eyes as though ashamed or embarrassed, then she finally replied, 'She said that she is the Queen of the women warriors who live between the Oxus and the shores of the Caspian Sea. She has heard that you are the strongest and most powerful man in the world and she thinks that only you are worthy of her. She awaits you in that tent and she invites you to spend the night with her. She hopes . . . that you will accept the invitation and that she will have a child by you: a boy or even a girl, who one day will receive the sceptre from her hands.'

Leptine covered her face with her hands and ran away in tears.

47

ALEXANDER LOOKED AT THE solitary tent that was just visible now in the semidarkness of the prairie while Leptine's quiet sobbing barely reached his ear. He was much moved when he thought of the double miracle that this land had worked: the appearance of a group of Amazons in a place so far from the River Thermodon, which flowed, as legend had it, along the borders of the women warriors' territory, and then the discovery of Leptine's origins and her recognition of her native tongue. He thought of how many things there were to be discovered in the world, how many mysteries to be resolved, and how many unknown lands to be explored in the brief day of a human life.

He would have liked to help Leptine who was so upset by the tumult and the emotions of the two such contrasting lives that had now suddenly clashed in her being, but Alexander's dominant concern was to get to know the mysterious woman who awaited him down there in the midst of the dark night of the steppe. He mounted his horse and headed off towards the solitary tent, armed only with his sword. Hephaestion saw him and nodded to some men of the Vanguard to move forward. 'Take up position around that tent without being noticed,' he ordered, 'and at the slightest sign of

anything suspicious, run to help the King. Take Peritas with you – if there is any danger he is much faster than anyone else.'

The men obeyed and they moved off in the dark, spreading out into a fan shape to surround the tent. One of them, the one who was holding Peritas, moved closer than the others and squatted down in the grass alongside the Molossian, but the night passed by peacefully and Peritas slept right through, lifting his ears and his nose only when he smelled some wild animal passing by in the silence of the steppe.

No one ever learned what happened that night nor whether Alexander planted a child in the belly of that Queen of endless solitude, a child who would grow up like a wild horse, running possessionless and free across that limitless territory, under the eyes of the sun and on the wings of the wind.

The King returned before dawn with an intense, febrile light in his eyes, as though he had just descended from Olympus.

*

They set off on the march westwards until they came to a river. Alexander wanted to travel down it to see how far it went and discover if it led towards the northern Ocean, but after three days' march the steppe had become a desert and the river had dried up among its burning sands. They pressed on again towards the west in a series of four stages, each lasting five parasangs until they came to another watercourse and started moving

down it, but it too was soon swallowed up by the cracks in the thirsty earth.

Ptolemy moved alongside the King, who was anxiously surveying the horizon, obscured as it was by the heat haze, and he put a hand on his shoulder. 'Let's go back, Alexander, there's nothing down there, apart from noonday spectres. If the earth here swallows up its rivers before they reach the sea, there must surely be some terrible reason that we are unaware of. Could a mother ever devour her child after having given birth to it?'

Even Callisthenes looked on that disturbing phenomenon with deep concern in his eyes. His knowledge of physics and philosophy suggested rational answers that were immediately quashed by the irrational fears that rose from the depths of his soul.

'I would like to find answers to these questions, Ptolemy,' said the King without turning round. 'If our energies were sufficient, I would like to follow these noontime heat demons, the spectres that inhabit the horizon. Ulysses, tied to the mast of his ship, was indeed a lucky man to hear the song of the sirens, but he never revealed to anyone what that song said. The secret died with him in a remote, hidden place, there where Tiresias's prophecy led him, the much-longed-for destination of his final journey . . .'

They once again took the road leading towards the south and day by day, as they approached the Margianian highlands, they came across more and more water and vegetation, plants and animals. On the banks of a river

the King founded another city and called it Alexandria of Margiana, peopling it with the semi-nomadic tribes that lived in the surrounding area and some of the men and women from his entourage. He left a garrison of five hundred men – Macedonian, Greek and Thessalian soldiers, all those who had set up families with the Asian women who continued to follow the army with incredible stamina and perseverance. He established those men who seemed to have forgotten the families they had left behind back home such a long time ago, a time that seemed infinitely farther than it was in reality.

They reached Bactra towards the end of the autumn with the intention of spending the winter there and it was while here that Alexander gave orders for Bessus's trial to take place, following Persian procedure. Oxhatres assembled the council of the eldest judges and had the prisoner dragged before them. The mutilations he had suffered that dark night in the countryside around Kurushkhat had healed now, but this gave his tormented face an even more disturbing appearance, like a living skull.

The trial was over extremely quickly, and when he was asked if he wanted to defend himself against the charges, Bessus said nothing at all. He stood in silence before his enemies with all the dignity of a man who had sought to redeem the honour of the Persian Empire, humiliated by the cowardice of Darius, the King who had twice fled from the battlefield. The dignity of a man who had sought to lead an uprising against the invader.

The sentence was passed – the worst imaginable one, the one inflicted on those who assassinate the sacred

person of the King of Kings and who usurp the throne of the Achaemenids – dismemberment.

Bessus was stripped and led to an open space that had been made ready for the sentence to be carried out. Two tall and slender willow trees, very close to one another, had been bent to the ground until they crossed and their tops had been fastened with a rope tied to a stake hammered into the ground. A sort of pointed arch was thus created by the two trunks and the prisoner was led there and tied by the ankles and the wrists to the two uprights as high as possible, so that he was left hanging above the ground by about five cubits. The Persians and local inhabitants were not the only ones to witness this barbarous rite; Macedonians and Greeks were among the crowds as well. Princess Stateira had come from Zadracarta specifically, impatient to see vengeance meted out for Darius, the father she had buried and mourned over for a long time in the royal necropolis of Persepolis, now abandoned. She sat there pale and motionless alongside Alexander.

At a simple nod from the supreme judge, the executioners moved towards the ropes brandishing their axes. At a second nod they both let fly with synchronized blows – straight blows that cut through them cleanly. The two trunks immediately straightened and for an instant Bessus's powerfully muscled body tightened in the impossible strain of the tension, then he was torn apart. The left-hand section, from his shoulder to his groin, remained attached to one of the trunks, while the other, with his head and his guts, hung from the other tree, and there was still some shadow of life in Bessus's

eyes when the birds of prey, ever vigilant in that place of punishment, came down to feed on his tortured flesh.

Alexander remained at Bactra with Stateira and the court for the entire winter, spending a lot of time with Eumenes writing to the satraps of his provinces: to Antigonus, known as 'One-eye', who governed Anatolia, to Mazaeus in Babylon, and even Artabazos in Pamphylia. He asked how Phraates was, if he had recovered from the grief of losing his near and dear ones and if he was living a quiet life in his palace on the sea. He had given orders for his blacksmiths to make a little carriage and to send it to Phraates as a gift together with two Scythian foals.

He also received a letter from his mother, Olympias, and from Cleopatra who told him all about her life in the palace at Buthrotum and all about her homesickness:

> News of your deeds reaches me somehow diluted and deformed by the distance and it seems to me to be impossible that I, your sister, cannot see you, that I cannot know when you will return, when you will call an end to this interminable expedition.
>
> I suffer because you are so far from me and I suffer in my solitude. I beg you to let me come to you as soon as possible, so that I may see the wonders you have achieved, the splendours of the cities you have conquered.
>
> I thank you for the gifts you send me continually, which make me most proud, but the greatest gift would be to be able to embrace you once again, it matters not where – the frozen wastes of Scythia or the deserts of Libya. I beg you, call me to you,

Aléxandre, and I will fly to you without delay, over stormy seas and against the strongest winds. Take good care.

Alexander dictated his reply, affectionate but inflexible, and he concluded with these words:

My empire is not as yet fully under control, my dearest sister, and I must ask you to wait for some time still. When everything is completed, I will call you to me so that you may participate in everyone's joy and witness the birth of a new world.

Then he turned to Eumenes. 'Cleopatra's prose improves with each letter she sends – she must be taking expensive lessons from some excellent teacher of rhetoric.'

'That's true,' said Eumenes. 'Yet, behind her flowery speech, behind the rhetorical ornament, there is sincere affection. Cleopatra has always loved you, she has always been a shield for you against your father's wrath. Don't you perhaps miss her?'

'Terribly,' replied Alexander. 'I miss those days, but I cannot let myself indulge my memories: the task I have set myself keeps coming back and demanding attention, like some imperative to which everything must be sacrificed and from which I cannot escape.'

'From which you have no wish to escape,' replied Eumenes.

'Do you really think I could, even if I wanted to? The gods put dreams in the hearts of men – dreams, desires, aspirations that are often much bigger than they are. The greatness of a man corresponds to that painful discrepancy

between the goal he sets for himself and the strength nature granted him when he came into the world.'

'Like Bessus.'

'And Philip.'

'And Philip,' said Eumenes, lowering his eyes.

They both fell silent, as though the spirit of the great assassinated King were somehow present in that place, evoked suddenly out of the silence and the oblivion.

Then Alexander dedicated time to maintaining contact with the cities he had founded in the farthest flung provinces of the Empire, the cities that carried his own name. He wrote personally to the military leaders and the magistrates of those small communities, encamped on the edges of inhospitable and unknown lands, and he wrote to Aristotle, describing the statutes and the constitutions of these cities, documents that would enrich the philosopher's collection.

Occasionally he also received missives from those remote outposts, written in very poor Greek or in Macedonian dialect; almost always they were requests for help against enemy attacks, against sieges from other peoples, all of them ferociously protective of their identities. Spitamenes' rebellion was spreading everywhere. Handing over Bessus had only cleared the way for the new leader who was now holed up in the snowy foothills of the Paropamisus.

Alexander had the same reply for everyone: 'Hold on. We are assembling more troops, we are waiting for new reinforcements to help you, to pacify the lands on which you are raising your children.'

The whole winter went by in this way. When spring

returned, fresh troops from Macedonia and Anatolia arrived, and the army set off on its march once more. On entering Bactriana, Alexander realized that the rebels had spread out into a great number of fortresses and castles and he decided to split up his forces in order to inflict a series of attacks, each aimed at a particular centre of resistance. However, when he communicated this strategy to his generals and his Companions, he found that almost no one agreed.

'Never divide your forces!' exclaimed the Black. 'As far as we can gather, Alexander of Epirus, your uncle and brother-in-law, was overwhelmed by the barbarians in Italy precisely because he was forced to split up his army. To do this same thing out of one's own free will . . . it seems like madness to me.'

'I think we would be better off staying united,' said Perdiccas. 'We will take them one by one and we will crush them like fleas.'

Leonnatus nodded in approval, as if there was not even any need to discuss matters.

'If you want to know what I think,' Eumenes began, but Alexander cut him short with the words still in his mouth:

'So we're agreed then. Craterus will remain in the south near Bactra while we move northwards and east-wards into Sogdiana to find the rebels up in the moun-tains and at a certain stage we will spread out into a fan – five units, one for each of you, one for each of the fortresses that must be taken. Diades has planned new long-range catapults and we'll be firing smaller, but equally effective harpoons.'

Leonnatus stopped nodding, realizing that the situation had changed and Alexander, who was watching him, asked, 'But weren't you in agreement?'

'I, really, I was in agreement with you . . .' he attempted to reply, but by now everyone was on their feet because there was nothing else to say and Alexander was accompanying them all to the door.

The plan was put into effect in the space of a few days: the King and his Companions, with more than half of the army, set off towards the entrances to the valleys where the armed rebels were waiting for them. They fought throughout the entire summer, wiping out some of the fortresses, but then the operations slowed down because of the enemy's evasive strategy – attacking and then retreating immediately – and because of the impervious nature of the terrain. When the weather began getting worse and foodstuffs became scarcer, Alexander led the army towards Samarkand.

*

Things went rather differently for Craterus. He had been left behind and failed to reach the capital of the province before a messenger from its garrison commander arrived.

'Spitamenes has invaded the area surrounding Bactra and has sacked the countryside and the villages. Our garrison made an initial sortie and was defeated, then we attempted a second one to give chase to Spitamenes, but we need reinforcements urgently.'

Craterus was suddenly overwhelmed by a dark presentiment. He knew Spitamenes' cunning very well and was almost certain that the incursion into the area surround-

ing Bactra was only a provocation to draw the capital's garrison into the open field and wipe it out.

'Which way did they go?' he asked the messenger.

'That way,' he said, pointing to the track that led towards the desert.

'We will go that way as well,' the Macedonian commander decided. 'After having rested a little. There is no point in our passing through the capital.'

They set off on their march before dawn, crossing over a torrent at a ford, and then approached a narrow pass flanked by acacia and tamarisk trees – an ideal site for an ambush. Suddenly Koinos, commander of the second *hetairoi* squadron, approached them: 'Look there,' he said, pointing towards the sky.

'What is it?' Craterus asked, lifting his hand to shield his eyes from the sun.

'Vultures,' replied the officer darkly.

48

THE SIGHT WAS TRULY horrendous. Hundreds of dead Macedonian soldiers lay there before them, their bodies horribly mutilated, many of them decapitated or scalped. Others had been put on stakes, others again had been tied to trees and bore the marks of terrible torture. The Commanders, two officers of the old guard, friends of Cleitus the Black, had been crucified.

'What are we to do now?' asked Koinos gravely.

'Assemble the cavalry; we'll attack now. The infantry will follow on at double-quick pace.'

Koinos had the fall in signal sounded and then had the cavalry cross the field of the massacre in a spectral silence. He wanted the soldiers to see exactly what the enemy had done to their comrades, he wanted the anger and the fury they bore within to grow out of all measure so that their thirst for revenge would drive them headlong into the chase.

As soon as the narrow passage opened up into a stepped and undulating plain, Craterus lined them all up in five rows of six hundred men and shouted to them, 'I will not stop until we have captured these barbarians and cut them to pieces. Follow me, men, and remember what they have done to your comrades!'

The enemy's tracks were fresh and clearly visible and

the squadrons were even able to maintain their formations. They set off at a gallop in a cloud of dust, rushing down into a steppe-like hollow and rising up the long slope on the other side until they came to a rise that hid another hollow from view. Koinos was among the first to reach the top, together with Craterus, and down below them they saw the enemy cavalry at a distance of less than three stadia, moving forwards at a walk and completely oblivious of the danger they were in.

'It's them!' shouted Craterus. 'Trumpets! Charge! Don't stop, men! Annihilate them! Tear them to pieces! Forward! Forward!'

The signal to attack was repeated several times and the cavalry set off down the slope like an avalanche. The earth shook, the air was rent by the bronze cry of the trumpets, by the fury of the attack. Spitamenes, who was leading an army made up of Bactrians and Massagetae Scythians, was taken by surprise and gave orders for his men to turn and face the enemy, but the manoeuvre succeeded only partially because the Macedonians were now on top of them with their spears lowered. They fell in hundreds in the first clash – thrown this way and that, dashed to the ground and trampled under the horses' hooves. The centre was completely overwhelmed and dispersed, the wings put up some resistance and sought to effect a series of diversionary manoeuvres, but Craterus did not bite. He called his men back, regrouped and led them once again in a second massive, frontal attack. In less than an hour Spitamenes' remaining troops were completely wiped out. The satrap barely managed to save himself together with

a few hundred Massagetae Scythians, all of them fleeing into the desert.

Craterus took his men back to put their fallen soldiers to rest, but before the funerals he called Koinos to one side and said, 'Do you know who our opponents are?'

'Scythians.'

'Massagetae, the tribe which two hundred years ago defeated and killed Cyrus the Great. I want you to spread sheer terror through their ranks, make sure they never dare attack us again . . . never again. Understand?'

'I understand,' replied Koinos, and then he added, 'Send me the ballistae, all you have, and a division of Agrianians.'

Craterus nodded and took his *hetairoi* back to the camp, the site of the massacre, which the infantry had already reached. The soldiers had laid down their arms and were now gathering up the dead, recomposing the mutilated bodies as best they could and carrying them with tears in their eyes to the edge of the field, where others were cutting down trees and building funeral pyres.

Koinos waited for the arrival of the ballistae and then had the Agrianians decapitate the bodies of all the Massagetae Scythians they could find. Then he went to the border of their land, marked by the river Artakoenes and watched over by patrols of their cavalry who rode up and down the opposite bank. He loaded the ballistae and fired the severed heads in clumps across to the other side, sending them rolling across the ground so that they ended up under the horses' hooves. Then he made an about turn to join up once again with the rest of the

army. They marched towards Bactra and along the way received the surrender of all the villages that had participated in Spitamenes' rebellion.

*

In the meantime the part of the army that had fought with Alexander had been quartered for some time at Samarkand and from there the Persian officers were recruiting as many young men from Bactriana and from Sogdiana as they could for the royal army, which was now very different from the one that had set off from Pella seven years before. This also left the enemy with ever dwindling human resources to help fuel its resistance against Alexander.

The fact remained that the successes of the expedition had been limited and this somewhat damaged the King's prestige, so that more than a few of his companions had sought to dissuade him from pursuing his strategy. Alexander for his part tried to make them all forget the precise nature of the situation they were in by throwing parties and banquets in which the Persian officers also took part and this once again created tension among the Macedonians and among his friends. Many of them now disliked Hephaestion because he seemed to appreciate Persian customs every bit as much as the King did and he often dressed in the oriental manner.

Many delegations came to negotiate, including the leader of a Scythian tribe who lived on the other side of the Oxus. On these occasions the King had the Persian protocol applied to everyone, including the 'prostration' ritual, and he often received guests while wearing a

kandys or even a tiara. This simply exacerbated the discontent.

From Greece and Anatolia came philosophers, seers, rhetoricians, poets and actors, all of them attracted by the King's fame and the news of his achievements, not to mention the rumours circulating regarding the limitless riches his army had expropriated. They all hoped they might be able to grab a little of that immense fortune, or at least be introduced to the young conqueror. Alexander received them and admitted them to the banquets. He liked to think that in this way a part of Greece was being transplanted to these remote regions; also he had a natural inclination for philosophical conversations and rhetorical disputes. All they had in mind, however, was to ingratiate themselves with the King and so they quite simply fawned over him in every possible way, often cunningly, so that it was not blatantly obvious what they were up to. This too irritated those Macedonians who were used to a relationship of rough camaraderie with their King where the only formal element was the kiss on the cheek reserved for those most intimate.

One day a man arrived with a load of dried fruit and nuts to offer the King. He had come directly from Greece with figs, almonds and walnuts. Alexander tasted the offerings and they seemed so good that he thought he would offer some of them to Cleitus the Black as a sign of friendship, following the numerous clashes they had had over protocol and his determination to introduce Persians and Asians not only into the court, but into the army as well. Indeed, some of these arguments had been quite heated.

The Black, despite his irascible and rather haughty character, was actually deeply religious and he was offering some sheep in sacrifice to the gods when the messenger arrived with the summons from the King. He left the sacrifice half-finished and followed the orderly, without realizing that a couple of sheep in their turn were following him.

When he reached the courtyard of the palace with his woolly entourage, Alexander started laughing: 'Black!' he exclaimed. 'Have you taken up shepherding now?' But when he learned that the animals were destined to be sacrificed he was troubled. He gave Black the gift of the fruit and nuts and as soon as he had left, he called Aristander and told him what had happened. The seer's face darkened. 'This is a bad sign,' he replied. 'It is a bad portent.'

That same night, perhaps influenced by the words of his seer, Alexander dreamed of Cleitus, dressed in black from head to toe, sitting alongside Parmenion's three sons, all of them dead. He woke up gripped by a most profound anxiety and did not dare recount the dream to Aristander. He chose instead to throw a party that very evening to chase away the deep sense of anguish that was crushing him. Despite their frequent clashes, he was deeply fond of Cleitus, the man whose sister had breast-fed Alexander; in Macedonian tradition this fact created a very strong bond, almost a blood tie.

That same evening Perdiccas was nominated master of the symposium, and he decreed immediately that there were to be two craters – one for the Macedonians with straight wine and another for the Greeks with one part

wine and four parts water. This decision in itself was enough to generate some dissatisfaction, and Alexander was somewhat disgruntled because the Persian guests were not even mentioned.

Among the Greeks, as well as Callisthenes, there was a philosopher by the name of Anaxarchus, a man who had arrived recently and who, despite being presumptuous and arrogant, was actually extremely able; he had also brought along with him two poets and they immediately set to drinking and stuffing their faces with food. The party had proceeded well with jokes, comments, and lewd stories, all this with the contribution of some women who were no less daring than any of the men. They had all started drinking too much and it was not long before everyone, especially the Macedonians and including the King, was merry.

At that stage one of the two poets who was with the philosopher, a man by the name of Pranikos, exclaimed, 'I have composed a small epic poem! Would anyone care to hear it?'

Alexander laughed, 'Why not?'

Encouraged by the King's approval, the poet began declaiming his masterpiece, soon provoking much laughter from his friends, but the Macedonians, as soon as they realized what the topic was, suddenly went quiet, even though they were all drunk, because they simply could not believe their ears. This pathetic poet was declaiming some sort of stupid satire on the commanders of the garrison at Bactra who fell in Spitamenes' ambush during the spring campaign, making fun above all things of their age:

The two old men croaked their cries of war,
Incapable of raising their rods from the floor;
Keen to charge, they should have stayed in their beds
And everyone laughed and called them eggheads

The Black stood up and threw his cup of wine in the poet's face, shouting, 'That's enough, you disgusting Greek shithead!'

Alexander was drunk and half naked as he sat between two female 'companions' who were doing all they could to keep him amused, and he had understood nothing of what he had seen take place before him, but simply that the Black had insulted his Greek guest, and so he shouted, 'How dare you! Apologize to him and let him continue! I like poetry.'

Cleitus, already very much under the influence of the wine, on hearing those words went completely out of his mind with rage. 'You short-legged, presumptuous, arrogant little boy! How dare you allow this shit of a Greek to fart over the memory of two valiant officers who gave their blood on the battlefield?'

'What did you say?' shouted Alexander, realizing the full enormity of the insult.

'You heard what I said! Who do you think you are? Do you really think you are the son of Zeus Ammon? Do you believe in the nonsense that freak your mother spreads around about your divine birth and all that claptrap? Just look at yourself! Look at the state you're in, dressed like a woman, with all that embroidery and all that lace!' He pointed at the Persian clothes the King had been wearing until the two girls had started undressing him.

Alexander stood up pale with rage and gave orders to his attendant: 'Sound the call for the shieldsmen! Sound it now I tell you!'

This was an extreme gesture that Macedonian Kings made only when their person was under direct threat, and as soon as the shieldsmen burst into the room they would immediately kill the guilty party; for this reason the attendant hesitated in astonishment at the command. Alexander punched the attendant in the face and as the man fell to the ground he called out with all the breath he could muster, 'Shieldsmen! Come here!'

'Yes!' shouted Cleitus in his rage. 'Call the shieldsmen! Call them right now! Do you want to know the truth? You are nothing without us ... nothing! We have won your battles, we have fought, we have conquered. You're not even worth one iota of Philip, your father!'

Ptolemy, alarmed at the way the argument was developing, grabbed Cleitus by the shoulders and tried to drag him out. 'Black, stop it now, you're drunk, don't offend the King! Come on now, come away!'

Perdiccas helped him as well and they had almost managed to drag him outside, but Cleitus got an arm free and started shouting, waving his hand in the air. 'Ha! Son of Zeus! See this hand? See it? This is what saved you at the Granicus ... had you forgotten about that?' He gave another powerful twist and pulled free, turning back, still shouting and insulting Alexander.

Alexander took an apple from the table and threw it at his head to drive him backwards, but Cleitus dodged it and came forwards, taunting the King even more. Blind with fury, outraged by the disobedience of his attendant,

and ridiculed before his guests, the King went wild: he grabbed a *sarissa* from one of the *pezhetairoi* standing behind him and threw it at Cleitus, never imagining that it would find its mark, wanting only to give him a fright, a lesson . . . it was an interminable instant, it seemed to last a lifetime, that moment in which the hand that had thrown the weapon, still extended, wanted to grab it back to stop it from reaching its target, and wanted the Black to save himself. But none of this happened – at this precise moment the Black was being held fast again by Ptolemy in an effort to save him from the King's wrath and drag him outside. The *sarissa* caught him in full, its iron head passing straight through his body.

Alexander cried out, 'No! Black, no! No!' and he ran towards his friend who lay vomiting blood on the pavement. He pulled the spear from his Companion's body, propped the shaft up on the wall and tried now to throw himself on its head. Seleucus and Ptolemy caught him just in time, and as he writhed like a man possessed, he shouted through his tears, 'Let me go! Let me go! I don't deserve to live!'

Leonnatus rushed to help his friends, but Alexander managed to free one hand and grab his sword and start another suicide attempt. They disarmed him and bodily carried him away.

Eumenes had not been able to do anything because he was sitting far away on the other side of the room, next to Callisthenes, and now, immobile, he surveyed the scene while the room, which just a moment before had resounded to the noise of an orgy of wine and blood, had suddenly precipitated into an absurd, unreal silence.

The squires standing upright against the wall in their dress uniforms looked at one another, all pale in their astonishment. Callisthenes turned to them and quoted a saying of Aristotle: 'He who commits a crime in a state of drunkenness is doubly guilty for he has become drunk and he has committed a crime.'

Eumenes stared at him, shaking his head in disbelief. 'What sort of man are you?' he asked. One of the pages, however, a boy by the name of Hermolaus, looked at him, his face full of admiration.

*

Alexander cried in desperation for three days and four nights, calling out the name of his murdered friend. He refused all food and water and was a shadow of his former self.

In the end his Companions, worried that he would lose his sanity and eventually his life, asked Aristander to intervene. The seer entered and spoke to him for a long time, reminding him of the dream he had had and the evil omen of the sheep that had left the sacrificial altar – an event already written by fate. Ineluctable. In the end he managed to call Alexander back to life, but the shadow of Cleitus the Black was to torment his existence with pain and remorse for the rest of his days and nights.

Alexander began drinking heavily again and the squires, who by tradition had the honour of taking turns in watching over the King's sleep, began to develop a certain contempt for him. On several occasions they saw him come back drunk, dragged into his room unable to

stand on his own feet, after which he would fall into a deep sleep, snoring and passing wind like an animal.

Only Leptine continued to serve him with the same affection as before, as always, without asking anything in return, praying in silence to her gods to bring some tranquillity back to his life.

At the beginning of autumn the two sections of the army were reunited at Samarkand and Craterus was much shocked by the news of the frightful events. In order to avoid the embarrassment of meeting the King, he set off on a march into the desert to give a final lesson to the Massagetae who supported Spitamenes' revolt. However, the tribe, realizing that the Satrap had no hope of leading a successful uprising against Alexander in Bactriana and Sogdiana, and still terrorized by events on the River Artakoenes, had also learned from Dravas that the King who had come from the west was an invincible demigod who was able to appear suddenly wherever he wanted and to strike with devastating violence. They called a council of all their leaders and agreed that they had to establish good relations with the new conqueror so as not to provoke his wrath. They cunningly captured Spitamenes, taking him by surprise in his sleep, decapitated him and gave his head to Craterus as a token of their good faith.

With the cold weather, the two parts of the Macedonian army, united once again at Samarkand, set off on the march to Bactra, to winter there.

49

During the following spring Alexander set off on his march again towards Sogdiana to wipe out the last pockets of resistance, in particular a fortress up in the mountains known as the Sogdian Rock. This was a completely inaccessible eagles' nest of a fortress, held by a lord of these lands by the name of Oxyartes, valiant and fearless, and unbeatable. The only way to reach the fortress was up a narrow, difficult pathway cut into the rock and leading to the only gate in the high walls, directly above the precipice. The rear area of the walls was built on a rocky peak that was covered in ice for almost all the year and which towered at least one thousand feet above the fortress.

Alexander sent a herald with an interpreter up the pathway and asked for the keepers of the rock to surrender, but Oxyartes himself shouted from the heights of the battlements: 'We will never surrender! We have enough foodstuffs to last for years while you all die of cold and hunger. Tell your King that the only soldiers capable of taking this rock of mine are soldiers with wings.'

'Soldiers with wings!' repeated Alexander as soon as the reply was reported to him. 'Soldiers with wings . . .' Diades of Larissa looked up, shielding his eyes from the dazzling snow with his hand. 'If you're thinking of

Daedalus and Icarus, I have to remind you right now that their story, unfortunately, is just a legend. Man will never be able to fly, not even by making wings. Believe me, it's impossible.'

'I do not know the meaning of that word,' replied the King, 'and there was a time when you did not know it either, my friend. I am afraid you are getting old.' Diades was silent in his embarrassment and moved on. No matter how much thought he gave to it, no idea for attacking such a place came to mind.

Alexander, however, had already come up with a plan. He called the herald he had sent to negotiate and ordered him to go through the camp offering twenty talents to whoever volunteered to scale, under cover of darkness, the peak above the fortress – a climb of at least two thousand feet from where they were camped at that moment.

'Twenty talents?' asked Eumenes. 'But that is too much money.'

'The reward must be commensurate with the impossible nature of the undertaking,' replied Alexander. 'Enough to render a family rich for five generations. I am quite convinced that money can make men grow wings.'

In less than an hour three hundred volunteers had come forward – more than half of them Agrianians, the others Macedonians from the more mountainous regions.

'We have had an idea,' said the man who seemed to be the leader. 'The Agrianians' knives are of no use to us in this situation. We will use the tent spikes, which are made of tempered iron, and we'll hammer them into the

ice, tie ropes around them and then we'll pull ourselves up one by one. I am sure we can manage it.'

'I am sure too,' replied the King. 'Have Eumenes give you a flag and fly it high as soon as you reach the top. We will then sound the trumpets and at that point all you will have to do is lean out so that they can see you from the fortress below.'

As night began to fall, the incredible undertaking got under way. The men climbed up on foot as far as they could, carrying their bags over their shoulders together with ropes and spikes. Then they began hammering the spikes into the ice and pulling themselves up, one by one.

Neither the King nor his companions slept that night; they were all awake, their faces turned skywards as they watched the men climbing slowly, struggling up the ice-covered face. Around midnight the wind started blowing, an icy wind that numbed their limbs and penetrated their bones to the marrow, but the warriors continued climbing and the dark line of their single-file formation could be made out against the impeccable white of the snow.

Thirty men fell to their deaths, smashed on the rocks below, but two hundred and seventy reached the summit with the first light of dawn.

'The flag!' shouted Perdiccas, pointing to a small red dot moving way up there. 'They've made it!'

'Oh! Gods above!' exclaimed Eumenes. 'If I hadn't seen it with my own eyes I would never have believed it. Quickly, sound the trumpets!'

The silence down below was broken by the insistent blare, echoed and refracted and the warriors all leaned out and shouted so that the inhabitants of the rock could

hear and see them. The sentries on the battlements struggled at first to understand where the voices were coming from, but then they lifted their eyes and saw Alexander's men up on the mountaintop. They ran to wake up their leader, who rushed out on to the battlements. Shortly afterwards, Alexander's herald again approached the fortress and shouted, 'As you can see, we do have soldiers with wings, and we have many of them. What is your decision?'

Oxyartes looked up, then looked down and looked up once more, 'I surrender,' he replied. 'Tell your King I am ready to receive him.'

Alexander, together with his Companions and the *hetairoi* of the Vanguard, went up to the fortress on the following day as darkness was falling. Formalities were exchanged and then the guest, together with his friends, was shown into the banquet hall, which had been prepared according to Sogdian custom – soft cushions in a double line on the floor with the tables in between. The King sat opposite Oxyartes, but his gaze was immediately caught by the person sitting to the right of the host – Oxyartes' daughter, Roxane!

She was an incredibly beautiful young woman with a godly figure who was already a legend among her people who called her by the name 'Little Star'.

She smiled at him and her teeth shone like pearls. Her face, a soft oval shape, was of a delicate but absolute perfection, her eyelashes were long and shining, her skin was as smooth as marble and was suffused with a pale amber glow. Her hair was so dark it emanated a blue sheen, framing a most finely drawn forehead, and when

she moved her head it shadowed the intense, sweet light of her large, dark, purple-tinted eyes.

Their gazes met and they were caught up in a whirlwind – a magical, shimmering aura, liquid and rarefied, like a morning dream. Nothing else existed for them now, the voices of the others faded far away and it was as if the room was empty – only the melody of an Indian harp, wavering now through the dilated, vibrating space, entered their souls and their bodies and even their voices, voices with different languages and yet equal in the music of an ineffable sentiment, a sublime transport.

Then Alexander understood that he had never really loved anyone up to that point, that he had lived through affairs of deep and intense passion, of burning desire, of affection, of admiration, but never love. This was love, the sensation he was feeling at that moment, this unquenchable thirst for her, that deep peace in his soul, accompanied at the same time by an uncontrollable perturbation, sheer happiness and undiluted fear. This was the love of which the poets wrote – an invincible, merciless god, an ineluctable force, a delirium of the mind and the senses, the only possible happiness. He forgot the bloody spectres of the past, the anguish and the terror, his anxious desire for infinity was appeased now and consumed in the light of those dark purple eyes, in that divine smile.

When he came out of his reverie he realized that everyone was looking at them and everyone had understood. So he stood up before the noble Oxyartes and said, his voice firm, but his eyes liquid with emotion:

'I know that we have been enemies up to just a few

hours ago, but I now offer you a long and solid friendship and in exchange for this friendship and out of the sincere and deep love I feel in this moment, I ask you for the hand of your daughter in marriage,' and as soon as the interpreter had finished translating, he turned to Roxane and added, 'If she so wishes.'

Roxane stood up and replied in her language, a tongue that was both so very strange and so very melodious at the same time, but she did pronounce his name just as she had heard it pronounced by his friends. She said, 'I want you, *Aléxandre*, for ever.'

*

The wedding took place in great style just three days later and Alexander asked for the Persian rite of the bread, but in the Macedonian manner, cutting it with his sword. The bride and the groom then ate of the bread, looking into each other's eyes and feeling that they would love each other to the very end. And even beyond. Roxane was dressed in her ceremonial clothes – a red tunic with a blue overdress, and around her waist a belt in discs of gold, and on her head a veil from which hung a drop-shaped pendant of pure gold, decorated with lapis lazuli.

During the supper that followed the rite, the King drank almost nothing and did very little apart from holding his bride by the hand and speaking to her quietly. He spoke words she could not understand – verses from great poets, images from his dreams, supplications, words of love. Alexander's tormented soul sought some relief in the eyes of this young virgin, in the feelings of love that

emanated from her hands while she caressed him, in her eyes when she looked at him with ingenuous and shameless desire, fiery and decorous at one and the same time. At each breath her blooming breasts rose and a slight blush spread over her cheeks, and in that breathing the King sought the meaning of this sudden and for the most part unknown feeling that he ardently hoped would live within him, immutable and eternal.

When they were finally alone and Roxane began to undress, her eyes lowered as she slowly revealed her divine body, filling their earthly nuptial bed with the godlike fragrance of her skin and her hair, Alexander found himself in the grip of the strongest and deepest emotion. It was like sliding into a warm bath after having walked for ages through a cutting blizzard and numbing ice. It was like drinking clear spring water after having wandered through the desert. He felt himself to be a man once again after having lived through depravation, violence, and brutality.

His eyes were moist with emotion when he pulled her to him and felt the touch of her naked skin, when he sought her inexpert lips, when he kissed her breasts, her belly, the inside of her thighs. He loved her with such intensity, with a total abandon he had never felt in his life before, and as their bodies writhed in the supreme spasm, he felt that he was pouring into her the life, the secret of that wild energy which had overwhelmed entire cities and armies, which had borne the pain of the most frightful wounds, which had crushed the most sacred sentiments, killed all pity and compassion. When he collapsed alongside her and abandoned himself to sleep,

he dreamed of setting off along a long, difficult road under a black sun until he came to the shore of a flat, cold and motionless ocean, like a sheet of polished steel. But he had no fear because Roxane's warmth enveloped him like a soft gown, like the mysterious happiness in a childhood memory.

*

When he woke up and found her lying there alongside him, more beautiful now and with the light of her dreams in her eyes, he caressed her with an infinite gentleness and said, 'We must leave now, my love, and we will not stop until I see the ends of the earth and the cities of the Ganges, the herons in the golden lakes and the shimmering peacocks of Palimbothra.'

Alexander turned his attention again to the preparations and reorganized the army, enlisting thousands of Asians from the provinces of Bactriana and Sogdiana, whose loyalty was now doubly ensured and bound by virtue of the marriage with the Princess, Oxyartes' daughter. Ten thousand Persians also arrived, trained and armed in the Macedonian manner, enlisted by his governors in the central provinces of the empire. So Alexander decided that for reasons of equality the custom of 'prostration' ought to be extended to all his subjects, but the Macedonians rebelled and Callisthenes faced him directly, reminding him just how absurd it was to expect this of his people. 'What will you do when you return home?' he asked. 'Will you ask the Greeks, the freest among men, to pay homage to you in the same way we pay homage to the gods? They are different, not even

Hercules was granted divine honours while he lived, and not even after his death for that matter, until the Oracle at Delphi requested it specifically. Do you want to be identified with these barbarian kings? Just think about what happened to them – Cambises was defeated by the Ethiopians, Darius by the Scythians, Xerxes by the Greeks and Artaxerxes by Xenophon's "ten thousand", which you know so well. They were all defeated by free men. It is certainly true that we are in foreign lands and to some extent we must think like these foreigners, but I beg you not to forget Greece! Remember the teachings of Aristotle. How can the Macedonians treat their King as though he were a god, and how can the Greeks treat the commander of their League as though he were a god? A man receives a handshake, a kiss; people build temples, offer sacrifices, sing hymns for gods. There is a difference between honouring a man and worshipping a god. You are worthy of the greatest honour among all men, because you have been the most valiant, the most courageous, the greatest, but please be satisfied with this, I beg you. Please accept the homage of free men and do not ask them to prostrate themselves before you like slaves!'

Alexander, who at that moment was sitting in audience, lowered his head and those near him heard him murmur, 'You don't understand me . . . you simply don't understand.'

One person who heard him was one of the squires, Hermolaus, the young man who thought so much of Callisthenes and held the King in such contempt. He had become chief of the squires now because Cebalinus, who had saved Alexander's life, had succumbed to the hard-

ships of military life and the bitter climate, falling ill with a raging fever during the campaign against the Scythians and dying some days later. Hermolaus spent as much time as possible listening to Callisthenes' advice and teachings and frequently neglected the work he was supposed to do.

The King in any case decreed that all those who did not feel they wanted to pay homage to him through the 'prostration' were not obliged to do so and he left the matter there, but not even this satisfied his critics. Many did not even tolerate the idea that he should accept 'prostration' from the Asians, for whom it was a perfectly natural, customary act, and they continued to label him as a presumptuous tyrant behind his back, blinded by power and by too much good luck.

Unfortunately the discontent did not stop at moanings and grumblings. Once again a plot developed, a conspiracy to kill the King, and this time it was the younger soldiers, those who were most closely involved in looking after his person – the squires whose job it was to watch over Alexander while he slept.

This terrible, painful event originated after the army returned to Bactra, on an occasion of relaxation and merriment. During a wild boar hunt, Hermolaus, as leader of the squires, was riding close by the King when suddenly, followed by Peritas and other dogs, a boar burst out of the undergrowth and charged at him. Alexander moved to one side and took aim with his javelin, but Hermolaus was so caught up in the excitement of the chase and was so anxious to have some hunting success for himself, that he struck first and killed

the boar, completely ignoring the King's right to pre-cedence in the situation.

It was a grave offence and a sign of arrogance and total contempt for court tradition and protocol. In such cases only the King himself was able to inflict corporal punishment on a squire or to decide who else could inflict it and Alexander made use of his prerogative: he had the boy tied up and beaten with canes.

This was severe punishment indeed, but considered normal for the Macedonian court. In their youth and childhood the companions had all been punished in that way – Leonnatus still bore the marks on his back, but even Hephaestion and Lysimachus had paid more than once for their own lack of discipline, on King Philip's orders or at Leonidas's or their weapon instructor's hand. The people who had written those rules perceived of them as a sort of exercise in bearing pain, a way of getting the youngsters used to obedience and of strength-ening body and soul in the face of difficulties. In Sparta boys were whipped with almost no punitive purpose, but simply as a form of education in valour and sacrifice, an exercise in the ability to withstand pain.

Hermolaus, however, considered himself a victim of a gratuitous, cruel and unjust humiliation and from that day onward he nurtured deep rancour against the King and even conceived of a plan to kill him. Although he would act on his own, he needed someone to help arrange his escape route. Fired by Callisthenes' ideas on freedom, he failed to realize that he himself was not an Athenian citizen engaged in defending his city's democ-racy against a tyrant, but was rather a Macedonian squire

in his King's service in a land far from home and in the midst of all sorts of danger. He also failed to realize that Callisthenes himself was dependent on Alexander, that the historian received from the King the food, the clothes and the blankets that sustained him and kept him warm through the cold nights up on the plateau.

With all the thoughtlessness that is typical of young men, Hermolaus spoke to a friend of his by the name of Epimenides, who promptly spoke about it with a friend – Charikles – whom he trusted blindly and who in his turn spoke with Epimenides' brother – Eurylochus – and this last, much frightened, sought to dissuade them in every way possible.

'Are you all mad?' he asked one day when they were gathered in a tent. 'You cannot do this.'

'Of course we can,' replied Hermolaus, 'and we will be doing the world a favour – freeing it of a hateful tyrant.'

Eurylochus shook his head, 'It was your fault – you know perfectly well that the first strike is the King's prerogative!'

'He had almost fallen from his horse, how could he have struck?'

'Alexander never falls from his horse, stupid, and in any case, how do you think you're going to do it? It's not easy to kill a King, you know.'

'Oh, but it is. Just think about how King Philip died, and he was much better than this one here, and no one has ever discovered who the assassin was.'

'But out here we're on our own, surrounded by barbarians and by the desert. They'll come looking for us

straight away. And then, if you really want to know, I have to tell you that there are already rumours doing the rounds about Callisthenes, rumours that would make you both prime suspects. Someone heard you asking him what one would have to do to become the most famous man in the world and he apparently replied, "Kill the most powerful man in the world." You are fortunate that these words have not yet reached the King's ears, but you cannot tempt fate too long without retribution.' He turned to Epimenides now and said, 'As for you, that's quite enough. I am your big brother and I order you to forget these wretches. And you two, if you know what's good for you, you'll forget it all. Behave respectably and perhaps all these rumours will fade away into nothing.'

Hermolaus shrugged his shoulders. 'I do whatever I wish, and if you don't intend to help me then that doesn't matter, I have other friends. It will be as easy as this,' and he spat a gob of saliva on the ground before turning his back and walking away.

The young conspirators waited for Alexander and his men to set out on an operation against a group of rebels; this way his death would appear to be the work of an enemy that had somehow infiltrated the camp. Then they debated the day and hour.

*

When the King left the palace at Bactra, Roxane embraced him hard and said, 'Don't go!'

'You are making great progress with your Greek,' replied Alexander. 'When you have learned it, I will teach you the Macedonian dialect as well.'

'Don't go!' repeated Roxane, her voice full of anguish.

Alexander gave her a kiss, 'But why shouldn't I go?'

The girl looked into his eyes and through her tears she said, 'Two days. I see . . . darkness.'

The King shook his head as though to chase away some irritating thought, then his attendants laced up his armour and accompanied him into the courtyard where his horsemen awaited, ready for the off.

Two days went by and the King, worried by Roxane's omen, spoke with Aristander. 'What do you think it might mean?'

'The women of this country practise divination and magic, they are able to feel menace when it is abroad, and what is more, Roxane loves you.'

'What should I do?'

'Do not sleep tonight. Read, drink, but keep your wits about you. You must remain awake.'

'I will do as you say,' replied Alexander and he waited for darkness to fall.

50

PTOLEMY SAW THAT A lamp was still burning in Alexander's tent and went in, saluted as he did so by the two squires who were on duty that night.

'Why are you still awake?' he asked. 'It's already the second watch.'

'I am not sleepy. I was reading.'

Ptolemy took a look, '*India* by Ctesias. You really can't wait, can you?'

'No. And when we have taken India, then we will be able to say that all Asia is in our hands. We will return then and we will begin to change the world, Ptolemy.'

'Do you really believe that the world can be changed? Do you think we can ever succeed in such an undertaking?'

Alexander lifted his eyes from the papyrus scroll that he was holding open before him, 'Yes, I do. Have you forgotten that evening in the sanctuary of Dionysius at Mieza?'

'I do remember. We were youngsters, full of enthusiasm, of hopes, of dreams . . .'

'Those youngsters have now conquered the world's largest empire – two thirds of the earth – and they have founded many cities of Greek culture and with Greek constitutions in the heart of Asia. Do you think this has

come about by chance? Do you think there is no meaning in all this? No purpose?'

'I would like to think there is. In any case, you can always count on my friendship, on my loyalty. I will never abandon you – you may be certain of this. As for all the rest, there are certain moments when I myself don't know what to think . . .'

At that moment Hermolaus entered. Peritas growled and Ptolemy turned towards him. 'Are you on watch tonight?'

'Yes, *Heghemón*,' replied the boy.

'So why were you outside?'

'The King was not sleeping and I did not want to disturb him.'

'You do not disturb me,' said Alexander. 'You may remain, if you wish.'

The young man sat in a corner of the tent. Ptolemy looked at him, and then at Alexander – he sensed something strange going on, an impalpable atmosphere of tension and repressed energy.

'He's the boy I had punished the other day, after the hunt.'

'Do you resent it, boy?' Ptolemy asked the squire, seeing the dark expression on his face. 'You mustn't, you know. If only you knew how many times I took a beating when I was your age. King Philip himself kicked me up the backside, and he even had me whipped once when I lamed one of his horses, but I never let it get to me because he was a great man and he did it for my own good.'

'Times have changed,' said Alexander. 'These lads

427

aren't like we were. They're . . . different. Or perhaps it's us, perhaps we're getting on. I'm thirty years old . . . would you credit it?'

'If it comes to that, I passed that mark some years ago. Good. I'll continue with my inspection rounds. Can I take the dog with me? He's good company,' at which Peritas wagged his tail.

'Take him. He's putting on weight and a bit of exercise will do him good.'

'I'm off then. If you need me just call.'

Alexander nodded and returned to his reading, every so often taking a sip from the cup on the table.

Hermolaus was sitting there before him in silence, his jaws clenched tight, his eyes lowered. Now and then the King lifted his head from the scroll and looked at him with a puzzled expression on his face. Eventually he said to him, 'You hate me, don't you? You hate me because I had you beaten.'

'That's not true, Sire. I . . .' but it was clear that he was lying and this convinced the King that the boy was a bad one because he had neither the courage to manifest his hatred nor to relinquish it.

'Forget it, it matters not.'

Almost all the night passed in this way – a cold, empty, useless night. The end of the watch was approaching now and dawn would soon be breaking. Hermolaus was tormented by doubts and continued to look at the King who kept lowering his head as though about to fall asleep.

Eurylochus too had stayed up all night because he had realized that all three of the squires on watch were

conspirators and he was sure they would decide to act, all the more so because Commander Ptolemy was in the habit of taking Peritas with him when it was his turn to inspect the guard. On seeing that the light in the royal tent kept burning, and that the King had not retired to bed despite the fact that there was no imminent danger of enemy incursions, he was sure that something terrible was about to happen: perhaps Alexander had discovered their plan. Perhaps Hermolaus and the others were about to strike. To think he had believed that words alone were enough to save those wretches. He saw Ptolemy coming to the end of his inspection and decided to speak to him, '*Heghemón* . . .'

'What's wrong, lad?'

'I . . . I must speak to you.'

'I am listening.'

'Not here.'

'In my tent then,' and he led him there and showed him the way in. 'So? What's all this secrecy about?'

'Listen, *Heghemón*,' began Eurylochus. 'My brother Epimenides, Hermolaus and other lads . . . how to put it . . . they have rather strange ideas . . . you know that Hermolaus together with my brother and some of their friends spend time with Callisthenes, and he's filled their heads with all sorts of stupid talk about democracy and tyranny and so . . .'

'So?' Ptolemy asked, his eyebrows bunching.

'They are only lads, *Heghemón*,' continued Eurylochus, no longer able to hold back the tears. 'Perhaps they've called it off this time, perhaps the King suspected something . . . I don't know . . . I decided to speak to you, so

that you might give them a good scare and then they'll get these stupid ideas out of their heads. It's all Callisthenes' fault, can't you see? They would never have thought of it. Even if the King did have Hermolaus beaten over that matter of the boar, I don't know if he would ever actually . . . but then you never know . . .'

'Oh, by Zeus!' exclaimed Ptolemy, then he shouted, 'Peritas! Run! Run to Alexander!' and the dog set off running as fast as his legs could carry him and he burst into the tent just as his master was nodding off, his head on the table, and Hermolaus's hand was moving stealthily to his belt, under his tunic. Peritas charged him to the ground and bit into the hand that held the dagger.

Ptolemy burst in immediately afterwards and managed to grab the dog just in time before he bit straight through the boy's hand. Alexander was woken suddenly from his dozing by all that noise and got to his feet, unsheathing his sword.

'They were out to kill you,' said Ptolemy, struggling for breath as he disarmed Hermolaus.

The boy writhed and kicked, shouting, 'Damned tyrant! You bloodthirsty monster! Your hands are stained with blood! You killed Parmenion and Philotas, you are an assassin!'

The other two who were on guard outside tried to slip away, but Ptolemy called the trumpeter and had him sound the call for the shieldsmen, and so the squires were stopped immediately as they sought to make their escape. Eurylochus was still crying as he arrived at a run and pleaded, 'Do not harm them, *Heghemón*! Don't hurt them.

They will do nothing more, I promise you. Give them to me, I'll punish them, I'll have them beaten, but do not harm them, I beg you!'

Alexander left, pale with rage, while Hermolaus continued shouting all types of insult and offence in the midst of the camp that was now seething with soldiers running from all directions.

'What are the just deserts of these men, Sire?' Ptolemy asked, using the ritual formula.

'Let the army decide their fate,' replied Alexander, and he retired to his tent.

The military judges assembled immediately and the squires underwent a trial which lasted all that day and all through the following night – they were asked to corroborate one another's stories, led into contradicting themselves and their fellow conspirators, beaten and whipped until they all confessed. None of them, not even under torture, mentioned Callisthenes, but Eurylochus, who had been spared for having saved the King's life, continued to say that those lads would never have thought up such a plan if Callisthenes had not filled their heads with his ideas. He continued to implore right up to the very end for them to be saved, but it was all in vain.

At dawn, a grey, drizzling daybreak, they were all stoned to death.

Eumenes, who witnessed both the trial and the execution, went to Callisthenes' tent and found him there, trembling and as pale as a corpse, wringing his hands in anguish.

'Your name was mentioned,' he said.

Callisthenes collapsed into a chair with a deep, rattling sigh. 'So this is the end, is it not?'

Eumenes did not reply.

'This is the end for me, is it not?' he shouted.

'Your ghosts have acquired physical form, Callisthenes, the bodies of those lads, who lie now under a heap of stones. A man like you . . . didn't you realize that words can kill just as easily as the sword?'

'Will they torture me? I'll never hold out, I won't resist. They can make me say whatever they want!' Callisthenes shouted as he sobbed.

Eumenes lowered his head in embarrassment. 'I am sorry. I only wanted to tell you that they will come before long. You don't have much time,' and he left under the beating rain.

Callisthenes looked around in desperation, searching for a weapon, a blade, but the only things available were rolls of papyrus, piled everywhere, his works, his *History of Alexander's Expedition*. Then he suddenly remembered something he should have destroyed a long time ago, but for some reason had kept. He went to a chest, rummaged through it, breathless in fear and anxiety, and finally he held firmly in his hands a metal box. He opened it and inside was a small sheet of papyrus and then, wrapped up in a cloth, a glass phial filled with a white powder. These words were written on the sheet:

No one can control the incubation of diseases, but this medicine gives the same symptoms.

One tenth of *leptón* gives high fever, vomit and

diarrhoea for two or three days. Then there is an improvement and it seems the patient is on the mend. On the fourth day the fever rises once more and immediately afterwards comes death.

Callisthenes burned the papyrus and then swallowed the entire contents of the phial. When the guards arrived, they found him collapsed among the scrolls of his *History*, his eyes wide open and full of terror, staring into nothing.

51

The coast of Phocis was clearly visible now, looming out of the evening mist, and the clouds in the sky and the waves in the sea were ablaze with the colours of the sunset. The boat sailed forward on a wind that blew from the Gulf of Aegina. Aristotle moved towards the bow to watch the manoeuvres as they moored and shortly afterwards he disembarked in the small harbour at Cyrra where seamen, port labourers and vendors of sacred objects were all busy at work.

'Want a sheep to offer in sacrifice?' one of them asked. 'Here they cost half of what they want at Delphi. Just take a look at this little lamb – four obols, that's all. A pair of pigeons then?'

'I need a donkey,' replied the philosopher.

'A donkey?' the merchant retorted in amazement. 'You've got to be joking . . . who on earth would ever offer a donkey in—'

'I do not intend to sacrifice it. I wish to ride it.'

'Ah! That's different then. In that case come right this way; I've got this old friend, a donkey specialist, and he has the most docile creatures you could ever ask for.' The merchant had already realized that the man before him was a scholar, a man of letters who was certainly poorly versed in matters equestrian.

They negotiated a price for three days' hire and a deposit to be refunded on return of the animal, and thus Aristotle set off for the sanctuary of Apollo, unaccompanied. It was late now and usually travellers preferred to climb up through the shining silver of the olive wood in the morning, in the full light of day, rather than in the darkness that transformed the centuries-old trunks into threatening, disturbing shapes. The calm gait of the philosopher's mount meant that he was able to think a little as the last rays of the setting sun warmed his limbs, somewhat cold as a result of the evening crossing and the wind that had evidently blown down across the first snows up on Mount Cithaeron.

He thought of the many years he had dedicated to his investigation of the death of King Philip, seeking out the elusive truth.

The news from Asia had not been encouraging for some time – Alexander seemed to have forgotten his teachings, at least as far as politics were concerned. He had put the barbarians on the same level as the Greeks, he dressed like a Persian despot, demanded *proskynesis* from those who approached him and gave credit to the rumours his mother Olympias had deliberately spread regarding his divine origin.

Poor King Philip! But it was said that it was the destiny of all great men to be the bastard offspring of a god or a goddess: Hercules, Castor and Pollux, Achilles, Theseus . . . Alexander could not be an exception to this rule. This was understandable, indeed it was only to be expected. And yet, despite all this he missed Alexander and would have given anything to be able to see him

once more. He wondered what he might look like, whether he still had that curious way of tilting his head towards his right shoulder when he was listening to or saying something that touched his soul.

And Callisthenes? Extremely able with the pen, no doubt about that, even though a trifle lacking in critical spirit, but definitely low on common sense. He wondered how he might be managing in those extreme situations, out in those inhospitable places, among those rough peoples and the intrigues of that movable court, unstable now and therefore even more dangerous. He had not received news from him for months, but of course lines of communication across such vast territories – deserts and highlands, fast-flowing rivers, mountain chains – would all be in some difficulty.

The philosopher hurried his donkey by digging his heels into its flanks because he wanted to reach the top before darkness. Indeed, Philip's assassin . . . whoever was behind it must have had a diabolic mind if up to that moment he had eluded him and any other investigators. The first clues suggested Queen Olympias, but she proved to be an unlikely culprit – why had Philip's wife made the dramatic gesture of crowning the body of the killer? There were still many friends of the King who would have been able to make her pay dearly for the assassination, all the more so because she was a foreigner and therefore doubly exposed and weak in that situation. Then he had followed the hypothesis of a crime of passion, a sordid story of male sex in which Pausanias, the killer, wreaked his revenge on Philip for an outrage he had suffered at the hands of Attalus, father of young

Eurydice and the King's latest father-in-law. But Attalus was dead now and the dead do not speak.

The regular noise of the donkey's hooves on the gravel of the road accompanied his meditations, almost marking out the quiet rhythm of his thought. There came to mind his interview with Pausanias's bride-to-be, at a graveside one cold winter's evening. Here was the third hypothesis: as soon as Philip's young bride, Eurydice, had given birth to a son, her father, Attalus, the boy's grandfather and the King's father-in-law, had thought up a daring scheme – to kill Philip and to proclaim himself regent in his grandson's name, the grandson who would take the throne on coming of age. The plan stood a good chance of being successful because the little boy's mother was pureblood Macedonian, unlike Olympias who was a foreigner. This plan would have had a perfect conclusion with the murder of Pausanias, the only witness to the conspiracy. But there was no proof for this theory because Attalus had made no attempt to take power following Philip's death – he had not marched on Pella with the army he led at that time in Asia. Perhaps he was afraid of Parmenion? Or of Alexander?

In any case, how to explain the words of Pausanias's betrothed? She was certainly well informed and seemed to believe that her lover had been raped in an orgy by Attalus's hunting stewards, which made no sense, if he was the assassin. He had searched for the girl again, but he was told that she had disappeared some time previously and that there had been no more news of her.

There was one last possibility – the clues leading to the Shrine at Delphi, the oracle that had issued an

apparently ambiguous, but ultimately accurate prophecy regarding the imminent death of Philip. And not far away from here there lived, under a false name, the man who had killed Pausanias, the only witness who might lead him to the person who ordered Philip's assassination.

The philosopher looked behind him and he saw that the dying light of the sunset had given a purple tinge to the waters of the gulf, a mirror enclosed between two promontories, and way up on high, to his left, was the great Doric temple of Apollo, already illuminated in the glow from the tripods and the lamps. At this point a melodious song rose into the clear silence of the evening:

> God with your silver bow, shining Phoebus,
> Who brings light now to the lands of Elysium,
> And the Isles of the Blessed, lost in the turbulent
> waters of the Ocean,
> Return, return now, Oh godly one! Bring us the
> dawn tomorrow,
> Your shining smile, after the dark night,
> Mother of nightmares, daughter of Chaos

He had arrived. He tied the donkey to a ring near the fountain and set off on foot along the sacred road, passing through the small votive temples of the Athenians, the Siphnians, the Thebans and the Spartans. They were all full of trophies of victories won by spilling fraternal blood, of Greeks who had killed other Greeks, and on looking at them he felt he knew what Alexander would have had to say about them if they could have spoken to each other at that moment.

The last pilgrims were leaving and the caretaker was about to close the doors of the deserted shrine.

He asked him to wait, and added, 'I have travelled here from far away and tomorrow I must leave. I beg you, give me just a moment, let me say a prayer to the god, a desperate request for I am victim of some terrible spell, of a curse that has persecuted me for many years,' and he slipped the caretaker a coin.

The man put it in his bag and said, 'Very well, but be quick,' and he set about brushing the steps of the podium.

Aristotle entered and slipped into the half-darkness of the left-hand aisle, taking small steps as he moved along and observed the thousands of votive objects that hung from the wall. It was intuition that guided him, the shadow of a memory from many years previously when as a child he had visited the temple, hand-in-hand with his father, Nicomachus. One votive object in particular had grabbed his attention. This memory, together with his suspicion, had led him here under this sacred roof.

He reached the end of the aisle and moved across to the other side, under the mother-of-pearl gaze of the god sitting on its throne. He continued his inspection, moving along the other aisle, looking carefully at the wall, but there was nothing that might confirm his memory, faded now in its remoteness. It was too dark. He took a lamp that hung from one of the columns, held it up to the wall, and immediately his face lit up in victory – he was right! There before him he could just make it out, faded by time, the mark left by an object that had hung in that place for many years.

He looked around to make sure no one was watching,

then with one hand he lifted the lamp while with the other he pulled out of his satchel the short Celtic sword that had killed King Philip that day at Aegae. He moved it towards the mark on the wall, slowly, almost as though afraid to do so . . . and the two coincided perfectly!

The two nails were still there in the wall, fitting the curves of the spiral handle and Aristotle hung it in its place.

'So . . . have you finished your prayers then?' came the voice of the guardian from outside. 'I have to lock up now.'

'I'm coming,' replied the philosopher, and he left quickly, thanking the caretaker as he passed by.

He spent the night under the portico, wrapped up in his cloak like all the other pilgrims, but he slept very little. The *amphictyony*! The league of Delphi! Was it possible? Was it possible that the most revered sanctuary in the Greek world had commissioned the death of King Philip? Perhaps that mark on the wall was just a strange coincidence, perhaps it was simply that Aristotle at all costs wanted to find a solution to the enigma that had defied his intelligence for so many years. And yet this theory was the only one for which there was objective proof – the weapon that had killed the King came from the temple! In the end it was even plausible – could the greatest authority in all Greece ever have allowed itself to be dominated by the will of one man alone? Was it not a manifestation of divine intelligence to kill a great King at a moment when almost anyone could have been accused of his assassination – Athenians who saw in him an oppressor and usurper of their supremacy, the Theban

survivors who hated him fiercely because of the rout at Chaeronaea, the Persians because they feared his invasion of Asia, Queen Olympias who hated him for having humiliated her and having chosen young Eurydice, Prince Amyntas to whom Philip had denied his legitimate succession? Even Alexander, ultimately, was under suspicion. Everyone, and therefore no one. Sublime – and the motive was one that justifies any crime: the power of the mind over men, much stronger and more important than any power in the world, the closest there is to the power of the gods.

There was one last link – the man who had killed Pausanias and who lived, as far as Aristotle had been able to gather, on a farm that belonged to the sanctuary.

It was still dark when he got up, loaded up his donkey and set off again. He went down the road that led to the sea for some ten stadia, then he turned on to a mule track that went towards the right and moved into a small plain arranged with terraces for the cultivation of vines.

The house was visible, down beyond the vines and standing next to an old oak tree: a small building with terracotta tiles on its roof and in front of it a small portico with olive wood columns.

He entered the yard where a small group of pigs were rooting around, eating the acorns scattered underneath the oak, and called, 'Is there anyone here? Is there anyone here?' but there came no reply. He dismounted and knocked at the door, which opened up, letting a ray of light into the interior.

It was him. And he hung from a rope tied to the ceiling beams.

Aristotle backed away in astonishment, hurried to his donkey and set off at a trot, trying to get away as quickly as he possibly could.

*

He wasted no time in reaching Athens and for several days refused to see anyone. He destroyed his notes and the copies of all the letters he had sent to his nephew regarding the matter. In the file on the assassination of Philip he left only the vaguest and most generic notes and began writing a conclusion: 'The true cause of the assassination probably lies in a sordid story of sexual relations between men . . .'

Towards the end of the month a messenger knocked at his door and handed him a bulky package. Aristotle opened it and found that it contained some of Callisthenes' personal effects and all the letters he had written to him. To one side was a roll of papyrus bearing the seal of Ptolemy, son of Lagos, King Alexander's bodyguard, Commander of an armoured division of the Macedonian army. His hands trembled as he opened it and read:

Ptolemy to Aristotle, Hail!
The fourth day of the month of Elaphebolion of the third year of the one hundred and thirteenth Olympiad, your nephew Callisthenes, official historian of Alexander's expedition, was found dead in his tent and Philip, the King's physician, certified that the death was the result of his having taken a powerful poison. A group of young squires had conspired to kill the King, and although none of the accused during the

trial mentioned Callisthenes by name, nevertheless there were those who attributed your nephew with a sort of moral responsibility for the criminal plot. It is indeed strange that such young men should take the decision to kill their King, without someone having planted the thought in their minds. There is reason to believe that by his suicide your nephew sought to avoid the pain of public judgement.

The King feels unable to write to you, his soul troubled as it is by so many and such conflicting feelings, and I decided to do this in his stead.

I know that this news will reach you with a great delay because as I began writing our army had already moved through some extremely inhospitable country in preparation for the invasion of India. I have also chosen to send you a copy of the *History of the Expedition of Alexander*, which Callisthenes had his own scribe make. Unfortunately the regrettable matter of his death leaves his work incomplete.

I thought anyway that it was best to send you news of events up to this point and the most important episodes in the Indian expedition, in case you want to finish the work of your nephew in whichever way you deem fit.

I would also like to tell you a story you may find interesting. A man from Elis, by the name of Pyrrho lived in the camp with us for some time. He had begun his career as a poor, almost unknown painter and had followed our expedition in the hope of making his fortune, but over the years he met the magi in Persia and then the wise men in India, after having spent much time with Callisthenes. From all these

experiences he is elaborating a new scheme of thought that may, as far as I can understand, enjoy some considerable renown throughout the world.

I hope this letter finds you in good health. Take good care.

52

ONLY AT THE END of the month, with the arrival of the cold weather, did Aristotle settle down to reading Ptolemy's report, a succinct but effective account that could have formed the basis for the continuation of Callisthenes' work.

The army set off through the Paropamisus or Indian Caucasus – as some prefer to call it – and this move cost great sacrifices. The cold was so severe at the pass that one night some sentries were found dead, still leaning against the trees at their posts, their eyes staring straight ahead and their moustaches and beards encrusted with ice. Alexander once again distinguished himself by virtue of his great humanity. He saw a veteran whose strength was obviously failing, shaking with cold, and had him take his throne, which was made of wood, and told him to burn it so that he might warm himself. After nine days' march we reached the city of Nisa, where the inhabitants claimed Dionysius had passed through on his journey towards India. The proof they offer for this is the presence of Mount Meru, which in Greek means 'thigh', for Dionysius was born of one of Zeus's thighs. What is more they maintain that this is the only place in all India where ivy grows, a plant that is sacred to the god.

Everyone crowned themselves with ivy and celebrated with great feasts and orgies, drinking, dancing the *komos* and shouting, '*Euoè!*'

There the army was divided into two contingents: Hephaestion and Perdiccas marched down the valley of a torrent from the highlands to its confluence with the Indus and built a bridge there; the other, of which I formed part together with the King and the other Companions, marched towards the high course of the Indus to take the cities lying in those valleys – Massaga, Bazeira and Orus, all of which fell after repeated attacks. The largest of them all was Aornos, over twenty miles in circumference and located at a height of eight thousand feet, defended by a deep gully all around.

The King had a dyke built and a ramp and I took up position one night at an outpost from which it was possible to attack the city at one of its weakest points. The Indians defended valiantly, but in the end the battering rams managed to open a breach and the army burst inside. We united our two divisions and took the city with a simultaneous attack. Alexander offered the Indians the opportunity to join his army as mercenaries, but they preferred to flee rather than fight against their brothers.

In these cities we captured a certain number of elephants, animals that Alexander was most pleased to have. They are truly extraordinary in their enormous mass, with their great tusks protruding from their mouths. They can carry towers with armed warriors on their backs and are led by a man who sits on their neck and spurs them on with his heels. If this man is

killed in battle then the elephant loses all sense of direction and knows not which way to go.

The Indians are a tall people, darker than all other men, with the exception of the Ethiopians, and they are most valiant in combat. After conquering Aornos, the King installed a garrison there, and as governor an Indian prince who initially had been with Bessus but then moved over to our side. His name is Sashagupta, in his language, but the Greeks call him Sisycottos. At Aornos we took two hundred and fifty thousand oxen as loot, out of which the strongest and the most handsome were chosen to be sent back to Macedonia to plough the fields and improve our breeds. Alexander then had boats built and even two ships, each with twenty-five oars, and we started moving down the River Indus, which is very wide and completely navigable, as far as I know, for its entire course.

Thus we reached the point where Perdiccas and Hephaestion had finished building their bridge over the river near a city called Taxila, whose people welcomed us in friendship. The Indian King of Taxila, who goes by the name of Taxiles, offered twenty-five elephants and three hundred talents of silver to Alexander. I have seen very little gold. As for the legends according to which there are giant ants in these lands that dig gold out of the mountains, which is then guarded by winged griffins, I found no evidence of this worthy of credit and I believe they must be considered groundless stories.

From there we went on as far as the banks of the River Hydaspes, the largest of all the Indus's tributaries, wide and fast-flowing because of the rains that

had fallen on the mountains. On the other side was an Indian king by the name of Porus with a large army – thirty thousand foot soldiers, four thousand horsemen, three hundred war chariots and two hundred elephants. It was impossible to cross the river because Porus shifted his own position each time we moved, preventing us from fording. Alexander then gave orders to the troops to move continuously, even at night, shouting and making as much noise as possible as they did so, and in this way our enemies no longer had any idea what our plans were and Porus had to pitch camp at one point and wait for us there.

We left Craterus opposite their camp with a certain number of soldiers and followed Alexander up the river with the *hetairoi* cavalry, the mounted archers, the Agrianians and the heavy infantry. In the meantime a storm had broken out, with deafening thunder and blinding lightning, which discouraged the Indians from venturing along the banks of the Hydaspes. The ford was extremely difficult, made possible only by the presence of an island in the middle of river. The men crossed with the water up to their shoulders, while the horses sank up to their withers. Alexander, even though he had promised not to take Bucephalas into battle any more after Gaugamela, decided to mount him on that occasion because only a horse of his size would allow him to crush the enemy cavalry with their faster, but smaller mounts.

At dawn Porus heard that the Macedonian troops had crossed the river and he sent his son at the head of a thousand horsemen to do battle with us. We

crushed them at their first charge and the young Prince himself was killed. Porus then realized that it was Alexander who had crossed the Hydaspes during that stormy night and he sent his entire army after him. He lined up the war chariots first of all, behind them the elephants and behind them again the foot soldiers, with the cavalry to the sides. He himself, built like a giant, rode an enormous elephant and as soon as the battle was under way he led the attack, shouting and spurring on his animal.

The chariots were the first to attack, but the terrain was so sodden with rain that they were slowed down to the point where it was an easy matter for our mounted archers to find their range and pick off the drivers.

On moving past the line of chariots, Alexander sent his cavalry to attack on the wings, engaging in furious hand-to-hand combat against the Indian cavalry that fought back with great valour. Porus in the meantime sent the elephants forward into our centre and these enormous beasts massacred our men, crashing through the tight ranks of the phalanx. Then Perdiccas and Hephaestion gave orders to break ranks and to let the elephants through while Lysimachus, having finally managed to assemble the engines after the river crossing, started aiming the catapults at them. We sent the mounted archers into the attack against those monsters as well, together with the javelin throwers who caused them all sorts of grief. The foot archers then came into play, taking aim at their riders and cutting them down one after another. Wild with pain and fear, the elephants started swaying and running

amok, even among their own soldiers, no longer able to distinguish enemies from friends.

At this point, with the elephants out of action, Perdiccas ordered the phalanx to close ranks again and sent them off to attack, shouting his war cry to encourage his men and taking up position in the front line. On the other side, Porus continued to move forward, fighting with incredible energy. His elephant was a fury, crushing everything in its path, its feet and legs dirty with blood and scraps of innards right up to its knees, while Porus, encased in his impenetrable armour, threw what seemed to be a constant stream of javelins with the force of a catapult.

The battle lasted eight hours, ceaseless, until in the end Alexander, leading the Vanguard out on the right flank, and Koinos, who led the left wing, managed to force the enemy cavalry into retreat and to converge on the centre. The Indians were completely surrounded now and they surrendered. Porus himself, wounded on his right shoulder, the only point of his body not protected by armour, began swaying.

It was touching to see how the elephant realized that his master was in trouble. The animal slowed down to a halt and knelt down, allowing Porus to slide gently to the ground and then, when it saw him lying there, it tried to draw the javelin from the wound. The elephant riders led it away, so that the Indian King could be handed over to our surgeons who immediately gave him treatment.

Alexander wanted to meet Porus as soon as he heard that he was able to stand and he was amazed at his enormous stature: more than seven feet tall and

his shining steel armour clung to his body like a second skin. He had initially sent King Taxiles, Porus's ally, as interpreter, but the giant King considered him a traitor and had tried to kill him. So he went in person with another interpreter and saluted him with great respect, praising him for his valour and expressing his sympathy for the loss of his sons, both of whom had fallen in battle. At the end of their meeting he asked, 'How do you wish to be treated?'

And Porus replied, 'Like a King.'

And he was treated like a King: Alexander let him govern over all the territories he had conquered up to that moment and let him take up his position again in his palace.

However, our joy at such a hard-fought victory over an almost superhuman enemy and against such monsters of physical strength and frightening appearance – animals that no Macedonian had ever come into contact with before – our joy was saddened by an event that threw the King into the deepest dismay. His horse Bucephalas, wounded during the battle and lamed in a clash with an elephant, died after four days of suffering.

The King cried for Bucephalas as though an intimate friend had passed away and he remained with him until he breathed his last breath. I was there and I saw him stroke the animal sweetly, speaking to him softly, reminding him of all the adventures they had lived together and Bucephalas neighed weakly as though seeking to reply. I saw the tears run down the King's cheeks and I saw his body racked by his sobbing when the animal slipped out of this world.

He had a tomb of stone constructed and founded a

city in his honour, calling it Alexandria Bucephala, an honour that no horse had ever received, not even the most famous victors of the races at Olympia. Alexander also buried a piece of his heart and the happiest period of his lost youth in that tomb.

Near the battlefield where he had defeated Porus, he founded another city, giving it the name of Alexandria Nicaea, in commemoration of the victory; he celebrated games there and offered sacrifices to the gods. From there we went eastwards, encouraged by Porus who gave us five thousand of his soldiers and we came to the Acesines, second largest tributary of the Indus, another fast-flowing river with many rapids and rocks with boiling, foaming waters. Several of our boats were dashed against the rocks and sank with their men, but then we found a point where the river was wider and calmer and we managed to cross. We conquered seventy cities, of which more than half had over five thousand inhabitants, and finally we have come to a halt under the walls of Sangala, on the banks of the Hydraotes.

I do not know what will happen now, whether we will succeed in taking this city too, whether we will cross this river as well. And after the river there is a desert and then an impenetrable forest and then other realms with hundreds of thousands of warriors. Our fatigue has become unbearable. In the forests there are snakes of fearful proportions, true monsters – Leonnatus killed one with his axe that measured sixteen cubits.

Aristotle sighed. Sixteen cubits! He stood up to measure that length with his steps and had to leave the room

because it was not long enough. He turned back to the table and continued reading.

The cultivated lands are most fertile, but the forest seems to surround them everywhere, attack them even, in a certain sense. There are monkeys of all sizes everywhere too and they have the curious habit of imitating everything they see. Some of them are amazing because of the expressions on their faces, which seem almost human, as you can see for yourself.

Alongside those words Ptolemy had had one of those monkeys drawn with charcoal, by a very skilled artist, and the animal's gaze indeed astonished the philosopher, almost provoking a sense of unease, a perturbing sensation.

There are also incredibly large trees that the Indians' call *banyan*. They reach heights of seventy cubits and their trunks are so big that not even fifty men together can embrace them. On one occasion I saw more than five hundred men in the shade of one of those giants.

There are snakes of all kinds. Some look like a bronze rod, others are dark in colour and their neck opens up into a sort of crest with two marks in the shape of circles. Their bite brings death almost immediately with unspeakable pain and heavy sweating. The first times we came across these animals we sat up all through the night, terrorized at the idea of being bitten in our sleep, but then we learned to light fires around the camp and the locals taught us how to use certain herbs as antidotes to the venom.

They are even more dangerous than the tiger that

frequents these impenetrable woods because at least there is a defence against the big cat, so they say, with a good sword, or a good javelin. The tiger is bigger than a lion and has a magnificently coloured coat with ochre and black stripes, and its roar makes the night air tremble at an unbelievable distance. I have never seen one, but I have seen a skin and this is how I am able to describe it.

Now I must stop. The torrential rains make it impossible for me to write any more – the humidity makes everything rot, the men fall ill, others end up in the jaws of the crocodiles that crawl everywhere here because the waters have caused the rivers to burst their banks and the fields and the countryside are flooded for thousands and thousands of stadia. I myself have no idea of when I may once again hope to live as a man and not as a beast.

Only he seems to know neither fatigue nor despondency of any kind. He always marches ahead of everyone, clearing the way through the thick vegetation with his sword, helping those who fall, encouraging those who are tired. And in his eyes is that burning light, the same light I saw so long ago when I saw him come out of the temple of Ammon in the midst of the desert sands of Libya.

Ptolemy's story finished at that point and Aristotle closed the scroll and put it on a shelf.

His thoughts turned to Callisthenes and his eyes filled with tears. His adventure had finished so sadly in some far-flung place near the ends of the earth and perhaps it really had been fear rather than the poison that had killed

him. He grieved for him now, knowing just how much stronger his ideas were compared to his soul and his courage. He would have liked to be there at the final moment and to have read to him Socrates' last words: 'But already it is time to depart, for me to die, for you to go on living . . .' but perhaps he would not even have heard, caught up as he was in the coils of sheer terror.

Aristotle put out the lamp and as he lay down and sighed in the empty room, in the diaphanous rays of the autumnal moon, he wondered if Alexander had felt any pity for Callisthenes.

53

HEPHAESTION RAN TO THE King's tent under the torrential rain, splashing mud as he went. The guards let him in and he moved over to the brazier in which a fire was burning, giving off more smoke than heat. Alexander moved over to greet him and Leptine appeared and gave him a dry cloak.

'Sangala has surrendered,' he announced. 'Eumenes is just finishing the count of the dead and the wounded.'

'Are there many?'

'Seventeen thousand dead.'

'A massacre. They obviously put up a strong fight.'

'We have an enormous quantity of prisoners. We have also taken three hundred war chariots and seventy elephants.'

Eumenes entered, he too soaked to the skin. 'I have the final count – five hundred dead on our side, one hundred and fifty of which are Macedonians and Greeks, and one thousand two hundred wounded. Lysimachus has a bad wound on his shoulder, but it's not dangerous, for the moment. Do you have other orders for me?'

'Yes,' replied Alexander. 'Tomorrow you must set off to the other two cities that lie between here and the Hyphasis. Take a few prisoners with you who can recount what happened at Sangala. If they recognize

my authority then there will be no more deaths or massacres. We'll follow on behind you with the rest of the army.'

Eumenes nodded and went out into the open with his cloak over his shoulders while a blinding bolt of lightning lit the entire camp up in a blue flash and a thunderclap exploded almost directly above the King's tent.

'I am going now to supervise the transfer of the prisoners,' said Hephaestion. 'If I can, I'll stop by again before nightfall to report.'

With his shield held over his head, he reached the palisade that surrounded the camp and saw that the prisoners were moving through two rows of stock-still *pezhetairoi* under the torrential rain, following two mounted officers who were leading them to a huge fenced area near the western gate, where enough tents for just over half of them had been pitched. Soldiers made sure that the women and children found shelter and then the men were taken care of, crammed in together in a tremendous crush, their feet caked in mud.

He lifted his eyes upwards and saw black clouds threatening even more rain, and then to the horizon where blinding flashes of lightning appeared increasingly frequently. It was an ugly sky and the rain was unrelenting, incessant. What was that land over there? What would they find on the other side of the river that Alexander was so determined to reach?

At that moment a lightning bolt cracked through the clouds, so strong it lit up the entire area and the city, and there appeared before him a spectral, ghost-like figure – a solitary man, semi-naked and skeletal, who moved

forward through the open gates of the camp. Hephaestion walked towards him in his astonishment and shouted over the deafening noise of the thunderclaps, 'Who are you? What do you want?'

The man uttered something incomprehensible in reply, but he did not stop, and continued to walk through the tents until he came to an enormous *banyan*. He sat down near the tree, crossed his hands and held them in his lap with his palms upwards and the index finger and thumb of his right hand united in a circle, motionless as a statue under the beating rain.

Not far away Aristander was busy just outside the small wooden temple they had built to protect the camp, sacrificing a sheep to the gods, asking them to stop the rain. Suddenly he felt a sharp pain in the back of his neck and heard a voice calling him. He turned immediately and he too saw the man walking slowly but surely through the camp. There was no one else nearby who could have called him and this intrigued him deeply. He went out into the rain, holding his cloak up over his head and walked towards the *banyan* tree. Hephaestion saw him try to communicate with the motionless, half-naked Indian and then he watched him as he in his turn first sought shelter in a cavity in the tree and then sat down on the ground.

Hephaestion shook his head and then, still holding his shield above his head, went to his own tent and dried himself as well as possible before putting on dry clothes.

It rained all night with frightful thunder and lightning crashing overhead, setting fire to trees and huts. The sun was shining in the morning, however, and when the King

came out of his tent he found Aristander standing there before him.

'What is the matter, seer?'

'Look. It is him,' and he pointed to the naked, skeletal man sitting under the *banyan*.

'Who is he?'

'Him. The naked man in my nightmares.'

'Are you sure?'

'I recognized him immediately. He has been sitting there motionless since last night. He has been in the same position, like a statue, all night, in the midst of the storm without even trembling, without batting an eyelid.'

'Who is he?'

'I asked the other Indians. No one knows. No one knows him.'

'Does he have a name?'

'I do not know. I believe he is a *samana*, one of their philosophers and wise men.'

'Take me to him.'

They set off walking through the thick mud that now covered the entire camp until they found themselves opposite the mysterious visitor. Alexander immediately thought of Diogenes, the naked philosopher he had met one warm autumn day lying in front of his churn, and he felt a lump grow in his throat.

'Who are you?' he asked.

The man opened his eyes and stared at him with a shocking intensity to his gaze, but he said nothing.

'Are you hungry? Do you wish to come to my tent?' and he turned to Aristander and said, 'Quickly, have an interpreter brought here.'

'Are you hungry? Do you want to come under my tent?' he repeated when the interpreter had arrived.

The man pointed to a small bowl there before him, and the interpreter explained that these holy men, ascetics who sought eternal bliss, lived off alms and that a handful of their boiled swamp grain, nothing more than that, would be enough.

'Why will you not come to my tent, dry yourself and get warm and have something to eat?'

'It is not possible,' said the interpreter. 'It would interrupt his journey towards perfection, his becoming one with everything; this is the only possible way to achieve peace, the only liberation from pain.'

'*Panta rei*,' thought Alexander. 'Democritus's ideas . . . everything dissolves and everything is reconstituted in different forms. Even the mind . . . breakdown as the only hope . . .

'Give him something to eat,' he ordered, 'and tell him I will be happy to speak with him whenever he wants.'

The interpreter replied, 'He says that he will speak with you just as soon as he has learned your language.'

Alexander bowed and returned to his tent, while the trumpets sounded the fall in for all the divisions. They set off in the direction of the Hyphasis, the last of the tributaries, the last obstacle before penetrating deep into the vastness of India, towards the Ganges, the wonders of Palimbothra, and the shores of the farthest Ocean.

The army set off into a sparsely wooded area that became thicker as they approached the river. On the second day it started raining heavily and it rained on the

third and fourth day as well, with deafening thunder and blinding lightning bolts. The Indian guides explained that this was the rainy season and that it usually lasted some seventy days. When they reached the banks of the Hyphasis, the river swollen and muddy, the King held a war council in his tent. Admiral Nearchus was present, together with the vice admiral Onesicritus, who had acquitted himself very well in the recent river crossings and in their voyage down the Indus from Aornos to Taxila. Also present were Hephaestion, Perdiccas, Craterus, Leonnatus, Seleucus, Ptolemy and Lysimachus. Philip's old guard had disappeared completely now and the lads from Mieza were the supreme commanders of all the army's largest units.

There was also an Indian ally, a King by the name of Phagaias, who knew the lands on the other side of the Hyphasis very well.

Alexander opened the council. 'My friends, we have come farther now than any Greeks had ever travelled previously, beyond the places visited by the god Dionysius in his peregrinations, and we owe this achievement to your incredible valour, to your exceptional fibre, your heroism and the qualities of our soldiers. All that remains now is the final step. On crossing the last tributary of the Indus, there will no longer be any obstacles on our march to the Ganges and the shores of the great Ocean. At that point we will have completed the greatest feat ever realized in the history of mankind and the gods. We will have given expression to the greatest dream ever imagined. I think our Admiral Nearchus should now illustrate

his project for crossing the river, after which the commanders of our combat units will expound their point of view on the march.'

A thunderclap broke above the tent at that moment, so strong it made the objects on the table tremble. There followed moments of interminable silence and then the noise of the rain seemed to grow deafeningly unreal.

Ptolemy exchanged a quick glance with Seleucus and spoke first, 'Listen, Alexander, we have followed you this far and we are ready to follow you even farther, to march through the mud, through the swamps, among the snakes and the crocodiles, we are prepared to cross more deserts and more mountains, but your soldiers are not.' Alexander looked at him in amazement, as though unable to believe what he was hearing. 'Your men have given their all and there is nothing left now.'

'This is not true!' exclaimed Alexander. 'They defeated Porus and conquered so many cities.'

'That is precisely why they are exhausted, at the end of their tether. Can't you see it? Look at them, Alexander, just stop and look at them as they march through the ceaseless rain with the mud up to their knees, their beards unkempt, their eyes red with lack of sleep. Have you counted how many of them have died in helping you fulfil your dream? Have you counted them, Alexander? Killed by loss of blood, by wounds that never healed, by gangrene, by snakebites, torn apart by crocodiles, burned up by fevers, consumed by dysentery. All skin and bone, they have dragged themselves this far, to the ends of the earth, and they are afraid – but not of the enemy, with their war chariots and their elephants, no!

They are afraid of this inhospitable and alien nature, of this sky that is perpetually rent by thunder and lightning, of the monsters that slither in the forests and in the swamps, they are even afraid of the night sky when they look up and see the constellations they have been familiar with since their childhood setting, almost disappearing below the horizon. Look at them, Alexander, they are not the same men – their clothes are all torn and they are forced to cover themselves with rags or with the clothes of the barbarians they have conquered. Their horses' hooves are worn down with these endless marches and they leave bloody trails across the land.'

'I have borne the same suffering, I have suffered the cold together with them – the hunger and the thirst, the rain and the wounds!' shouted the King, opening up his robe and showing all present the scars on his chest.

'Yes, but they are not you, they don't have your energy or your vital force. They are only men. They are exhausted, completely drained. They have heard nothing from their families for years – all they can do is dream of the wives and children they left behind so long ago.

'Think of those you forced into the garrisons, accusing those who did not wish to remain in the conquered cities of desertion. All of this is something that frightens them – they are afraid that one day a herald will arrive with orders for them to form part of the garrison of some godforsaken outpost, to forget for ever their family and their homeland. Take them back home, Alexander, in the name of the gods, take them back home.'

Ptolemy lowered his head as he stopped talking and all the other Companions remained silent. A lightning

bolt struck the ground with a tremendous crash and the thunder rumbled around the sky like the roll of a far off drum.

Alexander waited for it to die out before speaking: 'Spit it out, Ptolemy! Is this a mutiny? Is my army rebelling against me? And my officers, my closest friends, are they involved in it?'

'How can you say that? How can you accuse us and all your soldiers of such a crime?' spluttered Hephaestion, and at these words from the closest of all his companions, Alexander started. 'No one wants to disobey you, no one wants to force you into this. Ptolemy is right. If you want to go on, then we will follow you. We your friends have sworn never to leave you, not for any reason, but your soldiers have every right to return to their lives. They have paid enough and they have given all they could. They are completely drained. They have implored us to try to convince you and that is what we are doing. No more than that. Please think about it now. Send your herald to tell us what you want us to do and we will do it.'

They left one by one and went out into the fury of the storm.

The King stayed closed up in his tent for two days without seeing anyone, without eating, cursing the fate that was preventing him from reaching his goal when it was now so close at hand. Not even Roxane managed to console him, Roxane his beloved wife who had chosen to follow him at all costs and to share with him all the risks and the trials of the undertaking. 'Why don't you

want to listen to your friends?' she asked him in her still uncertain Greek. 'Why don't you want to listen to those who love you and who in all these years have never left your side? Why do you have no pity for your soldiers?'

Alexander gave her no response – he simply stared at her, his eyes full of despair.

'So is it really so important for you to conquer more lands beyond those you already possess? Do you think you might find happiness in taking control of yet more regions, more cities, more riches? Oh, *Aléxandre*, tell me what it is you desire so much on the other side of that river, I beg you. Tell Roxane, tell your wife who loves you so much.'

The King sighed deeply and said, 'I was five years old when I first ran away from my parents' house – I wanted to go to the mountain of the gods. Since then I have always wanted to know what lies beyond the dawn and beyond the sunset, beyond the mountains and the plains, beyond the light and the darkness, on the other side of light and darkness, of good and evil, beyond everything.'

Roxane shook her head for she could not understand. All these words were too difficult for her, but she understood the look in his eyes and felt the anguish coming from him.

'Let us go then,' she said. 'You and I. Let us go and see the world that lies beyond that river.'

'No,' replied Alexander. 'This is not my destiny, the oracles did not speak to me for this reason. I cannot leave my army, relinquish the glory . . . Roxane, I want to get as close as I possibly can to the gods, I want to go

beyond the limits of time, I want to surpass all those who came before me. I do not want to sink into oblivion when I go down in Hades.'

His wife's face expressed all her worry and anxiety as she looked at him: his speech had been too difficult for her to understand, but she felt there was a strength within him that nothing could defeat, a desire that nothing could ever satisfy. He was like a young boy chasing after a rainbow, like an eagle flying towards the sun. She caressed him and kissed him tenderly on the forehead, on the eyes, on the mouth and said in his language, 'Keep me with you, *Aléxandre*, don't ever leave me. I could never live without you.'

From that moment on she never left his side, not even for a moment. She sat in silence waiting for a look or a word, her gaze fixed on every movement of his eyelashes, every breath he took, but the King seemed to be made of stone now, closed up in his own impenetrable world, a prisoner of his own dreams and nightmares.

Then, on the evening of the third day, before sunset, while sitting in the dark in his tent, he suddenly felt a presence and lifted his eyes – there before him was the Indian sage, staring at him out of his deep, dark eyes. He realized that no one had seen the man, the guards had not stopped him and not even Peritas was aware of him being there; indeed the dog was curled up in a corner dozing.

The man said nothing but simply gestured with one hand towards the camp, and this movement emanated an incredible, irresistible force. The King went out and was amazed by what he saw there before him –

thousands of his soldiers were standing around his tent looking at him, their eyes red, their unkempt hair reaching down to their shoulders, their clothes torn, their eyes sad and anguish-ridden but firm, awaiting some response, and Alexander finally saw them and understood. He felt all their suffering bear down upon him and he spoke. He shouted out loud, 'I have been told that you no longer wish to continue. Is this true?'

No one replied. Only a deep grumbling ran through the ranks.

'I know it is not true. I know you are the best soldiers in the world and that you would never rebel against your King! My decision was to push onwards, to lead you further, but first I had to know the will of the gods and I have had some victims sacrificed. Unfortunately all the portents have repeatedly been negative, and no one may challenge the will of the gods. So get ready, men! Prepare yourselves, because the time has come for you to enjoy what you deserve and what you have conquered. We are turning back. We are going back home!'

There was no ovation, no shouting for joy, but simply a deep, intense emotion. Many of them cried in silence and the tears ran slowly down those bristly beards, down those faces worn with years of battles, of sleepless nights, of attacks, of frost and heat, of snow and rain. They cried because their King was not angry with them, he still loved them, as though they were his own sons, and now he was going to take them home. One veteran came out of the ranks and moved forward towards Alexander. He said, 'Thank you, Sire, for having let yourself be beaten by no one apart from your own soldiers. Thank you . . .

we want you to know that whatever happens, whatever destiny may have in store for us, we will never forget you.'

Alexander embraced him and then ordered them all to return to their tents to prepare for their departure. When the soldiers had moved off, Alexander went alone to the banks of the Hyphasis. The clouds had cleared somewhat, and the light of the sunset spread and illuminated the great river, giving a red tinge to the far off profile of the Paropamisus range with its high peaks, pillars of the sky. The King's gaze swept across to the other bank, across the infinite plain that extended over there towards the horizon, and the King cried; he cried as he had never cried before in his life. He never would see the great flow of the Ganges, nor would he ever walk on the banks of golden lakes, among the resplendent peacocks of Palimbothra. He cried from his blue eye, as blue as the sky; he cried from his black eye, as black as the night.

54

THERE WAS A BREAK in the bad weather for a day or two, as though the heavens themselves somehow approved of Alexander's decision, and the King divided the army into twelve groups, each of which was set to work building a gigantic stone altar along the banks of the Hyphasis. The structures were very high, each one in honour of one of the twelve gods of Olympus. Alexander then had a sacrifice made before the entire assembled army and prayed to the gods not to allow any other man to go beyond that mark. Then, the following day, they set off again in the direction of the Indus. Along the way they passed through Sangala and the cities he had recently founded – Alexandria Bucephala and Alexandria Nicaea.

It was here that Commander Koinos, who had fought so heroically at Gaugamela and then with Craterus in the campaign against Spitamenes in Bactriana, fell ill and died. Alexander had a grand funeral held for him and an impressive tomb built in perpetual memory of his heroism and his valour.

He left authority over all India in the hands of Porus, the man he had won the land from – seven nations and two thousand cities, with the obligation of providing tributes and contingents of troops to the Macedonian satrap he had installed at Alexandria Nicaea.

From there he set off again until he reached the Hydaspes and marched down it as far as the confluence with the Acesines. The Indian princes of these regions came spontaneously to pay homage and to perform acts of submission, but he was told that to the south, along the banks of the Indus, there were still many fiercely proud and independent peoples. Then they were joined by a contingent of twenty thousand soldiers recruited in Macedonia and Greece who brought with them new armaments, fresh clothes in the Greek style and eighty talents of medicines, together with bandages, surgical instruments, splints to immobilize fractured limbs and many other things that in all truth would have been extremely useful had they arrived previously.

Together with the reinforcements and the supplies, Alexander also received a letter from Stateira, and as he began reading memories of her came flooding into his soul and he felt deep regret at having neglected and almost forgotten her:

Stateira to Alexander, my dear husband, Hail!

I lived through a most sad time following the loss of our son and, not long afterwards, I received news that you have found a new love, the daughter of a Sogdian mountain leader, of whom it is said she is most beautiful and who you have proclaimed your Queen and mother of the future King. I would be lying if I told you that I did not feel sorry and disappointed and that I suffer no pangs of jealousy. Not because of the power and the glory of her being queen, but simply because she now enjoys your love, because she sleeps

alongside you and can listen to your breath through the night and smell the fragrance of your skin. Oh! If only I had given you a son! Now I would hold him in my arms and in his face I would see your face. But every human being has his or her fate assigned when he or she comes into this world; the gods decreed that I would lose my father and my son and then the love of my husband in such a short space of time. I have no wish to sadden you with my melancholy, I only hope that you are happy and that when you come back you might have some desire to see me again and to spend some time with me, even if only a day or a night. Since meeting you I have learned that one single instant can be worth as much as an entire life.

Keep out of harm's way, I beg you, and take good care.

Alexander replied that very day, while Roxane, who was still learning how to write, watched with growing curiosity. She asked him, 'Who are you writing to?'

'To the Princess Stateira whom I took as my wife before I met you.'

Roxane's face darkened, then she said in a tone of voice that Alexander had not heard before, 'I do not wish to know what you are writing to her, but just keep her away from me, if you want her to remain alive.'

*

Autumn was far advanced now and the rains had stopped. The King had decided to travel down the Indus to see how far it went. Indeed, some of his geographers felt that this river was nothing more than the early stage

of the Nile – like the Nile it was inhabited by crocodiles and along its banks there were dark-skinned men like Ethiopians. If this really were the case then the huge fleet would be able to sail down the river in triumph as far as Alexandria of Egypt.

The King was truly taken with this idea and he summoned Nearchus to the banks of the river, choosing a high point for their meeting from which they could see the entire army marching – now as splendid as it had been when they left Macedonia and now four times as large. 'Many of these men have walked for one hundred thousand stadia,' he said. 'I want them to be able to travel in comfort now at long last. I want you to build a fleet to transport both the men and the horses. We will travel down the river as far as the Indus and we will stop wherever we see a city, simply to reaffirm our authority over all that once belonged to Darius and now belongs to us.'

'Then what will you do?' asked Nearchus.

'I will send Craterus back with one half of the army through Arachosia and Carmania, while I continue down with you as far as the river will take us – as far as Alexandria, if it is true that this is the high course of the Nile, or even as far as the Ocean.'

'Do you have any idea of how many vessels we will need to transport all of our men?'

Alexander shook his head.

'No less than one thousand.'

'A thousand ships?'

'More or less.'

'Let's get working then,' Alexander encouraged him. 'As quickly as possible!'

'Finally!' exclaimed Nearchus. 'I think I must be the only admiral in the world with blistered feet.'

As they spoke the King's attention was drawn by the slender figure of Roxane, riding across the meadow that lay alongside the great river; she was astride a magnificent white horse, her hair flying in the wind.

'Is she not wonderful?' Alexander asked.

'She is,' replied the Admiral. 'The most beautiful woman that any man could ever imagine. The only woman in the world who is truly worthy of you.'

The girl saw him and pulled the reins to the left, setting the horse off on a gallop up the hill until she came before them. She rode to him, leaned out and kissed him on the lips. The soldiers who were marching by and noticed this amorous manoeuvre shouted, 'Alala-lài!' and the King, without taking his lips from those of his bride, lifted his hand in a joyful response to their salutation.

*

Nearchus sent a herald to all the divisions with orders for all those soldiers who hailed from coastal areas to fall in: Greeks from the mainland coast and the islands, Phoenicians, Cypriots, Pontics. Then he began construction of the boats. Hundreds of trees were felled and planks made of their trunks, then the master carpenters began the work of bending the boards and assembling the hulls with tenon joints.

Nearchus's calculations proved accurate – by the time they finished some thousand supply boats were ready for launch on the banks of the Hydaspes, together with eighty ships, each with thirty rowers, and the fleet took to the water in the midst of much applause and ovation from the crowds.

It was a sunny day and many inhabitants of the area had gathered along the banks to watch this wonderful spectacle. The men were all in extremely high spirits, thinking that the worst was now past and that they were leaving behind the most difficult and most dramatic period of their lives. In truth, they had no idea of what lay in store for them and the only information they had regarding the lands they were about to cross came from local guides, but none of them knew anything about what they would find beyond three or four days' navigation.

Nearchus took control of the largest vessel, which functioned as their flagship and carried both the King and the Queen. He gave the signal for them to depart, the oars dipped into the water and the ship glided out into the flow, quickly followed by the others. When the entire fleet was out there on the river, the spectacle became even more impressive with the foaming waters under the prows and the blades of the oars, the thousands of standards and other flags fluttering in the wind, the glinting of the shields and the weapons.

Among the philosophers who had been allowed on to the King's ship was Pyrrho of Elis who was now most highly thought of, and also on board were Aristander and the Indian sage who had appeared so mysteriously in the

camp at Sangala. He sat at the prow with his legs crossed, his arms resting on his knees as he looked straight ahead, like a figurehead.

'What have you discovered about him?' the King asked Aristander.

'His name is Kalan, Kalanos in Greek, he is a great sage among his own people and is gifted with extraordinary qualities that come from his lifelong practice of meditation.'

'These people,' added Pyrrho, 'believe that the souls of those who do not live a just life pass, following death, from one body to another until they have been completely purified by their pain and suffering like metal in a forge. Only then can they meld into a sort of eternal peace they call *nirvana*.'

'This reminds me of Pythagoras's thinking and a poem by Pindar.'

'That's right, and it is indeed most probable that these ideas reached Pythagoras from India.'

'How did you discover all this?'

'From Kalanos. He learned to speak Greek in less than a month.'

'In less than a month? How is that possible?'

'It is possible, because it has happened, but I don't know how to explain it. Even before he was able to speak, however,' Aristander continued, 'he managed to communicate with me. I would feel his thoughts entering my mind.'

Alexander's gaze turned to the wave that just then was breaking gently on the side of the ship, and then he lifted his eyes and looked out across the great expanse of

the river, over the teeming vessels in the flow. Pyrrho had moved away now to sit towards the stern on a coil of ropes where he was writing something on a slate he held on his knee. The King moved closer to Aristander and asked him, 'Did you speak to him about your nightmare?'

'No.'

'Do you still have it?'

'No. Not since he came to the camp.'

'And do you know why he came?'

'To meet you, and to help you. He had known for some time that a great man would come from the West, and he had decided to meet up with him.'

Alexander nodded, then he let go of the gunwale and moved towards Kalanos.

'What are you looking at, *Kalane*?' he asked.

'Your eyes,' replied the sage with a strange voice, resonant like the sound of a brass instrument. 'They are the image of the dark line that runs through your soul, a thin borderline between light and darkness, like the blade of a razor, and you are running along it. It is a difficult enterprise, often painful . . .'

The King replied in astonishment, 'How can you look into my eyes if you continue to stare into the waves and how can you speak my tongue so perfectly without anyone ever having taught it to you?'

'I saw your eyes even before meeting you. And then there is only one tongue, Sire. If a man can succeed in reaching the origins of his own soul and his own nature, he can understand, and be understood, by all humanity.'

'Why have you come to me?'

'To continue my quest.'

'And where does your quest lead you?'

'To peace.'

'But my path takes me to war. I have been readied for this, ever since I was a boy.'

'You were also made ready to receive knowledge. I see the shadow of a great wisdom in the depths of your eyes. Peace in the world is a supreme good and no supreme good can be achieved without passing through fire and sword. But this has already taken place. I want to help the wisdom of the great sovereign grow in you, the wisdom of he who one day will be father of all peoples. This is why I have come to you.'

'You are most welcome, *Kalane*, but my way was marked out for me when I first crossed the sea. I know not if I will succeed in altering its course.'

'Before long, this river will carry us into the flow of the great father Indus,' replied Kalanos, sending his gaze out over the fast-flowing water. 'If you travel up to its source, you will come to a small stream whose waters run clear, but then, down towards the bottom, you will see hundreds of other torrents mix their waters with it, changing its colour and its course, you will see the trees lower their canopies to touch its surface, you will see fishes of all kinds, snakes and crocodiles will appear suddenly, swimming in its flow, birds building their nests along its banks, the river you see now is all this and it will be something else again as it flows towards the Ocean. There it flows into the eternal waters, into the universal womb that surrounds all lands. At that point the great Indus exists no more, but is part of the only

vital fluid from which the clouds and the birds, the rivers and the lakes, the trees and the flowers are all reborn . . .'

He said nothing else and recomposed himself into his impenetrable silence.

Nearchus approached the King just then with a worried look on his face.

'What's wrong?' Alexander asked.

'Rapids,' he replied.

55

NEARCHUS POINTED AHEAD to where the river boiled threateningly, perhaps ten stadia away. 'We must stop immediately,' he said, 'and take a look from the bank before we attempt it with the fleet.'

He immediately had the alarm flag raised and ordered the helmsmen to turn towards the bank. The chief oarsman shouted, 'Starboard oars, out!' and the rowers on the right-hand side of the ship lifted their oars from the water while the port side continued rowing, pushing the ship into a wide turn towards the right-hand bank of the river. On seeing the signals and the manoeuvres carried out by the flagship, all the other vessels did likewise, approaching dry land and dropping their anchors. While the crews were busy mooring, however, there came a series of loud cries and from the hills towering above the river to the east there appeared thousands of warriors who immediately launched themselves into an attack.

Alexander had the trumpets sound and the shieldsmen and the assault troops leaped into the water and ran forward to engage the enemy who were now extremely close.

'Who are they?' asked the King.

'Mallians,' replied Nearchus. 'We are close to the

confluence with the Indus. They are fierce soldiers, unbeatable.'

'My weapons!' ordered Alexander, and his attendants came running with his breastplate, his greaves and his crested helmet.

'Don't go, *Aléxandre*!' Roxane pleaded as she wrapped her arms around his neck.

'I am the King! I must be the first!' and he gave her a hurried kiss and shouted, 'With me, men!' A moment later he grabbed his shield, jumped into the water and scrambled towards the shore.

In the meantime warriors were disembarking from the other ships by the thousand, and the trumpets blared and orders were shouted in all the languages of the great army.

As soon as Alexander reached land, the battalions of the heavy infantry came running, while higher up the river the horses were being disembarked to form the first cavalry squadrons.

The enemy, after the success of their initial impact, began retreating under the pressure of the Macedonian divisions that were gaining strength and attacking in compact formation. The Mallians, given the impossibility of forcing the Macedonians back, began an orderly retreat, still putting up a strong fight until, having backed up the hill, they found themselves in a more advantageous position and counterattacked with renewed vigour. The front line wavered as the Mallians and the Macedonians had the best of it alternately, but by late morning enough horses had been disembarked to form two entire squadrons of cavalry that proceeded to attack

the enemy's flanks. Alexander himself then mounted his horse and led the charge. At that very moment a long line of enemy horsemen appeared on the hills opposite and charged down to engage the King's squadrons.

The battle increased in intensity until about midday, when finally the Macedonians got the upper hand and pushed the Mallians back beyond the line of the hills. From there Alexander's gaze swept over five cities, one of which stood out because of its massive fortifications in rough brickwork.

He divided his army into five columns, and sent each one of them out towards one of the cities. He led the fifth and most numerous column himself, calling Perdiccas, Ptolemy and Leonnatus to attack the capital, but when he was about to order the assault, Leonnatus shouted to him: 'Alexander, look! Peritas has escaped from the ship.' Indeed, the Molossian was running as fast as his legs would carry him up the hill to join his master.

'By Zeus!' the King swore. 'If anything happens to him I shall have whoever it was who let him go whipped for this. Back! Peritas, back! Back to Roxane!'

The dog seemed to want to obey for a moment, but as soon as Alexander galloped off, leading his men, he started following once more.

Halfway through the afternoon, the column led by the King was already under the walls and the Mallians, the Macedonians at their heels, sought refuge within as they rushed through the three gates that had been left open for them.

Alexander was completely caught up in the excitement of the chase, and when he saw a section of the walls that

had in part collapsed because of the rain or lack of maintenance, he leaped from his mount and started running up the ramp to take the city. He reached the top without realizing he was alone. Leonnatus saw just how vulnerable he was, however, and he rushed after him shouting, 'Alexander! Stop! Wait!' But in the reel of battle and the chaos of the shouting, the King heard nothing as he went over the top and down the other side.

Leonnatus took his men up the ramp after Alexander to help him, but some enemy soldiers, having seen what had happened, rushed to form a barrier and block them, so that their companions could then kill the King within the walls.

In the meantime Alexander had realized the danger he was in and the fact that he was surrounded; he retreated until his back was against an enormous fig tree, where he was fighting desperately against a group of opponents. Leonnatus fought his own way through, swinging his axe, sending the enemy rolling down the ramp and shouting, 'Alexander, hold on! Hold on, we're coming!' But in his heart of hearts he knew that the King risked being completely overwhelmed at any moment. Right then he heard a howling come from behind him and he remembered the dog. He shouted as loudly as he could, without even turning round, 'Peritas! Run, Peritas! Run to Alexander!'

The Molossian ran up the ramp like a fury and reached the top at the very moment when his master collapsed, struck by a javelin; Alexander held his shield fast with the very last drop of strength he had. It took no more than a moment: Peritas leaped from the top of the walls, landing

like a lightning bolt in the midst of the enemy, sending them rolling backwards; he crushed one soldier's hand with a single bite, tore another's throat out, and ripped open the belly of a third, whose guts spilled to the ground. The magnificent animal fought like a lion, growling, baring his bloodied fangs, his eyes burning like those of a wild beast.

Alexander seized the moment to crawl backwards while Leonnatus, who had finally reached the top with his men, ran down shouting like a madman and swinging his cleaver in circles, opening up a path to the King. At that point he turned and faced the enemy who continued to attack: he split the first enemy soldier who came forward into two, from his head down to his groin, and the others, terrified by such frightful strength, retreated. In just a few instants hundreds of Macedonian assault troops and shieldsmen spread throughout the city, filling it as they went with fierce cries, with desperate screams, with the clangour of arms clashing in the fury of battle.

Leonnatus knelt down alongside the King and unlaced his breastplate, but at that moment Alexander turned his gaze and his eyes filled with tears and despair. 'Peritas! No! What have they done to you!'

The Molossian was covered with blood and sweat and was staggering towards him, whining, a javelin planted firmly between his ribs.

'Call Philip!' shouted Leonnatus. 'The King is wounded! The King is wounded!'

Peritas managed to reach his master's hand, to lick it for one last time before collapsing lifeless before him.

'Peritas! No!' Alexander moaned between his sobs,

pulling the dog to himself and embracing this friend who had made the ultimate sacrifice in order to save his life.

Perdiccas arrived, covered in blood and close to total exhaustion. 'Philip is not here; in the confusion of the attack no one thought to give him a horse.'

'What can we do now?' panted Leonnatus, his voice cracking.

'We can't move him in this state. We'll have to extract the weapon. Hold him, because this is going to hurt like hell.'

Leonnatus gripped Alexander's arms and held them behind his back while Perdiccas tore his *chiton*, exposing the wound; then, with one hand on the King's chest, he used the other to try to pull the bolt out, but the metal head was jammed between his collar bone and his shoulder bone and it simply would not budge.

'I'll have to use the blade of my sword as a lever,' he said. 'Shout, Alexander, shout as loudly as you can, for I have nothing to soothe the pain you will feel!'

He unsheathed his sword and put it into the wound. Alexander shouted, his body racked by the lancing pains. Perdiccas sought his shoulder blade with the point of the sword and pushed it backwards forcibly while with the other hand he pulled on the shaft of the bolt, which came free all of a sudden with a great spurt of blood. With one last shout, the King collapsed in a faint.

'Find some glowing embers, Leonnatus, quickly! We have to cauterise it or he'll bleed to death.'

Leonnatus ran off and returned quickly with a piece of a wooden beam from a burning house and plunged it into the wound. There was a nauseous smell of charring

flesh, but the blood stopped flowing. Perdiccas's men in the meantime had built a stretcher and now they moved the King on to it and carried him out of the gates of the city.

'Take him back as well,' said Leonnatus, his eyes red with tears and fatigue, pointing to the lifeless body of Peritas. 'He is the true hero of this battle.'

56

IN THE DEEP OF the night Alexander was taken, unconscious and burning up with fever, to the banks of the river where Nearchus had set up camp. Roxane ran to him shouting in despair, then she knelt alongside him and kissed his hand as she sobbed. Leptine looked on as she prepared clean bandages and water, her face pale and expressing all her terror and worry as they waited for Philip to arrive.

The physician appeared almost immediately and set to work straight away, leaning over the wounded man. He cut the rough dressing Perdiccas and Leonnatus had applied to the wound and began cleaning it with the water Leptine offered from a metal urn.

He put his ear to Alexander's chest and proceeded to examine him carefully while the King's friends, who one by one had entered in silence, waited anxiously for the verdict.

'Unfortunately this is not just any wound,' said Philip as he got to his feet. 'The point of the javelin has punctured his lung. I can hear the blood gurgling with every breath he takes.'

'What does that mean?' asked Hephaestion.

Philip, unable to speak, simply shook his head.

At that moment Alexander's breath rattled and saliva

mixed with blood ran from his mouth, spreading a large red stain on his pillow.

Ptolemy moved towards his friend and put a hand on his shoulder. 'It means that Alexander might die, Hephaestion,' he said, with a lump in his throat. 'Come on, let's leave him to rest for the moment.'

Seleucus, who had led the attack on the other cities, entered at that moment together with Craterus and Lysimachus and he immediately realized what had happened. He moved towards Philip and asked him in a whisper, 'Is there any hope?'

The physician lifted his eyes and in his gaze Seleucus saw such grief, such a sense of distress and impotence, that he said nothing else and left.

The tent was suddenly empty and quiet. All that could be heard was Roxane's soft lament as she cried disconsolately, covering her husband's motionless hand with kisses and tears.

Leptine, who in truth had always detested anyone who had ever become intimate with Alexander, approached slowly and put her hand on Roxane's shoulder. 'Do not cry, my Queen,' she whispered. 'I beg of you, do not cry. He can hear you. You must be strong. You must think . . . you must think that everyone loves him . . . we all love him and love is stronger than death.'

Philip took off his bloodstained apron, saying to the two women as he did so, 'Remember. Don't leave him unattended, not even for the briefest of moments. I am going now to get everything ready for a drain for the wound. If anything happens, send someone for me immediately.'

Leptine nodded and the physician took a lamp and left the tent. As he crossed the camp he saw Ptolemy and Leonnatus placing Peritas's body on a pile of wood; the dog's lead, decorated with silver studs, was laid alongside, like the ritual offering made on the pyre of a hero. He walked over to them.

'What a terrible day,' Ptolemy murmured. 'Just when it seemed that the pain and the fatigue were behind us . . .' He stroked the lifeless dog as it lay on a blanket of red wool. 'I'll miss him,' he said with tears in his eyes. 'He would always keep me company when I was on guard.' At that moment Craterus arrived with a patrol of *pezhetairoi* who lined up on the two sides of the pyre.

'We felt he deserved full honours,' Leonnatus explained. 'He was the King's first guard.'

Then he took a torch and lit the pyre. He waited until the flames took hold, crackling in the darkness, and then shouted, '*Pezhetairoi*, present arms!'

The infantrymen raised their *sarissae* in salute while Peritas's soul flew off on the wind, separated from his master for the very first time since Alexander of Epirus had given him to Alexander all those years ago.

*

Philip watched over the King all night, together with Roxane and Leptine. Only towards dawn did the Queen start dozing, exhausted after being without sleep for so long, but as she dozed she moaned continually, tormented by her anguish.

As day broke Hephaestion and Ptolemy entered and it

was clear they had had no rest either. 'How is he?' they asked.

'He has made it through the night. I can't tell you any more than that,' replied Philip.

'Should he die, we will burn those cities with all their inhabitants – this will be the funeral sacrifice in his honour,' said Hephaestion darkly.

'Let us wait and see,' replied Philip, his voice hoarse with fatigue. 'He is still alive.'

Another two days passed, but the King's condition seemed to be deteriorating beyond hope. His chest had swollen up despite the drain Philip had inserted, his fever was still burning, his breath came in fits and rattles, his skin was ashen, his eyes were circled with black and sinking into their sockets.

His Companions kept vigil outside the tent so as not to disturb him. They took turns watching over him, getting a little sleep only when they were completely exhausted. The camp, usually so bustling and noisy, was immersed in an unreal silence, as though time itself had stopped.

That evening, as Alexander's fever was rising once more and his breath seemed to come with ever-greater difficulty and suffering, Philip suddenly got to his feet and left the tent.

'Where is he going?' asked Leonnatus.

'I don't know,' replied Hephaestion. 'I don't know anything any more. There is nothing to know now . . .'

Philip walked across the camp, taking a quick look at Aristander who had continued to sacrifice victims on his

smoking altar during the night, and then he came to a place where a *banyan* tree rose majestically from the ground. He stood there before the skeletal figure of Kalanos who was lost in meditation.

'Wake up,' he said brusquely.

Kalanos opened his eyes.

'Our gods and our science have proved impotent. Save Alexander, if you can. Otherwise, leave us and never return.'

Kalanos stood up agilely, lightly, almost as though weightless. 'Where is he?' he asked.

'In his tent. Come with me,' replied Philip as he set off.

Kalanos followed and entered the royal quarters, all lit up with burning lamps.

'Extinguish them all,' he ordered, his voice firm, 'and leave us alone.'

Everyone obeyed Kalanos. He squatted on his heels behind Alexander's bed and simply stared through the darkness at the King's head, his body tensing up until it was like a block of stone.

They found him sitting there like that the following day, and the day after, and even on the following day. At dawn on the fourth day Philip entered to change the drain and pulled back a corner of the curtain that covered up the entrance to throw a little light on the scene. While he was washing his hands in a basin, before changing the dressings, he heard a weak voice calling out behind him, 'Philip . . .'

He turned sharply, 'My King!'

The fever had relented somewhat, his breathing was

regular, his heartbeat was weak but constant. He listened to his chest and the gurgling had gone. He called Leptine. 'Inform the Queen. Tell her the King is conscious. And make some broth immediately, we must feed him for he is more dead than alive.'

Leptine set about her duties while Philip immediately poked his head out of the tent where Lysimachus and Hephaestion were waiting. 'Tell the others,' he said. 'The King is awake.'

'How is he?' asked Hephaestion anxiously.

'How do you think he is?' replied the physician gruffly. 'Like someone who's had an iron bolt stuck in his shoulder.'

He went back to take care of Alexander and only then did he see Kalanos lying motionless on the ground, as still and cold as a corpse.

'Oh, by Zeus!' he exclaimed. 'Great Zeus!'

He had Kalanos taken to his own tent by his assistants and ordered them to warm him in every way they could think of and to give him something to eat, even by force if necessary, and then he returned to Alexander. Roxane was with him now, staring incredulously while Leptine tried to get him to take some broth in the only way possible – dipping some cloth in it and then holding it to his lips so that he could suck.

'What happened?' asked Alexander as soon he saw Philip.

'Everything, my King,' replied the physician, 'but you are still alive and I have every hope you will remain so. You cannot believe how happy I am,' he added, his voice trembling. 'You cannot believe . . . but please stop talking

now. It is a miracle you are alive, and I believe the miracle was worked by Kalanos.'

'Peritas . . .' Alexander managed to murmur.

'Peritas did not survive, my King. Leonnatus tells me he died saving your life. Now you must not render his sacrifice vain – try to eat and then rest, please rest.'

Alexander drank again from Leptine's hands and then fell back, closing his eyes, but even through his closed eyelids the tears escaped and ran down his cheeks to dampen his pillow.

57

THE KING LAY IN his bed hovering between life and death for many days and all the efforts expended in bringing him back to life definitively seemed to be in vain. Although his body had moved beyond the moment of greatest danger, his general condition remained so serious and the improvements so slight that Philip no longer knew if he could save him or if Thanatos, momentarily fended off by Kalanos's heroism, was about to attack again with the aim of taking possession of a soul he had already earmarked as his own. Only the Indian sage had no doubts whatsoever and he continued to say, 'I have made a pact. He will get better.' If anyone asked for details of this pact, he said nothing.

It was a month before Alexander was able to sit up, leaning against the head of his bed, and another twenty days before he was able to drink soup with Leptine's help as she spooned it into his mouth with Roxane looking on. He spoke very little and only with great difficulty, but every now and then he had Eumenes come to read him verses from Homer. With the unanimous approval of the Companions, the Secretary General had taken over the King's political role. At other times Roxane would sing songs from her mountain home, her voice quiet and

accompanied by her own playing on a stringed instrument with a simple and evocative timbre.

After two months, Philip agreed to his getting up and taking a few steps inside the tent, supported by Craterus and Leonnatus, but it was clear that even this minimal effort cost him tremendous fatigue and afterwards, dripping with sweat, he fell into deep sleep once more.

On one occasion Leonnatus entered together with Craterus and Hephaestion while Leptine struggled to have him swallow a decoction. The big man ran his hand through his ruffled hair and said, sincerely believing it was a good idea, 'And if we were to give him some "Nestor's Cup"?'

Philip looked at him with pity in his eyes. 'You don't know what you're saying. Honey, flour, wine and cheese – do you want to kill him?'

'You're probably right,' said Leonnatus, hurt to the quick, 'but do you have any idea what everyone out there is saying? The rumour is that the King is dead and that we are keeping him hidden so as to avoid creating panic.'

'How can they even think that?' exclaimed Philip. 'Everyone knows the King is alive.'

'That's not quite how things are,' said Hephaestion. 'We know it, but no one else does. I have given orders that not even the guards must see him in this state. The effect on the soldiers' morale would be the same as knowing he was dead.'

'Exactly,' Eumenes agreed. 'The truth is that the people have not seen him for months, while they see us coming and going continuously to and from his tent or

meeting together, and a few people have seen me use the King's seal on documents we have sent to the satrapies.'

'That's the way I feel as well,' confirmed Craterus. 'Some divisions are discussing the possibility of summoning the general assembly of the Macedonian army. Do you know what this means?'

Eumenes nodded. 'It means that they can force us to receive their delegation in the royal tent and show them Alexander in this state.'

Philip turned. 'As long as I am here, no one enters this tent without my permission: I am the King's private physician and I bear responsibility for—'

Craterus put a hand on his shoulder, 'Should the King be absent, then a plenary assembly of the army is sovereign in his place – they can do this thing and they almost certainly will.'

Seleucus and Lysimachus had entered to ask about the King's health and they could feel the tension in the air: 'What's happening?' Seleucus asked.

'The fact is . . .' began Craterus.

No one had given any thought to Alexander's presence since he had appeared to be fast asleep, but his voice suddenly shook them all: 'Listen to me.'

The Companions turned in surprise and embarrassment. Eumenes, realizing that the King must have heard everything, attempted to explain: 'Alexander, this is something we can easily resolve ourselves with—'

The King lifted his head and his right hand with an unequivocal gesture and everyone stopped talking.

'Seleucus . . .'

'At your service, Sire,' his friend replied instinctively, much moved to be receiving an order from Alexander after such a long time.

'Have the army fall in, a full assembly, after sunset.'

'Yes, Sire.'

'Leonnatus . . .'

'At your service, Sire,' replied Leonnatus, even more amazed than Seleucus.

'Have my horse prepared – the bay . . .'

'The Sarmatian bay, yes, yes. Of course, Sire.'

'Of course nothing!' exclaimed Philip. 'What is happening in here . . . have you all gone mad? The King is in no state to be—'

Alexander lifted his hand once more and Philip said nothing else out loud, but continued mumbling to himself.

'Hephaestion . . . '

'I am listening, *Aléxandre*.'

'Prepare my armour. It must be shining bright.'

'It shall be, *Aléxandre*,' replied Hephaestion with a lump in his throat. 'As bright and shining as the Argead star.'

Everyone was convinced now that the King no longer had any intention of fading away in his bed, that he had chosen to die on horseback, and even Philip was sure of this. He sat in a corner grumbling away to himself. 'Do whatever you want; if you want to kill him then go ahead. I'm having nothing to do with it . . .' and he could say nothing more, so moved was he by the thought of losing his King.

'Leonnatus,' said the King. 'I want the horse here, in the tent.'

'I will bring him here,' replied his friend, realizing that the King did not want his soldiers to see him being helped to mount the animal.

'You may all go now.'

They obeyed Alexander and as soon as they left he let himself go on his pillow and dozed. The voices of Hephaestion and Leonnatus woke him up. When he opened his eyes he found the tent full of the half-light of sunset.

'We are ready,' said Hephaestion.

Alexander nodded, struggled to lift himself up, sat on the edge of the bed and asked his friends to lead him to the bath. Leptine washed him and perfumed his body and his hair, then she began to dress him.

'Give me a bit of colour for my cheeks,' he said, and the girl obeyed. While she used some cosmetics to liven up his cheeks and cover up the dark rings under his eyes, he caressed her face and said, 'I will arrange a marriage for you with some great man of my empire and I will give you a dowry worthy of a Queen.' He spoke sincerely and with a tone of great security in his voice. When Leptine had finished, he asked his friends, 'How do I look?'

'Not bad,' replied Leonnatus with a half smile. 'You look like an actor.'

'And now for the armour.'

Hephaestion laced up his breastplate and his greaves, hung his sword by his side and arranged the diadem in his hair.

'Bring me the horse. Are the men lined up?'

'They are all in formation,' Hephaestion assured him.

Leonnatus went out and then led the fully decked Sarmatian bay by its bridle into the tent through the back entrance; Hephaestion knelt down and joined his hands to form a step for Alexander. The King put his foot in it and his friends all helped him get up there astride the horse.

Leonnatus approached with some straps in his hand, 'We thought it might be an idea to tie you to the horse. None of it will show, it will all be covered by your cloak.'

Alexander did not reply and his silence was interpreted as consent. They placed a large belt round his waist, from which hung four straps – two to the front and two to the rear, all of which were then attached to the horse's tack. Only then did they drape his purple cloak around him, so that it completely covered the improvised harness they had created.

'Let's go now,' he ordered.

Hephaestion looked out of the tent, Leonnatus nodded as though to say, 'Now!' and Hephaestion waved his hand – a prearranged signal. A dark rumble, like a far off thunderclap, broke the leaden silence of sunset. One blow, then another, and another again! Alexander put his hand to his ear, as though he could hardly believe what he was hearing and instinctively he straightened his back and touched the horse's belly with his heels. The bay moved out of the tent, walked around it and set off calmly along the long line of the assembled army.

The slow, solemn rumble continued, giving rhythm to the majestic pace of the powerful steed and Alexander struggled to hold back the tears that welled up as he felt

the air vibrate to the deep, thunderous voice of the drum of Chaeronaea!

The soldiers, motionless in their ranks, their hands tightly gripping the shafts of their *sarissae*, looked on in amazement as their King moved forwards, his gaze proud and firm and severe as he inspected them. As he approached each division, the officer in command stepped forward from the line, unsheathed his sword and shouted, 'Hail, Sire!' and Alexander responded with a slight bow of the head.

When he reached the end of the line the 'Thunder of Chaeronaea' fell silent. The most senior officer of the *hetairoi* front line pushed his horse forwards and exclaimed, 'At your service, Sire!'

'Sound the fall out,' said Alexander and while the trumpets sounded the order, he pulled on the reins of the bay and set off at a trot towards his tent.

'He's mad,' murmured Philip as he looked on from far away. 'Any one of those jolts could make him fall and—'

'He won't fall,' replied Seleucus, clapping the physician on the shoulder. 'He won't fall.'

Ptolemy could not take his eyes off him. 'So this is what he wanted; now they've all seen him, they know he's alive and that he's in command again.'

Alexander entered the tent still astride the horse and his friends unstrapped him and helped him dismount, then they began untying his cloak, his breastplate and greaves, together with his sword.

'Get him straight into his bed,' ordered Philip.

Alexander shook his head, walked slightly uncertainly towards his field chair, and put his hands on the table.

'I'm hungry,' he said. 'Would anyone like to eat something with me?'

Everyone looked at him in amazement and even Leonnatus stopped what he was doing and stood there holding the horse by its bridle.

'Leptine,' called the King. 'Clear this stuff off the table and bring me some "Nestor's Cup"!'

'"Nestor's Cup"?' replied Philip. 'So you really want to die? You'll never digest that concoction, you'll be ill and you'll vomit and your wounds will open up again and—'

'"Nestor's Cup"' Alexander repeated. Everyone stared at him with their mouths open – he seemed to have been reborn, to have been transfigured.

'It was the sound of that drum and the sight of his soldiers,' Craterus whispered to the doctor. 'Let him eat. He'll be fine, you'll see.'

Leptine brought 'the cup' and Alexander began eating. The only sign of fatigue was a slight band of perspiration that crowned his forehead. Philip was still stupefied as he watched, moving his own jaws as though seeking to help the King chew, and the others as well, all standing up around the table, could not believe what they were witnessing.

When Alexander had finished he cleaned his mouth and turned his gaze upwards towards the eyes of his amazed audience.

'What's up?' he asked. 'Haven't you ever seen me eat before?'

58

IN ANOTHER MONTH the King was back on his feet completely and was even running and going for horse rides and wrestling with Leonnatus. At the end of the summer he gave orders for the camp to be struck and for them to embark once more on the vessels.

They went downstream for two days until they came to the border with the region called Sindh and there Alexander asked Nearchus to moor the fleet. The guides explained that this was the starting point for the path that led to the mountain pass, through which they would be able to reach Alexandria of Arachosia.

He summoned his Companions to his tent for supper and showed them the map that the marching officers had drawn with the help of the local guides, both Indians and Persians. Then he spoke to Craterus: 'You will set off tomorrow with one half of the army; you will cross Arachosia and Drangiana and you will re-establish order wherever you find rebellions or any disorder. The Indian mariners have told us that the Indus is not a tributary river and it flows directly into the Ocean at Pattala. My plan then is that at Pattala Nearchus and Onesicritus will set off with the fleet along the southern coast of the Empire, while I will take the rest of the army across land, guaranteeing supplies for the ships at each landing point

following each day of navigation. We will all meet up on the plain of Hormuz, a city that dominates the straits between the Ocean and the Persian Gulf.'

'Why do you wish to pass through Gedrosia?' Craterus asked him. 'They say it's a frightful place, a desert burned by the sun throughout the year, completely lacking in vegetation – no grass, no trees.'

'The southern frontier of the Empire is the only one we do not know. We must move in that direction.'

They ate and drank in moderation because the King was still occasionally feeling the after effects of his wounds, and they went to sleep relatively early. At dawn the entire assembled army lined up to salute Craterus's contingent, which was just leaving. Alexander embraced him tightly and said, 'You are one of my dearest friends. I'll miss you.'

'I will miss you too, *Aléxandre*. Take good care of yourself, I beg you. Thus far you have tempted fate too much. May the gods smile upon you.'

'And may they smile upon you too, my friend.'

Craterus leaped astride his horse and raised his hand as the signal for the long column to set off amidst trumpet blasts and shouts of salutation from the Companions who were staying with Alexander. As soon as the last division of the rearguard had disappeared into the stepped expanse that led to the desert, Alexander had his men embark and start off. They sailed southwards and each time they stopped they received the submission and the homage of the local princes until they came to Pattala, the great city that stood at the very end of the Indus. It was heavily populated and rich, involved in all

sorts of trade with ships arriving from everywhere, many from a gigantic island to the east called Taprobane, which was said to be as big as all India.

From there the fleet moved on to the last stretch before the estuary. The river at that point was immense, so wide it was almost impossible to see from one bank across to the other and Onesicritus calculated that it must be some fifty stadia wide.

The evening of the last day of navigation found them at the mouth of the river and Nearchus decided he would anchor the ships at a point where the current was so slow-moving it was almost imperceptible. Indeed, he was afraid that if they were to venture out on to the open sea they would find no shelter in case of any sudden storms breaking out. What happened instead was a disaster no less terrible than a storm – during the night the level of the water descended to the point where the ships were stuck on the seabed and many of them capsized. Near-chus ordered everyone to stay at their stations and to wait until the waters started flowing once more. Then, considerably worried, he went to Alexander.

'I had no way of foreseeing this phenomenon, even although I have heard tale of a mariner from Massalia, a certain Pytheas, who described a point in the northern Ocean where a great hole swallows up the waters and then regurgitates them, uncovering and covering great swathes of the coast, but few people give him credit and this is not the northern Ocean. How could I ever have imagined such a thing might happen? It's a disaster . . . a disaster!'

'You have achieved the most extraordinary things,'

replied Alexander. 'You must not torment yourself. I know that we will emerge victorious from this battle with the river and the sea – my ancestor Achilles fought against the Scamander and won. I will win as well. Let us wait for the night to pass. The light of day will change many things.'

There was a new moon that night and the darkness added to the panic and the confusion. Nearchus had the alarm trumpets sounded and ordered the heralds to spread the word from one ship to another, instructing them all not to move for any reason, but many sailors, terrorized by this phenomenon and by the rumours they had heard in the ports and the taverns of their home cities, sought to escape under cover of darkness, seeking safety on dry land. They all died, swallowed up by the mud and the quicksand, and those who first tried to help their marooned companions were also swallowed up; their shouting and desperate cries for help rang through the night air, filling their companions who had stayed on board with anguish and terror – there was nothing they could do to help. Then the shouting died down and one by one the voices fell silent, and all that could be heard were the cries of the nocturnal birds and the far off roar of a tiger roaming through the woods in search of prey.

Out on the flagship Roxane clung to Alexander, trembling with fear, terrified by the hostile, inhuman nature all around them, so terribly different from the natural world of her native mountains and their clear sky. Nearchus and his mariners stood motionless and silent, whispering now and then of their sailing experiences.

Shortly before dawn there came a new, far off noise and the King turned his ear towards it.

'Did you hear that?' he asked.

Nearchus was already running towards the bow and when he got there he leaned out, trying to see what it was making the noise that was growing now with every instant. Suddenly he saw a sort of whitish band appear in the distance, moving towards them quickly in the pale light of dawn. It was a band of boiling, menacing foam, and the noise was the galloping of the white horses as they raced towards the helpless, motionless fleet marooned on the mudflats.

'Trumpets!' shouted the admiral. 'Sound the alarm! Sound the alarm! The waters are coming back! To your oars, men! The oars, quickly! Helmsmen, to your rudders!' and while the trumpet blasts rent the grey morning sky, he threw a rope to the King so that he could tie himself to the mast with Roxane and he himself rushed to the helm to help out, getting ready for the impact with the wave.

All the other crews heard the alarm and sounded their own trumpets and the great swampy expanse resounded with agitated shouting and crying.

The impact of the great wave was frightful – some ships were lifted and thrown backwards like twigs, while those that were firmly stuck in the mud were smashed to pieces, and yet others, whose sides were exposed to the wave, were overturned and crushed by the enormous mass of water.

Onesicritus, pilot of the royal quinquereme, was hanging on to the rudder and shouting to the men to row

with all their might to keep the vessel upright as he himself put his shoulder to the bar to fight against the force of the eddies that the flood-tide generated on the surface of the waters.

The great wave finally calmed, its thrust balancing out with the flow of the Indus, and Nearchus was able to look around and gauge the extent of the disaster. Hundreds of boats had been destroyed, many others damaged, and the surface of the water was littered with wreckage and with men frantically treading water, clutching at beams or planking as they floated by.

The whole day was spent recovering the shipwrecked survivors and Alexander himself did all he could to save his men, on occasions actually diving into the water to help those who were about to succumb to the fatigue of their ordeal.

That evening the ships dropped anchor just beyond the estuary, on the sandy shores of the Ocean, and the division commanders made the roll call: more than one thousand five hundred men had drowned. All the bodies they could manage to recover were placed on a pyre before the assembled army and the soldiers shouted the names of their dead companions to the wind and the waves so that their memory would not be lost for ever.

For all those whose bodies could not be found, the King officiated over a funeral rite and had a cenotaph built on the shore so that their souls would find peace in Hades, but he thanked the gods from the depths of his heart that none of his friends had perished in the disaster and that he had been able to embrace them all. He also read an encomium for Nearchus and Onesicritus – it was

only thanks to their courage and their skill that the disaster had not become a catastrophe.

The army remained camped on the shore for twenty days, to give time to everyone who had survived to join up with their divisions and to make sure all the damaged vessels were repaired.

They found a sheltered area not far off, surrounded by fertile fields and located at the border with the desert region inhabited by the wild Oritian tribes. Alexander founded a city there and had all those whose poor health meant they would not be able to face the long journey across the Gedrosian desert settled in it. He built a pier and a sheltered harbour and consecrated a closed area for the temples of the gods. He was then ready to make a decision regarding the day of their departure, both for the fleet and the army.

Nearchus was waiting for him on the newly completed pier and Alexander embraced him affectionately, just as he had embraced Craterus at the moment of his departure.

'It would have been wonderful if this river, as some maintained, had actually been the upper course of the Nile. We would have travelled together, all the way to Egypt.'

'Unfortunately it isn't so,' replied Nearchus. 'It takes more than dark-skinned men and crocodiles to make a Nile.'

'Indeed,' replied the King, 'but keep the coast and the army in sight all the time, and when you can, land wherever you see our fires: this will make it easier for us to supply you with food and water.'

'I will do so if it is possible, *Aléxandre*, but I must make

the most of this constant wind that blows westwards to save the energies of my sailors and I know not if you will manage to keep up with us. In any case, we will see each other at Hormuz. My vice-admiral Onesicritus would like to have the honour of bidding you farewell. He is an excellent sailor and deserves your esteem.'

As Onesicritus stepped forward and shook his hand, Alexander said, 'May the gods be with you and may Poseidon smile upon you. I made a sacrifice to the Ocean this morning, together with Aristander, and we invoked the clemency and the favour of the winds. The price we have already paid for this expedition is far too high.'

Nearchus and Onesicritus went to their ships and gave the order to release the moorings. The fleet moved off from the pier under power from its oarsmen, but immediately afterwards they hoisted the sails which filled with the brisk wind. In no time the mighty ships were as small as children's boats and Alexander went down to the sea and planted a lance there on the shore to indicate that he had taken possession of this remote region. Then he turned to his companions and shouted, 'It is now time for us to leave as well – give the signal!'

Everyone mounted their horses – Hephaestion, Leonnatus, Ptolemy, Seleucus, Lysimachus, Perdiccas, and they took up position at the head of their divisions. The King too mounted his steed, his banner flying before him, and then the long column moved off amidst trumpet blasts and the rolling of drums, its many flags and standards fluttering in the wind.

59

THE WOODED STRIP that ran along the banks of the Indus soon gave way to a sort of marshy prairie on which great buffalo with curved horns grazed, together with antelope and deer; in the distance small groups of lions could be made out, similar to the animals that were hunted in Macedonia. The trees were tall and full of all kinds of birds, including many brightly coloured parrots. Then the wetland prairie became a steppe with occasional bushes and small herds of oxen and sheep, led by wild, primitive-looking shepherds.

'Oritians,' explained the Indian guide. 'These are from the coastal tribe, but further on we will meet those from the steppes and the desert – truly savage and ferocious. They can be very dangerous, hiding in the sands like scorpions and jumping out suddenly to attack.'

'Pass the word on to everyone,' ordered Alexander, who then continued to move forward, gazing south-wards. Indeed, they had moved away from the coast to follow the track and the Ocean was now completely out of view.

On the fourth day of marching the army came to the edge of the desert and the men looked in astonishment at the great expanse of burning sand that spread out before them. This was hell – not even a blade of grass,

no shelter whatsoever, baked through all the seasons by the relentless rays of the sun.

The Indian guides turned back now and Alexander had to rely upon the experience of some Persian officers who had taken part in King Darius's expeditions to Drangiana and Arachosia.

Marching under those dreadful conditions soon proved to be a terrible ordeal, almost hopeless. The officers immediately sequestered the water supplies and kept them under constant surveillance so that they could be rationed, but this measure proved to be somewhat limited in its effectiveness – supplies ran out quickly anyway and they had to search out wells, which were few and far between, along the track through the sands. The food lasted longer because the plan to provide supplies to Nearchus's fleet proved to be impossible – the ships were no longer to be seen, the eastern wind having blown strong and hard to send them much further ahead.

At a certain point the Scythian guides saw prints near the track and reported this to their officers and the King. There was danger now of an ambush – in such arid terrain an invading army became legitimate prey because of the supplies it carried, together with the great number of pack animals and horses.

'Double the guards,' ordered Alexander, 'and keep fires burning if you can.' But wood was hard to come by – only a few skeletal trunks left by the tide on the seashore.

They attacked suddenly, one moonless night, and they began with Leonnatus's contingent, which was function-

ing as rearguard, marching some stadia behind the others. The precision of the ambush was deadly – like ghosts they appeared from the rocks, leaping like hellish furies on the warriors who were already seriously weakened by thirst and the long march; the result was a massacre. Leonnatus fought valiantly and when his trumpeter's throat was cut by an enemy who emerged suddenly from the sand, he himself picked up the trumpet and sent out long alarm blasts, calling for help from Alexander.

The King set off at a gallop with two squadrons and managed to break through the circle, freeing his friend, exhausted and wounded, just when he was being sur-rounded by a group of the enemy. When the sun rose, more than five hundred soldiers lay lifeless on the ground, many of them clinging on to their adversaries in the last spasm of their death throes.

They buried them all in the sand with their weapons because there was no wood for funeral pyres and their hearts were heavy with sadness as they moved on, knowing perfectly well that those hurried graves would soon be violated by the voracious savages.

One day a group of scouts returned from a reconnais-sance mission and reported they had discovered a group of villages near the coast, near the mouth of a small stream that brought a meagre flow of water to the sea. They decided to attack that very night. There was a full moon that lit up the chalky whiteness of the desert as if it were day.

Leonnatus hung his axe on its bracket, picked up his bronze shield, some sixteen minae in weight, and leaped

astride his stallion, but Alexander put out his arm to stop him. 'Your wound is still fresh. Stay here and let us deal with it.'

'Not even if you tie me up,' growled his friend. 'I'll make them pay for each soldier they killed, butchered in the darkness without even being able to defend themselves.'

The King, his Companions and the men selected to accompany them – some two hundred in total – had chosen black horses and wore black cloaks so as to blend in with the night shadows. Alexander gave the signal and all the steeds set off at full gallop, shoulder to shoulder, head to head across the deserted plain: demons born out of Hades.

It was too late when the Oritians spotted them, but they ran nevertheless to defend their villages, their children and their wives. They stood no chance at all with the first wave of attack, cut down like lambs at slaughter, while the Macedonians set about sacking and looting and Leonnatus let fly with his axe. The fleeing enemy fell like grain in the field; he massacred so many of them that at one point he felt his heart bursting in his breast and then he heard Alexander's voice shouting, 'That's enough, Leonnatus!'

Only then did he stop, dripping sweat and blood from his panting body.

A second squadron of light cavalry arrived soon after, bringing with them the pack animals and the water bottles and the carts for gathering provisions, but all they found were flocks of sheep and goats enclosed in stone

corrals. The thick layer of dry dung in the enclosures showed that they were taken out to pasture very rarely.

'I wonder what they feed them with,' said Eumenes, who had arrived with the supplies convoy.

'It looks like they use this stuff,' replied Seleucus, pointing to sacks made of dried seaweed fibre, full of a sort of whitish powder.

'It stinks of fish,' said Lysimachus.

'It is fish,' confirmed Eumenes, picking up a handful and bringing it to his nose. 'Dried fish ground into meal.'

They returned to camp with the water they had been able to collect and the flocks of sheep they had stolen, but when they slaughtered the animals the taste of the meat proved to be revolting, like putrefied fish. There was nothing else to eat, however, and so they had to make do with what they had scavenged.

For days they moved forward under the relentless sun, tormented by the heat and their thirst. At times the desert suddenly changed colour, becoming blinding white, and the army found itself having to march over a crust of salt deposited by the ancient marine lakes that corroded the horses' shoes and the infantrymen's footwear, penetrating their skin and causing first deep cracks and then extremely painful sores. Many pack animals and horses died of thirst or hunger and then the men started falling as well.

They had neither the time nor the strength to bury them or give them any type of funeral. There came a stage when the soldiers rarely took any notice when a companion collapsed, and even when they did notice

there was no help they could offer and the bodies were abandoned, prey for the jackals and the vultures – groups of the birds now circled continuously above the column as it marched. Not only did the King have to bear the pain of this ordeal, but he had to witness his young bride suffering such privations and difficulties, all of this combined with the anguish of not knowing what had become of the fleet; they had had no news of Nearchus since the day he left from Pattala.

In the midst of this terrible ordeal, while bearing all that suffering, only Kalanos seemed not to feel any pain or hardship: he walked barefoot across the burning sands, dressed scantily with a piece of cloth, and in the evening, when the darkness brought the cool air, he could be seen sitting alongside the King, teaching him his philosophy and the art of controlling the passions and the needs of one's own body. Roxane as well, despite being so young, behaved in an exemplary fashion, with incredible pride and strength of spirit. She was often to be seen riding alongside her husband, wearing the jerkin of the Sogdian horsemen, and more than once she was even seen hunting for passing birds with bow and arrow.

One day, when the men were on their last legs, a soldier of the royal guard found a hollow in which there seemed to be some dampness. He began to dig with the point of his sword until slowly, drop-by-drop, he saw water appear. He managed to collect enough to cover the bottom of his helmet and after having moistened his lips, he gave it to Alexander who was clearly struggling through this ordeal because of the after effects of his wound, which was still causing him no small amount of trouble.

The King thanked him, took the helmet and lifted it to his mouth, but at the same time he realized that all his men were watching him. Their eyes were red from the salt, their skin was dry, their lips cracked and he could not bring himself to drink. He poured the water to the ground, saying, 'Alexander cannot drink when his men are dying of thirst.' Then, seeing that many of them were about to give up, all their strength gone, he raised his voice, 'Men, take heart! Do you think the gods have let us perform such feats to then let us die here in this desert? No, believe me! I assure you that by tomorrow night we will be out of this furnace and you will have as much food and water as you wish! Do you want to give up now? Do you want to die just a few steps away from salvation?'

At those words the soldiers took courage and started marching again until darkness fell. They had left the sea behind them some time ago now and they were marching up towards a line of rocky hills where, as night fell, there was a minimum of freshness. On the following day, at sunset, they reached the pass and far off in the distance they saw a walled city.

'It is Pura,' said one of the Persian officers. 'We are safe now.'

Alexander shouted, 'Did you hear that, men? Did you hear? We're safe! See? Your King always keeps his promises!'

The soldiers, one by one as they reached the top and saw the city in the distance, cried out with joy, throwing their weapons in the air, embracing one another and moved to tears.

Ptolemy approached with an expression of sheer astonishment on his face: 'How did you manage it?' he asked incredulously.

'Do you remember yesterday when we came to that fork in the track? One arm that went westwards along the sea and the other climbing up towards the hills?'

'Yes, I remember.'

'Kalanos said to me, "The more difficult road is the better one."'

'That's it?'

'That's it.'

'So you took a risk.'

'Not for the first time.'

'Quite. It's certainly not the first time.'

They arrived at sunset, squeezing the last drops of energy from their exhausted limbs, and the commander of the stronghold at Pura came out, suspicious, to meet them.

'Who are you?' he asked.

Alexander turned to Ptolemy: 'Is Oxhatres still alive?'

'I believe so,' came the reply. 'I think I saw him a few days ago.'

'Find him for me.'

Ptolemy moved off and then came back a short time later with Oxhatres who explained to the Persian governor all he needed to know regarding the guest who had just arrived.

'Alexander?' asked the Governor of Pura in astonishment. 'Isn't he dead?'

'As you can see he is alive and well; but I beg you, let us in. We are exhausted.'

The governor gave orders immediately to all the men under his command and the gates of Pura opened to let in the army that everyone had believed to be lost and the king everyone had believed to be dead.

<p style="text-align:center">*</p>

They stopped at Pura for four days, to rest and eat after the hardships they had endured. Alexander asked the governor if news of their fleet had reached Hormuz, and the Persian replied that he had heard nothing, but that he would make enquiries and would let him know.

'I wouldn't bargain on their having made it,' said Seleucus. 'I have heard that these waters are very dangerous at certain points because of sandbanks and pirates who specialize in attacking grounded ships. If they had already landed here, there would certainly be news of them.'

'Perhaps you're right,' replied Alexander, 'but we too were given up for dead and we're here now. We should not give up hope.'

They started marching again in the direction of Persis, moving across burnt, arid terrain once more, but the commander of the garrison at Pura had given them expert guides who led them to wells with good water and to shepherd villages where they found milk and meat and dried pulses kept in large clay jars.

It was midwinter by the time the army came to Salmous, near the border with Persis. Alexander sent a group of scouts southwards to seek news of his fleet – a pair of Macedonian officers and a dozen auxiliaries with a Persian guide, together with half a dozen camels loaded with water bottles.

They moved forward for ten parasangs over completely deserted terrain with just one stop until, around midday, when the sun was at its highest, they saw something off in the distance.

'Can you make out what it is?' asked one of the auxiliaries, a Palestinian mercenary from Azotus.

'Looks like men,' replied a companion.

'Men?' asked one of the officers. 'Where?'

'Down there,' pointed the other officer, who now saw them distinctly. 'Look, they're making signs, shouting . . . I think they've seen us. Quickly, let's go!'

They set off at a gallop and soon found themselves before two men who barely resembled human beings – their clothes torn, their eyes sunken, their skin covered in sores and burned by the sun, their lips split with thirst. 'Who are you?' the wretches asked in Greek.

'We're the ones who should be asking that,' retorted the officer, 'and what are you doing here?'

'We are sailors of the royal fleet.'

'Are you telling us that Nearchus's fleet is . . .' the officer did not dare finish the sentence because the two men before him looked as though they had been through a shipwreck.

'Safe,' said the man with his last breath, 'but for the sake of the gods, give us some water if you want us to tell you the rest of the story.'

60

'MOUNT YOUR HORSES!' shouted the King, much agitated on hearing the news. 'Nearchus is on the coast with all the ships. He hasn't lost a single one! Eumenes, have the carts prepared – water, supplies, meat, sweets, honey, fruit and wine, by the gods! All the wine you can find. Follow me down there as soon as you can manage!'

'But this will all take time,' said his Secretary, trying to get him to reason.

'Starting by nightfall will be fine. I want these men to enjoy themselves, by Zeus! We will have a great banquet on the beach! We must celebrate, we must celebrate!'

His eyes shone with emotion and impatience; he looked like an excited young boy. 'And take care of these two sailors – treat them like princes, our honoured guests. And the Queen, I want the Queen with me as well.'

He set off at a gallop with all his Companions, followed by two squadrons of *hetairoi* cavalry. They came within sight of Nearchus's naval camp by sunset of their third day of travelling, all covered with dust and sweat, but the light was still shining in Alexander's eyes. The water gleamed splendidly with sparkling golden flashes and Nearchus's ships stood out in black silhouette against the shining mirror of the Ocean, all adorned with their pennants and standards.

Nearchus came to meet them at the entrance to the camp and Alexander, as soon as he saw him, dismounted, so that the two men walked the distance between the ranks of joyous sailors on the one hand and equally joyous cavalry on the other. As they came closer they started running towards one another, impatient to embrace, and in the end their meeting was more of a collision than a fraternal hug. When they pulled away to look at each other, their faces expressed sheer incredulity. Emotion got the upper hand and left them both speechless. In the end Alexander burst into a resounding laugh and shouted, 'You stink of rotten fish, Nearchus!'

'And you of horse sweat, *Aléxandre*!' retorted the admiral.

'I cannot believe that you are all alive,' said the King looking at the emaciated face of his navarch.

'It hasn't been easy,' replied Nearchus. 'At one stage I didn't think we would make it. We sailed through two storms, but above all else our problems were thirst and hunger.'

They started walking into the camp and such was the curiosity and the desire to recount their respective adventures that the two of them did not even notice that Ptolemy had lined up the cavalry to pay homage to them.

The commander's voice finally caught their attention: 'For King Alexander and for Admiral Nearchus, *Alalalài*!'

'*Alalalài*!' shouted the horsemen, lifting their spears and raising their cry to infinity, while the last rays of the sun were extinguished in the flaming Ocean waves.

'Allow me to mention Onesicritus as well,' added the admiral, nodding to his pilot to step forward. 'He has proved himself to be a great mariner.'

'Hail, Onesicritus,' Alexander saluted him. 'I am most glad to see you.'

'Hail, Sire,' replied the helmsman. 'I too am glad to see you.'

'I am sorry,' continued Nearchus, 'but we do not have much to offer you. We have fished all day, but our catch is poor. There are, however, a couple of tuna fish and they are on the grill as we speak.'

'Don't worry about that,' replied the King. 'I have a surprise for you all, although I am afraid it won't arrive until tomorrow.'

'If it's what I think it is, I can't wait!' exclaimed Nearchus. 'Did you know that one day we attempted an incursion into some villages along the coast? And do you know what the loot was?'

'No, but I think I can guess.'

'Fish meal. Sacks and sacks of fish meal. Those poor wretches had nothing else.'

'We know all about it.'

They went into Nearchus's tent and shortly afterwards Ptolemy, Hephaestion, Seleucus and the others arrived.

'Look,' said Nearchus, showing them a roll of papyrus open on a makeshift table. 'Onesicritus drew this map of our course from Pattala down here.'

'Splendid,' said Alexander, running his finger along the interminable desert coast where the vice-admiral had written the name 'Ichthyophages'.

'Fish-eaters,' Hephaestion repeated. 'You can say that again. Along there even the goats stink of fish. It makes my stomach turn just thinking about it.'

'You cannot imagine how worried we were after we lost contact with the fleet,' said Alexander.

'Just as we were,' replied Nearchus. 'The fact is that it was not easy to slow down to wait for you and when we did so there was never any sign of you. Perhaps you were ahead of us, or behind us. There was no way of telling.'

'The fish is ready,' announced one of the sailors.

'And it doesn't smell too bad,' said Seleucus.

'I think we'll have to sit on the shore to eat,' said the admiral. 'There aren't many dining beds and tables on board my ships.'

'We'll manage,' said Perdiccas. 'Hunger is hunger, wherever and whenever it comes.'

At that precise moment, just when everyone was moving off to sit down to supper, laughing and joking, the trumpets sounded the alarm.

'By Zeus!' exclaimed Alexander. 'Who on earth dares to attack us now?' He unsheathed his sword and shouted, '*Hetairoi*, follow me! Mount your horses! Mount your horses!'

Soon the camp resounded with trumpet blasts and the whinnying of the horses, the defensive palisade was opened and the squadrons prepared to charge out and deal with the enemy incursion. Indeed, a storm-like cloud of dust could be seen advancing threateningly towards them and in the midst of it they could make out metal weapons and shields.

'But they're Macedonians!' shouted a sentry.

'Macedonians?' asked Alexander in amazement as he blocked the charge of the *hetairoi* with a gesture.

There followed a moment in which all that could be heard was the noise of the galloping horses as they neared the camp. Then the sentry's voice rang out once more in the tension-filled silence, 'It's the wine!' he exclaimed. 'Eumenes has sent the wine with a squadron of assault troops!'

The tension collapsed into oceanic laughter and the assault troops paraded through the camp amidst the general applause of their companions, each of them carrying two bottles satchel-like across their horses' backs.

'So, is there anything to eat round here?' asked Leonnatus, dismounting and unlacing his breastplate.

'There's plenty to eat,' replied Nearchus.

'And to drink, by Zeus!' laughed Alexander. 'Thanks to our Secretary General!'

They sat down on the warm sand and the sailors began serving the fish.

'Fillet of tuna Cypriot style!' announced a sailor from Paphos pompously. 'Speciality of the house.'

Everyone tucked into the food and the conversation soon livened up because they all had their own stories to tell – stories of hardships and dangers, of storms and dead calms, of night attacks and marine monsters, stories of friends who for a long time they had worried they would never see again.

'Where do you think Craterus is?' Alexander asked at a certain point. And for a long moment all the Companions looked one another in the face, in silence.

61

CRATERUS REACHED SALMOUS with his army two weeks later and the exultation of Alexander and the Companions knew no bounds. The celebrations continued at length and when the army eventually set off on its march once more, the King wanted them to carry on. He had special carriages constructed and gave orders for dining beds and tables to be installed on them so that all the Companions lay there eating, drinking and laughing. The soldiers too were allowed to drink as much as they wanted from the wine supplies that followed the convoy.

Kalanos rode on one of the carriages and the King and his Companions all travelled with him to listen to his teachings.

The territory all around resounded with celebratory singing and chanting. This was no longer an army that advanced towards the heart of Persis, this was now a Dionysian *komos*, a procession in honour of the god that liberates the human heart from all struggles through the joy of wine and merriment.

In the meantime Nearchus had left with his fleet after having carried out the necessary repairs and loaded up the holds with everything required for a long voyage. They went through the Straits of Hormuz and entered the Persian Gulf, heading in the direction of mouth of

the Tigris. The meeting was to be at Susa, which could be reached by means of a navigable canal. At long last the hard times were behind them and the sailors rowed with renewed vigour and manoeuvred the rigging and the sails deftly, impatient to bring their adventure to an end and to be able to tell their loved ones all about it.

There was just one moment of tension for the fleet when out of the waves, not far from the flagship, great jets of spray appeared, followed by the glistening-wet backs of gigantic, shining creatures that immediately submerged again, waving their enormous tails out of the water.

'But . . . what are they?' asked the Cypriot sailor who had prepared supper for the King and his Companions on the beach, evidently terrorized.

'Whales,' replied the Phoenician boatswain who had sailed beyond the Pillars of Hercules. 'They pose no threat to us at all, as long as we don't ram them, because all it would take is a single blow from that tail and . . . goodbye flagship. They could swallow it up in a single gulp!'

'I prefer tunny fish,' stammered the sailor. He asked again, truly worried, 'But are you sure they won't attack us?'

'One can never be sure of anything at sea,' replied Nearchus. 'You ought to know that already. Return to your post now.'

*

Alexander's army continued its march along the road that led to Pasargadae and there the King discovered that

Cyrus's tomb had been violated – the sarcophagus had been opened and the Great King's body dragged out. He interrogated the magi who had been in charge of looking after the grave and had a trial held to try to find the culprits, but not even under torture did any of them offer any information. He let them all go, gave orders for the tomb to be restored to its original state and set off once more towards Persepolis. In the meantime rumours had spread that the King had returned and this news threw many satraps and even many Macedonian governors into considerable confusion because they had all been sure that he was dead and had all made the most of every opportunity to indulge in all sorts of stealing and looting.

Alexander saw the state to which the imperial palace had been reduced by the frightful fire that had destroyed it – only the stone columns and the gigantic entrance portals rose out of the enormous expanse of smoke-blackened and mud-covered ground. The gemstones had been prised from the reliefs, the lumps of precious metal that had melted during the fire had been stripped away. The only thing that recalled in some way the greatness of the Achaemenids was the flame burning before the funeral monument of Darius III.

The King thought of Stateira whom he had not seen for such a long time now, and he wondered if she had received the letter he had sent from the banks of the Indus. He wrote to her again, telling her that he loved her and that he would meet her at Susa.

One evening, some time later, while he was resting together with Roxane on the veranda of the satrap's palace, a visit was announced and a bald, stocky man was

shown in, a man who immediately greeted him with a broad smile.

'My King, my boy, you have no idea what a pleasure it is to see you once more. But ... where's the dog?' he added looking around suspiciously.

'Eumolpus of Soloi ... there's no need to worry, Peritas is no longer with us. He died in India, saving my life.'

'I am sorry,' replied the informer. 'Even though he didn't find me very agreeable. I know you loved him very much.'

Alexander lowered his head. 'Bucephalas is dead, as are many, too many friends. It has been hard going. But where have you come from? I'd given you up for dead – you disappeared into thin air without saying a word and I had no news whatsoever.'

'If it comes to that, I'd given you up for dead as well. And I'm not the only one. As for my disappearance, it's quite normal. Once I realized what you wanted from me I set off at the first favourable opportunity without a second thought – a good informer never lets anything out regarding his own movements, not even to the person who has commissioned his work.'

'If I know you,' said Alexander, 'you're certainly not here just for the pleasure of seeing me once more.'

Eumolpus handed him a scroll. 'Indeed. In your absence, my King, and, if I remember well, in full accordance with your wishes, I have been your eyes and your ears. I never forget those who have treated me well and you trusted me and you saved my life when every-one wanted to have me executed. There are things

written in here that will not please you: it is a complete
list of all the rum doings, the stealing, the corruption and
violence committed by the satraps and the governors,
Macedonians included, during your time away. There is
also a list of all the witnesses you may interrogate, should
you wish to begin trials against these people. The man in
charge of the royal treasure, for a start, that cripple . . .
Eumenes' friend . . .'

'Harpalus?'

'That's the one. He has taken five thousand talents
from the coffers, enlisted six thousand mercenaries and is
now marching towards Cilicia, if my latest information is
correct. I believe he is currently dealing with some of his
Athenian friends, men who are not exactly enamoured of
your own good self.'

'Demosthenes?'

Eumolpus nodded.

'Where do you think he is heading?'

'Athens, probably.'

At that moment Eumenes entered with an expression
of deep embarrassment on his face. '*Aléxandre*, unfortu-
nately I bring terrible news! I don't know where to start,
because . . . in a certain sense it's all my fault.'

'Harpalus? I know already,' and he nodded across to
Eumolpus who was sitting quietly in a corner and had
done nothing to bring himself to Eumenes' attention.
'And I know of many other things, all of them thoroughly
unpleasant. This is what must be done: you will immedi-
ately verify the allegations made in this document against
the people mentioned, whether they be of Macedonian,
Persian or Median race. After that, you will instigate all

the necessary trials. The Macedonians, if found guilty, will be sentenced by the assembled army and the verdicts will be carried out with full respect for our traditional rites.'

'And Harpalus?'

'Find the lame bastard, Eumenes,' ordered Alexander, pale with indignation, 'wherever he may be. And have him killed like a dog.'

Eumolpus of Soloi stood up. 'It seems to me that we have said all there is to be said.'

'Indeed. Eumenes will pay you handsomely.'

Eumenes nodded, even more embarrassed now.

'It is not your fault,' Alexander said to him as he got to his feet. 'You have never betrayed my trust and I know that you will never betray it.'

'I thank you, but this does not alleviate my disappointment.'

He left the room and as he walked away through the corridors of the palace he met Aristander. The seer had a strange light in his eyes, a look of madness, and did not greet him. Perhaps he did not even see him.

The seer entered Alexander's room and the expression on his face, so full of anguish and astonishment, struck the King profoundly.

'What has happened?' asked Alexander with the tone of someone who asks while fearing the answer that is bound to come.

'It is my nightmare. It has returned.'

'When?'

'Last night. And one more thing.'

'Tell me.'

'Kalanos is not well.'

'This is not possible!' exclaimed Alexander. 'He has undergone the worst hardships, the most demanding trials, the rain and the sun, hunger and thirst . . .'

'And yet he is very ill.'

'Since when?'

'Since we arrived at Persepolis.'

'Where is he now?'

'In the house you assigned to him.'

'Take me to him immediately.'

'As you wish. Follow me.'

'Where are you going, *Aléxandre*?' Roxane asked, worried.

'To visit a friend who is unwell, my love.'

They crossed the city, over which the evening shadows were just beginning to fall, and they found themselves standing before a fine house surrounded by a portico, the residence of a Persian nobleman who had fallen in battle at Gaugamela. Alexander had put Kalanos in this house so that he might enjoy some comfort after the difficulties of the expedition.

The King entered with Aristander and the two of them walked down the long, quiet corridors and came to a room that was barely illuminated by the last light of day. Kalanos lay on a mat on the floor. His eyes were closed and his body was shockingly emaciated.

'*Kalane* . . .' whispered the King.

The man opened his eyes, two black, immense, febrile eyes. 'I am not well, *Aléxandre*.'

'I cannot believe these words, master, I have seen you undergo every sort of hardship on a daily basis without you ever feeling pain or suffering in any way.'

'I am suffering now. And this suffering is unbearable.'

Alexander turned and met the frowning gaze of his seer.

'What is this suffering? Tell me, so that we may alleviate it.'

'It is the suffering of the soul, the most acute form of suffering, for which there is no remedy.'

'But what is it that makes you so unwell? Have you not walked the path that leads to imperturbability?'

Kalanos looked straight into Aristander's eyes and between the two sages there was a dark knowing. He struggled to move his lips, but he did manage to speak once more: 'Yes, I walked that path until I met you, until I saw in you the power of the Ocean in fury, the wild strength of the tiger, the supreme heights of the snow-capped mountains that hold up the sky. I wanted to know you and your world and I wanted to save you when your blind rage had brought you to the edge of destruction. But I knew what I would have to do if I failed. I made a pact with myself. I loved you, *Aléxandre*, just like all those who have known you, and I wanted to follow you to protect you from your natural instinct, to teach you a wisdom that is different from that of the sages who educated you, from that of the warriors who made you an invincible instrument of destruction. But your *tantra* cannot be bent in any way, I know this now; now I see what is looming, what is imminent.' He lifted his eyes to meet Aristander's wavering gaze once more. 'This is what makes my suffering so great. If I were to live to see what is about to happen, the pain would prevent me from ever attaining imperturbability, from

ever dissolving my soul in infinity. You do not want this, *Aléxandre*, tell me you do not want this.'

Alexander took his hand. 'No,' he replied, his voice quavering with emotion. 'I do not want this, *Kalane*. But tell me, I beg you, tell me what is this terrible thing that must come to pass.'

'I do not know. I can only feel it. And I cannot bear it. Let me die in the way I swore I would die.'

The King kissed the skeletal hand of the great sage, then he looked at Aristander and said, 'Listen to his last wishes and communicate them to Ptolemy in order that he may carry them out. I . . . I . . . I cannot . . .'

And he left Kalanos's quarters in tears.

★

When the time came Ptolemy carried out all he had been asked, and thus began Kalanos's last journey towards infinite imperturbability.

He had a pyre built that was ten cubits high and thirteen cubits wide. Along the access road he had five thousand *pezhetairoi* lined up wearing their parade armour and organized a march of young men who spread rose petals everywhere. Then came Kalanos, so weak and exhausted that he could no longer walk, carried by four men on a stretcher, with wreaths of flowers around his neck in accordance with Indian custom. He was placed on the pyre, as naked as the day he had come into the world, while choirs of young boys and girls sang the sweetest hymns ever heard on earth.

Alexander had decided from the very beginning not to watch the ceremony and for this reason he had asked

Ptolemy to carry out the Indian sage's last wishes. At the very last moment, however, he recalled how Kalanos had watched over him when he was close to death and he decided to pay his last respects; he walked along the ceremonial route until he came to the pyre and there he looked on Kalanos, so fragile and naked and he thought of Diogenes lying with his eyes half closed before his churn, in the remote evening sun, and at that moment he remembered what Diogenes had told him when they were alone – the very same thing that Kalanos had told him, without opening his mouth, in the darkness of the tent while he struggled with death: 'There is no conquest that has any meaning, there is no war worth fighting. In the end, the only earth left to us is the earth in which we are buried.'

He lifted his head and saw Kalanos's body enveloped in a vortex of flames. Incredibly he was smiling in the midst of that fiery plasma, and it seemed to Alexander that he was moving his lips, he was mumbling something. The roar of the flames was too loud to hear anything, but the voice of the sage resounded anyway:

'We will meet again in Babylon.'

62

ALEXANDER IMMEDIATELY LEFT Persis with all its sad memories and marched towards Susa, which he reached in midwinter.

As soon as he arrived, he went to visit Sisygambis who was much moved to see him and proffered greetings in the Greek manner with the most familiar of forms, 'Chaire, pai!'

'Your Greek is perfect, Mother,' Alexander complimented her. 'I am glad to find you in good health.'

'The joy is all mine for seeing you safe and sound,' replied the Queen Mother. 'I cried when news came that you had died. I imagine how your mother must have suffered, alone there in Macedonia.'

'I sent her a letter as soon as I reached Salmous and I think she will have received it by now and it will have assuaged her anguish.'

'May I hope that you might stay and eat with me?'

'Most certainly. It will be a great pleasure for me.'

'At my age I have no other satisfactions in life than receiving visits, and a visit from you is the most special of all. Sit down, my boy, don't stand there like that.'

Alexander sat down. 'Mother, I have not come simply to greet you.'

'Why else have you come? Speak freely.'

'I have heard tale that King Darius had another daughter.'

'This is true,' Sisygambis said.

'Well, I wish to marry her.'

'Why?'

'Because I intend to take up Darius's inheritance – his family must become my own family.'

'I understand.'

'May I hope that you will grant me her hand in marriage?'

'Even had her father survived she would have been granted to someone to consolidate some alliance or to assure the loyalty of some satrap. She is no great beauty, and yet her name will remind you of a great love that you have lost . . . do you know what her name is? It is Barsine.'

Alexander lowered his head, overwhelmed by memories. Images that had been faded by time suddenly leaped vividly and startlingly into his mind.

'That terrible day at Gaugamela,' continued the Queen Mother. 'I will never forget it . . . Stateira will be pleased to go and live with her elder sister. But Roxane?'

'Roxane loves me. She knows she is queen, but she also realizes exactly what a king's duties involve. I have already spoken to her.'

'And what did she say?'

'She cried. Just as my mother cried whenever my father Philip brought a new bride to the palace. But I love Roxane more than any thing or any one and she knows this.'

'I gladly grant you Barsine. Now you will unite the

Argead dynasty with the Achaemenids – now there will be neither victors nor vanquished. How will your men take it?'

'I will convince them.'

'You think so?'

'I am sure of it. And I have one more thing to ask of you – the hand of Barsine and Stateira's little sister.'

'You want Drypetis as well? I suppose it's only natural.'

'Not for me. For my friend Hephaestion. In our youth we thought it would be wonderful if we were to marry two sisters: that way our children would be cousins.'

'I can only be pleased to grant her to your friend. I only hope that this marriage is accepted by your noblemen and your soldiers.'

'Of course it will be,' replied Alexander. 'Many of my men already live with Persian or Median girls and even have children. It is right that they marry now, and for others I am selecting Persian brides. I have calculated that there will be, more or less, ten thousand weddings.'

The elderly queen opened her eyes wide in her heavily wrinkled face. 'Ten thousand, *pai*? Oh, great Ahura Mazda, this is something the world has never seen before!' She smiled with an expression of innocent wickedness. 'After all is said and done, I think you're right – the bed is the best place for building long-lasting peace.'

*

While organizing preparations for the weddings, Alexander began planning new expeditions to unknown lands

as well and it was for this reason that he waited impatiently for the arrival of Nearchus's fleet which was sighted, just as winter turned to spring, at the mouth of the Tigris.

The flagship flew the Argead standard with the golden star and dropped anchor in the canal that was almost directly below the city walls. Behind it the rest of the fleet moored to roaring acclaim and applause, amidst trumpet blasts and the rolling of drums.

Nearchus, all bedecked in his armour, received full honours from two battalions of *pezhetairoi* and then he was received by Alexander sitting on his throne with Roxane alongside him, stunning in her imperial gown all woven with gold and studded with gemstones.

As soon as he saw his admiral, the King went towards him and kissed him on both cheeks, then he received vice-admiral Onesicritus and all the commanders of each single ship to offer his congratulations and present each of them with a gift.

That same evening he summoned all his friends to supper, including Nearchus and Eumenes, to communicate his decisions. The banquet was set up in the throne room itself and the dining beds were arranged along three sides, so that all the guests could see and hear the King. There were neither women nor musicians present, which made it seem more like a war council than a banquet.

Alexander began, 'I have decided that the time has come for you all to marry.' They all looked at one another in amazement. 'You are getting on,' he continued, 'and

you ought to start thinking about setting up families. I have chosen beautiful brides who come from the highest social stations . . . all of them Persian.'

There followed a moment of silence.

'Not only this,' continued the King, 'but I have decided to celebrate weddings between the Macedonian and Asian couples that exist already. Many of them, as you know, already have children. I will provide money for the dowries of the brides for those who choose to get married now. Just so long as the bride is Persian, that is. This is the only way we can create a future for our conquest, to wipe out the rancour, the hatred, the desire for revenge – a single homeland, a single King, a single people. This is my plan and this is also my will. If any of you are against this, please speak up now.'

No one said a word. Only Eumenes lifted his hand. 'I am not Macedonian and I am not a hero like the rest of you and I have no intention to take part in the foundation of any empire – if I could be excused from having to take part in this springtime reproductive orgy, I would be most happy. The very idea of having a wife hanging around me gives me goose pimples and—'

'Your bride,' Alexander interrupted him with a smile, 'goes by the name of Artonis, daughter of the satrap Artaozos. She is most pretty and devout. I am sure you will be very happy together.'

The ceremony took place in the springtime, under a gigantic tent, with the Persian rite. High-backed arm-chairs were lined up in order and then the grooms arrived for the general toast and mutual wishes of happiness. Immediately afterwards the brides arrived, dressed in

their nuptial gowns and they each took their places alongside their spouses. Then, following the King's lead, each man took the woman's hand and kissed her. Each of the guests received a golden cup and then the banquet was set up, with a sumptuous supper for some twenty thousand people. The wine flowed from a fountain and everyone could drink at will. Choirs of young boys and girls sang nuptial hymns to the accompaniment of Babylonian and Indian harps, flutes and drums.

Stateira had arrived from Ecbatana two days previously and she took part in the ceremony as a lady-in-waiting to her sister Barsine, born of Darius's first marriage. When the time came to retire, she accompanied her as far as the threshold of the bedchamber where her new husband was due to join her. Alexander arrived before Stateira had left and she greeted him with a kiss.

'I am happy you have come, Stateira. It has been a long time since we last saw each other.'

'This is true, my Lord, it has been a long time.'

'I hope you are well.'

'I am fine,' replied Stateira with an enigmatic smile, 'but I find myself wondering just how well you are.'

'Perhaps I've had a bit too much to drink,' replied Alexander, 'but on a night like this the wine can only do me good.'

'Quite. An almost thirty-year-old virgin and a wife you haven't seen for almost four years are both desirous of your services.'

Alexander seemed to reflect for a moment on these words before he murmured, 'How time flies.'

Then he approached her, looked her straight in the eyes and asked, 'Have you come to offer me your love, or to challenge me?'

'To challenge you? Why should I? I will wait in the room next door while you make my sister happy – she is the newly wed and she has every right to the prime of your strength,' replied Stateira with the most inviting of smiles. She gave him a kiss and then retired to her room, closing the door behind her.

The King slept with both of his Persian wives that night, first with Barsine and then with Stateira, but when Stateira had fallen asleep, he covered her with a *chlamys* and went out into the corridor. He looked around and saw that everything was quiet, then he went down the stairs, walked across the courtyard and went to Roxane in the royal apartments. He tried not to make any noise, but when he lay down alongside her, she turned suddenly and lashed out like a fury, throwing punches and scratching him with her nails. 'You still smell of that woman and you dare come near me!' she shouted.

Alexander grabbed her wrists and pinned her down on the bed. She wriggled and twisted and panted beneath him, but Alexander said nothing. He let her shout and then cry disconsolately for as long as it took. In the end he let her go and he lay down alongside her once more, waiting for all her wrath and her pain to subside.

'I'll go if you want me to,' he said.

Roxane did not reply.

'I had explained to you that I was going to marry Barsine and that Stateira was to return. A king has certain duties—'

'But that makes no difference!' shouted Roxane. 'Do you think the fact it's your duty makes me feel any better?'

'No, I don't think that,' replied Alexander. 'That's why I asked you if you want me to leave.'

'And you really would go?' she asked.

'Only if you wanted me to,' replied the King, 'but I hope you don't ask me to because you are the only woman I will love for the rest of my days.'

Roxane was silent for a long time, then she said, '*Aléxandre . . .*'

'Yes.'

'If you do it again I will kill myself, and your child will die together with me. I am pregnant.'

Alexander held her hand firmly, in silence, in the dark.

*

On the following day the King announced that he personally would clear the debts of all those Macedonian soldiers who had borrowed money. Initially many of them did not dare report their debts because they thought that Alexander had worked out a plan to identify all those who had squandered their resources or who had not managed to get by on the generous pay they all received.

Alexander, on seeing that there were so few requests, spread word that he did not wish to know the identities of the debtors, but only the amount of the debt, and thus they all took heart and presented Eumenes with their applications and the documents proving the existence of the loans; in return they were issued with the monies necessary to clear the debt in full.

The Secretary General calculated the total cost of this operation at ten thousand talents.

Towards the end of the spring the King held manoeuvres at Opis, along the Tigris, where a new contingent of thirty thousand young Persian men had joined the army, all of them trained after the Macedonian fashion. There was a great parade in which the young Asian warriors, called the Successors, proved themselves to be exceptionally valiant and skilful. This irritated the Macedonian soldiers once again, who feared they might be put at the same level as those they had defeated and conquered on the battlefield. Their disappointment further increased when they heard that Alexander wanted to dismiss all the invalids and the wounded and send them all back, together with Craterus who was to substitute old Antipater as regent of Macedon.

'They are furious,' Craterus said to him. 'They are asking you to receive a delegation.'

The manoeuvres had finished and the young Successors had returned to their tents. Alexander had his throne brought out and said to his friend, 'Have them come to me.' It was clear that he was extremely angry and in a terrible mood.

Craterus moved off towards the Macedonian camp, which was clearly separated from the Persian camp, and not long afterwards there appeared a small company of soldiers representing the various divisions of the army: cavalry, heavy infantry, assault troops, shieldsmen, horseback archers.

'What do you want?' asked Alexander, coldly.

'Is it true that you are sending home the veterans, the

disabled, the maimed?' asked the commander of an infantry division, the oldest of the group.

'Yes,' replied the King.

'And you feel this is the right thing to do?'

'It is the necessary thing. There will be further expeditions and these men are no longer fit to fight.'

'What sort of a man are you?' shouted another. 'Now that you have these little barbarians all dressed like young girls doing their exercises and their pirouettes, you don't need your soldiers any more, the soldiers who conquered half the world for you with their sweat and their blood.'

'It's true!' exclaimed a third man. 'You plan on sending them back home now, but in what state? Are they the same men they were when you took them from their families ten years ago? No! Back then they were young and strong, in perfect shape! Now they are exhausted, emptied, wounded, maimed, invalids. What will their lives be like? And what about those who will never come back now? Those who died in the ambushes, who froze to death in the winters, who were smashed to pieces against the rocks, drowned in the muddy waters of the Indus, devoured by crocodiles, bitten by snakes, killed by thirst and hunger in the desert. Have you thought about them? Have you thought about the widows and the orphans? No, Sire, you obviously haven't, otherwise you would never have conceived an action of this kind. We have always listened to you, we have always obeyed you, but now you must listen to us! We, your soldiers, have met together in an assembly and we have decided. Either all of us, or none of us!'

'What are you trying to say?' asked Alexander, his face darkening.

'What I mean is,' replied the infantry division commander, 'if you send the invalid veterans back then you will have to send us all back. Yes, we are going home. You can keep your barbarians with their fine gold-plated breastplates and we will see if they're capable of doing as much for you as we have done, if they can sweat blood for you in the same way we have. Farewell, Sire.'

The small group of men bowed their heads slightly, then turned their backs and slow-marched back to the camp.

Alexander got to his feet, his face pale with rage and humiliation and he turned to the horsemen of his personal guard, 'Is this the way you see things as well?'

The commander was silent.

'Do you feel the same way?' he shouted once more.

'We agree with our companions, Sire,' came the reply.

'Then you may go. You are relieved of your duties – I no longer have any need of you.'

The commander nodded to indicate that he had understood, then he gathered his men and took them to the camp at a gallop.

Shortly afterwards their place was taken by a group of Persian Successors who from that moment onwards were on full display outside the royal tent, resplendent in their new armour and their embroidered gowns, their purple and gold standards.

For two days Alexander refused to see his soldiers, neither did he communicate to them what he intended to do, but in the camp his gesture had thrown everyone

into a state of considerable worry. They felt now like a flock of sheep without a shepherd, like children without a father, alone in the heart of a limitless land they had conquered, but which now threatened and derided them. And stronger than all these feelings was one other: the pain that came from having been excluded from the presence of their king, the thought that he was now making other plans, dreaming other dreams, conceiving of extraordinary adventures without them, the pain of not seeing him any more, of no longer having any contact with him, no relationship whatsoever.

Two days went by and the King did not show his face. On the third day some soldiers said, 'We've made a mistake. It was the wrong thing to do. After all, he has always loved us, he has gone through our hardships with us, he ate as we ate, he was wounded more than any of us, he has heaped gifts and favours on us. Let us go to his tent and beg his pardon.'

Others started laughing, 'Yes! That's it! Off you go and have your backsides kicked for your trouble!'

'Perhaps,' replied the man who had spoken first, 'but I will go anyway; you do whatever you want.' He took off all his weapons and wearing only his *chiton*, and, barefoot, he walked out of the camp. Others followed his example, increasing in numbers until more than half the army were there before the royal pavilion under the astonished gaze of the Persian guards.

Just at that moment Craterus passed by and saw them standing there. Ptolemy, who had returned from a mission along the Tigris, asked, 'What's happening here?'

They entered the tent and Craterus said, 'The men are outside, *Aléxandre*.'

They heard a voice cry out, 'Forgive us, Sire!'

'I hear them,' replied Alexander, apparently impassible.

'Alexander! Listen to us!' cried another voice.

Ptolemy could not manage to hide his emotions. 'Why don't you go to them? They are your soldiers.'

'Not any longer. I was not the one who rejected them – they rejected me. They failed me.'

Ptolemy added nothing else – he knew his friend too well to insist at that moment.

Another day and night and then another day went by and the soldiers' laments grew louder, their voices ever more insistent.

'That's enough now!' shouted Ptolemy. 'Enough! Those men have neither slept nor eaten for two days and two nights. If you are a man, go to them now! Is it truly so difficult for you to understand them? You are a king, you know everything of the workings of governments and politics, but they know only one thing: they have followed you to the ends of the earth, they have given blood for you and now you send them away and surround yourself with the very people you had asked them to fight against up until yesterday. Can you really not understand how they feel? Do you really think the money you have given them is any just compensation?'

Something in Alexander seemed to stir and he looked Ptolemy in the face, as though hearing these words for the very first time. Then he stood up and walked out, while the light of day was gradually fading away.

The entire army was out there – thousands of

unarmed soldiers, sitting on the dusty ground, many of them in tears.

'I have heard you, men!' he shouted. 'Do you think I am deaf? I have not slept for two nights because of you.'

'Neither have we slept for two nights, Sire!' replied an anonymous voice in the midst of the group.

'Because you are ingrates, because you failed to understand me, because . . .' Alexander started shouting.

A veteran soldier, with one hand missing and with a grey beard and long ruffled hair moved forward and looked Alexander square in the eyes, 'Because we love you, son,' he said.

Alexander bit his lip, realizing that at any moment he might start crying like a baby, he himself, King of Macedon, King of Kings, Pharaoh of Egypt, Sovereign of Babylon, was about to cry like a stupid little boy before his soldiers. And he did. Burning tears, shameless, without even covering his face. When he had finally calmed down, he replied, 'I love you too, you bastards!'

63

ALEXANDER, SITTING ON his throne on the podium, looked at the soldiers who had been summoned before him by the trumpets. Then he nodded to Eumenes, the signal for the Secretary General to start reading:

Alexander, King of Macedon and pan-Hellenic *Heghemón*, decrees:

The veterans who prove to be unfit for action after a medical examination will return home with General Craterus.

They will each receive a personal gift from the King, so that they will remember him for the rest of the days the gods grant them to live. They will also receive a gold crown each, which they will be entitled to wear at every and any public manifestation, when they are present at athletics or dramatic competitions. On such occasions they will be granted seats in the tribune of honour.

He further decrees that they will receive their wages for the rest of their lives, and, until they are twenty years of age, any orphans will receive the wages of their fathers who died in glory for the homeland.

The King's Macedonian guard is reinstated to its role. All those who are ill or are slightly wounded will

be treated and will rejoin the ranks. The King has asked Philip, his personal physician, to take care of them.

To all of you he expresses his deepest affection and gratitude. For ever!

Following those words there came a great explosive roar, the clangour of swords being beaten against shields, singing and shouting and cries of joy.

Four days later, the convoy led by Craterus set off on its march towards the Euphrates and the sea. Alexander stood there watching until the last man disappeared over the horizon. 'They have taken part of me with them.'

'You are right,' replied Eumenes, 'but the decree you have issued is excellent. They will all be there at the theatre, even those who have never set foot in one before, so as not to miss any chance of sitting in the special seats reserved for them, wearing in public the golden crown you have given them.'

'How do you think Antipater will take it?'

'Being substituted by Craterus? I don't know. He has always been loyal, he has served you faithfully. He may feel bitter, this is true, but it will pass. After all, he is the last one left of your father's old guard. What do you plan on doing now?'

'Do you remember the Ouxians?'

'Who could ever forget those savages?'

'To the north, there is an even more savage tribe that has supported attempts at restoring the Persian empire – the Cossaeans. I must sort out this business and then we will go to Ecbatana, the final capital, to reaffirm our

authority, to check up on the royal treasure and to put the corrupt governors on trial. Then we will march on Babylon, the future capital of the empire.'

'How long do you think it will take?'

'Two, perhaps three months.'

*

Alexander was wrong – it took all spring to subdue the Cossaeans and he remained at Ecbatana for much of the summer. Three high-ranking Macedonian officers – Heracles, Meleager and Aristonicus, were found guilty of corruption, theft and sacrilege with regard to the Persian sanctuaries and were immediately executed. In this way the King showed that he made no discrimination between Macedonians and Persians. Indeed, more than a few Persians who had proved to be corrupt administrators were condemned. In all these cases Eumolpus of Soloi's information proved to be correct.

Once these operations were complete, the King decided to organize a celebration with games and performances because some three thousand athletes, actors and impresarios had arrived from Greece. He then settled in the royal palace with Roxane. Stateira, in the meantime, with her sister who had married Alexander, had taken up residence in the palace at Susa. Thus they circumvented Roxane's jealousy, which became ever greater because she began to realize just how much power she wielded over her spouse – in his heart Alexander could never deny her anything. One evening, after having made love, while she lay alongside him as usual,

leaning her face on his chest, she said, 'Now, I am truly happy, *Aléxandre*.'

The King embraced her tightly. 'For me too this is a moment of great happiness. My fleet has returned safe and sound, I have completed all my military operations, I have made peace with my soldiers, I have united two races through marriage and soon I will have a son.'

'Wait a moment,' Roxane laughed. 'It might just be a daughter.'

'Oh no,' replied Alexander. 'I am sure it will be a boy – Alexander IV! You will be mother of my heir to the throne, Roxane, and to celebrate this moment I will proclaim great feasts, races and dramatic performances in the Greek manner. These are things that you have never experienced, but I am sure that you will immediately learn to appreciate them. Imagine hundreds of four-horse chariots racing round a track at breakneck speed, imagine stories represented on artificial stages with real men who pretend to be the characters in the stories, imagine athletes competing in races, wrestling, jumping, javelin throwing. And then dancing, music, singing . . .'

The girl looked at him, rapt with admiration. Since leaving her mountain home, peopled only by shepherds, she had seen all sorts of marvels and her life with Alexander, who in her eyes appeared omnipotent, was like an endless dream.

Thus the celebrations and the banquets began, but during these Hephaestion fell ill. As soon as Eumenes gave him the bad news, the King immediately ran to his bedside.

'What is wrong with him?' he asked straight away.

'High fever and nausea,' replied Eumenes.

'Call Philip.'

'Have you forgotten that we left him in Susa? I have sent for Glaucus – he is an excellent physician.'

Although feverish, Hephaestion was still able to joke: 'I don't want doctors – send me an amphora of Cypriot wine and I'll cure myself.'

'Don't be such a clown,' replied Alexander. 'You'll do exactly what the doctor tells you to do.'

Glaucus arrived quickly, uncovered the patient's chest and listened to it. 'Why is it that doctors' ears are always freezing?' exclaimed Hephaestion.

'If you want a doctor with warm ears all you have to do is ask,' joked Eumenes. 'Your friend is master of the world and he can find anything you want.'

Glaucus now began examining the abdomen and found it to be swollen and tense. 'I think he has eaten something that's had a bad effect on him. I'll prescribe a purge and then he'll have to fast for at least three days, drinking only water.'

'Are you sure this is the right cure?'

'I think Philip would tell you the same thing. If we weren't so far away, I would send a messenger for a consultation, but I really don't think it's necessary. An illness of this kind should clear up in less time that it would take the messenger to reach Susa.'

'That's fine, but make sure you keep an eye on him. Hephaestion is my dear friend. We have been close ever since we were children.' As he spoke Alexander's gaze fell on the golden pendant Hephaestion wore on his neck

with a small tooth mounted on it – the King's own milk tooth. Around his own neck was Hephaestion's tooth – the first token of eternal friendship they had exchanged.

'Have no fear, Sire,' replied the physician. 'We'll have Hephaestion back on his feet in no time.'

Alexander left and the doctor immediately had his patient swallow the purge and left instructions for his diet.

'In three days' time, if everything is going well, you'll be able to take some chicken broth.'

Indeed, three days later Hephaestion was better – the swelling in his abdomen had receded, and the fever had relented, although towards evening his temperature always rose slightly. That particular day the schedule for the games included the four-horse chariot race and Glaucus, who was particularly keen on horse racing, stopped by to examine his patient. On finding Hephaestion much improved, the physician asked if he might take a few hours off. 'General, there is an exciting chariot race taking place today. If you do not object, I would like to see it.'

'Of course I have no objections,' replied Hephaestion. 'Go and enjoy yourself.'

'And I can go without worrying? You will look after yourself?'

'Of course, Iatré. After everything I have been through in ten years of this military campaign, I'm certainly not afraid of a fever.'

'In any case, I will be back before nightfall.'

Glaucus left and Hephaestion, tired of fasting and the purges, called a servant and ordered him to roast up a couple of chickens and serve them with chilled wine.

'But, my Lord . . .' the man started to object.

'Are you going to obey me or do I have to have you whipped?' Hephaestion reprimanded him.

The servant found himself left with not much of a choice and he did what he had been ordered to do; he roasted the chickens and went to prepare the wine kept in pressed snow in the cellar.

*

The sun was setting and Glaucus was in excellent spirits as he entered his patient's bedchamber. 'How is our valiant warrior?' he asked, but his gaze fell immediately on the remains of two chickens and an empty amphora that had rolled into a corner. All the colour left his face. He turned slowly towards the bed – Hephaestion had not even managed to reach it. Alexander's friend lay on the floor where he had collapsed. Dead.

64

ALEXANDER WAS GIVEN the news immediately and he rushed to his friend's house with the hope that there had been some misunderstanding. When he arrived Eumenes, Ptolemy, Seleucus and Perdiccas were already there and, from the looks on their faces, from their eyes, he realized there was no hope at all.

His friend had been placed on the bed now, combed, shaved and dressed in clean clothes. Alexander threw himself on the body, shouting and crying in desperation. Then, having given vent to the sharpest grief, he sat in a corner with his head in his hands, crying silently, and he remained in that position all night and all the next day. The friends who were waiting outside the door heard him moan every now and then, his breath a dull rattle, or bursting out more than once into inconsolable sobbing.

At sunset on the following day, they decided to enter.

'Come,' said Ptolemy. 'Come away from here. All we can do for him now is prepare his funeral.'

'No, leave me be, I cannot abandon my poor friend!' shouted the King in his despair, but his companions forced him to stand up, almost bodily, and dragged him out to make way for the Egyptian embalmers who were waiting to prepare the body.

'It's my fault, it's all my fault,' moaned Alexander. 'If I hadn't left Philip in Susa he would have saved him and he would be alive now.'

'Unfortunately it was simply a momentary distraction,' said Seleucus. 'The physician left him alone while he went to the races and—'

'What did you say?' asked Alexander with an expression of utter horror on his face.

'That's what happened, unfortunately. Perhaps he thought there was no danger, but as soon as he found himself alone Hephaestion ate and drank too much – meat and chilled wine and—'

'Find him!' shouted Alexander. 'Find that rat and bring him here to me immediately!'

The poor doctor was rooted out by the guards who found him hidden away in the cellar, and they brought him before the King, white as a sheet, trembling all over. He sought to stutter some excuse, but Alexander shouted, 'Silence, you wretch!' And he hit Glaucus full in the face with his fist, so hard he sent him rolling in the dirt with his lip split.

'Have him executed straight away,' he ordered and the guards carried him away as he cried and begged for clemency. They led him down into the courtyard and propped him up against a wall where he continued to cry and beg. The officer shouted, 'Now!' and the archers all let fly at the same instant.

All the arrows hit their mark and Glaucus collapsed into a pool of blood and urine without uttering a sound.

*

Alexander was in total despair for days. Then, all of a sudden, he found himself in the grip of a strange, frenetic desire to honour his dearest friend with the most impressive funeral that had ever been celebrated in the entire world. He sent a delegation to the Oracle of Ammon at Siwa to ask the god if it was admissible for him to offer sacrifices to Hephaestion as one would to a hero, then he gave orders to the army to set off towards Babylon and to take with them the embalmed body of his friend to celebrate the funeral rites there.

Not all of his Companions understood this extravagant manifestation of grief, even though they had all loved Hephaestion. Leonnatus failed to see the point in Alexander's having sent the request to the Oracle at Siwa.

'Alexander is creating the religion of his new world,' Ptolemy explained, 'with his gods and his heroes. Hephaestion is dead, but he wants him to be among the very first of these heroes, so that he might live on as a myth. He has already started to carry us into the realm of legend. Do you understand?'

Leonnatus shook his head. 'He died of indigestion; I don't see anything heroic in that.'

'It is for this reason that he is preparing such an elaborate funeral ceremony for him. In the end this is what will remain in the people's memory: Alexander's grief for the death of Hephaestion is like Achilles' grief for the death of Patroclus. It doesn't matter how Hephaestion died, what is important is how he lived – as a great warrior, a great friend, a young man struck down by fate before his time.'

Leonnatus nodded, even though he was not at all

certain he had understood exactly what Ptolemy was trying to say, but instinctively he thought that Thanatos had worked his way into Alexander's troop, carrying off the first of the seven of them, and he wondered now who would be next.

During the march to Babylon, some Chaldaean seers came to warn Alexander not to enter the city – if he entered through its gates then he would never leave. He then consulted Aristander and asked him, 'What do you think?'

'Is there anything that might prevent you from doing the things you have decided to do?'

'No,' replied the King.

'Go then – our destiny is in any case in the hands of the gods.'

They entered the city at the beginning of spring. Alexander took up residence in the royal palace and began giving orders to prepare the pyre – a tower some one hundred and forty cubits high, resting on an artificial platform measuring half a stadium on each side.

The plan and the construction work were overseen by Alexander's chief engineer, Diades of Larissa, and by an army of carpenters, painters and sculptors. The magnificent structure rose up to five storeys in height and was adorned with statues representing elephants, lions and all sorts of mythological creatures, with great sculpted panels carrying scenes of gigantomachy and centauromachy. Enormous torches of pure gold laminate protruded from the corners and at the very top life-size statues of sirens supported the catafalque.

When the enormous pyre was completed, the embalmed body of Hephaestion was transported on the shoulders of the *hetairoi* of his battalion, followed by Alexander and the Companions, to the base of the tower. From there it was hoisted up using machines designed specifically for the job and was placed on the catafalque. Then, as soon as the sun disappeared below the horizon, the priests set fire to the structure. The flames took hold immediately, enveloping everything in their roar as they devoured the statues, the sculpted panels, the ornaments, the rich votive offerings.

Alexander watched the terrible, barbaric spectacle without shedding any tears, aware of the stupor he was creating in all the onlookers, among the people, awe-struck by this unheard-of manifestation of power, at this most exaggerated of events. Suddenly, while his eyes travelled upwards to look at the top of the tower that was just beginning to collapse with the accompaniment of sinister creaking noises, devoured by the fire, he had a vision of himself as a child once more in the courtyard of the palace at Pella, exchanging a token of eternal friendship with a small friend he had only just met. 'Until death?' Hephaestion had asked. 'Until death,' he had replied.

His hand moved instinctively to his throat and he searched for the token in its gold mount – the milk tooth. He tore the chain from his neck and threw it into the flames and as he did so he was overcome by an infinite melancholy, by the most profound and harrowing sadness. The first and the dearest of them, of the seven

friends united by the same promise and the same dream, had gone for ever. Death had taken him away and his ashes were now being borne off on the wind.

<center>★</center>

Spring came to an end and Alexander once again began pursuing his plans and his dreams of universal domination, while Roxane's belly grew as the pregnancy progressed. He had a gigantic harbour dug out of the banks of the Euphrates, capable of holding more than five hundred vessels, and together with Nearchus he planned the construction of a new fleet that would take them off to explore Arabia and the coastline of the Persian Gulf. The Phoenicians transported forty disassembled ships as far as the ford at Thapsacus in upper Syria and then they re-assembled them and launched them on the river. They went downstream with the flow as far as the capital, complete with crews from Sidon, Arados and Byblos, all of them ready to participate in this adventure that would take them to the far regions of mysterious Arabia. An entire fleet of two quinqueremes, two quadriremes, twenty triremes and thirty penteconters were transported in two months from the Mediterranean to the southern Ocean – nothing seemed out of the question for the young, indomitable sovereign.

Delegations from all over the world came to him – from Libya and Italy, from Iberia and Pontus, from Armenia and India – to pay homage, to bring him gifts and to ask to be allowed to enter into alliances, and he welcomed them all in his grand palace, among the

marvels of Babylon that was readying itself to become the capital of the known world.

One day, towards the beginning of summer, while the Euphrates was in full flood, Alexander decided to sail down the river and to enter the Pallacopas, a canal that was used to drain off the waters so that they did not flood the crops.

The King himself was at the rudder alongside Nearchus and he looked on in wonder at the huge lagoons that opened up here and there along the course of the canal, and out of which emerged, half hidden beneath the surface, the tombs of the ancient Chaldaean kings. Suddenly a gust of wind blew his wide-brimmed hat off, the hat he used to shield himself from the sun and around which a ribbon of gold had been tied, the diadem that symbolised his majesty.

The hat sank, but the ribbon became stuck in a tuft of canes.

A sailor dived into the water straight away, and managed to grab the diadem, but he was worried that he might ruin it by holding it in his hand while swimming towards the ship, so he put it on his head. When he was hauled on board, everyone was struck by this inauspicious event, and the Chaldaean seers who had followed the King suggested the sailor ought to be rewarded for having saved the royal diadem and immediately afterwards put to death in order to discourage any further ill fortune.

The King replied that a good whipping would be enough for the sacrilegious gesture and he arranged the diadem around his head once more.

Nearchus sought to distract him by talking of the great expedition to Arabia, but he saw that there was a shadow across Alexander's gaze, similar to the expression he had worn during the cremation of Kalanos.

A few days later Alexander was sitting on his throne, watching over the manoeuvres of his cavalry beyond the city walls. At a certain point he stood up to talk with the commanders and suddenly, while they were all distracted by the horsemen and their activity, a stranger passed through the chamberlains and sat himself down on the King's throne, laughing wildly. The Persian guards killed him instantly, but the Chaldaean priests beat their chests and scratched their faces, this being the worst of all possible omens.

And yet, despite all of these bad signs, his love for Roxane and the desire to see his child let him chase away his most melancholic thoughts.

'I wonder if he will look more like you or like me,' he said. 'My teacher, Aristotle, maintains that woman is only a vessel for the male seed, but in my opinion not even he really believes this – it is obvious that some individuals more resemble their mother than their father. I myself, for example.'

'Why, what is your mother like?'

'You will soon know – I will have her come here when my son is born. She was beautiful, but ten years have gone by . . . ten very difficult years for her.'

Rumours of all the bad omens had spread among his friends and they all vied with one another to invite him for meals to keep his spirits up. He accepted them all, never saying no to anyone and spending his days and

nights eating and drinking without restraint. One evening, on returning from such an invitation, he felt unwell – his head was heavy, his ears were buzzing, but he paid no heed. He took a bath and went to bed alongside Roxane who was already asleep with the lamp burning in the room.

He had a fever the following day, but he got to his feet nevertheless, despite the Queen's insistence that he should remain in bed. At midday he went to eat with a Greek friend of his who had joined him in Babylon some time previously, a certain Medius. As evening approached, while he was still at the table, he felt a sudden, sharp pain in his right side, so strong it made him cry out. The servants lifted him up, stretched him out on a bed and the pain seemed to calm down gradually.

A physician was called quickly to examine him, but he did not dare touch the area where the King had felt the knife-like pain. His fever was very high now and he felt mortally tired.

'I will have you transported to the palace, Sire.'

'No,' replied Alexander. 'I will stay here tonight. I am sure I will feel better in the morning.'

So he stayed at Medius's home that night, but in the morning his temperature, far from having fallen, was even higher.

On the third day he continued to deteriorate, but he did not seem to be particularly concerned. He called his chiefs of staff and, although Nearchus and his companions realized he was ill, they continued to discuss details of the expedition and the date of their departure.

'Why don't we put everything off for the moment?' suggested Ptolemy. 'You ought to rest for a while, have yourself looked after, try to get back on your feet. Perhaps you should move away from here – the heat is unbearable, it's difficult to sleep. Have you never wondered why King Darius spent his summers at Ecbatana, up in the mountains?'

'I don't have enough time to go up into the mountains,' replied Alexander, 'and I don't have enough time to wait for my fever to drop. When it decides to relent, it will relent. For the moment I simply want to continue forward. Nearchus, what do you know of Arabia and its extent?'

'Some say it is as large as India, but I find that hard to believe.'

'We will soon know, in any case,' replied Alexander. 'Just think about it, friends, the land of spices – incense, aloe, myrrh.'

The Companions feigned enthusiasm, but within themselves these words resounded like some grim portent – the King had just named a series of perfumes that were commonly used in embalming bodies.

Roxane sent for Philip who at that time was in a battalion of the army to the north of the city, taking care of an epidemic of dysentery, but when the Queen's orderly arrived in the camp he had already set off northwards without leaving precise indications of how he might be found.

For another three days Alexander continued to carry out his duties and attend his engagements, officiating at sacrifices to the gods and meeting with his Companions

to organize the expedition into Arabia, but it was apparent to everyone that his condition was still deteriorating.

When Philip was finally found, it seemed there had been some improvement – the fever had dropped and Alexander exchanged a few words with his physician. 'I knew you would come, *iatré*,' he said. 'Now I know that I will get better.'

'Of course you will get better,' replied Philip. 'Do you remember that time when you were half dead after going for a swim in that frozen river?'

'It's as though it happened yesterday.'

'And the note poor Parmenion sent to you?'

'Yes. The one that said you were poisoning me.'

'It was true,' Philip joked and laughed. 'I was administering a poison that would have killed an elephant, but it had no effect on you! You actually became fitter than you'd ever been, and so what do you think a bit of fever is going to do to you?'

Alexander smiled, 'I don't believe you, but it's nice to hear you say that.'

His condition worsened terribly the following day.

'Save him, *iatré*,' Roxane implored Philip. 'Save him, I beg you.' But Philip shook his head to indicate his impotence, while Leptine wept as she bathed Alexander's forehead in a vain attempt to give him some relief.

By the following day he could no longer stand up and the fever was truly violent. They carried him on a stretcher to the summer palace where there was some fresh air towards evening, and Philip made sure he was given cold-water baths to bring his temperature down, but all the physician's efforts proved useless now. Roxane,

in utter despair, would not leave him even for an instant and she covered him with kisses and caresses. His Companions watched over him day and night without ever resting, without eating.

Seleucus ran to the sanctuary of the god Marduk, patron of the city, a healing god, and asked the priests to take Alexander into the temple so that he might be healed, but the priests replied, 'The god does not want Alexander to be moved here.'

He returned disconsolately to the palace and met with the Companions and Philip to report on his mission.

'You should have killed those priests – if they don't know how to cure the King, why do they exist?' exclaimed Lysimachus.

'I think he'll pull through this time as well,' said Perdiccas. 'Don't worry, he's got over much worse than this.'

Philip stared at him with great sadness in his eyes and then entered the King's bedchamber. Alexander asked for water in a voice that was now almost imperceptible.

On the following day the King could no longer speak.

News had spread among the men that the King was very ill; some were saying he was already dead. Large groups of them appeared before the entrance to the palace and threatened to break down the doors if no one let them in.

'I'll go and see,' said Ptolemy, and he went down to the guardhouse.

'We want to know how the King is!' shouted a veteran.

Ptolemy lowered his head. 'The King is dying,' he

said. 'If you wish to see him, come up now, one by one, but in silence. Let him have some peace in his last hours.'

The soldiers went up, in single file, one after the other, up the stairs and along the corridors, to the King's deathbed. They walked before him in tears, saying good-bye with a gesture of their hands. And for each and every one of them Alexander had a look, a nod, a barely perceptible movement of the lips.

His men were all there before him, the soldiers who had accompanied him through a thousand adventures – the men of iron who had tamed the Nile, the Tigris, the Euphrates and the Indus. He saw their faces marked by ice and sun, he saw their bristly cheeks wet with tears and then suddenly he no longer saw anything. He heard Roxane's desperate crying and Leptine's sobbing and then Ptolemy's voice saying, 'It is over . . . Alexander is dead.'

★

He thought of his mother, he thought of how bitter and vain her wait had proved to be. He thought he could see her, way up in a tower of the palace, shouting and crying as she called him in desperation: 'Aléxandre, don't go . . . come back to me, I beg you!' That shout seemed to call him back for a moment, but only for a moment. Now those words, those shouts and that face faded away, far away, until they were lost in the wind . . . Now he saw before himself a limitless plain, a flower-filled meadow, and he heard a dog barking, but this was not the dark howling of Cerberus the watchdog – it was Peritas! He was running towards him, mad with joy just like the day when he had returned from exile, and then across the endless prairie came a thunderous gallop and suddenly an

echoing neigh. It was Bucephalas running towards him with his mane blowing in the wind, and he climbed astride him just as he had done that day in Mieza. And he shouted, 'Go, Bucephalas!' And the steed set off, like some burning Pegasus, in a reckless gallop towards the final horizon, towards the infinite light.

EPILOGUE

'YOUR BODY WAS still warm and we were already arguing over who was to succeed you and we fought over this for years. You weren't with us any more and with you the dream that had held us together had gone. Leptine chose to follow you and we found her dying at the foot of your bed, her wrists cut. The Queen Mother, Sisygambis, covered her face with a black veil and starved herself to death. Roxane chose to live in order that your child might live.

'Perdiccas finally realized his dream and married Cleopatra, but he was the first to fall in the attempt to keep your empire together. He fell in battle against my armies. Poor Perdiccas!

'The strange thing is that although we fought bitterly, making and undoing alliances, we never actually hated one another. The fact is that in a certain sense we all remained friends. Once, years after your death, we all met together at Babylon to seek some sort of agreement, but the meeting quickly degenerated into a fight. Eumenes appeared suddenly from behind a door and threw your cloak and your sceptre on to your empty throne; the arguing ceased as if by magic, our voices calmed down, our looks and the expressions suddenly became pensive. Even if only for a moment, you had

come back among us and we stood there, before that cloak and that empty throne as though you had suddenly reappeared, miraculously.

'We were not worthy of you, and yet we sought to imitate you in everything: we had ourselves depicted in the same poses, our heads tilted slightly towards our right shoulders, our hair combed high off our foreheads, even those of us who had very little hair, but it was all simply to try and exploit your image. We did not even have the courage to save your family – destroyed, annihilated mercilessly by a footnote at the bottom of a treaty: "If any misfortune should befall the child, Macedon will go to . . ." which was like condemning him to death. What horror – your wife, your mother, your child – all dead. Our thirst for power had left our souls parched, it had transformed us into monsters.

'And almost all of us wasted no time in repudiating the Persian wives you had chosen for us, apart from Seleucus who loved his Apama and dedicated beautiful cities to her.

'Seleucus . . . for some time he was the new Alexander and he almost succeeded in breathing life back into your empire. Now he is old like me, and full of aches and pains. We have waged war more than once, or rather our armies have clashed at the border with Celesyria, a frontier that was left too ill defined and too vague after another treaty, one of the many, but we have always been on good terms, like old friends.

'I don't know how he is now, but I suppose he too is nearing the end. As for me, it is two years since I left the

sceptre and the realm to my son, Ptolemy II, so that I could write this story. The only thing I can be proud of, apart from having known when to relinquish power before death forced me out, was to have brought you here, to your Alexandria, the only place worthy of you. Oh! How I would like you to be able to see it now! It is truly beautiful. It is a wonderful, thriving city, just as you dreamed it would be, remember?

'We were young men back then, and our souls burned with the dreams that you painted for us; we were like gods when we rode by your side, resplendent in our armour.

'Now I have written this the last chapter of my history and, as I was writing, it all echoed in my mind – almost as though it were all happening once again. I heard our conversations, the arguments, the jokes, Leonnatus horsing around, do you remember it all? Of course, it will all be transcribed properly; it will be a good text, edited in accordance with the rules taught us by our teachers at Pella and Mieza. But I prefer to remember it this way, our story, just as I have relived it, day-by-day, moment-by-moment, as I wrote it.

'I have done everything I had to and today, when I felt Thanatos's cold breath on my neck, I decided to come here so I could forget everything that happened after you left us, so I could fall asleep peacefully next to you, my dear friend.

'It is time now for Alexander's troop to reassemble, just like that day when we came to meet you in Illyria on that frozen lake, in the snow as it fell in sheets. It is

time now for us to close our eyes, those of us who have lived too long, and when we wake up we will be together once more, all young and handsome as we once were, ready to set off with you, to ride by your side towards the final adventure. And, this time, it will be for ever.'

AUTHOR'S NOTE

MY AIM IN writing this 'romance' of Alexander in a contemporary style has been to recount, in the most realistic and involving way possible, one of the greatest adventures of all time. I have always sought, however, to remain as faithful as possible to the sources, both literary and material.

I have made use of a language that is, overall, relatively modern – because the Hellenistic world was 'modern' in many ways: in artistic expressionism, in architectural innovation, in technical and scientific progress, in a taste for the new and the spectacular – trying, nevertheless, to avoid the use of gratuitously anachronistic expressions. For example in the military field I have used modern terms such as 'battalion' or 'general' to render *lóchos* or *strategós*, words which are perhaps difficult for most readers, and in the medical field words such as 'scalpel' to indicate a surgical instrument that is well documented in archaeological study. Wherever an ancient term remains understandable to today's reader, I have chosen to retain it.

I have also sought to restore the language typical of certain circles and of various characters (women, men, soldiers, prostitutes, doctors, artists, soothsayers). In doing so I have turned to the comic poets (particularly

Aristophanes and Menander) and the epigram writers above all others, because these writers were required by their art to reproduce a realistic language, even in its popular and vulgar aspects. The same poets were a precious source regarding many aspects of daily life – fashion, cuisine, sayings and proverbs.

At certain moments when one character addresses another I have used the Greek vocative case in order to render a particular sense of intimacy or intensity, or of acclamation, such as *Aléxandre* (Alexander), *iatré* (doctor), *heghemón* (commander).

As for historical events, principally I have made use of Plutarch, Diodorus Siculus, Arrian and Curtius Rufus, with occasional references to Trogus and the *Romance of Alexander*. For anthropological and behavioural background, I turned above all to the liveliest anecdotal evidence in certain passages of Pliny, Valerius Maximus, Theophrastus, Pausanias, Diogenes Laertius, but I also made use of a variety of sources such as Xenophon, Helian, Apollodorus, Strabo and, naturally, Demosthenes and Aristotle, as well as fragments of Greek historians' lost works. Archaeological sources generally provided support for the reconstruction of settings, interiors, furnishings, weaponry, decoration, furniture, machinery, utensils; and the recent discovery of the royal tomb at Verghina allowed me to reconstruct realistically the funeral of Philip II.

Where the story of the Macedonian leader moves into its truly historical vein, I had to make certain narrative choices that subsequently proved to be historical choices, sometimes going beyond traditional interpretations. A

case in point is the battle on the Granicus, where I preferred to apply what I believe is a more realistic reconstruction that owes little to Callisthenes' celebratory text.

I have amalgamated two distinct characters – Alexander of Lyncestis and Amyntas – into the single character of Amyntas so as to avoid confusion for the reader who already has to deal with two 'Alexanders'. In doing so, however, I have maintained the situational problems (dynastic, political, psychological) that arose around the two men.

I took great care with the topographical, tactical and strategic reconstruction of the sieges of Miletus, Halicarnassus and Tyre, as too with the battle of Issus, which involved a field visit. The literary sources of the second part are on the whole those already cited, with the addition of references from Herodotus (the flying snakes) and quotations from Homer and Hesiod, as well as some reference to the technical pages of the Aeneas Tacticus and Frontinus's *Strategemata*. Many material sources have also been used and the more alert reader will recognize some of them in works of art, coins and mosaics. Portrait work has been a constant inspiration, together with recent information from excavations in the various places named. Comprehensive field studies have been carried out on various occasions in all of these places.

*

The final part of Alexander's story is perhaps the most complex and the most demanding from the interpretative point of view. Indeed, many events in the sources are

not clear at all, such as the fire at Persepolis, the death of Cleitus the Black and the two conspiracies – the one involving Philotas and the other involving the 'squires'. Although it is not the task of a novel to unravel problems that have been widely debated in the historical literature, the narrative here offers considerable interpretative scope, precisely because it has to keep in mind a more general vision that is often lacking in specialist research. This is the case in the scene in which Parmenion asks Alexander for the reasoning behind the destruction of Persepolis.

The Macedonian conqueror is in any case depicted faithfully even in the most unattractive and least honourable moments of the story. Only some episodes, clearly presented with a negative slant in the sources, have been slightly improved to present what might have been the original and most authentic scenario.

Readers male and female, but above all else female, will have the impression that some women characters could have had a more significant place in the soul of our protagonist, but here again it was my intention to present matters as faithfully as possible with regard to the real situation of society at that time, and with regard to Alexander's character. In the ancient sources the female characters, even the most important, are barely mentioned; I have tried to give them some weight and to reconstruct, following logical processes, their presence and their influence on events narrated here.

The topographical reconstructions on the whole can only be considered approximate; unfortunately the loss of the *Ephemerides*, probably written by Eumenes of Cardia, and the reports of the Bematists ('march officers'

in this book), which provided extremely accurate descriptions of the itinerary, prevent us from building a more realistic picture.

<div align="center">*</div>

I would like to thank all of those friends who have helped and advised me, in particular Lorenzo Braccesi who has kept me company on this long and not always easy journey tracing Alexander's steps, and Laura Grandi and Stefano Tettamanti who have followed, page by page one might say, the birth of this novel.

Special thanks also go to Iain Halliday, English translator of this book, for the intelligent patience with which he has sought to follow my advice, and for striving to translate my text in the most faithful yet most creative way.

VALERIO MASSIMO MANFREDI